A RATIONAL MAN

Teresa Benison has been an antiques dealer in London and Cambridge and an auctioneer in Newmarket, running her own auctioneering company. She holds an Open University Arts degree and is currently writing her second novel.

Teresa Benison

A RATIONAL MAN

VINTAGE

Published by Vintage 1996

2 4 6 8 10 9 7 5 3

First published in Great Britain by
Hutchinson, 1996

VINTAGE
Random House, 20 Vauxhall Bridge Road, London SW1V 2SA

Random House Australia (Pty) Limited
20 Alfred Street, Milsons Point, Sydney,
New South Wales 2061, Australia

Random House New Zealand Limited, 18 Poland Road, Glenfield
Auckland 10, New Zealand

Random House South Africa (Pty) Limited
Endulini, 5a Jubilee Road, Parktown 2193, South Africa

Random House UK Limited Reg. No. 954009

A CIP catalogue record for this book
is available from the British Library

ISBN 0 09 959611 3

Papers used by Random House UK Limited
are natural, recyclable products made from wood grown in
sustainable forests. The manufacturing processes conform to
the environmental regulations of the country of origin

Printed and bound in Great Britain by
Cox & Wyman Ltd, Reading, Berkshire

For David

I honour that place in you
where the entire universe resides;
where, if you are in that place in you,
and I am in that place in me,
then we are One . . .

Namaste – Hindu greeting

Alex

1

My first mistake was thinking I knew Jonathan; my second was loving him too much. I've a friend who used to call him my 'mystery man' because he kept himself to himself. Nothing wrong in that. He'd had an odd childhood, living in that great big house with an embittered mother and a father incapable of hiding his distaste for his marriage. Jonathan had only told me the bare facts, but I had a pretty vivid picture of the people and the house with its tall rooms, its ceilings encrusted with plaster and windows draped with velvet.

The only members of Jonathan's family at our wedding were his Aunt Helen and her two sons. My lot swamped them; we make a fair old rumpus when we get together. I felt sorry for them, but wasn't comfortable with them. The first time I met his Aunt Helen was just after we'd decided to get married. Jonathan took me to meet her and she gave us tea in fluted bone china cups garlanded with roses, and served chocolate sponge on matching plates with real linen napkins and silver-plated cake forks. It seemed a bit over the top for a terraced cottage in Barnet.

I talked about the wedding, about how many of my family there'd be, how few of theirs, and saw her glance at Jonathan as if she'd forgotten her lines and needed prompting. I started to gush, prattling on about Jonathan's father, about what a shame it was he hadn't lived to see his son get a first at Cambridge.

Mopping chocolate icing from his fingers, Jonathan said, 'He'd probably say I was squandering it teaching.'

'You're too hard on him.' Turning to me, his aunt said, 'It wasn't his fault. He worked his way up the hard way; it was all he knew. He didn't understand about Jonathan and his books. That's not a crime, is it?'

3

'My dad's the same.'

'There you are, Jonathan.' She straightened her back and seemed to come to a decision. 'I want to show you something, Alex.' Getting up and crossing to the sideboard, she began rummaging in one of the drawers. 'Good. I knew it was here. Look.' She turned, flourishing an ageing manilla envelope. Jonathan shifted in his seat. His toe rucked the corner of the hearthrug. His aunt fumbled with the flap of the envelope and pulled out a yellowed newspaper cutting.

The photograph showed the buckled remains of a car twisted round a telegraph pole. According to the headline, the accident had been fatal. There was no text. Jonathan's aunt told me that it was her brother who had died.

My mum and dad thought it was morbid, keeping the photograph like that, producing it at such a moment. Still, they liked Jonathan, and they certainly didn't think he was wasting his talents by teaching. Actually they were quite proud of him, and were over the moon when Joanna was born.

Funny that, the way just mentioning her name brings me up in goosebumps. Particularly funny when I was never the sort to go soppy at the sight of a pram. The thing is, Jo's special – because she's mine, I suppose, and Jonathan's. He keeps teasing me because I spend so much time like this, watching her sleep. Regularly at two I put her down for her nap, and sit beside her with a folder-full of work lying open and unlooked at on my lap. My partner and I make our living reproducing and adapting antique fashions. Just lately we've moved into theatrical work and fancy dress, so I'm reading up on pageant costumes. Except that I'm not. I'm watching Joanna. What draws me isn't what she is but who she is. A part of me. A part of Jonathan. In a very real sense, she is me, and I'm her. Look at her, she's dreaming; her lips twitch and the muscles round her eyes clench, and the ground shivers under my feet because in another sense, and equally real, I'm excluded from her. We're separate. I don't know what she's dreaming or what she's thinking, any more than I know what Jonathan dreams or thinks.

I look at her, and ask questions. Will she be clever like Jonathan, or live on her wits like me? Will she be shy like him, or a show-off like me? I think she'll look like him, lean and dark – there, you see, physical separation – but I don't know how much any of it matters. I love her. I love both of them.

It frightens me, this burden. I think of all the things I can handle, like feeding her and bathing her and crooning her to sleep – and then I think of all the things that are beyond me. The invisible things, the vortex of genes that make her what she is. I want to scoop her up and hug her and keep control, keep the bad things at bay.

I sit up abruptly and my file slides off my lap scattering pages of sketches and reams of photocopied text across the floor. A breeze from the window makes the dove mobile above the cot rotate and tinkle. I can hear sparrows scrabbling in the gutter.

And then I hear a car pull into the drive.

Barney starts to bark, and as I run downstairs he skitters across the hall, scrunching the rug and clicking his claws against the parquet. I must look an idiot, answering the door Quasimodo-fashion as I grapple with Barney's collar. I tell him to sit and stay. The stranger on my doorstep laughs at the pantomine. He says, 'Hello. You must be Alex.'

'Yes.' I watch Barney out of the corner of my eye. Barney watches me, waiting for my attention to wander. I glance at my visitor and wonder what he wants, has he come to collect an order? He's in his mid to late fifties, balding with blue, almond-shaped eyes and an almost triangular face. He looks a bit like my Auntie Gwen's Siamese cat. The thought makes me want to laugh out loud.

He says, 'My name's Leonard Prentice. I'm a friend of Jonathan's father.'

'I see.' These days I'm a lot more curious about Jonathan's father – because of Joanna, I suppose – so the bait is irresistible. I say, 'You'd better come in.'

I show him into the living room and he perches on the edge of the Chesterfield like a budgie on a hot rail. I can't work him out: an elderly man in a sage green shirt buttoned to the neck and loose-fitting trousers a shade paler; he should look silly, but he doesn't. There's no vanity to him, nothing contrived. He just is. I think I'm going to like him.

He says, 'Here, I brought you something.' With a flourish he produces from a capacious trouser pocket a small package wrapped in blue paper covered with cavorting teddies. I take it but I must seem a bit sceptical because he says, 'Well all right, it's really for the baby.'

Never take sweets from strangers.

The paper is smooth and shiny; I run my fingers along the folded seam and think what a fool I am. I've invited a complete stranger into the house and now the three of us are locked together on the inside. The three of us and Barney.

Leonard Prentice smiles. 'It's okay.' He says, 'It's just a present, Alex, something I thought she'd like.'

'Who are you?'

'I told you. Go on, open it.' He speaks in a quiet, matter-of-fact voice as if it's no big deal, his being here. Barney nuzzles his knee and he scratches absentmindedly at the dog's wiry head and I think, well, dogs are reckoned to have pretty good instincts about people. So I open his parcel. I slide my nail under the strip of Sellotape and peel back the teddy-bear wrapping. Inside is a small box; inside this a nest of crackling black tissue paper. I feel as though I'm dismembering a black poppy as I fold back the paper to reveal an exquisite silver rattle.

'It's Georgian.'

'I can see that,' I say. Why is he doing this, why should he want to give Joanna such a special present? I finger the silky surface of the ivory handle and turn the little gadget over and over so that the tiny cluster of bells tickles against my palm.

'Do you like it?'

'It's lovely. Thank you.'

I glance up at him. He looks very serious. He says, 'Jonathan had one just like it, when he was a baby.'

My unease escalates into outright fear. Not of him, I sense somehow that the threat isn't in him, but in what he knows. I say, 'I'm sorry, Mr Prentice, but I don't remember Jonathan ever having mentioned you.'

He hesitates, then says, 'No Alex, I'm sorry, it was a mistake coming here.'

I rest the rattle on the arm of my chair. Very carefully I say,

'Perhaps. Only how can I judge? I'm confused. If you know Jonathan, why has he never mentioned you? And why did you bring this?' I gesture towards the rattle. 'Just because you used to be a friend of Jonathan's father – that doesn't explain anything, after all, he's been dead for years. . . .'

'Who told you that?' His voice becomes jagged. 'Who told you Charles was dead?'

Charles. So that was his name. Jonathan has never said. 'My father' is the phrase he uses – and rarely at that.

'Alex, who told you?'

'Jonathan told me. And his aunt. Everyone. Everyone said he was dead. . . .'

The implications clamour in my head. What possible justification can they have for such a monumental and well-coordinated lie?

He looks confused, as much at sea as I am. I say, 'What's going on?'

He takes a deep breath and I think, here it comes. Instead he asks if I mind him smoking. Although I do, I fetch him a dish to use as an ashtray. He produces a black Sobranie from a sleek tablet of a box and lights it with a heavy gold lighter. The smell of burnt earth fills the room. He uses the cigarette to create an interlude. I watch him manipulating the liquorice stem between his long fingers. His lips tremble as they accommodate the gold-foil tip. At last he says, 'Did they tell you how he was supposed to have died?' He gives a wry laugh and flicks some ash into the dish. 'I don't suppose for a moment it was peacefully in his bed.'

'In a car crash.'

'Of course. When lying, one's supposed to stick close to the truth, right?'

'I wouldn't know.'

'No.' He tugs at his cigarette, then says, 'It's true, there was an accident, but that's neither here nor there, and anyway it wasn't Charles who was killed.'

'They still lied, though. Why, Mr Prentice?'

'I wish you'd call me Leonard. Please, Alex.'

I'm so confused. What I'm learning frightens me, but at the same time I feel sorry for him. He hadn't expected this. I say, 'Tell me why they lied.'

'They have their reasons.'

'But what are they? And where do you fit in? Who are you, Leonard?'

'I look after him – Charles. I've known them a long time, Jonathan's family. Since before he was born. You must talk to him about it, Alex. It's not up to me.' He speaks in a breathless staccato; his rapid phrases offer tantalising fragments of a picture that doesn't make sense. He stubs out the half-finished cigarette and stands up. 'I'd better go.' He smooths down the scattered wisps of his hair with the flat of his palm. 'I made a mistake. I'm sorry.'

He gets as far as the door before it registers that he really means it. I panic, I go after him shouting, 'What the hell d'you think you're doing? You can't go.' I hear the tears in my voice and tell myself that they are due to frustration, not fear. 'Leonard!'

He says, 'Speak to Jonathan, Alex.'

'What did he do? What did Jonathan's father do that everyone wants him dead?' His eyes glitter, I can see that he's hurting, as if somehow Jonathan's lies affect him directly. Then Joanna starts to cry. His head jerks as he glances towards the stairs, and I think, he wants to see her. Is that why he came? I say, 'Tell me.'

He shakes his head. 'I can't bargain with you.' He turns to go.

I feel ashamed. He's right, it's wrong to use Jo as a bargaining counter. I call him back. 'I'm sorry, Leonard. I'll talk to Jonathan. Only don't go, please. Come and see Jo.'

He follows me upstairs. Jo is lying on her tummy and her fat little arms and legs are beating the mattress in frustration. Her face is all red and crumpled. I scoop her up and bob her on my shoulder and she gurgles and burps in my ear.

Leonard laughs. I glance at him and see how happy he looks. He reminds me of Jonathan the first time he saw her. I hug her closer, and the soft fuzz of dark hair tickles my cheek. She smells of talcum powder and milk. He steps closer and says, 'She's so beautiful, Alex.' Almost shyly, he brushes a finger against her cheek. She blinks at him and he laughs as if bewitched. Very gently, I give her into his arms.

He has held a baby before, I can see that. He's probably held Jonathan. He adjusts his hold and, carefully but firmly, shields the soft mushroom-cap of her head with his hand. Closing his eyes, he presses his lips againts her fragile crown and whispers, 'If only he could see her, Alex . . . . If only Charles could see her.'

2

I'd met Jonathan when my partner Penny and I moved to Cambridge. We'd decided that with all the students it'd probably be a pretty good place to set up shop, or rather stall.

The idea for the business came to us at school. We'd volunteered to do the wardrobe for the end of term production of The Crucible and everyone was very impressed. Apparently I had an excellent eye for colour and shape, and Penny a magical feel for fabric. When the production was over, the art teacher had the brilliant idea of auctioning off the costumes. We were amazed at how much money was raised.

The following summer, having jeopardised our exam results by spending every spare moment with our heads buried in books on costume and dress design, we moved to Cambridge and for the first nine months, shared a dingy bedsit. Not that we noticed our surroundings. We were working hard selecting designs, adapting them for modern wear, making up patterns and putting them together long into the night. Once a week we took a stall at the craft fair in the Fisher Hall, and there we learnt how to display and how to sell, and how to make a profit.

We decided we were doing well enough to expand and bought a little van. It was pretty knocked about but would do for us. And then we landed a contract for one of the fringe activities of the city's summer festival. Success shimmered before us like a heat-haze on an asphalt road. It went to our heads and we set about looking for somewhere better to live, eventually finding two rooms, one on the ground floor and another on the first, in a house on St Barnabas Road.

I loved the place the moment I saw it. It was a big semi-detached villa and had been quite grand once – you could tell that from the red and green stained-glass panels on either side of the front door, and the black and white tiling to the porch – but it had come down in the world. Now there was a black fracture through the petals of one of the roses, and several of the tiles had lifted and weeds were growing out of the gaps.

Fronting on to the road was an unkempt garden with a low wall which seemed to be steadily collapsing onto the pavement. The fine red brickwork was frost-flaked and crumbling, and the mortar had virtually all gone. In the middle of the uncut lawn was a shaggy lilac tree. Penny and I called it the Booby Trap because every time it rained it trapped bucketfuls of water which it then showered on the first person to pass. When the boy upstairs suggested we should trim it, the girl with the room next to Penny's said, 'Don't you dare. I love it. It's like life – great from a distance but get too close and it pisses on you.'

Inside, the house was even sadder and shabbier. The brown and yellow lino in the hall buckled as it met the skirting boards, and the dirty grey paint covering the walls looked as though it had been smeared on with an old rag. The whole of the downstairs smelt of rancid fat and stale beer and cigarettes.

We moved in in August and, because it was basically a student house, it was virtually empty. Which was nice because we got to know our way around, had the chance to get used to the place before the big influx.

Penny had the downstairs room at the front, the one with the bay window. It was bigger than mine, but as she did most of the pattern-work and needed plenty of floor-space, that seemed only fair. My room overlooked the back garden and, immediately below, a shed with a corrugated asbestos roof.

Throughout September the other tenants trickled back. There was a girl with spiky blonde hair who played the flute, in the next room there was a graduate who'd not yet found a job – 'doesn't relate well to employers', we were told – and in the room next to mine an Italian boy who turned out to be a girl. Jonathan's room was on the floor above.

This house was much bigger than our last one, and much

noisier. There was always someone thumping up and down the stairs, and music playing – usually rock underlaid and punctuated by Judith's flute. We were all constantly in and out of one another's rooms, on the borrow – sugar, butter, money, tapes. From us they usually wanted a sympathetic ear, or advice as to what they should wear – we were both part of them, and separate.

All this toing and froing, coming and going, didn't touch Jonathan. The first couple of times I passed him on the stairs, the only response to my greeting was a curt nod. Judith came round one evening just after one of these abortive attempts at communication and, as we sat round Penny's sewing machine drinking cider out of pottery mugs, I asked her what she knew about him.

'Oh, him. Old po-face. Why d'you want to know about him?'

I shrugged. 'No reason, just curious. Seems a bit standoffish, that's all.'

'You could say that. Personally, I've never spoken to him. Nice-looking, though.'

That was true. He had lovely dark hair, silky, and eyes like freshly hulled chestnuts.

After that I asked one or two of the others about him, but none of them knew anything, and none of them cared. With a bit of practice you barely noticed him. He didn't feature in the life of the house, wasn't invited to any of the parties. When the house throbbed and seethed to music, I imagined him in his chaste bed, cotton-wool plugs stuffed in his ears.

And then we had a particularly loud party. There were so many people that we left the front door open so that they could spill out into the garden. I'd got hot and gone outside to cool down. I sat on the step watching the way the dying leaves of the lilac seemed to dance to the music, thinking of the past, of the people who had lived here a hundred years ago or so, wondering what they'd make of the noise and the mess.

Rod, the unemployed graduate, came to sit beside me. He grumbled about the latest rent rise, demanded to know how he was supposed to afford the increase when all he had was his dole cheque – why didn't people understand, why wouldn't anyone give him a job, and why wouldn't I go to bed with him? He pretended to be hurt when I laughed.

And then I saw Jonathan.

Rod called out, 'Hey, look, it's the invisible man. Why don't you join us? Why don't you ever speak to us?'

Jonathan didn't even glance at him as he stepped over his outstretched legs. He looked at me though, when I said, 'Don't, Rod. Leave him.' The light from the hall glittered against his eyes as they focused fleetingly on mine. Then he shrugged, and went inside.

The next morning I went up to his room and banged on the door. It took him a moment to answer and, when he did, he stood there blinking at me as if he'd never seen me before. I said, 'Hello there, I'm Alex. I live downstairs.'

'I know.'

I thought, I like his voice too, as well as his eyes. He was very slim – lean rather than skinny, and wore faded jeans and a dark blue sweatshirt. He hadn't shaved yet and ran a self-conscious hand over the stubble.

I said, 'Look, I just wanted to say, I'm sorry about Rod. He was bloody rude, but you mustn't mind him.'

'I don't.'

He looked faintly amused. I thought how well the colour of the sweatshirt suited him. I bit my lip, and said, 'And the rest of us were a bit noisy, weren't we?'

'A bit, yes.'

'Did we keep you awake? Were you wearing earplugs?'

He laughed, and it transformed him. He said, 'What did you say your name was?'

'Alex.'

'Jonathan.' For a moment I thought he was going to shake hands. 'Don't worry about the noise,' he said, 'I don't notice.' He made a throwaway gesture towards the cluttered desk. 'Only thing that really gets through is that bloody flute.'

I laughed. 'I'll pass on the complaint, shall I?'

He shuddered. 'I don't think so. She looks a bit fierce.'

'She is, yes.'

That could easily have been the end of it. We'd run out of things to say. But then I've never known when to leave well alone. I said, 'There's some wine left. I put it in my fridge. Why don't you come down, we'll finish it off.'

*

Penny said, 'And then what?'

'Nothing. He said he had an essay to write.'

He'd sat on the edge of my bed, cradling his mug of wine and, because I was nervous, I went into performance mode. I started to tell him about our business, about what we did and how it started; I even pulled a couple of items off the rack and, holding them against me, pranced back and forth in front of him, the perfect parody of a model. I made him laugh. I liked that.

A couple of days later I bumped into him in the town and we had coffee. I let slip that I was going to see Valmont *at the Arts that evening – mainly for the costumes, though I didn't confess that – and suggested he might like to come too.*

After the film we sat talking till the early hours. He knew a lot; he was reading history and he brought the film and its period to life. He told me he wanted to teach. It worried him that children were given so little sense of history. Without understanding the past, what chance did they have of constructing a viable future? His eyes glistened and his face became more and more animated. I felt tender and proprietorial as he explained his mission.

I had a mission too. I was going to go into period millinery. He didn't laugh and treat it as trivial as he might well have done. He asked questions, about research mainly. A couple of days later he knocked on my door and presented me with a book he'd picked up in a second-hand shop. I invited him in and we sat side by side on the bed as I slowly leafed through it. It was a beautiful book with detailed engravings and little captions to the pictures – widow's cap of tarlatan with fine folds across the crown and crepe ruching, a lace bonnet of tan-coloured lisse . . . it made my mouth water.

'So now what?' he said, a smile in his voice.

'Now I must see if we can buy the shapes, or whether we have to start from scratch.' I closed the book, smoothing the cover with the flat of my palms. I said, 'It's exquisite, Jonathan, thank you.' He shrugged dismissively, and I leant against him, kissing his cheek.

A few days later he invited me out for a drink. We went to a pub called the Anchor and although the evening was chilly, we sat outside on a low wall overlooking the river. He fussed, saying, 'Are you sure you're okay? It's very cold.'

I laughed, 'I'm hardly the delicate type.'

The lights from the pub striped the ripples of the water. The noise and the glitter pressed against the windows, and the other drinkers began to spill out onto the terrace which up until now we'd had to ourselves. It happens on the stall too. If it's quiet, you only need a couple of people out front and before you know it you've got a crowd. Everyone's terrified they might be missing something.

Jonathan balanced his glass of cider on his knee, and said, 'They don't much like me – Rod and the others – do they?'

'They don't know you. You should make more effort.'

'How?'

'Well, it doesn't take much to pass the time of day, does it?'

'I've never been much good at that sort of thing, making friends.'

'I doubt you've ever tried. And if you don't make a start, you're going to have a bloody lonely life, Jonathan Wade. Not everyone's as pushy as me.'

The next time we had a party, I managed to persuade Jonathan to come. I even lent him a burgundy and cream brocade waistcoat to wear over his tee shirt. 'Smart,' I said, tweaking it. 'Sexy, even.'

I expected him to be embarrassed, but he wasn't. He put his hands over mine and we stood there for a moment, and then he said, 'Let's go down. They've started without us.'

They finished without us too.

The noise was tremendous and at first he stuck close to me. The pounding of the music made him screw up his eyes and frown and every time he wanted to say something he leant close and bellowed in my ear. And then, somehow, we became separated and I got cornered by Rod. Rod had at long last been offered a job, and now he didn't know whether to take it or not. 'I mean, what d'you think, is it a good career move?'

'You haven't got a career,' I told him. He didn't like that. He scowled and shifted restlessly from one foot to another and lectured me on my intolerance. He told me I had no heart, no soul. I was an empty vessel.

Then a hand came to rest on my shoulder, and I knew without looking that it was Jonathan.

I'm not sure whose idea it actually was, but we found our way up to my room and he sat on my bed with his back against the wall and I lit an apple-shaped, apple-scented candle and balanced it on a saucer on the seat of the chair I used as a bedside table.

The walls shivered with the beat of the music and the floor-boards vibrated beneath my bare feet. I thought how funny it was that I should be here with gentle Jonathan – and I pulled him closer and the candle-flame limned his hair and made the shiny skin on his shoulder glow.

Penny and I went back to Wisbech for Christmas. My sister Mel had a new boyfriend, a reporter on the local paper, and he came over on Boxing Day. I wished then I'd invited Jonathan. He was staying with his aunt and cousins and if I'd known where exactly I'd have rung him and asked him up. Not that it mattered. We were all back in Cambridge in time for Judith's New Year's Eve bash. It was a fancy-dress party. I went as the Tree of Knowledge, and Jonathan as the Serpent.

A couple of weeks later, Penny and I were still laughing at the inappropriateness of dressing Jonathan as a serpent. We'd been to the warehouse to buy fabric. I was on my hands and knees in the back of the van, hauling the bolts towards the door, when Penny said, 'You didn't tell me Jonathan had a brother.'

'He hasn't.'

'Well who's that, then?' she said as I scrambled back out onto the pavement. A little way along the road, a man in a grey suit was locking an expensive-looking car. It was dark green and low-slung and looked like a tropical beetle – totally out of place amongst the rusty Citröens and Renault 4s that habitually lined our road. I bit my lip. He just had to be Jonathan's brother; they were so much alike. They dressed differently, that was all. Jonathan gener-ally slouched around in jeans, whereas the newcomer wore a double-breasted suit and a flash crimson and blue tie. And as he came closer, I saw that there were other differences. He wasn't as tall as Jonathan, was slightly stockier in build. Also his hair was coarser.

When he reached us, he stopped. I suppose we'd been staring. He smiled. And of course, it was Jonathan's smile. He said, 'I'm looking for Jonathan Wade.'

'Thought you might be,' said Penny, her eyes narrowed, her head cocked on one side.

'In there,' I said, pointing towards the house. 'Top floor.'

By the time we'd got the first of the bolts of cloth into Penny's room, we could hear them shouting. Both of them. Jonathan's voice was deeper and more angry, his brother's lighter, almost pleading as he crashed down the stairs, herded by Jonathan whose arms flailed and whose face was red, his voice by now so thick with anger that he could barely articulate.

'All right.' His brother glanced at Penny and me where we stood, mouths agape, in her doorway. 'Enough, Jonathan, okay? I made a mistake. I'm going.'

And as he made for the front door, for a moment we stood face to face and his eyes – Jonathan's eyes – glistened with hurt.

I went after him, following him to his car. 'Are you okay?' I said as I caught up. He nodded, but didn't look at me and I didn't know what else to say. My instinct was to apologise – but what for? This was Jonathan's brother. It was none of my business. I could almost hear Penny saying, *And when has that ever stopped you?*

He said, 'It's all right. Forget it.' He got into his car and his hand shook as he put the key in the ignition.

'Come back tomorrow,' I said. 'I'll talk to him.'

'And say what? He's right. I shouldn't have come.'

I stood at the kerb, watching him drive away. When he reached the end of the road and turned, I went back inside and slowly climbed the stairs to Jonathan's room.

He'd drawn the curtains and was sitting cross-legged on the bed. There was an old-fashioned gas fire in the room and he'd turned it up high so that the ceramic waffle glowed orange and the blue flames hissed like water on hot stones.

I said, 'He's really upset, you know? He was shaking.' Jonathan didn't answer. I knelt on the bed beside him. 'What's going on? Why did you shout at him like that?'

'What's he told you?' He plucked at a loose thread in the seam of his jeans.

'Nothing.' I bent down so that I could look into his face. He closed his eyes and I drew back. 'Why didn't you tell me you had a brother?'

'Half-brother. He's my half-brother, and I shouted at him because he had no business coming here.' He jerked up his head and his eyes were sharp points in the gloom. The light from the fire armoured his dark hair. He said, 'What is it with you, Alex?' and his words spat like burning fat. 'Why d'you do it, why d'you always have to have all the details?'

'You're right. I'm sorry. It's none of my business. Forget it.' I started to move away, swinging my legs down over the edge of the bed.

And he said, 'His name's Nicholas.' I half turned. His head was lowered, his face in shadow. 'We only ever met once. When I was twelve.'

The year his father died.

I reached out and touched his hand where it rested on his knee. He didn't move. His voice was flat as he said, 'He took me to see him. They made us play chess.'

'Who made you, your father?'

'No. His mother.'

My hand jumped, a reflex I suppose, as all the questions jostled in my mind – how? Where? Why?

He took a deep breath, and the tension began to drain away, and his shoulders sagged as he said, 'I wanted to hate her, Alex – his mother – but I couldn't. I wanted her to be ugly and evil, you know, like a witch in a fairytale. Or else so beautiful that I could despise her and call her shallow. But she wasn't like that. She was like a fire. A little fire crackling in a grate. She was everything my mother wasn't – and d'you know, I almost understood why it was he didn't love us . . . I almost forgave him. He was so different with her. He touched her. He put his arms round her, in front of me, and I'd never seen him like that with my mother. And Nicholas' – suddenly his voice hardened again. 'Nicholas was the son he should have had. . . . He could have been proud of Nicholas – would have been, if he'd lived.' He clenched his fist and banged it back against the wall once, twice, three times as he repeated 'if he'd lived . . . if he'd lived . . . if he'd lived.'

3

The day after his visit, Leonard Prentice telephoned to make sure I was okay. He'd had no idea, he said. He'd assumed I knew about Charles. Had I spoken to Jonathan?

'I've tried,' I said, and described his dazed response to the news of Leonard's visit, his stark portrayal of the facts of his father's life.

Leonard said, 'And that's it, is it? The prosecution rests its case.'

'No. There has to be more to it than that.'

'There is, Alex. Of course there is. We'd better meet, don't you think?'

I left Jo with Penny, explaining that I had to go to London, I needed to do some research. It was sort of true. I'd arranged to meet Leonard at the National Portrait Gallery and, getting there half an hour early, I pulled out my sketch-pad. Perched on the edge of a leather-covered bench with my pad balanced on my knee, I began a copy of an Elizabethan bonnet. It wouldn't come right. I tried to concentrate, from pad to painting and painting to pad like a nervous driver checking his rear-view mirror, but another image kept interposing itself – Jonathan's face as he came into the living room and caught the taint of Leonard's Russian tobacco, the way he clutched at the silver rattle, his knuckles protruding as he gripped the ivory shank.

A creaking tread on the wooden floor alerted me to Leonard's arrival. 'Hello, Alex,' he said, sinking down on to the bench. I glanced sideways at him, but didn't answer. I was too nervous. He took the pad out of my hand and examined it, comparing it with the painting. I said, 'It's rubbish.'

He laughed, and it was an unnatural sound in the hushed intimacy of the old-fashioned gallery. 'Don't be so hard on yourself.' He handed the pad back. 'Listen, why don't we pop next door for a coffee.'

The National Gallery was noisy and crowded. Downstairs in the coffee shop, Leonard queued while I found us a table. The painted walls of the subterranean room were decorated with posters of past exhibitions and, on the table next to ours, a middle-aged Japanese lady poured tea with precision while her husband surgically dissected a piece of cake. I watched with fascination until Leonard blocked my view as he unloaded the tray and sat down. Stirring a minute amount of sugar into his coffee, he said, 'Does Jonathan know you're here?' I shook my head. He said, 'That's probably wise, at this stage. You know, I can't stop thinking about him. He must be terrified – he could lose you and Joanna over this.' He continued to stir his coffee, though the sugar must have dissolved long ago. Eventually he said, 'But you do love him and you're here to try to understand. Am I right? You want to salvage something from all this.' Gently replacing his spoon in the saucer he said, 'So perhaps you should tell me exactly what Jonathan has told you.'

'That he was crazy.' The words gagged in my throat. I had to take a deep breath before continuing. 'He said his father was out of his mind, that he didn't know what he was doing. Is that supposed to reassure me, d'you suppose?' I shivered. I was frightened. Out of his mind and locked away for years. Joanna. I dreamt about her last night, saw her lying in her cot encased from top to toe in a bitter tangle of roots, unable to move, her future determined by her grandfather's past.

It hardly seemed possible that forty-eight hours ago my biggest concern about Jo had been whether or not she'd inherit my looks or Jonathan's, his meticulous logic or my flair.

Leonard said, 'I don't know about reassurance, but it's true, up to a point. You must understand, Alex, these things don't happen in isolation. If I can explain how it came about, maybe that'll help.'

Maybe it would. I agreed to see him again, and went on seeing him over the next few months. There was a lot to tell, a lot to understand and, between meetings, I did my own research. I visited the library and looked up the old newspapers; I read all the reports and each time came away choking on questions there was no point in putting to Jonathan because he refused to discuss the matter. They had to wait till I next saw Leonard.

They were strange occasions, these meetings of ours. On one level, two people who enjoyed one another's company, met for lunch. Leonard liked good food and enjoyed sharing his culinary discoveries and we would order the most interesting sounding dishes, occasionally sharing fragments from each other's plates, and laughing a great deal, to the extent that it occurred to me that despite the disparity in our ages, people might think we were a couple. And when, halfway through the main course, we became serious and earnest in our conversation, then these same people might think we were talking about our relationship and our future, when in reality we were talking about Charles, and the past.

They wouldn't have thought that the day Nickie joined us. Leonard didn't forewarn me but was keen that I should be on time. As a result I was a few minutes early, arriving to find him already waiting. He seemed nervous. Glancing at his watch, he said, 'I hope you don't mind, but I've asked Nicholas along.' Ridiculous, but I felt put out; I treasured our lunches and I didn't want to share him. I had to remind myself why I was there: not for fun but for Jonathan and Joanna.

When Nickie arrived they embraced and Leonard said, 'You've met Alex, haven't you?'

I laughed, 'Not met, exactly,' I said. Nickie looked none too pleased to see me. He was stern for one so young, had an authoritative air that I'd have probably found intimidating had our previous encounter not been on the day Jonathan ejected him from the house on St Barnabas Road. He looked from me to Leonard and back again, then relented with a shrug. He gave an embarrassed smile and I felt sorry for him. We were both of us out of our depth.

After we'd ordered Leonard explained to Nickie about his visit to my house and his discovery that Jonathan had lied to me about his father. When our first course arrived the conversation shifted to the food, the service, a play they'd both seen. Not until coffee did he bring us back to the subject he'd brought us here to discuss.

Nickie accepted one of Leonard's Sobranies. Lighting first Nickie's cigarette, then his own, he confessed he had a favour to ask.

Nickie waited. 'Your mother's diaries,' he began tentatively. 'I was wondering if you'd be prepared to let Alex read them?'

Nickie was furious. Come to that, so was I. The diaries belonged to him and to his mother, they weren't for general scrutiny. I said, 'It's okay, Nickie. Leonard, you've no right . . . .'

'It's important, Nickie.' Leonard leant forward, urging his point. He said, 'This affects Alex, she's part of it now.'

'I know that. I'm sorry, it's not personal, Alex, but she's my mother.'

'It's okay. I understand.' I touched the back of his hand, half expecting him to pull away.

It must have been about a fortnight later that he telephoned to say he'd talked again with Leonard, and had changed his mind.

So gradually, one way and another, I began to construct a rationale for what had happened. Eventually even Aunt Helen agreed to talk to me and what she had to tell, combined with what I already knew from the diaries and from Leonard, gave me a strong sense of the personalities and circumstances that had propelled Jonathan's father headlong into the abyss. And then, when I had it all – or thought I had – Leonard said, 'Am I right then, you don't hate him any more?' I shook my head. It was bizarre but true. 'You see, I told you. Once you understand the circumstances, you start to see how it happened – how easy it really was.' He stubbed out a cigarette and the bent tip crouched against the glass ashtray like a crumpled golden caterpillar. He took a breath, and said, 'Just one more thing, Alex. Will you meet him?' My breath froze. It was one thing to understand, quite another to confront. He said, 'Do this for me, Alex, please. Come and see him.'

I heard myself agree. I even allowed him to persuade me to bring Joanna. She was his only grandchild, he said. It sounded so reasonable. I told Jonathan I had to meet a client and that as Penny was busy I'd be taking Jo with me. I said the meeting was liable to drag on and I didn't know when I'd be back. I hated lying, but the truth would have hurt him more.

I did my best to feel optimistic about the visit, but it was a thin effort. Deep down I was shaking; it seemed I hadn't stopped shaking from the moment I'd agreed to this. It was all very well to be liberal-minded and generous and say, of course I'll come, but what if he turns out to be a monster after all? What if all my rationalisations have been nothing more than arm's-length sympathy? I might be like those people who write hefty cheques to charities but recoil at the sight of the diseased child. What if I'm just not up to the reality of meeting him face to face?

Leonard Prentice and my father-in-law lived in a small, neat house in Chelsea. I got the cab to drop me at the end of the street and took my time finding number eighteen. Odd that it never occurred to me to back out; all I wanted was to delay things a little.

With Joanna lodged firmly on my hip, I rang the bell. No answer. Maybe they've forgotten; they're out. I was about to ring again when Leonard opened the door.

He looked very fresh and cool in a pale apricot shirt, but harrassed too. I said, 'Have I got the right day?'

He laughed. 'Of course you have.' He brushed Jo's cheek with his finger. 'Hello, Jo-jo. Bet you don't remember me.' I think she did; at any rate the sound of his voice made her chuckle and reach out, and I let him take her. He looked at me over her head and said, 'Are you okay?' I gave an exaggerated shudder and a nod. 'Don't worry. It'll be fine. He's looking forward to meeting you. Come on, Joanna, come and meet your granddad.'

Leonard led the way through to the drawing room. Jonathan's father certainly didn't look pleased to see us. He gave the impression of being supremely irritated.

But I was beyond caring. I had my own concerns and, now that I was here, I was alert to every detail. All the things I knew about him, the good things and the bad, came flooding back in a nightmare jumble. There was so much to assimilate, to understand. I felt threatened by him, by the strengths and weaknesses, the blindness and the insight that made up this man and, by extension, Jonathan and Joanna. What he was and what he'd done would shadow her all her life – but from the inside, not the out.

I told myself not to be so melodramatic. There was more to Jonathan's father than the nuances of his mind. What about the physical legacy?

I made an effort to focus, to concentrate on the outside.

He'd been tall once, and broad, but now he was withered and his shoulders sagged and he leant heavily on a walking stick. His hair was very thick, much thicker than Jonathan's – more like Nicholas's – and completely white. There was a scrubbed, clean look about him. In fact much the same could be said about the whole house.

The drawing room was painted magnolia white, with a dark blue carpet and matching curtains. The furniture was antique, of the spindly-legged variety, with everything placed just so. The room looked as if it was about to be photographed for a home-decor magazine.

Leonard said, 'Here they are, Charles. They found us. This is Alex.' My father-in-law nodded, but didn't speak. 'And this,' Leonard adjusted his hold on Jo and straightened the collar of her dress, 'is your granddaughter.' Overwhelmed by the sudden intensity of attention, Jo buried her face against Leonard's cheek and wrapped her arms throttle-tight around his neck. I was amazed at how totally she trusted him. I remembered the reassurance I'd gleaned from the fact that Barney had trusted him. Animals and children can't be fooled. No doubt she was right to be wary of her grandfather.

Leonard said, 'Come on, Jo-jo, don't be shy.'

'Let her be.' His voice was deeper than Jonathan's and shivered with authority.

Leonard had told me that both Charles's sons resembled him, but I couldn't see it. Except for the dense colour of his eyes which narrowed as he said, 'She's terrified. Don't force her. Why don't you get her something to drink, and make us some tea while you're at it.'

I was amazed at the way he spoke to Leonard, as if he were a servant. But Leonard caught my eye and smiled. *It's okay,* he seemed to be saying, *he doesn't mean it how it sounds.* What he actually said was, 'There's an idea! Why didn't I think of that. Come on, Jo, let's make Mummy some tea.'

After they'd gone, Jonathan's father swayed slightly against his stick, and said, 'Do you mind if we sit down?'

He pointed me to the sofa, and sank heavily into a deep armchair. I was fascinated by him. If he was a broken man, he hid it well. His expression was austere, the only giveaway being the studied blankness of his eyes, as if he'd learnt to keep all feeling out of them.

I realised that I was staring. I looked quickly away and he said, 'It's all right, Alex. Look as much as you like. What did you expect? To find it stamped across my brow in letters of fire? I think that's a bit biblical for this day and age, don't you?'

'I'm sorry.' I saw that I'd been wrong. The temporary disguise was already dissolving. The masonry of his face crumbled as I watched. Again I looked away. On the table by the window stood a bronze bust. Next to it was a photograph of Jonathan as a boy. Or Nicholas. From this distance I couldn't be sure.

He said, 'Jonathan . . . I hear he's doing well.' I nodded. 'Teaching, is that right?'

'History, yes.'

'He always spent too much time with his head in a book.' I drew breath to defend Jonathan, but he said, 'So long as he's happy. He is happy, isn't he, Alex?'

And his voice carried so much pain and so much longing, I didn't know what to say. In the end I blurted out, 'I'm sorry about Jo. She's shy, and strange surroundings. . . .'

'It's all right. I've never been very good with children. But then I imagine Jonathan's told you all about that.' From the kitchen came the sound of Leonard explaining something to Jo, and Jo gurgling with laughter. 'Leonard, on the other hand,' Charles's voice softened and he even smiled faintly, 'has everything it takes.'

For a while we sat in silence, listening to the happy sounds coming from the kitchen, to the chink of china and the rattle of spoons in saucers. Then he said, 'It wasn't my idea that you should bring Joanna. It was you I wanted to see. Leonard's told me what's been going on, that you know, that you understand.' His hands lay knotted in his lap. They clenched tighter still as he said, 'Jonathan hates me, I know that. I don't blame him. I hate myself. I expect you hate me too. I do realise, Alex, that what I did affects you – through Jonathan, through your child.' He paused, then said, 'I frighten you, don't I?'

'Yes.'

'Of course I do. But there's no need.' For the first time I heard a faint echo of Jonathan. 'But I think you should know. You seem to have found out so much, through Leonard and Nicholas. I want you to know it all, Alex – from the inside.'

'No.'

'It can't hurt you. It'll help. What I am Jonathan is and Joanna is. You might need to know some day. Don't look at me like that. Don't be afraid, Alex, please.'

'I don't want you to do this. Please. I don't need any more.' I begged him for myself, out of fear, but also for his own sake. I could feel the pain radiating from him like heat from an open fire. 'Let it rest. Don't go digging it all up, there's no point. It was a long time ago – they've told me enough, all I need to know. I understand. . . .'

'Understand!' he barked. 'How can you understand? Look at you – you're still afraid.'

'Of course I am – because of Jo, and Jonathan. But that's my problem. I can handle it. What more can you possibly say? I know what you did and I know why, what else is there? It's over.'

'How can it ever be over? You want to bury the past but it won't be buried. It's here, Alex, inside me all the time, every day and every night, rolling round and round my head like a great fireball – and there's never a moment when I can forget. Think of perpetual noise and perpetual light; that's what it's like.' He stopped. Then continued more quietly, 'And now you think, it's right what they said, that he's mad, he didn't know what he did. . . .'

At our second meeting, Leonard had almost broken down as he told me how it had been going on for so long that he couldn't remember what it had been like before, what it felt like to live an ordinary life. For twenty-five years he'd lived and breathed this man's madness until it was his too, a shared breath.

I remembered his anguish as I looked into Charles's dark eyes, but there was no madness there. They were clear and lucid, and incandescent with purpose. 'I knew then, Alex – and I know now. I did forget for a while. I locked it up inside me, and I stopped living. Jonathan told you the truth, I did die. But it wasn't allowed to last, they forced resurrection on me. They brought me back, bit by bit. But even then, knowing I was alive, I didn't know where I was or why – but they kept on and on, they wouldn't let me rest. Bring it all out in the open, they said, face the monster, that's the only way you'll defeat it.

'But it's me, Alex. I'm the monster. I did that thing, nobody else, and they kept on and on until I faced it, and even that wasn't good enough. They wanted the words. Words make it real. They wanted me to say it out loud, because once I'd done that, I'd be cured.

'So I did. I said it. I said the words they wanted.' He leant forward and peered into my face. 'Did it work, d'you think? Do I look cured to you, Alex?'

4

How could I possibly answer such a question? In this context, I didn't even know what "cured" meant. If it referred to a mind that had careered out of control being once again firmly harnessed, then yes, he was probably cured. But the cure itself had debilitated him. It would have been kinder to allow him to forget.

He said, 'I want you to understand, but I think there are things you expect me to say. I think you want reassurance, want me to tell you that it could have been different, that there was something I could have done to prevent it. But there wasn't, Alex, there was nothing I could have done, I swear. Not without help, not on my own.'

'You weren't on your own. You had Leonard.'

He didn't answer. He looked angry and I thought, what am I doing here, what do I expect to gain from all this? And as for Leonard, if there are questions I'm not supposed to ask, then he should have told me.

At last Charles said, 'Not then. He wasn't there then.'

'But he said he knew you before you ever met her. I thought that was the point.'

'I knew him before, yes.' He spoke softly now, no longer angry. 'But not during.'

At that point the door opened and Leonard came in carrying a tray of tea. Joanna tottered behind him, every now and then reaching a tentative hand to steady herself against his leg. He sat down on the sofa beside me and poured tea into bone china cups. He handed one to me, another to Charles, and gave Jo a chocolate biscuit. She laughed and leant against him, nuzzling his knee much the way Barney had done. Sucking at her biscuit, covering her chin in melted chocolate, she watched her grandfather out of the corner of her eye.

'Well,' Leonard coaxed. 'How far have we got?'

Charles tried his tea. It was too hot; he put it aside. His hands were unsteady. He said, 'I can't work out where it started to go wrong – before I met her, before I met you . . . I don't know. Don't they say it's our parents who make us what we are? Is that true, d'you think?'

'Up to a point,' said Leonard, glancing at me as he slowly stirred his tea. 'But that isn't to say you don't have to take some of the responsibility.'

'Yes.' He sounded almost meek. 'I realise that. But the things I did, they didn't seem so wrong at the time. I knew what I wanted, that's all, and I went all out to get it. No harm in that. I was a success, I had my own company, a big house. . . . Have you seen the house, Alex?' I shook my head. 'I thought Jonathan might have taken you. Or Leonard.' He sounded hurt. I suppose it was important to him because whatever he had since become, once upon a time he had been a man of consequence.

I'd been tempted to visit the house. I knew the address and had located it on the map; it would have been no problem to find. But it was where Jonathan had grown up and it didn't seem right to go there without him. To Charles, though, it must have seemed as if I wasn't interested. I started to explain, but didn't get very far because Joanna dropped her biscuit and, in fumbling for it, lost her footing and trod it into the carpet. Seeing the mess, she started to cry and I gathered her to me, shushing her, afraid she'd make him angry.

He said, 'For goodness sake, give the child another one.' He sounded irritable but when I looked up he was busy selecting a biscuit from the plate beside him. 'Here,' he said, holding it out to her. She stiffened, and pressed back against me. I sat perfectly still, waiting to see what she'd do. She made up her mind. She pulled away, and took two steps towards him. She paused. I held my breath. I had a sudden compulsion to call her back, to hold her safe. At the same time I wanted her to go to him. He smiled at her. She wobbled. He said her name, and she reached out and her fingers brushed his as she took the biscuit. Then, instead of coming back to me or to Leonard, she stayed where she was, clutching her biscuit, watching him. He held out his hand and, when she put her little fingers in his palm, he gathered her to him and I winced at the chocolate on his sleeve, but he didn't seem to notice. As he began to speak, I held my breath, all my attention on Jo, on the way his arm curved round her. Speaking slowly, as if feeling his way, he began to tell me about his own father who had died suddenly of a heart attack when Charles was forty. At first his voice was unsteady; it was as if the words came of their own accord, telling him a story he either didn't know, or had long forgotten, but then gradually he gained confidence. His voice grew stronger, and his manner urgent. He leant forward slightly in his seat and his elbow nudged the plate balanced on the arm of the chair. And all the while he continued to caress Jo's cloud of dark hair, touching it with the tips of his fingers, warily, wonderingly, skimming it with his hand as if it were made of spun-glass, as if it might break.

Sophie

1

Helen wept. Dust to dust, ashes to ashes – poor Dad, reduced to a handful of ash, sprinkled over a floribunda rose in some draughty corner of the Garden of Remembrance, and then forgotten. So much for the ascendency of Man.

And on top of everything else, now she had to endure her mother's cronies, ghastly old women with faces wrinkled like fingers soaked too long in bath water, dressed in stretchy Crimplene which swelled and strained across their massive bosoms. Funny how, at a certain age, breasts become a bosom, are reduced from the plural to the singular, to an armoured mass of one.

She shuddered.

Coming out of the church she'd heard one of the harpies murmur consolingly to her mother, 'Lovely service, dear. I always say as you can't beat a nice funeral.'

Helen remembered the funerals of her pre-war childhood. The whole street would be involved, everybody doing their bit, making tea and cutting sandwiches and lending crockery.

Not much had changed since then, except there was more food on the table and wall-to-wall carpet, courtesy of Charles, though Mum would insist on scattering it with offcuts of the old turkey rug in an attempt to guard against wear.

Helen wondered what Dad would make of it, his front room crowded with plump Crimplene dolls stuffing Mum's crustless ham sandwiches into their mouths, swilling them down with tea. Their curly white heads bobbed and bounced and their croaky voices clattered round the room, ringing against the vases and clashing with the crash of spoons in saucers, like starlings hogging a bird table. She glanced over to where Mum was talking to Auntie

31

Peg. Helen was fond of Peg, though sad to see how out of place she looked, like an ageing cocktail waitress in her little black dress and pillbox hat. Behind Mum and Aunt Peg, Anthony had been cornered by old Mrs Cotton. Serve him right.

'Hello there, dear. Lovely spread.' The voice came from behind her. As she turned, Mrs Lloyd patted her arm. 'Mind you, always did have a dainty touch you did, even when you was little. Here,' the pat became a pinch, 'where's your brother gone and hid himself? I haven't seen him, not since we got back from church . . . .Oh look, here comes your mum. She'll know. Mary,' her voice twisted itself into a parody of compassion, 'how you feeling, love? Was just saying to your Helen, haven't seen your youngest. You must be pleased, really done you proud, he has.' Mum gave a stiff little nod. 'Daresay you'll move in with him now, what with him not being married. Life of Riley you'll live in that great house of his, you mark my words.'

Charles wondered how long it would take his mother to root him out of his hiding place. Not long. She'd realise he wasn't around, ask Helen if she'd seen him, then come looking. She'd find him easily. She always did – always had.

When they were little he and Helen used to play hide-and-seek and, as he huddled in his dark corner with his feet shuffling amongst the empty wellington boots and his face pressed against Dad's old gaberdine mac – the one that for no reason he'd ever been able to fathom always smelt of damp chalk – he'd hear the tramp of Helen's feet on the stairs above him, and the crackling music from Mum's wireless, and then her calling to Helen, 'Under the stairs, Helen, he's under the stairs.'

He hadn't hidden under the stairs this time. He smiled to think of the effort it would take, how he'd have to hunch his shoulders and duck his head under the shelf, the way the stiff brushes and feather dusters swinging from their hooks would powder his dark suit with dust. Imagine having to explain that to Emmy.

He wondered if the coat was still there, or if his mother had already got rid of it. Over the years it had become scruffier, smellier; more and more like something a tramp might wear – or so his mother said. Time and again Dad had rescued it from the jumble-sale bag.

He could remember further back than that, to when his father had brought the coat home, all spanking new and crisp and folded up and layered with rustling tissue paper. It had a narrow belt and pockets with flaps and big shiny buttons like Pontefract cakes. And he also remembered it as the wind-whipped garment Dad used when gardening, frayed raffia trailing from the pockets and a trowel hooked in the belt.

From his hiding place in the little dining room at the back of the house, Charles listened to the erratic clacking of his mother's friends. God, he hated them. His brother, too. Anthony was in there, giving himself airs and graces – he was the eldest, head of the family now. Until the bills started coming in, then it would be, 'Charles, have you seen the price of this? It's wicked', then, after an almost imperceptible interval, an oblique reference to the state of the property market. Not that he begrudged it, if money was all they wanted, that was easy.

He ran his hands through his hair. He didn't want to be here. The house buzzed – like a bumblebee trapped in a jam-jar. It was over, they'd had their fun, why couldn't they just go home?

Any minute now she'll be here, wanting to know why I'm hiding, why I'm not doing my duty. What more do they want?

He'd done all that could reasonably be expected of him. He'd gone to the church and sung the hymns his mother had chosen for her own pleasure, not for their relevance to his father. Yes, he'd done his bit and if none of it meant anything, well, he kept that to himself. He'd said his goodbyes to his father last Sunday, saying his own prayers to his own God in his own church. Today was a matter of form, done for the living, not for the dead.

Shrugging off an involuntary shiver, he caught his reflection in the overmantel mirror. The mantelpiece was crowded with china pots and figurines, mementoes of long-forgotten holidays. In the middle, half-obscured by a faded postcard of Blackpool Tower, was an oak photograph frame. He reached for it, knocking over a china dog which in turn toppled and dislodged an egg-timer, a present from Southend. He and Helen had pooled the last of their holiday money to buy that for Mum. They'd had just enough left over to buy a stick of rock to share. As they trundled along the pier crunching on the pink and white rods of sugar, their clattering footsteps echoing on the wooden planks, Anthony came up behind them and started making fun of Charles for still believing in the tooth-fairy.

Clumsy-fingered, he fumbled the ornaments back into some kind of order, guessing as best he could the proper positioning of the dog and the egg-timer. When it looked about right, he lifted down the photograph and rubbed his palm over the smeared glass. It was a black-and-white snap of his parents standing side by side in the garden. Dad's sleeves were rolled up and his mother's arms were folded across her swollen bosom. Behind them, the roses on the trellis were in bloom.

Dad used to say, 'Don't be too hard on her, lad, she means well.' Why did he do that? He always stood up for her, why did he never take Charles's side?

His father's eyes, dark like his own, looked back at him from the photograph. Would his mother miss it? Surely she never noticed it amongst all the other clutter. He ran his thumb along the carved edge, outlining an acorn with his nail. He gnawed his lip for a moment, then slid the photograph into his pocket. He felt as though he'd committed a crime. He told himself not to be such a fool and crossed the room to the French windows.

Heavy rain streaked the glass, fragmenting his view of the garden. It was less than a week since Dad had died. He'd collapsed while hoeing the tiny vegetable patch concealed behind the trellis. Less than a week, and yet the grass already needed mowing, and the rain had beaten the petals from the roses, leaving the stalks naked and brown, the grass strewn with irreverent confetti.

He tried to imagine his mother's panic at finding his father like that, lying with his face pressed into the crumbled earth, ants crawling in his hair.

He desperately needed to believe in her grief.

He pressed his hand against the cold glass. If nobody grieved for him, really grieved, then what had his life amounted to?

Not much. He'd been plucked out of life and the soil had tumbled down into the hole, filling it, obliterating it almost at once. It was as if he'd never lived.

'Charles! Charles, are you in there?' She'd found him, though it had taken longer than he'd expected. The door opened a crack. 'Thought I'd find you in here.' Her cheeks were flushed and rosy. She looked radiant, more newly wed than newly widowed. 'Everyone keeps asking where you are. It really won't do, Charles, hiding away like this.'

He hated her. The realisation was as sharp and unexpected as a bee sting. Until today he'd felt only a dull resentment, occasionally spiked with a sense of injustice. There'd never been anything like this urge to hit back. He felt a biting need to exact retribution for all she'd done to him and to Dad, for all the little ways she'd hurt and belittled them.

He caught a movement behind his mother's shoulder as Helen performed a dumb-show: *don't say anything, don't let her stir you up, you'll only make it worse.*

The guests were beginning to edge their way out into the hall. Time to go home. He stood at Helen's side, accepting the string of insincere condolences, tolerating Mrs Lloyd and Mrs Cotton and all the rest as they patted his arm and squeezed his fingers as if he were still eight years old. He half expected one of them to slip him a sixpenny bit. He whispered the thought to Helen and she laughed out loud.

When the starlings had flown the house felt awkward with itself, as if uncomfortable at what it had witnessed. In the front room the antimacassars were all skewed and the cushions dented. Cups and saucers littered every surface, plates had been left lying just anywhere, some empty, others with denture-dented sandwich crusts smeared with lipstick.

'Come on, Mum, come and put your feet up.'

'She's not an invalid,' muttered Charles as his brother plumped a cushion and packed it behind their mother's back.

'She's tired, she's had a hard day.'

'Haven't we all,' said Helen as she gathered the crockery on to a tray patterned with a thatched cottage surrounded by hollyhocks. 'Mrs Lloyd's enough to knock the stuffing out of anyone.'

Having escaped to the kitchen, Helen toyed with the idea of putting on the radio. Last Christmas she'd given Mum a transistor – a Roberts, cased in wood and leather, but Mum would have none of it. She still used the old wireless in the bakelite case, keeping it permanently tuned to the Home Service. The wireless went with the kitchen – Mum didn't like change and the room was just as Helen remembered it from childhood, its walls covered in shiny green paint, the tall tap with the green rubber spout, the roller towel on the back of the door.

She decided against the radio. Unloading the tray on to the table she hummed to herself. Who'd have thought a dozen old ladies could create so much mess? Good job we didn't give them a sit-down meal. She smiled to herself as she set about stacking the saucers and rinsing the dregs from the cups.

'Want a hand?'

He made her jump. She swung round, one soapy hand pressed to her chest. 'Charles, you shouldn't creep up on people like that.'

'Sorry.' He closed the door and leant against it, his hand resting on the big old-fashioned key jutting from the mortice. 'I've this terrible urge,' he said, 'to lock them out. Or us in.'

'I wouldn't, if I were you.'

'You're probably right.' He straightened and, adjusting the roller towel, turned back into the room. 'What d'you want me to do then? You wash and I'll dry?'

She laughed. He was so tall and solid, he reminded her of Dad. She said, 'Honestly, Charles, when did you last wash up? I can't imagine Emmy letting you within a mile of her kitchen.'

'She is a bit territorial, but I seem to have a vague memory of how it's done.'

She gnawed her lip and peered into his face. He was making a pretty good job of it, but he didn't fool her. She knew him too well. She knew what they meant – those tight little lines bracketing his mouth and the rigid set of his shoulders. She said, 'You really shouldn't let Anthony get to you.'

'Easier said than done, sis.' He lifted a soiled tea towel from the back of a chair and, flinging it on to the table, sat down. His shoulders sagged and, leaning forward, he massaged the back of his neck.

'Are you all right?'

'Fine.' He glanced up. There were shadows under his eyes. 'Bit of a headache, that's all.'

'I'll get you something.' She started towards the cupboard where Mum kept the plasters and antiseptic cream.

'No,' he said sharply. 'It'll go in a minute.'

With a shrug, she went back to her washing up. No point arguing with him, not in this mood. Besides, there was something she needed to discuss. She turned on the hot tap and the water gushed and splashed. One by one, she slid the saucers into the bowl and watched as they sank beneath the snow of bubbles. 'Charles,' she said slowly, as if musing, as if it had only just occurred to her, 'about Mum . . . .'

'What?'

She took a breath and said, 'Do you think she ought to be living on her own? She's getting on, you know.' As she swirled the dish-mop round the outside of one of the fluted cups she noticed a fine crack, like a single hair, stained with tannin.

'I can't see her wanting to move, can you?' His voice was hard. 'Besides, where would she go?'

She leant a saucer against the cup to drain. 'I suppose one of us should offer.' She waited for him to respond. He met her eye and, picking up a bone-handled teak knife, tapped out three beats against the melamine table top. 'Charles?'

'Me, you mean.'

'You've got more room than the rest of us – and Emmy to help you.'

'No.' He tossed the knife aside and it chinked against a plate.

She sighed. 'I thought you'd say that. Oh well, I said I'd ask.'

'This was Anthony's idea?' She nodded. 'Anything else, Helen, but not that. If she wants me to find her somewhere more convenient, a flat or a bungalow, all she has to do is say. But I won't have her to live with me.'

'She's not so bad, you know. You just get on her wrong side. She only ever wanted what was best for you.'

'Is that so? Well, it's not how it feels. You remember what it was like – the way she nagged at me? Nothing I did was ever good enough – always pestering me about school, why didn't I try harder, why didn't I get good marks like Anthony? Anthony, for heaven's sake. Much good it did him. Then all that stuff about God. Dragging me to church every Sunday, filling me with hellfire and damnation – not much in the way of salvation where she's concerned, is there? Suffering and punishment from here to eternity. And all for my own good! Look at me, Helen. Just look at me and see what a success she made.' He stopped. He'd never let go like this before, never let the bitterness come tumbling out – and even now, this was only the tip of it.

No, oh no. Keep control. Big boys don't cry. Damn this headache. He massaged his brow. 'She must have done it to save her own soul, Helen – it did damn all for mine.'

Oh but the power of the woman, the insight. She'd known exactly what he needed. She'd offered him magic, the promise of escape as, Sunday after Sunday, he'd knelt with her at the altar rail, receiving the bread and the wine as he begged forgiveness for sins he'd never committed. What were those sins? Of all mankind, or just his own insignificant variants on the theme? It didn't matter that he didn't understand; he'd never be free of it. The fabric, the essence of worship still stirred an ache in him, a sense of the unattainable something that he knew was there, above or behind or within the vaulted stone and the stained glass. Yet it was neither a someone, a something nor a somewhere he sought. The knowledge made him shiver, but didn't shake his faith.

'I worry about you,' said Helen. He opened his eyes and slowly raised his head. She stood watching him, her hands dribbling soapsuds on to the red and black dandycord mat.

He pressed his hands flat on the table and pushed himself up. He said, 'You mustn't.' He smiled at her, 'So long as I don't have to have Mother come and live with me.' And before she could answer, he said, 'Listen sis, I'm sorry about this, but I've got to go. I've got a meeting. I'm late as it is.'

Helen stood by the front room window, struggling to disentangle the net curtain from the chrome-plated rosebowl so that she could wave to Charles. The car pulled away from the kerb. Anthony said, 'I reckon that takes some beating, going off like that, today of all days.'

'No more than I've come to expect,' said their mother in a pained voice. 'It's all you ever get with him, self, self, self.'

'It's not his fault,' said Helen. 'The meeting was set up weeks ago. How was he to know . . . .'

'Was it indeed. Well, I'll tell you this much, if I'd known this was how it'd turn out, I'd never have let your father encourage him.' Helen shrugged. Charles hadn't needed much encouragement. Like her, he'd upped and left home at the first opportunity. 'We mortgaged this house for him, you know.' Helen knew, she'd heard it all before. 'Give the boy a leg-up, your father used to say.'

'And you never let him forget it, do you? It's not as if he didn't pay you back – and the interest, don't forget that. He paid you interest, just like you were a bank.'

'I didn't want his money.'

'You'd have griped if you hadn't got it.'

'Oh that's all it is with him. Money. Just look at him, coming here in that great car, but could he stay? Could he bring himself to give his mum a bit of comfort? No! He could hardly wait to get away.'

'It isn't like that. You don't understand.'

'Oh I understand all right. I've seen it all before, my girl. He swans around doing just as he pleases with never a thought to the rest of us, and then as soon as it gets a bit difficult, he's off. He's always running away, he always has.'

'That isn't fair.' Helen almost shouted. Too loud, too vehement. Why? Because it wasn't entirely unjust. She remembered Charles as a boy, awkward and preoccupied, with eyes like black shadows, glazing over whenever Mum's carping got too much for him, his face a mask, his mouth rigid. She used to wonder where he went, what it was like, that deep dark place where none of them could follow. She wondered if he still went there.

2

The sparks flew, crackling in the cold air, then cascading and dying before they hit the bench. Sophie MacKenzie pressed the shaft of the brass candlestick harder, then harder still against the spinning wheel, and the whirring electric motor altered its pitch. She peered through the scratched windows of her goggles as the sparks performed their dance of death, relishing the alchemy, the transmutation of black metal into bright gold.

Stepping back, she switched off the motor. As the wheel slowed, sighing into silence, she gave the candlestick a final rub with a scrap of purple rag. God, it was hot work, this. She tugged off her goggles and wiped the sweat from her face with the flat of her palm. She knew without looking that her cheeks would be covered in smuts, all except for the white panda-patches round her eyes where the goggles had been. What she needed now was a long hot soak in water lavishly laced with lavender bath salts.

She wrapped the candlestick and its mate in a sheet of newspaper and added them to the others already packed into the two wooden crates stacked on the floor. James was calling in at the shop some time tomorrow, and James was heavily into candlesticks. 'As many as you can get your hands on, Sophie my pet. Pairs, singles, I'm not picky. Don't even have to be antique, so long as they look like they've knocked about a bit. Do what you can, eh? I've got this Yank coming over at the end of the month – he's opening a hotel in New England. Butter knives too – about fifty. And wooden clogs, would you believe, to serve the bread in. Disgusting. Still, ours not to reason why. See what you can come up with, right?'

She grinned as she pressed down the lids of the crates. This was the way to do business. When she'd met James Peterson, a year or so ago, she'd had just about enough of selling Staffordshire dogs and twee shepherdesses to the general public; James's enquiries had revealed an entire area of the trade she'd been neglecting.

Over the following weeks she toured the capital's trade markets, checking on prices and chatting up the traders until she had a fair idea of the kind of goods they wanted and how much they were prepared to pay. In the end it was easy to establish contacts and build relationships; they were as keen to find new and interesting stock as she was to provide it.

She was lucky to be able to make a living doing something she enjoyed so much. She loved it. At least, she loved the actual dealing but not this, not the cleaning and polishing and generally tarting up. She grimaced at the tang of burnt buffing soap and, lifting one of the crates on to her hip, carried it out to the car.

The little Morris Traveller was parked between the barn and the cottage, its back doors gaping. The low winter sun hadn't reached the yard and frost still furred the tufts of dead grass thrusting up between the cracks in the concrete. As she fastened the back doors, Jerry the postman came pedalling perilously down the lane brandishing a fistful of envelopes.

Two hours later, deliciously soft, fragrant and wrinkled from her bath, she wrapped herself in an emerald kaftan, twisted her hair into a towelled turban and, putting a pot of coffee on to brew, leant back against the Rayburn and began to open her post. First a letter from an old schoolfriend who had moved to Wiltshire, then a notification of interest on a building society account and, finally, two auction catalogues.

She poured the coffee into a treacle-glazed pottery mug and carried it through to the dining room. From one of the drawers in the pine dresser she rummaged a pen. Settling herself at the table, she started to go through the catalogues, reading the description of each lot then, if it sounded her kind of thing, marking it with a cross in the margin. The first sale looked to be a waste of time, but the second had a couple of dinner services and one or two other interesting bits and pieces. She thought she'd give it a go.

Charles's study was at the front of the house, on the opposite side of the hallway to the drawing room. He was fond of his study. Emmy thought it gloomy, said it gave her the creeps. Her latest suggestion had been 'A nice cream carpet, and some paint to brighten it up. Beige . . .' she'd mused, turning slowly on her heel to survey the room.

He'd laughed and leant back in his chair. 'Not my style,' he said, 'and well you know it.'

He felt safe here; he liked the way the dark walls enclosed and protected him. Whenever he had a problem, he'd shut himself in his study to soak up the silence and think things through. He wondered if this was how monks felt when closeted in their cells, or hermits in their caves.

It was here, long ago, that he'd interviewed Emmy for the job of housekeeper. He'd thought her a bit young, no more than a couple of years older than himself, but in the end it was this that decided him; she was so much less formidable than the other applicants. Now the house wouldn't be the same without her.

As for Em, only much later had she confided how the agency had described him as a property developer, a successful man, wealthy and very choosy, having already turned down several highly suitable applicants. She'd expected someone middle-aged with a paunch and a cigar. Instead she'd found a diffident twenty-nine-year-old rattling about a massive house in the final stages of refurbishment, who'd conducted the interview perched on a dusty packing case.

Emmy wasn't unanimously welcomed. His mother thought she'd only be there five minutes, 'Then you'll get married and won't need a housekeeper.'

'Married?' He'd laughed. 'What makes you think I'll get married? There aren't enough hours in the day as it is.'

His mother had been affronted. Perhaps she felt he'd trivialised the institution she revered so highly by treating it as a time-share option. He smiled as he refilled his fountain pen. He glanced at his watch. Eight-fifteen. He ought to be going. He was driving to Essex to look at some land. He'd arranged to meet the local planners and the agents dealing with the sale. The project was routine. His greatest challenge would be persuading the architects to curb their creativity and accept that they were designing industrial units, not a prestigious residential development. Today's little jaunt wasn't likely to win them any prizes.

He flicked through the file to make sure he had everything he needed. On the desk in front of him was Dad's photograph, filched six months ago on the day of the funeral. If his mother had missed it, she hadn't let on. He tucked the file into his briefcase, relishing the rippled surface, the smell of calf-leather. He liked the feel of it, the authoritative slap as he flicked over the tab and fastened the brass lock.

In the hall, Emmy helped him into his coat. Brushing his shoulders, she said 'Tonight?'

'Usual time.' He completed their ritual with a smile and stepped out into the square where his car was waiting. It was a brilliant January morning, cold as glass, the sky a pale, translucent blue. The low orange sun scalded the white-rendered buildings. The fizzy-cold air caught at the back of his throat and made him gasp.

He decided to drive himself, take control, to choose, if he wished, to drive off into the wide blue yonder. A grand delusion. He was his own destination. And yet sometimes, just sometimes, he needed the fantasy of free will.

He demanded the keys from his driver and, sliding into the driving seat, allowed his hands to linger on the steering wheel. Then he slowly slipped the car into gear and pulled away from the kerb. Glancing in the mirror, he smiled fleetingly at the sight of Thompson looking formal and foolish as the car went off without him.

He drove carefully, exchanging the elegant squares of Belgravia for Whitechapel and the Mile End Road. It was good to be behind the wheel, an unfamiliar pleasure these days. It took an age to get out of London, but he didn't regret his decision and eventually the big car was lumbering along the winding A11 drawing curious stares as he passed through one straggling village after another. He was observed, but untouched, distanced by the tinted windows, by the gentle rhythm of the engine which seemed a part of him, bonding him to its world.

Observed, but untouched. That's what it all comes down to. Nothing touches me.

Panic made him clutch the steering wheel. Taking his foot off the accelerator, he allowed the car's massive weight to act as a brake as he entered yet another village. Three women, congregated outside the post office, craned curiously.

He thought, it's true. I don't feel. Not how I'm supposed to. Even when Dad died, even then it wasn't as it should have been.

At first he'd been angry – a selfish rage at having been abandoned so abruptly. Anguish had followed, and with it the usual agonisings over all the things that must now remain unsaid, the taunting inadequacy of their last conversation – but very soon all that had been forced into the shadow of his resentment towards his mother.

That was no excuse. It should have hurt more than that. He wanted it to hurt. He needed to suffer. Suffering gives meaning to life.

Our Father, which art in Heaven . . . now that moves me. Incantation and incense have the power to reach me.

Hallowed be Thy name.

That was the nearest he could get to love, but it gave him no sense of being loved in return. Which it should. He knew the rules – repent your sins, and God will repay with His love and His grace.

But I haven't committed any sins.

And why does nothing touch me?

His eyes ached with the effort of watching the road and negotiating the bends. He was driving along a stretch with a red-brick estate wall on his right, and a crackling black canopy of trees on his left.

Untouched, untouchable – has this been done to me, or have I done it to myself? I don't understand. What is it that alienates me from the world?

What particular thing, above all others, sets me apart?

He reached inward, and touched his isolation. Facing the thing that kept him apart, he recoiled from his difference.

All the things he would never know clustered at the margins of his mind. Flesh against flesh – the hair on his nape stirred – a coaxing voice whispering in his ear, the touch of sweet breath on his cheek, soft skin sliding against him.

No.

He spoke aloud.

If he'd wanted any of this, he could have had it. But he hadn't, he'd wanted something else, something more tangible. Freedom from want, from family – independence. Freedom from, not freedom to. He had no regrets.

3

His meeting with the planners went well even by his standards – and God knows, he was used to getting his own way. Afterwards he went straight to the agent's office.

The partner he'd arranged to see wasn't there. 'Oh dear, I am sorry, Mr Wade.' The secretary was badly flustered; she wriggled uncomfortably in her stiff blue suit and the white flounce of her blouse fluttered and writhed. 'But we weren't expecting you just yet. Mr Lambton's still out on his last appointment.'

'I see.' He was curt. He kept his eyes on a vague point just beyond her left shoulder. Encounters like this invariably brought out the boorish side of his nature.

In a hopeful, placating voice she said, 'I could make you some coffee, if you'd like.'

Regretting his rudeness, he smiled and said yes, thank you. Coffee would be most welcome. With obvious relief, she led him up a flight of narrow stairs to an unoccupied office. Apologising for the chill, she snapped on the two-bar electric fire, and hurried off to make the coffee.

Left to himself, his unease returned. He couldn't settle. Uncomfortable questions forced their way to the front of his mind. What was he doing here? Was this all his life amounted to, the endless buying, developing and selling of one site after another? What choice did he have? It was all he knew. All the same, it was irksome being cooped up in here. He should have said no to the coffee and taken a stroll round the town instead. He started to pace. Brushing against the ancient desk left an exclamation mark of dust on his trousers. He flicked at it with forefinger and thumb and went over to the window. The glass was dirty and the pane cracked across one corner. In the yard below a row of grey metal dustbins, their lids all askew, clustered against the wall. Next to these was a precarious stack of stationery boxes. As he watched, a black and white tomcat systematically marked its territory with much stamping of its feet and shuddering of its tail.

The secretary returned with the coffee. It was thick and dark, like the mud-coffee he and Helen used to make, mixing it in a rubber bucket with a stick filched from their mother's kindling pile.

He came to a decision. Thanking her, he said he'd changed his mind. He was going for a walk.

In the white-gold sunlight his ill-temper vanished, leaving him liberated and light, like a snake that has just shed its skin. On the other side of the road was a cattle market. Although it wasn't market day and the cobbled yards were empty, the sweet smell of decay lingered in the straw-filled gutters. Running alongside the market was a building, a long, single-storey timber construction which had a board outside announcing that an auction of antiques was in progress. His interest in antiques was vague and of a purely practical nature. He had a friend, James Peterson, who exported to the States and who, some years ago, had furnished his house for him. Maybe James was here, and if not, well, it was as good a way as any of wasting half an hour.

The crowded auction room contrived to be both cluttered and cavernous – this last resulting from the pitched roof which rose to a cobwebby height, punctuated by sloping skylights through which occasional shafts of winter sun penetrated. Halfway along, the roof space was spanned by a broad beam from which hung various items: a tarnished copper warming pan with a handle honeycombed by woodworm, a bedraggled and snarling lop-eared bear's head, and a collection of vicious-looking iron implements which made him wonder whether the auctioneers were selling the contents of a local torture chamber. He decided with wry disappointment that they were more likely to be domestic items, the sort of things that dangle over kitchen ranges, or are found propped in inglenook fireplaces.

As for the floor space, most of this was taken up with dusty furniture, much of it heavily carved, some of it spindly-legged and dainty, but none of it, so far as he could tell, of any great quality. At the far end of the room, directly in front of the auctioneer's rostrum, was a broad table covered with blue cloth and stacked with an array of china and silver-plate. The auctioneer was a round man with a red, pendulous face, a dusty serge suit and a plum-coloured bow tie. As he announced each lot the porters put their heads together in a whispered consultation before finally locating the item and holding it up for display.

'Lot two-three-two.' The auctioneer's disdainful voice hissed from beneath a white moustache stained yellow at the edges like the fur round a poodle's genitals. 'Lot two-three-two, three nineteenth-century chamber pots. Where do we start, then?' The two porters bickered over which pot to hold up and ended by making a juggler's attempt at all three.

Resisting an urge to applaud, Charles eased his way between the furniture, excusing himself as he edged round the preoccupied buyers, until he found a space next to the black iron pot-bellied stove which appeared to be the room's only source of heat. After the fierce cold of the January day, the warmth made his sinuses tingle. He leant back against the rough pine walls and closed his eyes. Immediately the voice of the auctioneer and the hum of voices round him took on a sing-song quality. As he dozed, images darted into his mind: Dad confiding the best way to get a good shine on his shoes, his mother jabbing her finger at a passage in the Gospels that he'd failed to learn by heart. He started to protest, and his head rolled sideways and his hair snagged on a splinter in the panelling and he woke with a start to the suddenly noisy auction room.

He took a steadying breath and smoothed down his hair. If possible the room was more crowded now than when he'd arrived. There were groups of rough-looking, youngish men with greasy hair straggling over the shoulders of their sheepskin coats; older men in shabby waistcoats; middle-aged women with gloves, handbags and headscarves. There were some younger women too, these more haphazardly dressed. In all more of this sex than his own.

He shuddered, and huddled deeper into his coat.

And then he saw her.

He noticed her because she stood apart from the others. She was totally absorbed in what she was doing, bidding for each lot with an amused toss of her head. The auctioneer clearly knew her because not once did he ask her name. One by one the lots were knocked down to her and she added them to the list on the back of her Gestetnered catalogue. From where he stood, he could just make out the blurring of purple machine-ink and her wavering columns of pounds, shillings and pence.

He continued to watch her, fascinated by the way she stood, the way she wrinkled her nose and shook her head at the auctioneer when she wasn't prepared to pay any more – and the way, now and again, she suddenly re-entered the bidding, wrong-footing her opponent to win the prize. And yet he was confused; there was something odd about her. Perhaps it was to do with the fact that, though small, she gave a sense of occupying a much larger space than her body required. She had presence. He had a weird feeling that there was more to her than he could see, that she was some-how all-knowing – a sibyl or a sorceress unconcerned with disguise as she stood secure within her magic circle.

Absurd. Sorceress indeed. Apart from her hair, a torrent of auburn curls showering her shoulders, she was remarkably ordi-nary. To break the spell, he described her to himself – a short woman in jeans and a suede jerkin trimmed with fur and decorated with green embroidery scrolls. She wore open-toed clogs on her bare feet and a coin bracelet jangled at her wrist. Gipsy or hippie, either or both. Her feet must be frozen.

He allowed his gaze to rake upwards from the curled toes, past the ringed hands clutching catalogue and pen, to the wide, stern eyes that locked on to his and held him. His face burnt. She grinned. And then she winked at him, and turned back to her buying.

With a grunt of annoyance, he thrust his hands deep into the pockets of his coat. He was cold; he shivered and moved closer to the stove. His fingers tangled with the reassuring jumble of his car keys and he shifted his feet as the chill from the concrete floor seeped through the soles of his shoes.

No point in staying here. He'd seen a pub across the road. God, it was cold.

He adjusted his scarf, ready to go back outside. Just then the auctioneer announced that there would be a short break before he commenced the next stage of the sale, the silver and jewellery. There was an immediate upheaval in the room and a roar of conversation. Charles was jostled and almost lost his balance in the surge towards the table. He waited for the crush to ease, then turned to leave.

At which point, a voice behind him said, 'Excuse me, but do I know you?'

4

Twenty minutes later, as he waited his turn at the crowded bar, he wondered how on earth he'd managed to get himself in this position.

She'd come up behind him saying, 'Excuse me, but do I know you?' and he'd swung round to find her standing so close that she bumped his arm when someone nudged against her, and he had to put out a hand to steady her. He withdrew it quickly. She was smiling up at him, waiting for his answer. Her eyes were a turbulent grey flecked with gold, like sun on a winter sea. 'Well do I?' she persisted.

'No, I don't believe so.'

'Then do you know me from somewhere, is that it? Did I sell you something, a dinner service or a coal helmet – or a suit of armour?' She laughed. He wondered why.

'Not that I'm aware.' He heard, as if from the outside, the way he clipped his words, like shears snipping tin.

'You were staring,' she said. 'Perhaps you didn't realise.'

'I realised,' he said. How had he got sucked into this conversation? He wanted to get away. He said, 'You winked at me.' She nodded and grinned. 'Why would you do a thing like that?'

'Not very ladylike, was it?'

He thought, she's making fun of me, she's saying what she thinks I think. 'Why?' he persisted. 'Why did you do it?'

'I don't know.' She was tiring of the game. Her attention wandered and she smiled at someone behind him. He resisted the urge to turn and see who it was. Then she wriggled her shoulders and her mischievous gaze danced up and across his face and she said, 'I honestly don't know why – to put you in your place, perhaps.' She considered him with her head cocked on one side, like Auntie Peg's budgie sizing up its cuttlefish. 'Well, whatever.' She shrugged and, folding her catalogue, stuffed it into her carpet shoulder-bag with much jingling of her bracelet. 'I'm done for the day,' she said. 'Don't need any furniture. Nice meeting you.' She started to turn away.

'Wait.' His voice came too loud, and he was startled by the effort it took not to grab her by the arm. 'Do you have to go?'

He was gripping his car keys so tightly that they dug into his palm. Don't do this, said the voice inside him, let her go, shut the door, turn out the light.

He said, 'I'm sorry I stared and made you uncomfortable.' She waited. 'I'd like to apologise properly. Let me buy you lunch.' She scowled and adjusted the strap of her bag. Quite right. He was being crass. Still, no matter. If she was offended – too bad. It wasn't as if he wanted to have lunch with her, in fact he couldn't think what had prompted him to ask.

I don't know you.

She said, 'No, I don't think so, thank you.'

'Why not?' He sounded aggressive – he was confused. If he genuinely didn't want her to say yes, why was he so terrified of being turned down?

She said, 'Because you're a complete stranger. Never talk to strange men, my mum used to say.'

'I don't think I'm particularly strange,' he said, then laughed. 'My mother used to say things like that, except she was more concerned about strange women.'

'Speaking for myself,' she said, 'I rather like the idea of being a strange woman.' She bit her lip, considered him for a moment, then came to a decision. 'Okay, a drink – not lunch, just a drink. But you'll have to help me load my car.'

Before he could agree or argue, she'd slipped through the crowd like water through fingers. She approached a porter who greeted her with a grin and produced some boxes from beneath the display table. The two of them chatted and joked as they wrapped her purchases – a dinner service, two tea services, various teapots and jugs, a couple of Staffordshire figures and several brass candlesticks – and packed them into the boxes. When they were done, Charles saw her slip something into the old man's palm before turning to beckon him.

He picked up one of the boxes, she took the other and he followed her out of the sale room, staggering across the yard to where her car was parked. She opened the back doors of the Morris Traveller and shoved the boxes inside. Considering the breakable nature of their contents, she was remarkably cavalier with them. As she slammed shut the doors, little flakes of varnish showered off the wooden struts. She turned the key in the lock and, turning to face him, said, 'Oh dear, look at you; you didn't exactly come dressed for this, did you?' Before he could stop her, she had him by the arm and was brushing the dust off him with short sharp strokes of the flat of her hand.

The pub was dreadful, all mock beams and flock wallpaper, glittering embossed brass plaques, horse brasses and hunting prints. Standing at the bar and huddled round the little tables were people he recognised from the auction room. Several of them waved or called to his companion and one man beckoned her with a lift of his chin. Out of the corner of his eye, Charles saw her shake her head and indicate that she wasn't alone.

She found them a seat by the window and he went to the bar to order their drinks, draught Guinness for her and whisky and water for himself. He glanced back at her. She'd taken off her jerkin and draped it over the back of the seat. The man who'd beckoned was standing over her, one foot lodged on the strut of her chair. He said something, and Charles heard her laugh. He spoke again and she shook her head and her bronze hair coiled against the bright yellow ribbing of her polo-necked sweater.

The drinks arrived and he made his way to the table. Her friend had gone. He passed her her glass and as he sat down, she saluted him. She sipped her drink and he was captivated by the way the coffee-coloured froth lined her lips, by the unselfconscious dart of her tongue. He said, 'You haven't told me your name.'

She glanced up. 'No, but then you haven't told me yours. Officially you're still a stranger . . .'

'Charles Wade,' he said.

'Sophie,' she responded. 'Sophie MacKenzie.' She held out her hand. To take it he had to half rise and reach across the table. He released himself quickly from her dry grip and sank back into his seat. She said, 'Tell me, are you always so formal, or have I caught you on a bad day?'

'No, I'd say this is about the norm,' he said, and felt the tug of a grin. She was forthright; he liked that. He had a tendency to be forthright himself. Blunt, Leonard always said, but then Leonard was prone to overstatement. He said, 'You know, you were pretty formidable in there. That was why I was staring. I can't imagine how anyone dare bid against you.'

Lest you put a hex on them, he thought with a clutch of hysteria.

She shrugged, 'All part of the act.' She changed the subject. 'What were you doing at the sale? I haven't seen you before; you're not a dealer.'

'As a matter of fact, I am,' he said, 'but in property, not antiques.'

'Ah,' she was amused. 'That Charles Wade. So go on, tell me. What were you doing at the auction?'

He settled in his seat and began to tell her, sketchily at first, then in more depth, about the site he'd come to see and his plans for it, and about the enthusiasm of the planners. Even as he spoke he marvelled at his indiscretion. What if a rival bidder was in the pub, at the next table? He didn't mention figures, but he did talk about ideas; what if the phantom eavesdropper hadn't seen the site's potential? Or perhaps this MacKenzie woman was in the pay of a rival. He almost laughed at his mounting paranoia. Ridiculous. They weren't even talking about him any more; she was telling him about her shop in Cambridge, about her husband and Enid who helped her out three days a week. It was all perfectly ordinary, perfectly natural. He'd lived alone too long and had become obsessed with secrecy.

The barman flickered the lights. Charles looked up, blinking, as he rose from the soft, rounded dark of baptismal immersion to the glittering surface and the scything sunlight.

They were almost the last people to leave. She grinned at him as she wriggled her arms into the stiff suede sleeves of her jerkin. He tried to help her. He felt awkward and the fur trim left a slightly greasy deposit on his fingers.

They crossed the road side by side, and he held her car door for her as she settled herself in the driving seat. When he pushed the door shut she cranked down the window. She said, 'Thank you for the drink, strange man.'

'My pleasure.'

'Oh dear, he's gone all formal again.' She laughed, and the gold flecks danced in her eyes.

He smiled, but wished it didn't have to end in such a rush. If only he could have shaken her hand, made some contact; but it was too late, she was cocooned in her car. He said, 'You'll be all right driving home, will you?'

She contorted her face into an expression of exaggerated innocence, 'It were only the one, officer.'

'Just take care, that's all.'

'You sound like my father.'

'Really.'

'Fussing, I mean.' She was laughing at him again, he was sure. She said, 'Of course I'll take care. Don't worry. Deep down I'm a responsible type.' She started the engine and adjusted her rear-view mirror. She slipped the car into gear, then slipped it straight back out again and dived into her Axminster bag. She hunted for a moment, then found what she was looking for. 'Here, take this,' she said, handing him a business card. 'Just in case you ever come to Cambridge. Might be worth your while, rumour has it we undervalue our property.' She re-engaged the gear and released the handbrake. She seemed suddenly embarrassed. 'Must go. See you.'

He thought, I don't suppose you will, and watched as she pulled out on to the main road, disappearing round the corner with a final wave from the open window.

When she was out of sight, he remembered Lambton and his appointment. Stuffing her card into his pocket, he crossed the road to the agent's office.

All through the meeting he fingered her unread card, turning it over and over, running his nail along the edge and folding down the corner. The meeting went well, Lambton would put his offer to his clients. He would let Charles know in a day or two. Charles said, 'Make it a day. The offer stands till five pm tomorrow.'

On the way back to London he wondered why he'd made that proviso. It wasn't necessary. He wasn't in that much of a hurry. Still, it could do no harm to chivvy them along and if it backfired, well, the site wasn't that exceptional.

It was dark by the time he arrived home. It had turned foggy and the light from the fanlight over his front door transformed the grey, moisture-laden air into a golden fuzz. And then a honey-coloured rug rippled down the front steps as Emmy opened the door smiling a greeting and reaching to help him with his coat. He could smell his dinner cooking. 'Nice piece of beef,' said Emmy. 'About twenty minutes, is that all right?'

He went into his study and crossing to the desk, switched on the lamp and sat down. The buttoned leather of the chair was cold and it creaked as he moved. He sat for a moment, staring into the shadows, then pulled Mrs MacKenzie's card from his pocket.

It was printed in gold on dark red. The lettering, which had a Celtic look, told him that she traded under the name of Dragon's Lair Antiques, and that her shop was situated in the Market Place, Cambridge.

The card, which had been crisp and new when she'd handed it over, was now tired and buckled. And slightly unreal. He gave a little self-conscious laugh as he pushed at it with his forefinger, half expecting it to merge with the red-gold of the mahogany, and disappear.

5

You know, after all these years he's still got that card, keeping it safe like a relic, like the mouldering finger joint of some long-dead saint.

He said, 'I suppose you'll want to see it, won't you?'

'No, it doesn't matter, it's okay.'

But he didn't seem to hear me. He turned to Leonard saying, 'Will you fetch it. Fetch the tin. You know where it is.'

When Leonard had gone, Jonathan's father sat back in his chair. I thought about what he'd told me, about his first sight of Sophie and his fantasy that she was some kind of a sibyl or a witch. Was he speaking with the benefit of hindsight, or was that really how he'd seen her? On balance, I decided he was telling the truth. The only thing I wasn't sure about was his supposed innocence. After all, it was the tail end of the 1960s when he met her – 1968, I think – and he wasn't young, so just how credible was his sexual naivety?

It was as if I'd asked the question out loud. He said, 'I suppose it must seem odd. People have this idea that in those days everybody was jumping into bed with everybody else at every opportunity. But it wasn't like that, Alex. Only for the few. And for people my age – think of our upbringing. I can remember the war, Alex, what it was like in those shelters, smelling of metal and wet cement with the bombers overhead throbbing as if they were inside your head, like a pulse.' He stopped. Above us the floorboards creaked. Jo, who'd fallen asleep on the sofa, was making little sucking noises. He said, 'I was the parent generation. Sophie could almost have passed for my daughter.'

'But not quite. The difference wasn't that great. . . .'

'Twelve, thirteen years. That's not really the point. It seemed more. Sometimes, anyway. But she was old, too. Older than me. I never could really tell. It was as though she was two people.' As he spoke, he tugged at the pad of skin next to his thumbnail. The flesh beneath was red and sore.

Then Leonard came in. Perching beside me on the arm of the sofa, he handed Charles a red-tartan shortbread tin. With great concentration, Charles prised off the lid. For a moment or two his fingers probed amongst the contents, and then he found what he was looking for.

Sophie MacKenzie's business card had been much handled. Its deep colour had become diluted and it was paler at the softened edges than at the middle. I read the address. I knew the place. It was a jeweller's now, I told him, and his blank eyes stared back at me as if the information was worse than meaningless. I looked down at the card. How on earth had he managed to hold on to his relic? He'd left that house, the house where Jonathan had been brought up, in a frenzy of violence. I could hardly imagine him careering down those steps and out into the square with a tartan biscuit tin tucked under his arm.

Then I realised. Of course, it was Leonard. At some point he would have crept back to the house – perhaps on his own, perhaps with Emmy's connivance – and searched through all the cupboards and drawers . . . for what? Anything incriminating? No. What Leonard had been looking for was anything precious, all those tender personal things that shouldn't be looked on, or even touched, by others. It was Leonard who had left the house with a biscuit tin under his arm, Leonard who had kept it safe until Charles was free to reclaim it.

By noon the following day Lambton had telephoned to confirm acceptance of his offer. Charles promptly instructed Peter Knight, his solicitor. He then arranged for his architect to visit the site to work out detailed plans for development. All in all, it had been a satisfactory excursion. The only matter outstanding was Mrs Mac-Kenzie.

She'd as good as invited him to Cambridge. Not that he'd go. His schedule was far too tight, there was no way he could fit in a trip to Cambridge.

And yet he couldn't settle, couldn't shake off the flickering memory of gold-flecked eyes and supernatural fantasies. Perhaps he should go – if he saw her again, he'd see her for what she really was, and lay her irritating ghost.

Once again he dismissed his chauffeur and drove himself. This time the journey was longer. He was tired by the time he reached Cambridge. His concentration waned and he lost himself in the maze of narrow streets. As he edged the big car between the old buildings with their sooty facades punched with black windows glittering like split coal, he fervently wished he'd allowed Thompson to drive.

He took a turn, and then another and another, and suddenly he wasn't in the centre any more. That's it, he thought, this was a stupid idea. If I see a sign to the London road I'll take it.

The next road he turned into was inappropriately called Gold Street. On either side the houses had been demolished and the cleared sites were being used as a car park. The chalky rubble crunched beneath his tyres and the bonnet of the car bounced as he dipped first into, then out of, a large pothole. He found a space next to a pale blue Morris 1000 with orange sunbursts painted on the doors and roof, and a straw hat on the parcel shelf.

As he climbed out of the car a woman with a pushchair came towards him along what had once been the pavement. The pushchair wheels bounced and rattled against the stones and the baby grizzled. Charles called to her, asking the way to the city centre.

It turned out he'd parked on the fringes of what she called the "Kite". 'Because of its shape, see,' she explained. It would take him ten, maybe fifteen minutes to walk into town. He thought it was probably best to do this rather than get back into the car and risk getting lost again. He followed the woman's directions, along Fitzroy Street, through another car park, this time enclosed by a square of Georgian cottages, and into the town. Suddenly the quiet of the winter afternoon gave way to a heaving bubble of noise. He asked directions again, this time being more specific about his destination. It turned out he was quite close.

On the corner of the market square a busker played a violin. As her bow leapt and danced across the strings, sending the notes ricocheting off the buildings, he realised he knew this piece.

Paganini.

He dug some coins from his pocket and tossed them into the violin case lying open on the pavement in front of her.

He was sure it was Paganini. Leonard had tried to educate him but had been forced to concede that he was musically illiterate.

He should telephone Leonard. Peter Knight had offered him a junior partnership. Leonard deserved it. Some time ago he'd toyed with the idea of forming his own legal department, with Leonard at its head. Luckily, he'd never actually made the offer.

Luckily. Why? It was impossible for him to articulate the nature of their misunderstanding.

Leonard's birthday – yes – and a shop in Bond Street; a bronze in the window, a fine piece perched on a Grecian type column, surrounded by disembodied plaster hands and feet painted silver, sprinkled with red metallic dust. Perfect for Leonard's flat. Leonard had laughed when he'd unwrapped it, 'It looks like you,' he said. And then he'd brought out the Paganini. Charles remembered the way he'd balanced the record on his long, delicate fingers, taking care not to touch the playing surface as he lowered it over the chrome spindle – and how they'd sat side by side, and Leonard had said, 'When I'm on my own, I like to lie on the floor.'

'What?'

'Improves the sound. Shall we try it?' Positioning himself between the speakers, Leonard stretched himself full-length on the floor.

Charles wondered if the floor was dusty, if he'd mess up his suit and how he'd explain it to Em. Gingerly, he lowered himself down beside Leonard and slowly uncoiled his spine against the pine boards. The floor was hard, it dug into his shoulders and heels. A draught sliced under the door. Above, the ceiling was wreathed in shadow. Through the enclosing bars of the music he could hear the steady sigh of Leonard's breathing. He tried to match the other man's rhythm.

'This is ridiculous,' he muttered and rolled his head sideways. Leonard's pale face and almond-shaped eyes were very close to his.

And since that day, they had barely spoken.

He shook himself free of the memory. Sophie MacKenzie – soon he'd see her again. It was unnerving the way she haunted him.

The cobbled market square was flanked on one side by a church, on another by a massive, flat-fronted building that looked like a temple. He stepped between stalls selling vegetables caked in black fen soil, and others set out with sheepskin goods and Indian cotton skirts and tops, suede shoulder-bags and gaudy waistcoats. He paused by a display of second-hand books and picked up a volume on twentieth-century architecture. 'Five bob, that one,' called the stallholder from the shadows at the back. 'Nice condition.' Charles nodded, and replaced the book.

The day was very cold and grey clouds scudded low, scouring the tops of the buildings. He turned up his collar against the spiteful wind that whipped between the stalls, flapping their awnings and cartwheeling litter across the cobbles. He called to the stallholder that he was looking for an antique shop called Dragon's Lair. 'Sophie's place, you mean? Through there, mate.' He pointed. 'On the corner.'

Sophie MacKenzie. He formed her name with his lips, but made no sound. He'd been deluded, of course. There was nothing special about her, she was just an unremarkable woman trying to scratch a living from her antique shop; the wicked, glittering eyes, the teasing laugh, were his own invention.

He skirted the edge of the market and a gust of wind caught him from behind, lifting his hair. As he smoothed it down, he caught his first sight of her shop. It was quite small and situated on the corner of a paved alley. One of its windows looked on to the alley itself, the other overlooked the market. The door was set at an angle across the corner.

He stepped closer. Her display was not brightly lit but the hectic jumble emitted the occasional dull gleam of brass or silver or the sheen of a glaze. Like any shopper, he leant forward with his nose close to the glass, as if examining the goods, searching for a particular item amongst the clutter of jugs and basins, oil lamps and figurines. But what he was searching for wasn't in the window. He waited until his eyes became accustomed to the gloom and he was able to penetrate the dim interior.

And then he saw her. She was sitting at the back of the shop at a small, untidy desk and was speaking on the telephone with much gesticulation. He was so close to the glass that he could feel the cold radiating from it. He must have moved, certainly something made her look up. She recognised him and, apparently without pausing in her conversation, waved and gestured to him to come in.

He closed the shop door behind him, shutting out the noise of the traffic and the jangling bicycles with their trilling bells, and she signalled that she wouldn't be long. Crouching back over her phone, she said, 'Yes, I know. But listen, tell me again. The sale's when?' She fell silent and, wedging the heavy handset between her chin and shoulder, pulled a pad of paper towards her and began to write.

Charles waited. The tiny shop made him feel ungainly. He wanted to hunch his shoulders and duck his head, make himself inconspicuous. And not just because of his size. His flimsy excuse for being here had something to do with it.

Willing himself to relax, he took a deep breath, inhaling a magic cocktail of beeswax and vinegar and something more acrid which he couldn't identify. And something else – lavender; he was sure he could smell lavender.

From the rear of the shop, from behind a half-open door, came the sound of spoons chinking against cups and the hiss of a kettle.

He took a step forward. He hardly knew where to put his feet, the place was so cluttered. Small items – ring-trees and silver boxes, even a darning mushroom – lay scattered over every surface. Wall brackets and tables and chests of drawers had been pressed into service, presumably until they were sold. Bits and bobs were piled on the furniture and under it, were hung from the walls and from chair-backs, and even from the ceiling.

He took another step, and blundered into a table, almost breaking a jug. She laughed as he saved it with an improbable juggle, then said to her caller, 'Hey Bill, I'll have to go, there's a thumping great bull just blundered into my china shop. I'll see you Tuesday, okay?' She put down the phone and tossing back her hair, opened her arms in welcome. 'Behold,' she said, 'the dragon in her lair.'

He said, 'Looks to me like you could do with larger premises.'

'Ever the professional,' she accused. 'Come on, pull up a chair. Coffee?'

'Black. No sugar.'

60

Her eyes danced and she bit her lip. She found his taste in coffee amusing. He felt the beginnings of a scowl and she said, 'Don't do that, it makes you look old.' Turning, she called over her shoulder, 'Enid, can we have an extra coffee please? Black.'

He busied himself clearing a chair, lifting a box off the seat and removing a lace christening gown from the back.

She said, 'I didn't think you'd come.'

'Neither did I.'

Enid arrived with two speckled mugs of coffee. As she set them down, she asked if it was all right if she left a bit early. Sophie said fine and a few minutes later she emerged from the back room wearing a big brown tweed coat, a woolly hat and carrying a black handbag. She said, 'Two o'clock Saturday, that okay with you, Sophie?' Sophie nodded and smiled.

As the door swung shut behind her, Charles saw that the afternoon had faded into an early dusk and the bulbs lighting the stalls dangled like strings of glowing skulls over the fruit and veg. Inside, it was so dark that he could barely make out the glimmering shape of Sophie's face. She reached out and switched on the anglepoise lamp perched like a jagged crow on the corner of her desk. She fiddled with the shade until it threw a disk of yellow light round her mug.

He was happy, he realised with a tingle of surprise. He stretched his legs, and crossed his ankles; the tension, the weariness of the long drive and the weight of anticipation, began to ebb. It was delicious, like getting straight out of a hot bath and into bed.

The shop door banged open and an icy gust of air chilled away the cosiness. The customer was middle-aged with blonde hair fading to grey. She seemed embarrassed by the violence of her entry. 'Are you still open?' she asked. 'Could I look round?'

'Go ahead,' Sophie reassured her. 'Shout if you need anything.'

The woman began to edge round the shop, like a suicide skirting the parapet of a building. Charles felt sorry for her. After a few minutes of superficial browsing, she picked up the jug he'd almost broken. Holding it gingerly towards the light she said, 'It is pretty, isn't it?' He sensed that she half-expected Sophie to contradict her. 'Such a nice colour,' she continued, growing bold.

'Never mind the colour.' Sophie went to join her. 'Feel it. Go on.

Just feel the quality of the glaze.' She took the jug from the woman and slid her hand seductively round its belly, watching the woman's reaction as her fingers lingered over the caress.

Ten minutes later the woman left with the jug cocooned in great swathes of crimson tissue paper. Sophie closed the till on the laboriously filled-in cheque and said, 'That's that then. Time to shut up shop. Are you in a mad rush to get back to the big city?'

'No.'

'No one waiting for you? Your wife?'

He shook his head. She waited. He said, 'I'm not married.'

'Yes,' she mused. 'I had a feeling that was the case. Which means,' she became brusque, 'you can come home with me, have dinner, meet Michael.'

She drove him to Gold Street and he was relieved to find his car still there. They must have looked a strange little cavalcade, the big black Rolls following the little Morris Traveller through the winding lanes to the village where she lived.

They entered her cottage by the back door which led straight into a kitchen lined with pine units topped with mustard-coloured tiles. There was a straw mat on the red, quarry-tiled floor and trailing pot-plants hung from the ceiling in woven string nets.

Several doors led off the kitchen and, taking his coat, Sophie disappeared through one of them. When she came back, he said, 'Look, I don't have a wife but I do have a housekeeper. Could I use your phone?' She directed him through to the hall. There was yet another plant on the telephone table; its striped green and white blades tangled with his fingers as he dialled.

Back in the kitchen, Sophie was standing over by the sink topping and tailing carrots. 'That was quick,' she said without looking round. He didn't answer. He was having trouble associating this domestic scene with the woman he'd met at the auction. Not that she was any less enchanting, but it was difficult to reconcile, to see clearly – she was like a window winking in the sun, many colours, many elements. Or like water. Yes, a stream sometimes turbulent and dashing itself against rocks, sometimes tranquil, but the same water with the same destination.

She was talking. He said, 'Sorry. What did you say?'

'If you go through there,' she directed him towards one of the other doors, pointing with her peeler, 'you'll find some sherry. If you'd like some, that is. It's not mandatory.'

'Right. Thank you.'

'And while you're at it, I need the Calvados – right-hand cupboard of the dresser.'

The walls and ceiling of her dining room were painted a deep, midnight blue. Over the waxy, antique pine refectory table hung a tarnished brass chandelier. The dresser was also pine. Pottery plates decorated with primary splashes of red and green lined its shelves and in the centre was a brass tray with a cut-glass decanter two-thirds full of a tawny sherry and, clustered around this like pupils round a teacher, a set of matching glasses. He poured sherry for them both, took it through to her, then went back for the Calvados.

On his return, he found the kitchen occupied by a large, bearded ginger-haired man in a baggy buff sweater. 'Hey, Soph,' he said. 'What's that bloody great Roller doing parked in the drive? How am I supposed to. . . .'

'It's mine,' said Charles. The man swung round and Sophie touched his arm, restraining him with the lightest possible pressure, before stepping forward to relieve Charles of the Calvados. 'Is it in your way, would you like me to move it?'

'This is Michael,' Sophie interrupted. 'Michael, this is Mr Wade, I told you about him, remember?'

Michael MacKenzie squared his shoulders and didn't answer at once. He was a fraction taller than Charles, and bulky with it. He seemed to fill the kitchen like a teddy bear crammed into a doll's house.

'The property man,' Sophie persisted, at the same time urging Michael forward with a hand on his shoulder. It was an inappropriate gesture, more the way a parent might urge a shy child to make friends.

Charles said, 'Perhaps I'd better be going.'

'Of course you're not going. You're staying to dinner. I invited you.'

'I know, but I don't want to intrude. . . .'

'You're not. Is he, Michael?'

'Of course not.' The voice was wary, but not grudging.

'If you're sure. . . .'

'Sure we're sure.' This time Michael was emphatic.

'About the car. . . .'

'The car's fine. Leave it where it is.' Stepping forward, Michael took Charles's hand in a big-boned grasp and belatedly pumped his welcome. 'Soph says you're in the property business. What are you? An estate agent?'

'Not exactly.' He saw a flicker of amusement pass across Sophie's face.

She said, 'Don't bicker – you hardly know one another! You're in my way, the pair of you. Michael, take Charles out to the barn, show him that box you're working on.'

Michael looked Charles up and down. 'Are you interested?' he demanded.

'Charles.' Sophie treated him to the full force of her gold-flecked eyes. 'The choice is yours, workshop or sitting room?'

Michael grimaced. 'Don't be fooled,' he said. 'That's not a choice she's giving you, it's a thinly disguised order.'

The barn was across the yard. Charles waited while Michael fumbled with the padlock on a small wooden door set into a much larger one. They had to duck their heads as they stepped over the sill.

It was draughty inside, a great cavern of a place. Scattered about were bits and pieces of broken furniture, tables without legs, chairs without seats. Up in the rafters fluorescent tubes hung festooned with cobwebs. The floor was covered with varicoloured curls of woodshavings. As he shuffled his feet, Michael explained, 'Insulation. Leastways, that's what I tell Soph when she nags me to clear up.' He glanced sideways at Charles. 'You didn't ought to let her bully you.'

'I wasn't aware that she was.'

'Well, she does it with a smile. But take no notice of me – what do I know?' He gave a harsh laugh. 'Here, come and look at this.' They crossed to the bench, their feet scuffing the shavings, crushing them. All around rose the smell of turpentine and linseed oil and resin.

Charles said, 'Does she bully you?'

Michael glanced at him, then looked away. 'Always has,' he said lightly. 'We were in the same class at school – it was hell. Come on, I want to show you something.' Sitting on the bench was a large rosewood jewellery box. 'What d'you reckon?' said Michael. 'Beautiful, eh?' He ran his large, freckled hand tenderly across its surface, pointing out the almost unnoticeable repairs and displaying the quirks and individualities of the original manufacture. 'Now what d'you make of that? See, it's got a Bramah lock.'

'A what?' Charles brushed sawdust from his jacket.

'Bramah.' Michael chuckled. 'Go on, try it, feel that movement.' And Charles had to turn the key back and forth to sense the quality of the unseen mechanism.

Dad would have loved this place. Odd, Dad jumping into his mind like that. Back at home he'd fitted a bench at one end of the garage and would spend hours in there. He said, 'My father would have been in seventh heaven here.'

'His line of work, was it?'

He shook his head, remembering the gaberdine mac back in the days when it was new, and the bulging briefcase and the harassed expression on his father's face as he left for work. 'No, he was a bank clerk; but he pottered about doing bits and pieces of woodwork in his spare time.'

'You didn't take after him.'

'No, not really.'

'Each to his own. Let's go back, shall we? I imagine she's calmed down by now.'

To his surprise, he found he was enjoying Michael's company and they entered the kitchen still talking. The room was muggy and moist with condensation and Sophie was flushed as she hustled them through to the dining room. Only as he sat down at the table did he realise just how hungry he was.

Sophie had made a dish of chicken pieces in a cream sauce spiked with Calvados. There was wine as well, and a basket piled with wedges of french bread. They finished off with fruit – Sophie ate a pear, slicing it with a pearl-handled knife – and then went through to the sitting room where a fire had been lit. He and Michael sat in deep armchairs, Sophie on the sofa with her bare feet tucked under her.

Michael poured generous glasses of apricot brandy, and Charles leant back in his chair enjoying the spread of warmth, the ease of their company.

'Come on then, tell us about this property business of yours.' Michael leant forward and peered into the log basket as if choosing a chocolate from a Christmas selection. 'Not into slum clearance and intimidating little old ladies, I hope.'

'Certainly not.'

'Michael!' Sophie hissed.

Michael considered his chosen log, then glanced across at his wife. 'Just asking, no harm in that.' He tossed the log on to the fire and it landed in a shower of sparks.

'It's all right,' said Charles. 'He's quite right. There's a lot of sharp practice goes on, but I don't get involved in that sort of thing.'

'So what do you do?' she demanded, wriggling down in her seat and rolling her glass against her chin.

'Retail development, industrial. Some residential, but not so much.'

She ruffled her curls. 'You're very rich then, are you, Charles?'

'Hey, Soph.' Now Michael was embarrassed.

To Sophie Charles said, 'Yes. Very.' And she raised her glass in a mock salute.

After that it was his turn to do the quizzing. He wanted to know how she'd got into the antiques trade. She explained that she'd begun by working for an auction room, learnt her trade watching other people deal before branching out on her own. He listened drowsily, watching as the heat from the fire forced the resin to ooze from the cut ends of the logs. The sound of her voice, the peaks and troughs of emphasis and conspiracy, enthralled him. There was something truly special about her. Did Michael realise how lucky he was? He glanced across at him. Yes, he did. He was listening with pride to a story he must have heard a hundred times and, as he listened, an indulgent smile softened his bluff face and his eyes followed every movement of her hypnotically darting hands. Charles felt a voyeuristic frisson, and thought what a delight it must be, what a terror, to be so enslaved.

Much later he noticed that the fire had dulled to a glowing

honeycomb and, checking his watch, saw that it was well after midnight. He said, 'Look, I'm sorry. I had no idea it was so late.' He edged forward in his chair and reached behind him for his jacket. 'I've had a marvellous evening, thank you. Both of you.'

Sophie said to Michael, 'Should he be driving back to London at this hour?'

'I'll be fine,' he said in an over-loud voice.

'Soph's right,' said Michael. 'We've had a fair bit to drink, and it's a bad road,'

'All the same. . . .'

'You must stay.' Sophie was firm. 'We always keep a bed made up for Michael's brother.' She stood up and began gathering together the glasses.

Looking from one to the other, Charles realised that so far as they were concerned, the matter was settled. He was annoyed, he didn't want to be coerced like this but, as he pushed himself out of his chair, he realised that they were right. He swayed slightly, and had to steady himself against the mantelpiece. To his relief, neither Sophie nor Michael appeared to notice. Waiting for the dizziness to pass, he made a show of examining the contents of the mantelpiece. It was well ordered and symmetrical, very different from the one in his mother's dining room. Brass candlesticks stood at either end, next to these a pair of bronze greyhounds. In the centre was a weird little carving. It appeared to be made of stone. It was a head, surely. He picked it up and weighed it in his hand. It was more or less spherical and had been crudely carved with a blank-eyed face. 'What's this?' he demanded of Michael.

'Ah, that.' Michael spoke in a conspiratorial whisper. 'I'd put that back if I were you. It's just something of Soph's. Celtic, I think. Best put it back. Come on, I'll show you your room.'

He slept well that night, despite the deafening country silence. He felt almost drugged as he buttoned his borrowed pyjamas and crawled between the sheets. As his head sank into the pillow he thought he detected a fluid quality to the darkness and, when he closed his eyes, he dissolved into that darkness, became one with it.

The following morning, after Michael had left for work, he and

Sophie lingered over their breakfast. They finished one pot of coffee and she went through to the kitchen to make another. When she returned, she brought with her a rack of fresh toast.

They sat facing one another across the pine dining table. They didn't say a great deal. She'd had a catalogue come in the post and was checking through it, marking it up and making notes in the margin. He had the newspaper open at the business page. It was like being married. He finished his coffee in a single gulp, folded the paper and stood up to leave. Sophie looked surprised, but didn't comment.

As they walked to his car, she linked her arm in his and leant against him. 'Tell me, Mr Wade, aren't you glad you came? It's been fun, hasn't it?'

'If you call getting me drunk fun. . . .'

'Don't be so stuffy. Anyway, you weren't drunk, just a bit unsteady. Hey,' she stopped and pulled him round to face her, and now she wasn't Michael's wife any longer, she was the sibyl from the sale room. 'You'll come again, won't you?'

'I don't know.'

'You will,' she told him.

'Won't Michael mind?'

'You got on okay, didn't you?' He nodded. 'Good. Come for a weekend.'

'I don't know. I'm very busy.'

'Right. Fine.' She released him. 'Have it your own way.' He was suddenly alarmed; she was angry and he didn't know what to do, how to say he was sorry. He hadn't meant it how it sounded.

Or had he?

He climbed into the car and started the engine. She stood at the edge of the drive with her arms folded and her bare toes curled into the chill gravel. He said, 'You'll get frostbite.'

She shrugged and said, 'I'll live, don't worry about me. Go on, Charles. Go home.'

6

The galvanised metal meathook hung from a brass rail salvaged by Michael from an old plywood wardrobe. The chandelier suspended from the meathook swung to and fro at Sophie's touch. The glass tinkled; she hissed threateningly as she struggled to reassemble the jumble of crystal fragments. Each drop was threaded with a thin curl of rusted wire which had to be eased through tiny holes in the chandelier's series of brass hoops. Both drops and hoops were graded by size.

'Bloody thing!' Sophie cursed as a piece of wire jabbed under a fingernail and drew blood.

'Are you all right?' Enid appeared with a box of self-assembly chandelier parts. 'Where d'you want these?' Sophie pulled up a rickety bamboo table with a frayed raffia top. 'D'you want some TCP for that?'

'No. It'll stop in a minute.' She dabbed her bloody finger with a tissue. Pulling the box towards her, she rifled through it, measuring the crystal spears against the tier on which she was working. She wondered what Charles was doing. It was almost lunchtime. He'd be in his office, dictating letters to a bouffant secretary with a short skirt and stilettos. God no, that wasn't Charles's style. But what was his style? Where did he work, what sort of people did he employ? And a housekeeper, for God's sake. Who had a housekeeper these days? She tried to picture him, upright and immaculately groomed in his dark suit, his dark hair brushed back, his shirt crisp and white, gold glinting at his cuffs as he addressed a board meeting. It didn't feel right, he just wasn't part of the modern world.

The fact that he was such an oddity, such a misfit, lay at the root of her fascination. That day in the saleroom he'd stood all on his own, buttoned into his heavy overcoat, a stern man and a lost child, and in that bright and passing moment of insight she'd seen and understood and been filled with the desire to help. That was why she'd spoken to him, why she'd encouraged him to come to Cambridge, brought him back to the cottage and filled and refilled his glass until he had no choice but to stay.

Michael didn't understand. Or rather, he understood her impulse, but thought she was wrong. 'It's crazy, Soph. He's not like that. The man's rich, he's got influence – he's not some half-drowned kitten you can take in and feed.'

'I know,' she said. She wasn't stupid, she sensed the danger in him, but a wounded bear is as much entitled to healing as an injured kitten. She said, 'He's lonely. . . .'

'For Christ's sake!'

'I know what I know, Michael . . . I wish sometimes you'd look, really look. You take everything at face value, you get it all twisted. Life's not like that.'

'And what would you know about life?' His freckled face was flushed and angry. 'Theories and patterns and shapes – all up here.' He tapped his forehead. 'Bubbles, Soph. Join us down in the real world for once, why don't you?'

Charles sat at his desk listening to the clatter of Betty's typewriter and the distant trill of telephones, congratulating himself because it was Wednesday afternoon, and still he hadn't succumbed to the temptation to telephone Sophie MacKenzie. He leant back in his chair. Dusk had fallen and the bright office lights turned his window into a darkened mirror occupied by a man whose movements uncannily echoed his own.

To go back there – a pulse flickered at his throat – what a wild idea. Pointless. He had nothing in common with the MacKenzies. They were pleasant enough, but they'd soon run out of things to say to one another. Far better to let the friendship end now than have it fizzle out like a damp squib in a few months' time.

'And what sort of noise does a damp squib make?' The question bounced off the blank corridors of his mind, and Sophie MacKenzie's mocking voice replied, 'A sort of hissing slurp, like a balloon going down too fast.'

He laughed out loud – he should have more control. He picked up his fountain pen and rolled the fat, marbled body between his fingers. The gold clip glinted at him. The staccato chatter of the typewriter in the next room and the intermittent ping of its carriage return became intrusive. He slipped his hand into his jacket pocket and drew out his wallet. The crimson business card with the celtic writing was still there, crumpled but safe.

The man in the window-mirror picked up the telephone, and dialled.

Enid answered on the second ring. She told him Sophie was at home. As the dial whirred and the mechanism clicked through the new set of digits, he remembered the way Sophie MacKenzie had held his arm – not a loose, casual gesture but a tightening grip as she urged him to come again. The ringing tone vibrated; the handset's black plastic casing felt clammy against his palm. Wedging it between chin and shoulder, he fiddled with his pen. He made an ink blot on the file in front of him.

The phone rang on. He'd lost all sense of how long he'd been waiting. He made an awkward effort to blot up the inky mess and thought, enough is enough. And then he heard the click of the receiver being lifted.

She was out of breath. 'Yes?' she snapped and, for a wild moment, he considered hanging up on her. 'Hello, who is it? Who's there?' She sounded so cross.

'Me,' he said. 'Charles. Charles Wade. I rang the shop. Edith gave me your number.' He waited. 'Am I disturbing you?'

And she laughed. 'Yes, Charles,' she said. 'Of course you're disturbing me. But never mind. How are you?'

On Friday he returned to Cambridge. The night was wet. He ducked his head and ran to the porch. The conifers bordering the drive bent their heads towards one another in a sighing conspiracy.

Michael's welcome was immediate. He drew him in, taking his bag and slapping him on the back. Sophie was in the kitchen, standing by the Rayburn stirring the contents of a bright orange saucepan. She grinned at him over her shoulder. 'You made it then. Good. Michael, take his coat. Are you hungry? I hope you're starving!'

At breakfast on Saturday morning, Sophie thought how relaxed Charles looked. The bear was sleepy, his claws sheathed. She poured more coffee and he helped himself to the toast. 'Try this,' she said, pushing the jam-pot towards him. 'Marrow-ginger.'

'Go easy,' warned Michael. 'She's got a heavy hand with the ginger.'

She watched Charles spoon the tawny preserve on to the side of his plate. He looked up, and smiled. She liked that, the way he could look so solemn, but then his smile would transform him. There was a great deal about him to like – all the contradictions apparent but not understood, the depth of his voice, the sudden lightness of his laugh, and his thick dark hair and dark eyes and yes, dark, that was it, the word that summed him up. He was dark inside, as well as out. And so was she – she felt the jolt of recognition – that was why she wanted to gather him to her, to protect him, because in so many ways they were very much alike and she could help him, she could show him a trick or two worth having, a knack, a sleight of hand, a way of shielding the darkness with the light.

Michael said, 'Pass the sugar, Soph.'

She passed the bowl, and said to Charles, 'Did the owls keep you awake? They can be frightening if they come too close. Last summer one perched on the open casement, it scared me half to death. They scream too, sometimes. It's a horrible sound, like a child caught in a mantrap.'

'I remember that,' said Jonathan's father. The mechanism of the brass-framed carriage clock clicked against the silence. I was alone with my father-in-law; Leonard had taken Joanna to the park. 'I used to dream about it,' he said, describing a nightmare where the bird came into the room, its wings beating desperately against the ceiling, its fixed eyes in their feathered saucers staring wildly and the hooked beak lashing and gashing its terror.

I listen to him, and hear truth, the accuracy of his fear. His memory is wonderfully intact, but disordered. He remembers the actual events, but is confused about the chronology. Maybe it's his age, but he's not so very old, not seventy yet. Is it to do with the treatment they gave him in that place? You hear such terrible

72

stories about those days, experimental drugs and electric shocks – is that what they did? Did they plant their wires in his tortured brain and try to take the Temple by storm?

He said, 'There was a cottage. On the corner of a field. Or rather there wasn't, not any more. Maybe I dreamt that. I don't know.'

Sophie and Michael had taken him for a tour of the village and she pointed out the spot, now ploughed with dun-coloured furrows, where old Mrs Gower had lived. Mrs Gower did the paper round on her bike. It took forever because she was always stopping to chat. But then she died, quite suddenly, and they demolished her cottage and incorporated it into the field and soon it was as if she'd never existed.

And on that walk, or another just like it, they passed the church and Charles stopped to look. It was squat, flint-faced with a square tower and a lychgate. Michael said, 'It's Saxon,' and carried on walking. Charles hung back, then stepped up and under the lychgate. The path stretched straight and level to the porch. On either side the graveyard grass had been roughly cut and the headstones leant together in friendship, or apart in eternal quarrel. Some were so worn that it wasn't easy to see which way they faced.

A gust of wind caught a scrap of paper, whisking it against Charles's ankle. He retrieved it. It was a handwritten notice rendered illegible by the weather. Sophie was waiting for him by the gate. He called out, 'Could we go inside?' She shook her head. Beyond her, on the far side of the village green, Michael was talking to a woman with a big white dog. Returning his attention to Sophie, he said, 'Why not?'

'You can, if you want. I'll wait here.'

'It doesn't matter.' Screwing up the piece of paper, he stuffed it in his pocket and joined her. She was annoyed. He said, 'What is it? Don't you like churches?'

She shrugged, 'They have connotations.'

'Personal?'

She laughed. 'In a way. Do you believe in God, Charles?'

'Yes. Don't you?'

'Not one that you would recognise. Not an interventionist god, not a creator . . . .'

And he thought, what does that leave? She frightened him. In his experience people either believed or affected a superior disbelief. It was a theme with few variations. Never before had he experienced this sense of somebody nursing a real alternative.

7

When Nicholas and Leonard talked about Sophie's diaries, I'd imagined something calf-bound with gold-tooled pages. In fact she used a series of exercise books dated only on the first page. The one relating to this period has a red cover which has bled into the edges of the pages. Her writing's weird, very bold with some odd curls and flourishes, and she's not as laid back about Charles as she'd have him believe. Or as she'd have herself believe. Listening to him and reading her account, it seems incredible that neither of them realised where it was leading. If he was naive, then surely she wasn't. Unless they were too self-absorbed to see, blinded by a mistaken sense of self.

Leonard and Jo were still out, so I went to the kitchen to make some tea. Waiting for the kettle to boil, I tried to picture the two of them – and Michael. What did Michael see, what did he make of his wife playing Dr Frankenstein to Charles's monster?

'New life,' she wrote. 'I'm giving him new life, the way a mother does. He was dead when he came here, huddled and dull, and look at him now. Oh just look at him now.'

I loaded the tea onto a tray and carried it back through to the drawing room. Jonathan's father was sitting where I'd left him, sorting through the contents of this tartan biscuit tin. 'Look at these,' he said, handing me two yellowed photographs. They had been taken on the day Sophie and Michael took him punting. Sophie had teased and bullied him into having a go with the pole. He got to his feet, the punt rocked wildly. Sophie laughed and, gripping the side, leant over to compensate. Charles braced himself, then edged towards Michael who was standing, feet apart and perfectly at ease, on the platform at the far end.

The pole was slippery and very long. It was also extremely heavy and he had difficulty getting the balance right. Michael stood beside him for a while, showing him how to dig the metal-feruled end into the river bed, then push hand over hand to propel the punt along before loosening the pole and using it as a rudder. That was the hardest part. Twice he steered them into the bank and once he almost lost his footing. And then there was a click and a laugh – Sophie had taken a photograph of him. As if that wasn't bad enough, the pole was dripping water onto his shirt and depositing long strands of weed all over his trousers.

'Oh dear,' she was still laughing. 'Look at you, you'd better let Michael take over.'

He lowered himself beside her and stretched his legs along the bottom of the punt. Michael resumed his position, then called to them, 'Come on, you two, let's have a smile.' He had the camera poised. 'Put your arm round her, Charles. She won't bite.' Forcing a smile, he laid his arm along the back of the seat. She nestled against him and gathered his hand on to her shoulder.

Sitting this close, Sophie could feel the warmth radiating from him, the lift and fall of his breathing, the drum of his heart. And she wanted to be closer still, not physically – more deeply than that. She wanted to know what he was thinking and feeling, she wanted to know what he dreamt at night.

I wonder if Michael deliberately steered the punt under the willow tree. I would have, in his position. He certainly succeeded in rousing the two of them as the tattered trails of its veil brushed their faces, sprinkling them with water. Sophie laughed. And Charles tightened his arm around her as for the third time that day the punt collided with the bank.

Back in London that Monday night, Charles stood under the shower letting the water spatter against his brow and his closed eyelids, gasping and choking as it trickled like tears down his face. Tears of laughter. He grinned as he lathered the shampoo, digging his fingers deep into the foam and massaging his scalp. The water continued to beat a tattoo against the shower-tray and the sides of the cubicle, drowning out all outside sound, keeping him apart, separate.

It had been hard leaving Cambridge. It got harder every week. After Michael left for work he dawdled at the breakfast table. He saw his life in tones of London-grey, and lived for the vivid splashes of weekend colour.

He titled his head so the force of the water could rinse the soap from his hair. The suds dribbled down his back and streaked the insides of his thighs. He lingered under the spray long after all the soap had washed away.

On Saturday, Sophie had had him making apple strudel. He'd rolled up his sleeves, and she'd wrapped him in a red and white striped apron. As she tied the tapes, he'd felt the warm nudge of her knuckles. Then, standing either side of the kitchen table, they'd stretched the strudel dough on the backs of their hands until it was so thin they could see the pattern on the floured tea towel beneath. She'd teased him about the smudges on his face. As he brushed them away, he saw how the white powder clung to the dark hair of his arms.

Last week he'd helped Michael clear out the barn. The week before he'd minded the shop for a couple of hours while she and Michael went shopping.

Arriving home, Emmy asked if he'd had a good weekend. She wasn't used to him going away and he'd offered no explanation. Being Emmy, she was worried rather than curious and he'd come close to telling her.

He sat on his bed, drying his hair. Why so coy, why not tell her? He ought to share the MacKenzies, invite them down, introduce them to his friends, to Helen perhaps? Though God knows what his sister would say if she knew some of the things Sophie had him doing. Yes, he could have the MacKenzies to stay, invite some people over, Peter and Abigail would be sure to come . . . .

No.

Why not?

Superstition.

Ridiculous. What d'you think will happen? He shivered. It was an irrational fear, that if he told tales on them, they would disappear. They didn't seem quite real, at any moment the carriage might become a pumpkin, the bag of gold a sack of dust.

On Wednesday he came home from work, changed and went down to the drawing room to await Emmy's call to dinner. The late sun had a tarnished tint as it slanted through the drawing-room window, catching the brass frame of the carriage clock, making it flare like a struck match. He sat listening to the click of the clock's mechanism as it punched against the deep silence of the house. It would soon be Friday.

Surely they'd noticed how one-sided the relationship was. He really ought to invite them, it was foolish to be so superstitious. He crossed to the sideboard and poured a measure of dark sherry from a crystal decanter. He didn't much like sherry – so why perform this ritual every evening? He could almost hear Sophie laughing at him. See her too, standing by the fireplace, her hair glinting in the sun.

To have her here – what would she make of his home?

His mother had said, 'I dare say it'll impress all the right people.' But impressing people wasn't what it was about. The house, the car, Emmy and Thompson weren't a means of flaunting his success, they were there to help maintain the barriers.

Sophie would understand. He knew that whatever she thought of the house, she would see why he lived as he did. Probably she already suspected, already understood.

In which case, what could be the harm in inviting them? He settled back in his chair, the glass of barely tasted sherry abandoned on the Chinese table beside him. He'd have to think it through, of course, make sure he gave them a good time. They could go to the theatre. Sophie would like that. He'd need to find out what was on. He could ring Leonard, get his advice; maybe even ask him along.

To have her here – surely something of her would linger, and afterwards his London life wouldn't be so grey. Stretching his legs, he rubbed his toe against the polished steel fender. Probably she'd take a professional interest in things like the fender. James had been particularly pleased with it, a real bargain, apparently, though Charles paid scant attention to individual prices. That's it! The thought startled him. James! He'd throw a dinner party, invite James, and Cathy of course, and Peter and Abigail Knight. He'd get Em to put on a show, dig out all the best tableware.

'Charles!' James greeted him with exaggerated enthusiasm and an outstretched hand. 'Can it be you? I can't be sure, only it's been so long . . . memory starts to go, know what I mean?'

'James.' He allowed his hand to be shaken. James had a light, restless touch.

'I won't say it's not great to see you, but my God, you're in big trouble, I hope you realise.'

'In what way?' It was a game they sometimes played, straight-man and comic.

'Cathy.' He pulled a face. The waiter led them to their table and the antique wall mirrors threw back a smudged replica of James's jittery figure. 'You are not her favourite person just at the moment,' James continued. 'We've not seen you since before Christmas. She says if you're determined to drop out of sight, then you could at least arrange a nice funeral. She's fond of you, is Cath.' Charles laughed. As they sat down, James said, 'You know, you should have married Cath when you had the chance.' It was an old joke. 'She'd have had you like a shot.'

'I don't think so.'

'Trust me, I know my sister. Too late now, of course. You're on her blacklist. Right at the top and double-underlined.'

'I wasn't aware that she had a blacklist. Is it very long?'

'To be frank, no. In fact, you're the only name on it at the moment. So if I were you, I'd start explaining pretty quick. What the hell have you been up to? You're never at home, you don't return calls – and Emmy doesn't give a lot away. Anyone but you and I'd say there was a woman behind it.'

He had a dream that night. He'd never had one like it. He went to Cambridge – to Sophie's shop – and it wasn't there. Or rather, the name was different and the window was full of second-hand books with prices handwritten on pieces of white card tucked into their pages. He went in. The proprietor was the man who'd had the stall on the market, who'd directed him to her shop. But he said he'd never heard of Sophie MacKenzie, that he'd had this shop for twenty years. Before that, it had been a tobacconist's.

The scene shifted. He was in the countryside, driving to her village – then nosing along the lane to her cottage. But the cottage was gone. The ploughed field that had once stopped at her back fence now came right up to the road and, borne on the wind, rippling across the furrows, came the torn scream of something or someone caught in a trap.

He woke with the sweat running down his sides and his heart crashing against his ribs. The sense of loss was an ache like a bruise, swelling and spreading and throbbing through his body.

He was late leaving for Cambridge on Friday. Peter Knight telephoned, wanting to discuss a clause he didn't much like on a contract that had just come through. They talked at length, then agreed to meet on Monday afternoon. As a consequence it was after eight o'clock when he pulled into the MacKenzies' drive.

Sophie was in an uncharacteristic fluster when she opened the door. She said, 'Where have you been? We've been worried.' She caught his hand and tugged him into the hall, then suddenly smiled and said, 'Well, you're here now.' And she squeezed his arm and kissed his cheek. 'Dump your things. We're eating out.'

The local pub had a restaurant. It wasn't much of a place but Sophie knew the landlord. The dining room had wheel-back chairs and polished refectory type tables, hunting prints and cheap blue and white plates. The waitress looked about fifteen. She led them to a table by the inglenook and had to lean across Charles to light a stub of red candle pressed into a leaf-shaped brass ashtray. Sophie smiled at him through the crook of the girl's arm.

He glanced at the menu. The choice was basic and he went for peppered steak. Michael ordered the wine, explaining that this was a celebration – he'd been promoted. Charles congratulated him and made a show of listening as the fifteen-year-old served them with unripe avocados and overdone steak. And all the while he watched Sophie, how she loaded her fork, the way she occasionally looked beyond Michael's shoulder to take stock of the other diners, her absentminded fingertip-caress of the rim of her glass.

He realised with a shock how familiar all her gestures were. He knew them by heart.

Knew them by heart . . . what did that mean? He remembered the dream. Anyone but you, James had said.

He shivered. He'd shivered that day in the sale room, and blamed it on the cold.

She'd winked at him, then asked, 'Do I know you?'

Anyone but you. You're wrong, James.

Do I know you? – how could I have been so wrong?

Again and again you turn to the darkness, denying the light.

Yes, I see that now.

Then say it.

She is the light.

Of course she is. Go on.

He closed his eyes, but the light that was Sophie burned on, blinding him – and then it didn't matter any more because he knew what lay behind the light, hiding its face, whispering its name.

'Charles? Charles, are you all right?' Sophie was leaning across the table, shaking his arm, peering into his face.

'Yes, fine. I'm sorry. Dizzy, that's all. It's hot in here. Go on. What were you saying?'

'Nothing.' She withdrew her hand. 'It doesn't matter.'

'It does, I want to hear.'

'Tell him, Soph, go on, it's a good story. He'll like it.'

So she continued with her tale of a cloisonné pot which another dealer had turned down the opportunity of buying when it was in her shop, only to pay three times the price when she put it in the local auction. It was a typical Sophie story. Charles raised his glass in a toast, all the while asking himself, how could I not have seen? All those precious things about her that I love – the way she touches me, holds my hand, leans against me. Nobody touches me like that. How come I didn't realise that all those little things add up to something so much more?

The sudden clamour in the restaurant, cutlery chattering against plates, subdued conversation erupting into laughter, broke in on him, making him lift his head. He intercepted a conspiratorial, questioning glance between Sophie and Michael.

Jealousy. Sudden. Sharp. Like lemon juice in a cut.

They were a couple. So what if Michael did seem occasionally disaffected and was happy to leave his wife in Charles's company at weekends – 'he finds me wearing,' she'd once explained – what if he now and then heard them bickering in their bedroom? It didn't matter, they were a couple, it was a marriage. And he stood alone, on the outside.

After the meal they went back to the cottage for coffee and apricot brandy. Then he went up to bed. Undressing in the dark, he listened to the floorboards creaking in the next room, and to the murmur of voices. He crossed to the window and opened the casement. The night was warm and faint rustling sounds came from the garden, from the trees and from the spaces beneath the shrubs. He pictured a whole alternative world of beetles and bugs, of hedgehogs and mice, but by no stretch of the imagination could he see himself and Sophie as a couple. They were too different, there was too much to overcome.

He took a deep breath, inhaling the sweet summer night.

It shouldn't be like this. He was in love. He should be happy – he should be bouncing off the walls.

But what did 'love' mean? It was on everybody's lips, scrawled in lurid letters on the sides of bridges, punctuating the conversation of the young like a veiled command . . . the word was meaningless.

Yet the feeling was real.

The question remained, where to from here? What would another man do? James?

Not a good model. His second wife had been married when they met and, if his sister was to be believed, they'd barely exchanged names before jumping into bed.

Thou shalt not commit adultery.

Okay, fine. I'm not at all sure that I want to.

Then what do you want?

To be with her. To talk to her. To be just as we are.

But tonight you were jealous of Michael.

The night turned cold and the chill breeze prickled the hair on his arms. 'It's over, then, is it?' he whispered to the beetles and the hedgehogs and the night.

Yes. All over. Say goodbye, go home. Forget.

8

At breakfast Sophie announced that she needed more stock and intended doing the rounds of the fenland villages to see what she could pick up. Michael wasn't keen. He said, 'Charles'll keep you company.'

They'd had days like this before; he acknowledged now how glad he'd always been when Michael decided to stay at home. He loved watching her do business; he loved the poky little shops with their lintels so low that he had to duck to get through the doors, the uneven floors stacked with piles of dusty plates, and hoards of old prints leaning against the walls. These were the places where Sophie was most likely to pick up bargains: bits and bobs bought from villagers only too delighted to find they had anything of worth. The people who ran these shops were honest enough, but they were remote from the capital and had no idea what a voracious appetite it had.

That Saturday in July, they called at a village on the far side of Ely, parking alongside the green, close by a small shop with a row of cane-seated chairs and a couple of black iron cooking pots ranged on the pavement. In the tiny window, surrounded by grubby pressed glass dressing-table pots and cheap brass ornaments, was a pair of vases, maybe eighteen inches tall, and a matching clock. Sophie gestured towards them, and grinned.

'But they're ugly,' Charles protested. She bit her lip and laughed and pushed open the door.

They were just as hideous on closer inspection. The glaze was a smudgy red splashed with gold, and each piece had a transfer print of eighteenth-century ladies and gentlemen promenading in a garden. The woman who ran the shop lifted them from the window and handed them over, one at a time, with great ceremony. She was obviously very proud of them. Sophie turned them over and over, checking for damage and wear. Charles felt sorry for the woman, there was something inherently critical in Sophie's examination. When at last she was satisfied, Sophie turned to her and asked the price. A figure was mentioned which made her smile and shake her head. She then offered a much lower sum. The woman argued, but Charles could sense her lack of conviction. She tried for another figure, a little less than her first. Sophie returned the vase with a regretful shrug. And with that supremely casual bluff – he could see it, how could the woman be so blind? – they settled on an amount only marginally more than Sophie's original offer.

By early afternoon the car was full. There were several sets of vases, a couple of chandeliers, a Parian figure of a woman in classical dress attended by two little cherubs, not to mention a dinner service or two. Sophie slammed the doors on the last of these and said, 'Shall we call it a day?'

He thought, now for it. I'm going to have to tell her. I can't lie and I can't just stop coming.

He sat beside her in the little car, feeling too large, just as he always did in her shop. A bump in the road made the boxes in the back jump and rattle; he feared for the ugly vases. She slowed for a corner. As she reached to change gear her bracelet – the one with the amethyst drops that reminded him of her chandeliers – slithered down over the back of her hand.

After a few more miles they were in the fens proper. There were no more bends on this sword-slash of a road cutting its way through the black fields. He glanced sideways at her. She was wearing an orange and green Indian skirt that rippled almost to her ankles, and an off-white cheesecloth top, laced at the front. Her hair snaked across her shoulders as she half-turned towards him, catching his eye. And then, without warning, she swerved off the road and into a farm gateway. The ratchet of the handbrake grated his nerves. She switched off the engine and sat back. Neither of them spoke. The wind that whipped across the black expanse of the fens rocked against the car.

She said, 'What's going on, Charles?' He didn't answer, he couldn't. 'Something,' she murmured, gazing out of the window, her fingers outlining the hard rim of the steering wheel. 'Something's wrong.' A tiny black dart, a low-flying military plane from one of the US bases, skimmed the distant horizon. 'Even Michael's noticed.' She turned to look at him. She was so close that he could see the threads of mascara clinging to her lashes, 'Oh no,' she said, understanding, turning away from him. 'Oh Christ, Charles, no. You bloody fool.' And she punched the palm of her hand hard down on the horn so that it blared out, deafening and ringing and challenging the wind. He grabbed her wrist and pulled her hand away. He held on to her, but she wouldn't look at him. 'Not like this,' she said, and he heard the deep pity in her voice. 'I could have helped you, I wanted to, but not like this.'

Pity. Not love, but pity – such as she might feel for anyone, for a sick child, a rabbit maimed by a car.

Dad. Dad and Anthony rummaging in the toolbox, the grind of metal, the rabbit's frightened eye and his gentle father kneeling on the road, the spanner poised above the frail skull. The rabbit knew. The rabbit knew.

He got out of the car. The wind buffeted his ears and the air smelt of celery. He took a few unsteady steps to the edge of the field, to where the uneven verge gave way to a ditch puddled with stagnant water.

And then she was beside him and he was aware of her skirt flapping in the wind and her auburn hair bobbing and writhing as if being tugged and teased by a spiteful child. She said, 'What do you want me to say? This isn't what you want, Charles, not really.'

'I love you.'

'All right.' Her voice became hard. He stared down at her and her hair twisted Medusa-like in the wind and the bare skin of her arms was scattered with goose bumps. 'So what if I said fine, I love you too, I'll come to London with you, we'll be together . . . . What would you say, Charles?' He continued to stare. The wind blinded him and deafened him, and yet he could still see her – but only her – and he thought that he saw something other than pity flickering behind her grey eyes, something indefinable and dark that turned his skin to ice in the moment before she masked it with the gold.

'Well?' she persisted, and he shook his head and looked away. She knew the answer. She'd only put the question to be sure that he knew too. He had nothing to say. He had nothing to give. It was over.

9

Sophie stood just a little inside the redbrick wall that enclosed the kitchen garden of the big house. The warm air was sweet with the smell of crushed grass and all around her the murmur of voices was like the buzz of bees collecting pollen. It was a comparison Charles would have appreciated: the dealers were the bees, the goods they'd come to buy the pollen which they would convert into life-sustaining cash.

She began to stroll down one of the brick-paved paths. Once this area had provided vegetables for the whole house. Now, instead of rows of lettuces and ferny carrots, there were rows of garden tools, rakes and hoes and forks and spades, all tied in bundles with fraying string. She passed an old galvanised wheelbarrow stacked with terracotta flowerpots caked with dried soil and smudged with sooty cobwebs. Prospective buyers hovered and wandered, inspecting the lots on offer and consulting their catalogues.

For the most part the lots that interested her were in the marquee on the lawn. There was some porcelain and one or two respectable bronzes. Not that she stood much chance. The big guns were out today. She glanced up. James Peterson approached, a paper cup of steaming tea in each hand.

At first she hadn't thought it worth her while driving all the way to Lincolnshire, but after the fiasco with Charles at the weekend, it became most urgent for her to get away.

James handed her her tea and from his pocket produced a hip

flask. 'Here, this should liven it up a bit.' With a flourish he topped the cups to the rim.

Bumping into James put the tin lid on any hopes of making a profit on the day, most of the stuff she picked up in places like this was passed straight on to him. 'Fancy another look inside?' he said when she'd finished her tea.

'Why not.' He took her empty cup and tucked it, with his, inside one of the flowerpots.

In the marquee, the insufferable heat fermented the trampled grass. They had a quick look round, then went into the house. It was a fine eighteenth-century building. The auctioneers had draw-ing-pinned arrows to the door frames, directing them to the main part of the house. 'Like a party game, isn't it?' she commented as they passed from arrow to arrow and through a servants' door to emerge into the hall.

The carpets had all been taken up and the dark oak floorboards echoed and the ceiling creaked as people tramped overhead and clattered on the stairs. A man with an eyeglass had unhooked a painting and was examining it closely. Sophie wondered what he was looking for. Maybe he just wanted to know what the subject matter was. To her untutored eye, all the detail seemed to have melted together in a marmite-coloured mess.

James was marking some hunting prints in his catalogue. Above them, draped over the galleried landing, hung a series of Persian rugs and runners.

When they'd done, James said, 'So what are you doing? Are you staying over?'

She nodded. 'Might as well, now I'm here.'

'Great.' He grinned. 'Let's have dinner. Seven-thirty suit you?'

Later that night, back in her room, she thought about James Peterson and how different he was from Charles. He was a self-conscious charmer, whereas Charles charmed almost despite him-self. Strange to think they were friends. Not that she knew much about James' private life, apart from passing references to failed relationships and the fact that following his divorce, he'd set up house with his sister. Over dinner he talked about the house, a neo-gothic mansion bought from a friend who'd originally acquired it with the intention of knocking it down. 'He can be a bit of a philistine,' he'd said, laughing affectionately, and she'd thought, it's Charles he's talking about.

She'd deliberately not let either of them know that she knew the other. At first it was just mischief, but after so many months she found it curious, this lack of communication between them. Surely Charles would have mentioned that he'd met someone else in the antiques trade? Apparently not.

She sat cross-legged on the bed. She'd drunk too much. The dark ceiling beams swung low, the room felt claustrophobic and the breeze from the open window rustled the curtains, making her think of birds trapped in a chimney.

On the bedside table, next to the telephone, lay her Celtic head. She'd got it years ago as part of a job lot. At first she'd used it as a paperweight, but then it had taken on a different significance. She picked it up. Charles had shown an interest in it once, and she'd been tempted to tell him – but then, surely, he knew. Then again, maybe not. He lacked wisdom. He loved her, and that shouldn't have happened. She should have put a stop to it, but she hadn't seen it coming – she was no more wise than he.

That day in the fens she'd ached to comfort him. They'd stood so close that when the wind whipped at her skirt it tangled with his legs. She'd wanted to cradle him and say, it's all right, I'm here. But she had no intention of being there. Instead she'd shown him his weakness and, if admitting it hurt him, then it hurt her too. Her vulnerability filled her with fear – of her quaking flesh, of the darkness she recognised, of the terrible unreflecting blackness that threatened to mingle with her own and obliterate her.

She closed her fingers round the little head, hiding its blank, mocking eyes, then placed it face down on the bedside table. In her bag she had both his home and his work telephone numbers. She glanced at the clock. Not too late, just after ten. She flipped open her diary to the relevant page. His writing was bold and controlled, with here and there a flourish breaking through.

The telephone was answered promptly by a woman who gave his number in a friendly, confiding way. This, no doubt, was his housekeeper. What had he called her? Emmy, yes, that was it.

Her voice shook as she asked to speak to Charles. She gave her name, and the woman asked her to wait. She heard the light tap as the receiver was laid down.

The stone head wasn't looking at her, but she could feel the hard press of its disapproval. She swivelled and turned her back to it.

Any minute now, Charles would come on the line. What was she going to say to him? Hello, did you have a good journey? Am I disturbing you? Are you missing me yet?

A scraping sound warned her that the receiver was being picked up. She drew breath to speak, but the woman's voice pre-empted her. 'Hello, Mrs MacKenzie? I'm sorry, but Mr Wade's out, I'll let him know you rang, shall I?'

10

On a hard bright night in November, Leonard Prentice arrived home late and, standing on the kerb as the cab pulled away, took several deep gulps of the sharp, stinging air. It was a fine night with the frost sparkling on the pavements like crushed glass. His breath formed a grey-white vapour, as if with every exhalation he lost a little part of himself.

It was very late. He was tired. He'd been to the theatre – something unmemorably experimental in the upstairs room of a pub – and afterwards a crowd of them had gone to a cheap Italian place to eat pasta and drink too much Chianti.

This new freedom was hard to grasp. The law had changed, and yet he didn't truly feel it. All his life he'd occupied the world as an imposter. Was today really so different from yesterday? If Peter Knight or Anthony Wade or the rest of them knew the kind of company he'd kept tonight, what price his professional future?

The steps down to the area were slippery and he slithered and had to make a grab for the handrail.

Once inside his bolthole, he poured a drink and sipped it as he played back the answering machine. His mother wanted him to stay with her down in Brighton for a few days; a client wanted him to get in touch first thing in the morning. The third message was breathless and reproachful. 'Lenny? Hey, are you there? It's me. Danny. I called yesterday. Why don't you ring me? What did I say, Lenny, what did I do?'

Danny was becoming a nuisance. Leonard rolled his glass between his palms and considered the bronze bust that stood on a pedestal in the alcove. Charles. He'd seen him this morning, at Bernstein's. They'd passed in the corridor with the briefest of nods. No doubt he was on his way to consult Peter.

Something wasn't quite right. What? A touch more grey in his hair, and he'd lost weight; he looked tired, but then he always pushed himself too hard. Ran hard too, ran away from anything that didn't fit the pattern he'd forced on to his life, yet underneath Leonard sensed he wanted to be stopped, wanted someone to stand in his path, make him turn and confront himself. Leonard ran a finger down the hard line of the bronze jaw. But he hadn't been running today. There was something else. Charles had presence. Authority. When he entered a room, you noticed. And that was what was missing. It was as if he'd sprung a leak and a little part of him had seeped away.

A friend – albeit a lapsed one – would get in touch to see if he could help. But whatever the problem, Charles was unlikely to confide in him. More likely to slam down the phone. He trailed his fingers across the sculpted bronze lips, and withdrew his hand. No, not a wise move. Draining his glass, he picked up the phone and rang Danny instead.

11

On Christmas Day, Charles woke late to a chill silence and the nasty aftertaste of a dream he couldn't remember.

It was a little after nine. He was due at his mother's between ten-thirty and eleven. They'd all be there, Anthony and Susan, Helen, Brian, all the nephews and nieces. God, what a sham. He pushed back the covers and climbed out of bed.

He lingered over his shave, slowly building up a good foam and working it into his sleep-numbed skin with the soft bush of the badger-brush. Less pleasant was the rasp of the razor being dragged from cheekbone to chin. Flicking the blade under the tap, he glanced up and met his own gaze in the mirror. It was eerie, the sight of those dark eyes watching him from above the gashed foam-mask – as if a stranger lurked in the mirror. Or behind the eyes.

Fool. He finished his shave with a succession of quick, decisive strokes, swabbed his face with a towel, and it was his face again, his eyes.

What if he rang his mother, told her what she could do with her Christmas dinner, or that something had cropped up and he couldn't come? No, she'd want to know what and why. He'd have to make something up, and she'd know he was lying. She always did.

Emmy was in the dining room. The toast stood like a fan of cards in the silver rack. Beside his plate was a parcel wrapped in scarlet paper covered with holly. 'Merry Christmas,' said Em as she poured his coffee. They sat amiably across the table from one another and she unwrapped her presents, some perfume and a terracotta birdfeeder to hang outside her kitchen window. Then she said, 'Well go on, aren't you going to open yours?'

He drew the parcel towards him and ran his fingers along the folded seam. Then set about cutting the Sellotape and peeling back the wrapping paper. Inside was a canary yellow polo-neck sweater. He had never worn such a thing. He glanced at Emmy, and saw at once that she knew how unsuitable it was. She said, 'If it's the wrong size, I can change it.'

'You know my size.' He grinned. 'I'll wear it today, shall I?'

Breakfast over, Emmy left to spend the day with her sister. Watching her cross the square, he thought how odd it was that he knew neither where her sister lived, nor whether she ever called here.

He moved away from the window and poured himself a glass of whisky. The carriage clock struck the hour. He should be at his mother's. He poured another drink. The decanter clashed against the glass and the liquid stung the back of his throat.

The telephone rang. He went out into the hall, then stopped. It'd be her, his mother. He stood two feet from the phone and let it go on ringing and ringing, echoing across the hall and up the stairway of the empty house.

Then it stopped. The sudden silence made the air tingle.

But what if it wasn't her?

Who else could it be?

Sophie.

Why would Sophie ring after so long? Last time she phoned he wouldn't speak to her. Oh, but it would be good to hear her voice again, and all he had to do was pick up the phone and dial.

The phone started up again, jangling and clanging against the silence. It wasn't Sophie. No chance. The phone was still ringing as he left the house.

He parked a little way along from his mother's house and, as he locked the car, the curtains flicked in Mrs Lloyd's window opposite. In the house next to his mother's an over-large Christmas tree pressed against the panes, as if trying to escape, its red and white Santa Claus lights blinking on and off too fast for comfort.

His sister answered the door but, as he stepped into the cluttered hallway, his mother emerged from the kitchen, fumbling to untie her apron. She said, 'So, you managed to get here. I've been trying to ring you.'

'I got held up.'

'Did you, now.'

Helen came up behind, whispering, 'And a merry Christmas to you, little brother.'

His mother said, 'What's so important that you couldn't get here on time?' He tucked his gloves into his pocket and began to unbutton his coat. 'Well really! If you can't make a bit of an effort at Christmas – it's only once a year you know.' She stopped short as he took off his coat to reveal his new sweater.

Helen hooted. 'Well, look what Santa brought you.'

'Emmy, as a matter of fact.' He grinned. 'What d'you think?'

'It's great!'

'I think that woman takes liberties.' His mother had never liked Emmy. He saw no point in arguing.

They were ten to lunch. They sat elbow to elbow round the table, red crepe-paper crackers crowding the stainless-steel cutlery and up above, red and yellow paper chains swaying in the draught from the French windows.

'I'll pop over next week, see if I can't do something about that.' Helen's husband brandished his fork in the direction of the draught.

'Thank you, Brian.' His mother spoke pointedly, with a glance at Charles.

Charles ignored her. He held a bowl of bread sauce for Helen to help first herself, then him. At the far end of the table Anthony was saying something about buying a cottage on the Norfolk coast.

'My,' said Charles in an undertone to his sister, 'we are going up in the world.'

Susan heard him. 'Easy for you to sneer,' she spat. 'Anyway, we're only talking about it. Can't afford to do much else.'

Charles felt Helen nudge his foot. He nudged her back, and passed the bowl of bread sauce to Brian. His mother poured a glutinous dollop of gravy on to her turkey, saying, 'Auntie Eileen rang this morning. Sends you her love, Helen, and the boys. She's upset with you, Charles, says you never go to see her.'

'We went up a few weeks ago.' Helen tried to draw the fire.

'So she said.'

'What use is that,' snarled Anthony. 'She doesn't want us, it's

Charles she wants to see. Probably intends leaving him her collection of rare knitting needles. Oh yes, everyone's favourite, is Charles.'

Charles speared a piece of turkey. It tasted bitter. He carefully sliced through a brussel sprout, admiring the tight layers of shaded green. It was almost too good to eat.

His mother was speaking again. 'I told her – no good expecting you to go and see her when you can't even find time to visit your own mother.'

'I've been busy.'

'How is business?' Helen tried again.

'Busy, he says. Too busy for his own mother. Doesn't even telephone. I told her.'

'I bet you did.'

'Really! You're getting worse Charles, d'you know that? So rude.' She looked round the table, silently enlisting support. 'I don't know what your father would have said.'

Give it a rest, eh love? Give the boy some more wine – Charles smiled, and reached for the bottle.

'I'm glad you find it a laughing matter . . . .'

He refilled Helen's glass, then his own. Helen said, 'Come on, Mum, leave it. It's Christmas.'

'Yes, you'd think he could make an effort at Christmas. He's got no consideration, that boy.' Turning to Charles, she said, 'And for God's sake, take that dreadful jumper off.'

'I like it,' said Helen. 'I've been telling him for ages he ought to brighten up his image.'

'You're wasting your time, sis.' He spoke quietly, though still loud enough for his mother to hear. 'She's been looking forward to this, building herself up to it.'

'Don't, Charles,' she warned softly.

'Why not? Why are we all so bloody frightened of the truth? We just sit here and take it, year after year. I get the worst of it, but I'm not the only one, not by any means.' His voice deepened. His diction became tight. They stared at him, their knives and forks frozen in mid-air. He couldn't stop. He'd choked it back for years, resentment at the injustices, bitterness at minor cruelties magnified by time. Now it all came bubbling up. He threw down his knife. It clattered against the plate and splashed gravy across the white damask tablecloth. 'She's been working herself up to this. She does it every year.' His stomach churned and waves of fire and ice washed over him. He faced his mother. She was ugly, her face contorted with fury. 'Okay, so I never come to see you – and you can't think why not!' He heard the hysteria edging his voice. 'Let me tell you . . . .'

'That's enough, Charles.'

'No. It isn't. Nowhere near. Nothing I have ever done has been good enough. It doesn't matter how hard I try, it never comes up to scratch. I don't even know what you expect of me any more. Tell me. Go on. There must be something. You sit there disapproving and I have to guess, and I always guess wrong. Tell me what you want. You want me to buy Anthony and Suffering-Sue their holiday cottage? Okay. Fine. Consider it done. You need money? For what – a bedroom suite, a new carpet? Just say how much. Cash or cheque?'

'Charles!'

'But no, it's not that, is it? It's not my money you want, it's me. You want some kind of lap-dog or mummy's boy running errands – but every move I make in the world takes me farther from you and you can't stand it . . . .'

'I don't know what he's talking about. Helen, do something. He listens to you.'

'Don't go dragging Helen in, she's always putting herself between us, and you've used that – well, now you can leave her out of it. Just listen, that's all you have to do. Listen and I'll tell you what really hurts. It's the fact that I've tried. All the things I thought – I guessed – you wanted from me, I've tried to give you. I was fool enough to think my success would please you. I thought it was what you wanted and I tried so hard, so bloody hard – and you didn't . . . you didn't even notice. Did you? Did you?'

He choked on the sudden silence. His family sat round the table in a stunned tableau. He felt sick. He held his breath, willing the nausea to go. Then, in a deceptively quiet voice, his mother said, 'It's not the time, Charles. It's not the place.'

'When is it ever the time or the place?'

'Oh dear,' she said, and the glaze of her smile embraced her

94

family, uniting them against him. 'Whatever happened to the Christmas spirit.'

She always did this. She'd set about him, making him shout back at her, and then turn it round so that it was his fault. How many times as a child had he run crying from a scene like this?

No, never quite like this.

He stood up.

'Where do you think you're going? Sit down.'

'How dare you speak to me like that. How old,' his lips were stiff like wood and it was hard to articulate, 'how old do you think I am? You've no respect for me. None whatever . . . .'

'Respect has to be earned.'

'On that at least we can agree.' Thrusting back his chair, he started to cross the room. It was such a small, crowded room, and yet it was a terrible distance from table to door. It took a great effort of concentration. He turned the cold, bakelite knob and found himself in the chill of the hall. He pulled the door shut behind him.

He was shaking, and still nauseous. His head was spinning and his surroundings seemed to advance and retreat, advance and retreat, and the shaking became more violent and he wrapped his arms across his chest, hugging his shoulders, fighting the convulsion.

And then someone said his name. The voice was very close, which was odd because he hadn't heard the door open, hadn't realised anyone had joined him in the hall.

'Charles? Charles, are you all right?' It was Helen. 'Come and sit down. I'll fetch you some water.'

'No. I'm okay.' The nausea ebbed. He lowered his arms. He was still shaking but now it was more of a shiver and could be blamed on the cold. Helen was touching him, her hand resting on his arm, her face close to his. He moved away, clumsily disentangling his coat from the hallstand.

'Don't go, Charles. Not like this.' He didn't answer. He fumbled with the buttons. She said, 'Why did you do it? She's old, Charles, she doesn't mean any harm.'

'How can you say that?'

She adjusted the folds of his scarf. She said, 'Where will you go?' He shrugged. 'Home?'

'I expect so.' Where else was there?

Leonard. With a jab of regret he remembered Leonard's flat with its stripped pine floors and its stark furnishings, and the bronze bust.

'Shall I drive you?' Helen offered. He shook his head and opened the front door. A gust of wind sprayed his face with rain. 'I'll ring,' she said. 'Tomorrow.'

'If you want.'

'Charles.'

He turned back. She stood on the doorstep, her hands pressed together as if in prayer. She looked so worried. He thought, she really cares about me, my big sister. He remembered how he used to throw his arms round her when he was frightened or unhappy, how she'd pick him up – struggling because he was heavy and almost as big as her – and carry him to one of their nooks behind the sofa or in the kneehole of her dressing table with the candy-pink curtains drawn along their kidney-shaped rail, and there snuggle him against her and tell him a story and make all his troubles go away.

He didn't go to see Leonard. He drove home through the battering rain, his windscreen wipers slashing hypnotically and his wheels churning dirty waves of water up on to the empty pavements.

Once home, he stood for a moment in the hall, dribbling pools of water on to the black and white chequered marble floor, listening to the silence of the house and the drumming of the rain outside.

In the drawing room, Emmy had laid a fire. He was damp and incredibly cold. It took him several minutes to locate the matches. Finding them, he slid the box open with shaking hands and spilled the slivers of wood all over the hearthrug. He swore and, going down on his heels, selected a match, struck it and applied it first to one screw of paper, then to another, working from left to right. The paper caught and blazed and almost at once the coal began to smoke.

He was tired, and still cold. Sinking into the armchair, he stretched his legs towards the fire. He hadn't bothered to draw the curtains. The low cloud had hastened the winter dusk, and rain streamed down the glass, diffusing the glow of the streetlamps.

They were probably talking about him, sitting round the mince pies, bemoaning his appalling behaviour. And they were right. He shouldn't have spoken to his mother like that. But it didn't matter now. None of it mattered. He was safe. No one could touch him here.

Holding his breath, he listened to the strange suspended silence of Christmas Day, no traffic, no people, everybody imprisoned with their families.

Oh but how he ached. His body felt heavy as a water-sodden sponge. He didn't feel sick any more, but was still dizzy, and he couldn't keep his eyes open.

Sleep. That was the answer. If he could sleep his life away and wake to find he'd died – now wouldn't that solve a lot of problems.

Or would it? Would it put an end to doubt and disappointment, to the voices that called him and the faces that formed in his mind – the faces of all those who thought they had a claim on him, demanding his attention: now, at once, without delay – Helen and Anthony, James and Cathy, his mother.

Leonard and the MacKenzies.

Sophie. Oh Sophie, do you ever think of me?

You were so sure, so generous, you were good to me – and for me – you warmed my life for just a while and now I'm so dreadfully, so terribly cold.

You used to touch me. I like that. I can still feel it, feel you, isn't that funny? It's like you're with me still, I can feel the pressure of your body leaning against mine, and your hand on my arm, and the touch of your breath on my cheek – and now, not then but now, you're touching me now, but not so gently shaking me and calling me. Sophie.

12

As Helen locked her car, Emmy opened the front door. She looked white and frightened. Helen took the steps two at a time, the questions spilling from her lips: 'What happened, where is he, is he all right?'

'Upstairs. He's upstairs. Asleep. You'd better come in.'

The drawing-room fire had been lit but had not burned through. The newspaper was singed along its edges, but the print was still legible; the sticks were partly charred and the hearthrug strewn with unspent matches.

Helen had rung this morning, as promised, to be told by Emmy that Charles had been taken ill. 'There.' Emmy pointed shakily at the chair. 'That's where I found him, all slumped to one side. I thought he was dead. I thought he'd had a heart attack or something.'

'But he's okay?' Emmy nodded. Helen took hold of her arm. 'Poor you, poor Em. You look all in. Come and sit down, tell me.'

'All these years.' Emmy kneaded her hands in her lap. 'He's never been ill, never so much as a cold. The doctor says he's run down, but I don't like it, I don't believe it.'

Helen agreed. Charles had always been aggressively healthy. To be ill was to be out of control and that he never allowed. Leaving Emmy to rest, she crept up to his room. He was sprawled across the bed in a most unCharles-like way. She saw that his skin was damp, his hair clinging to his brow in dark strands.

Little brother.

She drew up a chair and sat down. The last time she'd seen him like this he'd been eleven years old. He'd failed to get the scholarship their mother had set her heart on. Dad said to leave him be, leave the academic stuff to Anthony; but Mum wouldn't have it, she said he'd done it deliberately, to spite her. She didn't just say it to Dad. She said it to Charles, she shouted at him, said he was an ungrateful, lazy boy and he'd best buck his ideas up or he'd end up working in a factory. Even at fourteen Helen could have told her mother she was going about it the wrong way. Or could have if she'd dared. You couldn't push Charles.

Was that why he'd never married, because he wasn't prepared to let anyone have that much power over him again?

Mum had got it fixed in her mind that he'd failed on purpose. She would not let it go. She went on and on at him, until one morning he didn't come down to breakfast and Helen was sent to call him. She'd found him lying in his bed with his eyes open, not seeming to see or hear her. The doctor agreed with Mum, that he was malingering. 'He'll come down when he's hungry. He's trying it on, that's all.'

It had lasted over a week and ended on a Thursday morning with him coming to the breakfast table, thin and shaky, acting as if nothing had happened, daring them to say anything.

And no one had dared. She was inclined to think that, consciously or not, it had been a tactical withdrawal. And now it was happening again. She took hold of his hand. It was broad and strong. She stroked his fingers. He became restless, twisting back and forth, tossing his head on the pillow. She called his name and pushed his hair up off his brow, whispering that it was all right, she was here, she'd look after him.

Gradually it became clear to Charles that he wasn't alone, that there was someone in the room, leaning over him, touching him.

He opened his eyes. The room was hazy, as if a bright light was shining through fog. He blinked. Who was with him? Sophie? Must concentrate, try to see. He blinked again, squeezing his eyes tight shut before opening them. It wasn't Sophie.

Helen smiled.

He turned his head away. He didn't want her here, to have to answer her questions, be dragged back to the world. He wanted to stay in that other place, where night and day slid into one so there was no knowing which was which, and memories darted along the corridors of his mind, vanishing round this corner, reappearing round the next – and Sophie, wonderful Sophie with her cascade of auburn hair, watching him with grey eyes prickled with gold.

Why did you marry Michael? The question rang out, rattling the bars between one world and the other. Did you love him? If I'd found you first, I'd have made you love me. I know exactly how it would have been. Our children – oh can't you see them, can't you hear them? I can hear them. I can hear their laughter and their feet clattering up and down the stairs and along the corridors. They look like you, they sound like you. Your laughter shaking the windowpanes, shivering the chandeliers.

Then silence. The laughter subsides and the tinkling chandeliers become still. In the sudden hush his bones ache and crumble, and his blood thins to water.

Helen stood by the window. It was dark now. By the glow of the streetlamps she could see a cat patrolling the railings of the communal garden. It was fluffy and white, Persian maybe, the sort of cat that, on a December night, should be in a padded velvet box by an open fire.

'Sis?'

She swung round. He'd slept so long that she hadn't expected him to wake much before morning. She saw with relief that this time he was properly awake. She sat down on the edge of the bed. In a husky voice he asked, 'What time is it?'

'Almost eleven. Do you want a drink?'

'You shouldn't be here. Why are you here?'

'To look after you. And help Emmy. You gave her a fright.'

'You should be with Brian, with your family.'

'You're my family.' She fussed at the rumpled bedcovers.

He said, 'It's not the same.' He disentangled himself from the sheets and reached for her hand. Awkwardly stroking her fingers, he continued, 'It's odd the way we hardly ever touch one another in our family. Ours, I mean, not yours. I imagine it's different there.'

'Yes.' The affirmation chilled and isolated him. She said, 'It doesn't have to be like this. You don't have to be alone. You're too independent – if you'd married. . . .'

'No.'

'But if you had – it could still happen.'

'No.' He released her hand and lay back against the pillows. Closing his eyes, he heard quite distinctly a distant shout in the high, piping voice of a child, and sensed the vibration and heard the receding bounce of a ball along the corridor. Then silence again, and darkness, and a dragging sense of being utterly alone.

13

Sophie was in her bedroom washing the paintwork. From the open casement she could just see the fuzzy ginger nest of Michael's hair. He was having trouble with the mower. He tugged at the cord; the machine gave a smoker's cough, whirred, spluttered and died.

She was confused about Michael. She could hardly remember when he hadn't been around. They'd gone to school together. When she moved to Cambridge, he followed. He'd always been there, an unlikely knight standing between her and the hard edges of the world; but just recently his armour had acquired a tarnished look.

They'd had a row this morning. His brother had written suggesting that she and Michael, Clive and his latest girlfriend – emptyheaded with long blonde hair reaching almost to the tops of her shiny white thigh-hugging boots – should take a villa in Italy. It was a far cry from Clive's usual excursions, backpacking in India, but then Terri was a departure from his usual run of beaded and belled girlfriends.

Michael passed her the letter. She read it, then tossed it back saying, 'Whatever happened to bedrolls under the stars?' Michael shrugged. 'I'm sorry. There's no way I'm spending a fortnight with those two.'

'Typical.' His explosion startled her. 'When you had that bloody estate agent here every weekend I had to grin and bear it, but as soon as it comes to something I want. . . .'

He shouldn't have invoked Charles like that. She dunked her sponge in the soapy water and set about the greasy film coating the top edge of the picture rail.

This time last year, Charles had still been visiting them. God, but she missed him.

She scrubbed at a speckled patch of fly-dirt. Michael had finally got the mower going and its engine throbbed against the heavy summer air.

If I'd said yes, I love you too. . . . What would you have said, what would you have done?

She'd known the answer before posing the question. Because she knew him. At least, she'd known him then. What about now? Had he changed? Did he miss her, wish he'd handled things differently?

No point; she'd been down this path too many times – the same old questions representing themselves like bounced cheques.

She got down off the stool and wrung the dirty sponge into the bucket. What had happened to him? Had he gone back to being the huddled, unhappy man he'd been when they met? Or had he built on what she'd given him?

James would know. She'd bumped into James last Saturday on Portobello Road. Outside the Red Lion Arcade she was fingering the drops of a very ornate, very ugly chandelier, when she heard him shout, 'Hey, it's the queen of the chandeliers. How's it going? You look great. I'm due up in Cambridge – got anything lined up for me?'

'One or two bits. . . .'

'Okay,' he took her by the elbow and drew her away from the stall, 'tell me.'

As they browsed she described what she'd put aside for him. He said he'd call the following week. And all the while the little voice in her head whispered, ask him, go on. Ask him about Charles – your friend, the one who almost demolished your house – how is he?

Does he miss me?

She said, 'What d'you think of this?' A silk shawl hung from the crossbar of a stall. It was embroidered with green vines, vivid against the black background, jet encrusted with emeralds. The long fringe tickled the back of her hand and the embroidery curled in tight weals along the border.

James flicked over the price tag. 'Too much,' he murmured.

'To sell, yes, but I want it for me.' She tested the weight. 'What d'you think?' She unhooked it and, swinging it round her shoulders, pirouetted up the narrow aisle, very nearly dislodging a copper warming pan from the cross-rail of the bay opposite.

She paid for the shawl. James had to go – he was meeting someone – but he and Cathy were having some people round tonight, why didn't she join them?

She said no. She too had arranged to see someone. Jazz. She would go and see Jazz, that way it wasn't a lie. James said, 'Not to worry. Another time.'

Jazz sold 1930s china, Susie Cooper and Clarice Cliff, from a pitch in Camden Passage. Edging between a stall selling walking sticks topped with ivory and cloisonné and silver, and another offering silver pocket-watches, Sophie spotted Jazz's outlandish collection of angular orange and yellow pottery. She couldn't understand the craze for Art Deco.

Jazz was surprised to see her – they usually met at auctions; it was only by a fluke that Jazz hadn't been with her the day she'd met Charles. Would it have made any difference? What would Jazz have made of him? Sophie smiled. Easy. So far as Jazz was concerned, men might have their uses, but it didn't do to take them seriously.

They sat behind the stall discussing trade, swapping silly stories – Sophie had one about a couple who'd bought an Edwardian bureau with the intention of converting it into a Shinto shrine – and drinking coffee from a flask.

On the way home she got caught in the late afternoon traffic. Trapped in the car, tapping out her impatience on the rim of the steering wheel, the thoughts crowded in. Why had she refused James's invitation?

Out of pride. And fear. There was a chance, admittedly remote, that Charles would have been there.

It was hot. She opened the passenger side window. The traffic was snarled like a piece of string. She eased forward, and came to a halt beside a building site. It was surrounded by a tall yellow hoarding with viewing panels meshed with rusty wire. With a jolt, she recognised the company emblem – a tawny eagle with half-mantled wings and outstretched talons. Only Charles could be naive enough to use a bird of prey to represent a property company. And probably only Charles was honest enough to get away with it.

She smiled to think of the man responsible for all this standing in her kitchen wrapped in a red and white pinny, the dark hair on his arms frosted with flour. God, it was hot. She pushed her tangle of hair up off her brow. 'Bloody man!' she whispered to the ghost in her mind. 'God but I miss you, you stupid, stupid man.'

14

Charles accepted Cathy's invitation to her firework party – it wasn't really his sort of thing, but this year was different. His illness had made him realise that there was something very wrong with his life. But what? The symptoms were easily identified – depression, paranoia, the conviction that everyone but him possessed a secret formula for happiness. So much for the symptoms, but what of their cause? He wasn't such a romantic as to put it all down to his obsession with Sophie MacKenzie.

Why was it that the things that had once given him pleasure – the neat conclusion of a deal, a site transformed – had lost their sharpness? He hungered for something new. Sophie had shown him that there were other pleasures to be had. She'd shown him himself as he never allowed himself to be seen. He knew now that the pattern could be broken. He could build on that, he would change his life.

Cathy greeted him with a hug and a laugh. She took him upstairs to show him his room, then linked her arm through his and said, 'Come on, don't hang about. Come and meet everyone.' He glanced sideways at her as she led him across the hall and into the drawing room. She had changed. Her hair was the same, long and straight and dark, falling from a centre parting, but the face it framed had become heavy at the chin, and the skin round her eyes was puffy and pale. It made him sad to see how plump she'd become under the ballooning paisley bedcover of a dress. But then, maybe she was looking at him and thinking how grey he'd become, how dull.

She squeezed his arm, interrupting his cruel dissection. All around them were well-dressed men and women sipping sherry and talking. The accumulated noise heaved and surged like a sluggish tide, crested here by a shrill laugh, there by the clash of glasses. A pearly pall, a swirling moonlight haze of cigarette smoke, hung above their heads. Cathy's pudgy hand, heavy with angular rings incised and set with oddly shaped amber stones, rested on his arm. 'Let's find James.'

James stood with his elbow resting on the mantelpiece, immersed in conversation with a woman in a green dress who had her back to Charles. As he spoke, he flicked his hand to emphasise a point, and the woman nodded. She was small and neat-bodied and over her crushed-velvet dress she'd draped a black silk shawl embroidered with brilliant green leaves and vines. Her long auburn hair had been lifted off her neck and loosely fastened with a pair of ornate tortoiseshell combs.

Cathy called to her brother, who looked up and waved, then said something to the woman. The woman turned.

The weight of Cathy's hand dragged at his arm and there was a sudden increase in the noise level – in the room or in his head, he couldn't tell which.

James said, 'Charles. Glad you could make it. Meet Sophie. Sophie, this is Charles. He's the philistine who wanted to raze this place to the ground.'

'But instead,' she smiled at Charles and the familiar gold flecks flickered in her eyes, 'sold it to you in the name of friendship. How do you do – Charles?'

James said, 'Sophie's in the antiques business.'

Cathy laughed. 'So are most of the people here – except Charles. Oh look,' she peered past him to the dining room, 'I think Donna's ready.' She raised her voice, 'Shall we go through, everybody.'

He sat on the opposite side of the table and four places down from Sophie. Throughout the meal he was presented with her profile as she talked with her neighbours. She never once looked fully in his direction. He ate without knowing what, talked without knowing what he said. And all the time he studied her, the untidy pile of her wonderful hair, its weight inadequately supported by the antique combs so that all over little curls escaped, muzzing the outline, shimmering in the candlelight. When she turned away to the fullest extent to say something to James, he saw how the pale tendrils gauzing her nape shifted like flames, catching the light with every movement.

James had said something and she laughed and, sitting back, began to explain or describe an object or an idea to the man opposite. As she spoke, her hands batted the air like fluttering moths. Charles held his breath as every gesture clicked into place in his memory.

He hadn't expected ever to see her again.

His neighbour asked him something about the state of the property market. He answered automatically. He could hear nothing now but the sound of his chasing blood as it swelled his veins, making him ache with unfamiliar longing, making him aware of his body and its frontiers as never before. He felt the constriction of his shirt-collar, tight and hard as it pressed against the tender part of his neck, was acutely aware of the sore patch on his ankle where his shoe had rubbed, and of the intense bubbling heat of the room that no one else seemed to notice. The sting of candle-smoke and the smell of hot wax made his eyes smart and his throat dry. He finished his wine. The neck of a bottle appeared over his shoulder and someone topped up his glass. He played with his food, shifting it round the plate, making patterns out of slivers of meat and scraps of carrot. His plate was removed and replaced with a crystal goblet of sorbet, sharp against his tongue, chilling the roof of his mouth.

Why wouldn't she look at him? Her silver spoon flashed as she used it to orchestrate an argument. The man opposite jabbed an urgent finger at her, daring to disagree, and she laughed and rapped his knuckle gently with her spoon. He saw the man's resistance dissolve, and wondered what Michael would make of it all.

The meal ended with the pushing back of chairs and the tossing of napkins onto the table and a general drift towards the drawing room. Sophie didn't move. Would James never shut up, never leave her alone, give someone else a chance?

The old Charles would have waited his turn. Most likely that turn would never have come. Forceful in business, he'd never acquired the knack in situations such as this. But he would learn. It was possible to change. He stood up and edged his way round the table. James straightened and slapped him on the back. 'Charles! How goes it? Enjoying yourself? Listen, I've got some things to do, why don't you keep Sophie company. That okay, Sophie?'

And Charles thought, as easy as that.

Everyone had left the dining room, but still Sophie didn't move. He hadn't a clue what to say or do next. And then she looked up at him and said, 'For God's sake, Charles, sit down. You look like you're waiting for a bus.'

He laughed and, straightening a chair, sat down beside her. Suddenly he felt amazingly light-hearted. Light-headed too, though that was probably the wine.

From the hallway came the clatter and babble of yet more guests arriving. Sophie said, 'I'm glad you're here. I hoped you would be.'

So it was no accident. He was indignant. He was delighted. He said, 'I didn't know you knew James.' The words came out clipped, an official statement. If only he could be less formal. He wanted to loosen his tie, undo the top button of his shirt. Touch her. Instead he stared at the damasked battleground of the table, rendered virtually speechless by the knowledge that she hadn't forgotten him, that in some obscure way he mattered to her.

Out of the corner of his eye he could see the line of her dress as it draped her knee, the black silk fringe of her shawl looping down over her arm. She moved, and the shawl slithered lower to trail the carpet.

'How's Michael?'

'Michael,' she murmured. He could hear the smile in her voice, but didn't dare look at her. Leaning forward, he began to gather the scattered breadcrumbs, debris of the meal, into a small pile. His fingernail rasped against the nap. 'Michael's fine. You know what he's like. Doesn't go in for this sort of thing.'

'No.'

'Don't be like this,' she chided. 'Don't be angry. I've missed you – Charles?' He heard her move, the sigh of silk against velvet, felt her touch his arm. 'Are you listening?'

Of course he was. He was the reason she'd come. And she'd missed him. His heart rattled like a dinghy ripped from its moorings. He didn't want this. Freedom to change, yes, to discover his own self – but not this.

She withdrew her hand. Her fingers dragged against the stuff of his sleeve. He looked at her. Her face was white. Crimson splashes heightened her cheekbones. She looked frightened. Why should she be frightened? Because he was angry? He was, but not with her. It was his own weakness that infuriated him. He should say something, reassure her, but he couldn't. His mind was empty, his throat frozen. No. Not true. His mind wasn't empty, the thoughts rose like bubbles, bursting when they hit the surface, but every one of them was either too important or too banal.

How's business?

I love you.

Bought any good chandeliers lately?

I meant it, what I said about loving you.

She sat back in her chair. She said, 'All you have to do is say it. If you don't want me here, say so. I'll find an excuse. I'll go. Tell me what you want.'

Stay. He thought it, but didn't say it aloud. He didn't get the chance. James came back. Charles followed them through to the drawing room.

Cathy bustled over and thrust a ridiculously small cup of coffee into his hand. She asked what he'd thought of the sorbet and though she didn't really want to know, he told her anyway. She lit a cigarette, took a couple of deep draughts, and moved closer to him, saying, 'He's at it again, isn't he?' She nodded towards her brother. James was absorbed in conversation with Sophie. 'I can talk to you, Charles, you're his friend – why does he do it?'

'Do what? I don't understand . . . Sophie?' Realisation dawned. 'James and Sophie?'

'God, just listen to you, you're as bad as he is. What is it about her, what's so special? She's just a cocky little red-head. . . .'

'Red? I wouldn't call it red, exactly. . . .'

'Well what is it, then, exactly?'

She was upset and he was sorry, but he didn't like what she was implying. He said gently, 'You mustn't be jealous, Cath.'

'Jealous? What's to be jealous of? Her not-exactly red hair?'

'That's not what I meant.'

'I know what you meant,' she said, murderously jabbing her cigarette at the ashtray. 'Okay. You're right, I take things too seriously. But you know what he's like. I can't face it again, all the upheaval and upset.' He took her hand and gave it a squeeze. She smiled and said, 'God, I'm so sorry, Charles. I get like this some-times – maudlin.' She hugged his arm, then released him and waved to her brother. 'James,' she called, 'are you ready? When are we going to see these fireworks?'

The night was mild. The fireworks were splendid, exploding in great showers of red and silver, green and gold, following one after the other with hardly a break, whizzing and banging and whorling and flashing.

Tilting his head back to watch the display gave Charles a crick in the neck. Worse, he could feel a headache coming on. A fluttering pain above his right eye made him frown.

Sophie. Where was Sophie? There: over to his left, leaning against James with her foxy face lifted skywards. She must have sensed him watching her; she turned and, by the flare of a rocket, met his eye and winked.

The display ended with a series of rattling explosions as a great rose and gold umbrella burst and hovered tantalisingly, terrifyingly above them. They stood, holding their breath, as the cascade dissipated in a series of sad spirals and wisps of smoke, blue against the black night sky. When the last sparkling star had vanished, James stepped forward to light the bonfire which at once erupted into an eight-foot pyre of crackling orange flame.

There was now no sign of Sophie.

All around him people laughed and exclaimed over the fireworks, pointing delightedly at red against black, sparks dancing upwards in the current of the heat, swirling in fiery constellations, living then dying, falling back to the fire, their source.

Music. Loud. Raucous. A heavy drumbeat thrumming like a pulse. People dancing, gyrating across the terrace, spilling over on-to the lawn, crushing the damp grass. Charles made his way round to the far side of the fire where the sounds of the party were distanced and overlaid by the infernal roar. He stood alone, watch-ing the flames turn from red to orange to yellow-gold as the heat intensified, listening to the crackling and snapping of the fire as its outline shifted and its inner structure began to crumble and give way.

And she came to him out of the fire.

At least, that's how it seemed. One moment it was all leaping colour and scorching heat, the next there was a coolness and a blackness at its heart. The blackness moved, detached itself, and came towards him.

She was smiling. The sparks from the fire, transmuted to gold, sailed across her eyes. Her lips moved, but he couldn't hear what she was saying. She tipped her head to one side, waiting for an answer to a question he hadn't heard. He nodded, and she tossed her head and laughed and, taking him by the hand, led him towards the house.

Hand in hand, they made their way through the drawing room, across the hall and up the stairs – the nearer the top, the tighter her grip.

You know where this is leading, don't you?

Yes, I know.

You don't want it. You said so.

I lied.

Her room was dark. He reached for the light switch but her fingers fluttered over his. 'No,' she said. 'Wait.' He heard her cross the room, then the swish of the curtains as she swept them aside, setting the room alight with the dancing, grotesque shadows of the flame, making the massive Victorian furniture glow red as if tor-ched from the inside.

She stood silhouetted against the crimson window, a figure poised at the mouth of hell.

Then she moved to adjust her shawl, and the image changed, the analogy became absurd.

I love her – the thought roared in his head. His throbbing blood matched the pounding of the music. He went to stand beside her. Below the party racketted on and the electric guitars overlaid the subterranean beat with their twanging and whining.

He said, 'Look, there's James. What's he doing, is he looking for you?'

'Probably.'

'Perhaps we should go down.'

'No.'

'No,' he agreed.

She looked up at him; one side of her face glowed rosy-gold, the other was in black shadow. 'What are you thinking?' she whispered, and when he didn't respond she said, 'Are you afraid?'

'Yes. Are you?'

'Yes.' He believed her. She held up a hand, palm outward and at shoulder height, like a Red Indian greeting. He matched his hand to hers, fingertip to fingertip, and the space between fizzed and flared. Her fingers curled, locking with his. He bent over her, blocking out the treacherous firelight, kissing her, pulling her against him, feeling her melt and mould to him and this was it, he knew, the point on which his future hinged, the door flapping back and forth in the unseen breeze and a trickle of perspiration runnelling down his spine and the fire so fierce that he knew the wood would burn.

But you're not made of wood – the voice of reason screamed.

And he answered – So? Flesh also burns . . . the martyr strapped to the stake, the gridiron saint, blistering skin and curling flesh and sizzling hair.

You must not burn. Mind defeats fire, mind above all.

But see how my mind is in thrall, encircled by flames, I'm blinded by smoke.

Fight. You have to fight – the hated voice hissed against the snare-drum slide of blood in his ears.

I don't want to fight. Not any more.

He held on to her, crushing her tighter and tighter, and where he gripped the small of her back the cool silk of her shawl bathed his hand like the cascade of a forest waterfall.

No good will come of it – no good ever comes of it.

I don't care. I love her.

And he held her welded tight and she moved and rippled against him, sinuous and strong like a snake.

Not a snake, but a serpent.

Sin.

Damnation.

His mind clenched and his body failed; he tore himself from her. His chest heaved as he struggled for breath. He stared at her and saw how her face had softened and her eyes were heavy and her hair gleamed bronze in the up-shining firelight – and where was the sin?

Here. Here. Here.

He started towards the door, step by step, his body like a marionette. But all she had to do was say his name in a voice that carried the dark brown resonance of a double bass. 'I love you. You know that, don't you. You do know that?'

He swayed, and clutched at the ruby-glowing mahogany bed-end. Down in the garden, someone turned the music even higher. 'Don't go.'

No. He mouthed the word, but no sound came. He didn't even know what he meant – no he wouldn't go; or no, he couldn't stay. It didn't matter which. Even as his brain struggled with the conundrum his hands were tugging at his tie and he heard the rasp of his breath as he fumbled with the buttons of his shirt. He bent to struggle with a knotted shoelace. She said, 'Hurry, Charles.' And her voice goose-pimpled his flesh. He kicked off his shoe with such sudden violence that it disappeared under the bed.

And now he was done. His clothes lay scattered all around him and the cool air made the hair on his body rise. His body? This vessel of sinew and flesh and writhing arteries had nothing to do with him; he was hidden deep inside, the slippery white kernel buried in the bruised heart of the fruit.

What now, where next. . . . Nothing had prepared him for the ferocity of this moment, the wonder and horror of his shape-shifting body, the alienation from self and then, in a moment of dazzling realisation, the bursting of the kernel, and his own being growing and swelling inside to match the raw inner surface of its vessel.

He turned to face her.

Like him, she had shed her clothes and the lessening glow from the bonfire rippled across her skin, sending her shadow trailing across the carpet like a discarded robe. Sibyl. Once he had called her that; and sorceress; now she was a pagan priestess poised for sacrifice.

But she'd said she was afraid, and on one level he believed her. But fear only strengthened the illusion, sharpening the sense of danger. As the lift and tremor of her breasts echoed her deep, shuddering breaths, he saw that she was both more and less than human, a mythical creature of fire and shadow. And as he stood close to her, face to face, he saw through the fire of her, and into the terrifying darkness beyond, and he couldn't bear to see that and he bent over her, enclosing her – and all his senses focused on her and what she was and what she wasn't until there was no space, no distinction between them, and they rocked together to the sound of raging guitars, clutched by a flame-filled trance that tore them back and forth, flesh against flesh, sliding and sighing and grunting until the bellow of his ursine roar roused him to the room and the bed and the puffy feather mattress that supported and surrounded them, to the dented pillows littered with her hair, the tortoiseshell combs still clinging to its tangled strands, and to the grating rattle in his throat as he struggled for breath.

He pushed himself back till he could see her parted lips, her unfocusing eyes flecked with fire by the ebbing light. His heavy body was a burden to him, and surely to her. He started to lift himself away but, with an intake of breath, she pulled him back down and into her, twisting against him, her arms tightening convulsively as she moved beneath him, and then her head tossing from side to side on the pillow, her fierce teeth whitening her lower lip.

Then she lay still. He moved over to the cool side of the bed. He stared up at the rosy glow pulsing across the ceiling. He felt tired, his limbs gripped by a terribly lethargy. He closed his eyes, too weary to be either glad or sad, exultant or guilty.

It's a sin, you know, what you've just done.

I know. So what. Who cares.

He must have slept. Not deeply and not for long, but enough. He woke to find her leaning over him. The combs were gone from her hair and her face was in shadow. Stroking his temple, she ran her fingers rasping over his stubbled cheek, down again to outline the shadowed cleft of his collarbone, then further still, under the sheets and the heavy eiderdown. She touched him, and he grew to fit her palm. She laughed and said, 'No regrets?'

'None,' he spoke on a breath as she flexed her fingers, defining him, threatening and thrilling. Gingerly, he touched the tip of her breast and as he too began to massage and coax, she closed her eyes and her lips parted and he heard the altered sound of her breathing, watched entranced as her face took on a closed, concentrated look – and then she moved, sliding onto him and astride him and she was laughing and so was he and she rode him with her head thrown back and her hair flying, as a child rides a hobbyhorse, except that it was much more than that. They were no longer two but one, a single creature – a pivoting beast, a Trinity. . . . The blasphemy speared him and he shifted beneath her, rolling her over as he delved deeper and deeper to find the kernel, the ark of life, the altar of death. She was the Host on his tongue, the wine in his throat and in this moment of union, this point of communion there was no difference – no difference between body and mind, pure and pagan, male and female, all division is illusion, the only truth the blinding unity of this moment.

They lay facing one another. Her shoulder gleamed like a golden apple and he cupped it in his palm, then slid his hand under her unruly hair. She closed her eyes and, in a voice laden with sleep, said, 'I love you. Are you happy?'

He answered, 'Yes.' And heard the laughter and the breathlessness in his voice. 'I'm happy. I understand – I don't know how to say it, how to make you see. Am I crazy, Sophie? I feel as though I've seen the face of God.'

15

Charles woke as the first touch of dawn lightened the window. Sophie was stretched beside him, breathing steadily. Careful not to disturb her, he peeled back the heavy covers and slid out of bed. She stirred and curled into a foetal ball along the edge of the mattress.

He had trouble locating his clothes. He was usually so methodical, but last night he'd shed his outer skin just anywhere. He glanced back at the hunched mound cushioned by feathers. If only she'd wake up. They could talk, plan – how would she tell Michael? Better to write than phone – he'd have to warn Emmy.

He began to dress. The fabric rasped against his newly sensitised skin. He had to fight to suppress the harsh, panicky sound of his breathing. Why was he so anxious? Because he was in the wrong room, was going to have to creep back down the passage in his stockinged feet and hope the other guests wouldn't hear him. He was both horrified and excited by the need for subterfuge.

Going down on his hands and knees, he rummaged a shoe from under the bed. Before leaving, he stood over her for a moment. The dim light filtering through the window offered him the outline of her features. He thought, so this is it, the great mystery. And the mystery wasn't diminished by revelation. Strange how she'd stayed with him during all these months, the way she stirred him as no one else had ever done, seemed to contain within her the answers to questions he was only now beginning to ask. So wise, Sophie, lying there like a child. No one would ever guess – but he saw, he knew what she was.

Very gently, he touched her cheek. Her lips twitched, her eyes opened a fraction. But she didn't wake.

Sophie took a deep breath, held it for a beat, then allowed it to trickle out through the slit of her lips. Charles must not realise she was awake.

She lay curled along the edge of the mattress, her eyes tight shut, listening to the scuffle of his surreptitious dressing, to the rustle of an arm seeking a sleeve, the teetering thrust of leg in trouser. She heard the thud of a dropped shoe and a hissing intake of breath. When he bumped against the bed-end, making it shudder, he disrupted the regular pattern of her breathing. She almost gave the game away when he leant over her. The touch of his fingers triggered a moist flutter and an aching reminder.

Don't think of that. Don't weaken.

The door clicked shut behind him. Grabbing the pillow she hugged it to her, stuffing it against her mouth. Panic came first, at what she'd done, the betrayal – not of Michael but of herself. And then panic was replaced by anger and indignation. She sat up, still clutching the pillow. Her eyes and cheeks stung like hot sand. Stupid man. You weren't supposed to go so far. I only wanted to see if you were as innocent as you seemed.

Not true. I wanted more than that.

She'd been right though – about his inexperience. Everything about him, his reverence towards her, his bewilderment and exhilaration at the excesses of his body, confirmed what she'd believed from the start. Which meant that, having behaved as she had, it was inevitable that it should end like this. She rocked forward over the pillow, her arms throttle-tight about its middle. He'd tried though, he'd tried to call a halt, but she wouldn't allow it, oh no, not her. She had to keep on at him, push it just that one stage further, and then further and further still, edging them ever closer to the brink.

And what lay down there in the abyss? Shared darkness, abandonment to desire and the annihilation of Self. She'd wanted to jump. She had jumped. And so had he – it had been the same for him. She knew because even now he didn't shield himself well, not from her. They were too much alike. They had fought the same battle tonight, between thought and feeling, sense and sensuality. He was like her, her dark side, her negative image.

He should have woken her, shaken her awake and made her sit up, embroiled her with plans and promises – forced a commitment from her, got the contract signed before any of the parties could think twice.

But he hadn't. He was too bloody considerate. He'd let her go on sleeping. When he got down to breakfast she'd disappeared on some jaunt with James.

One or two guests lingered at the breakfast table. He sat next to Cathy who poured him some coffee. He asked where James and Sophie had gone. She shrugged. 'To look at some furniture, or something. Not sure exactly. He wasn't too communicative this morning. You upset him, sneaking off like that.' He concentrated on buttering his toast. Cathy said, 'When I think of all the years we've known you – you've always been so discreet. But you were seen, Charles. You and the redhead creeping into the house hand in hand like a couple of naughty children.' He laughed. 'Yes, well, James laughed too. Great joke. Except you stole a march on him. He's none too pleased, Charles.'

The day passed slowly. The weekend guests trickled back for lunch. Sophie and James were not among them. As the afternoon dragged on, he grew more and more restless. When he could bear it no longer, he escaped into the grounds.

Dusk had fallen early. It was cold and misty. Huddling into his coat he dug his hands deep into his pockets.

Why was she doing this? She'd run off without a word. Where had they gone? Last night must have meant something to her. It had meant so much to him. He could still feel the lingering traces of her touch, as if she'd left a physical residue on his skin. It wasn't possible their lines of intent had become so thoroughly tangled.

God, she's made a fool of you. No sense hiding your head in the sand. Think how thick she is with James. They probably set the whole thing up between them. Let's take him down a peg or two – yes, a put-up job. They've had a bet on it, they're probably out celebrating and she's giving him all the details, about how easily led you were, how clumsy – didn't put up much of a show, did you – and all that noise, and talk of God. . . .

He kicked at the debris from last night's fireworks, their fairy splendour reduced to a scattering of bent wire and scraps of scorched paper.

It had been the most sacred moment of his life. Hers too, he was sure. Because she loved him. She'd said so, hadn't she?

Back at the house several new cars were parked in the drive and lights blazed in the downstairs windows. He pushed open the front door; Cathy crossed the hall laden with coats. She said, 'They're all early tonight. You'd better get changed.' He asked if Sophie was back. And James. Cathy said, 'Yes, about ten minutes ago.'

He changed quickly, then sat on the edge of the bed with his fists clenched into the mattress. If Sophie had got back before him, she must be dressed and ready by now. Maybe she'd come to his room. He braced himself for the knock on his door.

It didn't come.

He waited.

More cars arrived, he heard the scudding of gravel and the slamming doors and shouted greetings. The house throbbed with movement and music, an intrusive bass thump made the floors and walls shudder.

She's not going to come. If he didn't go down soon, Cathy would come looking for him. He stirred himself, and went out on to the landing. He paused at the top of the stairs to smooth his hair, then went down.

Nobody noticed his arrival. The party had already reached the seething, oceanic stage where bodies move individually, jigging and swaying, but at the same time form a uniform movement, order out of chaos.

He saw Cathy dancing with a bearded man in a red shirt. Sophie was dancing with James. Once again she'd fastened her hair with the tortoiseshell combs. As she bounced to the music the diaphanous fabric of her dress glinted and whirled in the flickering lights.

James gave him a tight nod, and said something to Sophie. She shrugged and shook her head.

Then Cathy saw him and made her way over. 'You're not drinking,' she accused. 'Come on, I'll get you something.'

The buffet was laid out on the dining table and the sideboard was a forest of bottles. Cathy poured him some wine. He sipped it. It was too acid. Cathy said, 'Now go back in there and ask your not-exactly redhead to dance with you.' He shook his head and swirled the wine in the glass. 'Don't let him cut you out, Charles. He will if you let him. You're going to have to fight for her.'

'I don't want her,' he said. 'I don't want to fight. Here comes your friend.' The bearded man approached. 'Go and dance.'

After she'd gone, he abandoned the wine and poured himself a whisky. He downed it in one. That was better. He poured another. The glow, the slight lightheadedness was immediate. He was on his third hefty measure when a hand reached to take the glass from him. Sophie sniffed it and pulled a face. 'How can you drink this stuff?' He snatched the glass back and drained it. 'That doesn't solve anything.' The dim light gave her hair a mahogany tone. An escaping strand trailed her neck. A pulse flickered in her throat. She said, 'Would you like to dance?'

'I don't dance.'

'Please yourself.' She made to leave. His throat cracked and he barked her name and grabbed her by the arm.

Fight for her, Cathy had said.

'I need to talk to you.'

'Not now.' She tried to turn away, but he held on to her.

'Now,' he said, and manoeuvred her across the room and out into the hall. She didn't resist. Perhaps he'd caught her by surprise. He'd certainly surprised himself.

In the hall, a couple careering out of the drawing room bumped into Sophie, knocking her against him. He took the opportunity to shift his grip from her arm to her hand. 'Well, well,' she mocked. 'How masterful.' And he squeezed her hand. A flicker of pain passed across her face. His mind was taut as a drum-skin. The sounds of the party, the music and the voices skittered across its surface like water on a griddle.

He said, 'What's going on? Where have you been all day?'

'With James, and some of his cronies. Looking at a furniture shipment, visiting a couple of warehouses, that sort of thing.'

'Why?'

'What?'

'You just went. You didn't say. I've a right to know. . . .'

'No you don't. Oh, unless you mean right of tenure – is that it? Possession being nine-tenths. . . .'

He yanked her hand, pulling her across the hall and out of the front door. The cold air checked him. The heavy door banged shut, muting the music and the babble. He took a deep breath. The night smelt of damp leaves and bonfires and incense. He dragged her down the steps, over the crunching gravel drive and onto the wet lawn. She floundered after him, yelling his name. 'Stop this. You're hurting me. What the hell d'you think you're doing? Charles!'

The further they went, the harder it was for her to keep up and her breath came in jumping gasps. Every time she stumbled, she jerked his arm in its socket. And then suddenly it seemed they'd gone far enough. He stopped so abruptly that she blundered into him.

She looked ragged and vulnerable. She fumbled at his fingers, trying to prise them open. He released her and she stood, head bent, massaging her wrist. He said, 'Tell me about James.' She didn't answer. His voice raked in his throat. 'How long have you known him . . . how well? Is he your lover?'

She became still. She said, 'No. You are. Remember?' The words kicked and winded him. She looked up. 'What's this about, Charles? What do you want?'

'To marry you.' He hadn't meant to say it, just as he hadn't meant to ask her to lunch that first day. The devil on his shoulder spoke, but it wasn't what he wanted.

'Don't be so bloody ridiculous.'

'Why? Why is it ridiculous? You love me, you said so.'

'Did I? Was it true, d'you think? Would you know the difference?'

The night was cold. He shivered. 'You said it. I remember. I believed you.'

'Maybe that's why I said it, because it was something you needed to believe.'

'Don't do this!' He grabbed her and shook her. 'You said it. You meant it. You know you did – you can't walk away, not after last night. D'you know what you did, d'you have the least idea? You changed me, made me do things I'd never have done – and now you want to walk away, as if it never happened. You can't just go. You owe me something.'

'I owe you nothing. You don't want to marry me, you just want to fuck me again.'

He stepped back and stumbled against a tussock of grass.

'Oh dear. Now I've shocked you. Come on, Charles, face it. That's all it was, you know, one long, glorious. . . .'

'Don't say that.'

'You used me. All right, I used you too. I wanted to know just how innocent you really were, and you wanted to know what it was like. You're nothing but a pathetic middle-aged virgin who wanted to find out what he'd been missing – and now you're riddled with guilt and you're trying to offload it on to me, and it won't do.'

'I thought you loved me.' His lips were rigid. He could scarcely articulate. 'Otherwise I wouldn't have, I'd never . . . I swear.'

'Oh yes you would,' she spat. Then, more quietly, 'Dear God, Charles, just listen to us, shouting and sniping, saying things we don't mean. Listen to me.' She slid her hands up his arms, crumpling the damp cotton of his shirt. 'I only said it to make you see. Please, try to understand.' He hardly heard her. He stared at the house, the figures moving at the dimly lit windows, and he was still shivering. She was running her hands up and down his arms as if to warm him. She said, 'You're so cold, you'll get a chill. It's raining.' He hadn't noticed but now he felt the rain like tears on his face. She said, 'Let's go in.' He shook his head. 'We needn't go back to the house. Come on.'

They climbed the shallow steps of the summerhouse. The wooden floor echoed to their footsteps as they scuffled through the dried leaves. She gave a nervous laugh. 'There,' she said, 'that's better.'

They stood close. The rain was heavy now, pattering on the roof like a rodent army. Sophie straightened his tie and rested her hands on his shoulders. She was warm, but when he tried to move closer, she pushed him down on to the bench.

They sat shoulder to shoulder. His damp shirt chilled him. The rain gauzed the doorway and a sudden breeze curled across the floor, rustling the dead leaves. They reminded him of the wood-shavings in Michael's barn and the smell of resin they threw up when trodden on and crushed. He said, 'Why did you marry Michael?'

She said nothing. She gathered the dead leaves from the bench beside her and crumbled them into her lap where they lay like tawny confetti, like dead moths.

'Did you love him?' he insisted. 'Do you still?'

'I've always known him. He loves me more than anything. I think I married him because he was safe. I shall stay with him for the same reason.'

16

Lying in his bed with the folded sheet chill and taut against his chin, he fretted over her words. She'd said Michael was safe. Did that mean she regarded him as unsafe? It made no sense. He was safe to the point of tedium. The slightest whisper of danger and he was guaranteed to flee. Ask Leonard.

Or was it the danger he represented that she feared?

She'd come here hoping to see him. She'd said as much and, despite her taunt, he knew how to recognise truth. So why reject him? Because, like him, she feared the burden of dependence? Even now he didn't feel totally disentangled from their love-making.

They were a stubborn pair, unaccustomed to compromise, and, if he wanted her, he was going to have to learn to bend, to accommodate her weaknesses as well as his own. He should have left her alone this evening. She'd probably have come to him in her own time. But oh no, he'd gone crashing in, making demands. What if he placed himself entirely in her hands? He could say, tell me what you want from this relationship; whatever it is – even if you tell me to go – I'll respect that. It might work; she would appreciate an approach like that. She wasn't unreasonable, and she did love him. And if her answer was the same as last night's, well, he had already learned to live without her.

He slept after that, waking early to a prickly-cold morning. Dressing hurriedly, he pulled on a sweater and took particular care brushing his hair.

He hesitated outside her door. Adjusting the knot of his tie, he smoothed back his hair, knocked and went in. She was up and dressed, standing by the bed folding her nightdress. A suitcase lay open on the tousled candlewick cover. She glanced up at him, then carefully placed the nightdress in the case.

Reason fled. 'What the hell are you doing? You were going to sneak off, weren't you, without a word.' She tucked a hairbrush into the pocket at the side of the case. 'Say something,' he demanded. 'Tell me I've got it wrong. Look at me, Sophie.'

There were shadows under her eyes, her cheeks were puffy, but there was a hardness too, an edge of defiance as she said, 'I thought if I slipped away it'd save all this fuss.'

'Why did you come here? If this is all there is, one night and a lot of heartbreak, why bother? Or is it only me that's hurting? Just a bit of fun to you, is it? Let's see if we can't make him squirm a bit – like tying a can to a cat's tail, or pulling the legs off spiders. . . .'

'If you think that,' she began. Then, 'No, I came because I'd forgotten.' She spoke softly, almost to herself. 'I'd got so that I could only remember the easier things about you – our similarities. I'd forgotten the differences. But now I realise how elusive you are. I don't know you, Charles. You seem to expect me to change my entire way of life and commit myself to you.'

'Why not?'

'Because I don't know you; I'd be marrying a chimera. Every time I see you, you change, become someone else. Whoever you seem to be, there's always someone else lurking underneath. I can't even get you into focus by talking to other people. The man James knows has nothing to do with the man I met in the sale room, who came to Cambridge, who fucked me. You say you love me, but I think that's something you need to believe – how else can you justify what's happened? But Michael, he loves me. Do you know what he'd do if he knew what we'd done? He'd forgive me. Would you do that, in his place?'

'No.' She turned back to her packing. 'But that doesn't prove anything. That's not love, that's someone who doesn't care, doesn't value you.'

'I have no value, Charles.' She looked at him over her shoulder. 'Take a tip from the man who knows. You're better off without me.'

'You don't have the least idea what my life's like without you.'

'D'you think I haven't thought about it? You have a life, Charles, and when you get back to it you'll see you've got it out of all proportion. You're an intelligent, capable man, you'll shrug this off in no time. You've got friends, a family, your career. And your faith, don't forget that, your interventionist god.'

'As you say, you don't know me.'

She shrugged and crossed the room to the dressing table. She clattered and chinked glass against glass as she gathered together pots of cream and little tablets of make-up. It struck him as an intimate thing to be witnessing. He looked away. And spotted the Celtic head. It was lying in the corner of the suitcase, nestling against the folds of last night's dress.

He edged closer. The oval face stared up at him. The blank eyes were knowing and the straight mouth mocked him. He picked it up.

'Don't. Put it back.' Her voice was like glass. He thought, She always reacts to this. He tested its weight. Why had she brought it with her? She said, 'Will you please put it back where you found it.'

'What's it doing here? What's so special about it? Oh no you don't,' he laughed angrily as she made a grab for it. He held it high up, out of her reach. 'Tell me.'

'It's nothing, just a bit of stone, a paperweight.'

'Well in that case. . . .' He started towards the door.

She said, 'You're being bloody childish, you know that, don't you?'

He was conscious of the stone's weight. He ran the ball of his thumb over its gritty surface. 'Yes, but then so are you.'

'It's a symbol,' she spoke without looking at him. 'That's all. It means something to me, but only to me.'

'What?'

'It's complicated.'

'Try.'

She took a breath. 'Life. I suppose it means life, survival. You believe in the Trinity, salvation through sacrifice and all that – and the crucifix is the symbol of your belief.'

'So?'

'So that's what the stone means to me. It represents what I believe. It's a reminder. Now give it to me. I want to go home.'

17

When he'd said he'd seen the face of God, he hadn't meant the features, the fullness or thinness of God's lips, the outline of his jaw. He'd always found such anthropomorphism absurd. He knew that some faiths contained mystical strands which believed man contained a spark of the godhead, was capable, through discipline or insight, of reuniting, merging with the entity inadequately labelled 'god'. Charles wasn't sure whether this involved conscious absorption or the annihilation of Self. He found both concepts exciting and terrifying, the implications made him dizzy – more than ever now that he'd experienced some degree of insight. In that moment of sexually inspired theophany he'd seen himself not as an isolated atom, but as part of something greater. Like the dancers at the party he was autonomous, and yet contributed to a uniform movement. At first this vision seemed to place his life in context, but examining his revelation more closely, he became frightened. All very well to theorise in the abstract, but daily life is run by other rules. He felt disorientated, as if the rules had been changed when he wasn't looking and now he had to make sense of the new order on his own. He needed mystery, he always had, but he needed guidance also.

He used to use St Matthew's fairly regularly. It was the antithesis of his weekday life. But all that had changed. Today the irrelevant service rumbled on and he sat, hands folded in his lap, trying not to fidget. The upright back of the pew dug into the knuckles of his spine, thrusting him forward so that his knees grazed the tongued and grooved planks of the pew in front. He remembered a time when he'd been tolerant of discomfort, almost unaware, his body only a vehicle – but that had also changed. Now he was permeated by a sense of Self that ripped through his blood and along his nerves, until it reached the outer surfaces where it stretched and spread, redefining the boundaries. Sometimes he was startled by his reflection in a darkened window, or by his hand reaching wilfully for the telephone. He would stare at it, fascinated by its broad strength, the scattering of dark hair and the square-cut nails.

Those hands lay clenched in his lap. He didn't want to be here. He'd lost track of the service. No matter. If the magic had gone, he still had the building. He loved this church, so tall and wide and gracious. He'd brought Leonard here once, to show him the stained glass, particularly the window commemorating the Great War. They'd barely started when the vicar joined them. Lawrence May had researched the history of the church. It was only natural that he should take over from Charles. Later, Leonard accused him of sulking.

He tried hard to draw solace from the building. Churches could be pretty gloomy places, but not this one. This was all leaping vaults and crisp arches, the bright white light searing through the clerestory windows giving a vertiginous sense of space that once would have promised access to God. Not any longer. Now he believed that gateway to be within himself and he ached with the cold of the stone, and the clean-cut arches and the whitewashed roof exposed him, a sacrifice stretched upon the altar.

He wanted to leave, but that would be too blatant a rejection. May would probably come to visit him. Had the church been fuller he might have slipped away. But the congregation was scattered like currants in a teacake. All the little movements, the snapping clasp of a handbag, the shuffling of cold feet, chattered like goblin footfalls.

Let us pray.

From habit he lowered his head and fixed his eyes on the maroon hymnbook with the gold-tooled cross lying on the shelf in front of him. He could hear the rest of the congregation wriggling to its knees, but couldn't force his own conformity so far.

He closed his eyes, and saw Sophie nursing her wretched stone as if it were an injured bird.

Our Father, which art in Heaven. . . .

And then returning it to its cloth-of-gold nest.

What the crucifix represents to you. . . . He raised his eyes to the caramel-glazed figure spread-eagled on the cross on the pillar behind the lectern. He didn't understand.

May finished the prayer and looked straight at Charles as he announced another hymn. Across the stretch of pews cadaverous fingers rustled flimsy pages and discreet coughs joined with the sound of shuffling feet to echo and bounce from vault to vault, from arch to arch. The organ groaned the opening notes and the old ladies raised their shrill voices and when Charles tried to join them, his voice came too loud, too harsh.

Everything was out of kilter today, the alienation was almost physical. He felt like a child crammed into a jacket two sizes too small.

Surely I can find my way back, with just a little more effort.

Another command to pray. He slid forward off the comfortless seat and knelt on the dull red plush of the threadbare hassock. Dust drifted up, catching in his throat, making him cough. A stab of cramp in his right calf almost made him cry out. He gripped the back of the pew in front until his fingers ached and whitened.

No prayer came. A snowstorm white-out filled his mind, cutting and cold. He had changed irrevocably, had lost his place here, forfeiting the comfort of this beautiful building with its sprinting arches and carved wood and sculpted stone and the brilliant fragmentation of stained glass. He had lost Sophie, and lost this. He had only himself.

So be it.

A finger of warmth touched the back of his neck. The low winter sun, slanting through the window to his left, kindled the lurid reds and blues into a burst of reminiscent fire – and the prayer came, scorching the snowfield: tell me. Explain. Who are you?

You are the bread on my tongue and the wine in my throat. . . .

He knelt at the altar rail and took the proffered bread and it was dry. The silver goblet chilled his lips, the wine was gall. All the magic had fled. What he was doing here wasn't even sacrilege. It was nothing.

18

Sophie leant against the deep stone sink in the little room at the back of the shop, scouring at a tannin stain on a blue and white teapot. Her wrist ached. She dropped the teapot back into the bowl where it bobbed and bubbled and the distended chinamen prancing round its bulge had to struggle to keep their heads above water. Spreading her fingers, she examined their wrinkled pads; they smelt faintly of bleach. She poked at the teapot, submerging it, drowning the chinamen. A puff of suds trickled from the spout.

The trick was not to think. But thought was her refuge. When her parents had died, when Michael was being difficult, or the shop going through a bad patch, she'd retreat to that inner place where no one could follow. But someone had followed, occupied her, colonised her thoughts.

She fished for the teapot. The window by the sink looked out on a sun-blocking expanse of grubby Cambridge brick. She knew by heart the pattern of the bricks, every flake and chip, every gobbet of missing mortar. The colour of the clay had the sheen of dead skin.

She set the teapot to drain and rummaged in the bowl for its lid. After this she had a dinner service to pack, then she might do a bit of dusting in the shop.

No good. Charles's dark-eyed face wavered between her and the foamy water like a reflection in a shop window. Charles. A corkscrew of desire spiralled through her. She despised that kind of weakness, in herself no less than in others.

She gripped the edge of the sink. The teapot had disgorged its suds on to the blanched and swollen wood of the drainer. She noticed a fine star-crack in the base, fine enough to pass as crazing, but even so she should have spotted it before buying.

The door bell jangled, startling her. A customer. Good. Another distraction. She dried her hands and went through to the shop.

It wasn't a customer. It was Charles. He stood just inside the door, all buttoned up in his overcoat, grim as the day she'd met him. She felt a fluttering tenderness and swore silently. That trick of his, the vulnerability, the impression he gave of being permanently out of his depth, it got to her every time. Tricks and illusions, that's all they were.

He said, 'I should have telephoned, but I thought if I did you'd refuse to see me.'

'Yes.' She fixed her attention on the point where his tie peeked out from between the burgundy folds of his scarf. 'Yes, I would.'

'But now that I'm here. . . .'

His deep voice tugged her attention back to his face. The corkscrew gave another quarter-turn. She said, 'You'd better come in. Lock the door.'

He followed her through to the back room. Very slowly he pulled off his gloves and slapped them on to the corner of the table. He unbuttoned his coat, pulled out one of the slatback chairs, and sat down. She stood over him, indulging the memory of how she'd held that stern face between her hands, seen its lines dissolve with pleasure, how she'd buried her fingers in the thick hair and felt the hard contours of bone beneath.

He said, 'Don't hover, Sophie, please.' She set a chair at right angles to his and sat down. In the silence she could hear the deflating bubbles sighing in the sink. He said, 'I haven't come to pester you. I'm not trying to make you change your mind. You must be clear about that.' She nodded, but wondered if this was the truth or a negotiating ploy. He continued, 'You don't want me, and that's fine.' He stopped. 'I don't mean that. It's not fine at all, and I don't understand, but. . . .' He took a breath. 'But I promised myself to abide by whatever decision you made.' He paused. His face had lost its colour, even his lips were pale. He said, 'But I need your help.' He picked up his gloves and fidgeted with the stitching round the fingers. 'It meant a lot to me, that night. And afterwards, I said something.'

'Yes.'

'And you didn't laugh, or tell me not to be a fool. It was almost as if you were expecting it.'

'The face of God.'

'It made sense at the time. As if all my life, all my attempts to understand, to find meaning in the world, crystallised in that moment. It was like a sunrise, Sophie, a great fireball of illumination. But I can't hold on to it, it's fading, it's dying. Do I sound crazy? I think you understand, it was the same for you, wasn't it? You said something once about not believing in God, but I don't think that matters; this goes further, deeper than that.'

'I said I didn't believe in a god you'd recognise – an interventionist god, a creator.'

He gave a frightened laugh. 'Yes, I remember. But I've never understood.'

'What you saw that night – it was the fragmented god, the fractured soul, the godhead within.'

'I don't understand.'

'You didn't see the face of God, you saw his splintered reflection in the mirror of your Self. And not "his" because just as he has no face, God has no gender. You've gone beyond such expediences, you don't need the trimmings any more, the stepping stones of liturgy and church. You've your own Temple, a Temple of blood and bone.

'Listen to me, Charles. The Celts believed that the head was the seat of the soul. They decapitated their enemies to be sure they had conquered utterly. The head is like the crucifix, it's a symbol.'

'I still don't. . . .'

'I'll show you.' She laid her hands over his. The silk fringe of his scarf trailed her knuckles. 'Close your eyes and tell me what you see.'

'Nothing. I can't see anything.' He heard the edge of hysteria in his voice.

'Try. Please.'

He tried. In a way it was a relief to shut her out. He shouldn't have come. To please her, he accepted the darkness – only it wasn't dark. Lights danced across the inner surfaces of his eyelids like streetlamps through fog.

She said, 'Remember that bit in the bible about each man being a temple?' He nodded. 'Think of it like that – your mind as an actual place made up of branching tunnels and vaulted chambers – it's beautiful, isn't it? Lovelier than any church.' She curled her fingers round his, squeezing, crushing. 'You can see it, I know you can. It's real, Charles. It sighs with your blood, its hymns are your thoughts. You can go there whenever you want, for as long as you want, and no one can touch you, reach you, know where you are. Do you understand what I'm saying? It's a safe place, a haven. If you can find it, you don't need me beside you in the flesh. It's better this way, living on the outside is too dangerous.'

He tugged his hand violently from her grip. Why had it never occurred to him that she behaved as she did, playing games with his feelings, advancing and retreating, and now this crazy talk of temples because, quite simply, she was crazy.

Did Michael know? Living with her day in, day out, he must see the cracks in her reason. Unless familiarity had blinded him.

He stood up and backed away from her. She frightened him, this woman, this bright-eyed devil from hell snapping at his heels, dragging him down to the fire.

No. Not so. The devil snapped at her heels too – they were in this together and he should pity her, try to help her, but he couldn't. He hurt too much, he felt cheated.

Slowly, she rose to her feet – her burning hair a symbol of damnation. She took a step towards him. He took two steps back. Fear flickered across her face; he knew that she knew what he was thinking. The gold in her eyes glittered like sunlight on a puddle. She drew breath to speak, then pressed the tips of her fingers against her lips as if to push back the words. And then she gave a hopeless little shrug, and started to turn away. It was such an ordinary gesture, so human and sane, that his devils fled and she was just Sophie again. Sophie loading tinkling boxes of chandelier parts into her car, haggling and bidding against the hubbub of an auction; in her kitchen, her sleeves rolled to the elbow, face filmed with flour. He saw how good she was, how strong. Strong enough to let him believe she was out of her mind if it would help him let her go – she knew, as he should have known, that this was why he'd come. His sense of her strength overwhelmed him. The black depth of his feeling revealed itself like a river of tar, and he reached for her and pulled her towards him. Her face was filmed with tears. Her arms slid under his coat, fluttering like a caged bird in the space between jacket and shirt. Her flesh was smooth and warm beneath the puffy bulk of her sweater, their staccato breath a clashing symphony as they backed towards the store, tugging at one another's clothes, laughing and shivering in the draught.

She made him wait. She pulled a blanket from a shelf and it tumbled down in a shower of dust that made them cough and gag. She blinked and rubbed the corner of her eye with the back of her hand, then flicked the blanket across the old chaise longue that stood rammed against the wall beneath the shelves. They stumbled towards it and he stubbed his toe on a fender. He almost fell onto her, but saved himself in time to see her face and her heavy-lidded eyes and hear her whisper his name as she wrapped herself round him, enclosing him with fire and shadow, so that time held still and motion was all as the rocking and the thrusting took his senses in thrall, and he filled his vaulted chamber right up to the roof before heaving the door to and ramming the bolt home.

<u>Alex</u>

1

I only went to the house in Chelsea once. I'd promised Leonard I'd go again, but there was Jo to think about and the business to run – and processing all the information I'd gathered.

Jonathan insisted he wasn't interested. 'I don't care why he did it. I don't want to know. I hate him.' And yet he lingered by the desk, his eyes averted from the screen as he fiddled with my pencil sharpener.

It was in March the following year that Leonard rang to say Charles was ill. Cancer. I told Jonathan. He was sitting at the dining table marking homework. He stopped writing, but didn't look up. Is this what Sophie felt, faced with Charles's inability to express feeling – the frustration, the violence, the desire to shake a response out of him? Then the longing to enfold, to use tenderness to teach tenderness.

A couple of weeks later I woke late one night to find Jonathan wasn't beside me. I went downstairs. He was sprawled on the sofa. He had my notes and was drinking the Scotch we kept for guests. It wasn't like Jonathan to drink.

I perched on the arm of the sofa. Stroking his hair, I said, 'Are you okay?'

He pulled away. He said, 'Why are you doing this?'

'You know why. I need to understand, it helps.'

'Well, it doesn't help me. I've spent most of my life trying to forget, and now you're digging it all up, you won't let it rest till you've got every last detail. I wish you'd stop.'

'I can't. It scares me, Jonathan.'

'D'you think I'm not scared?' His voice grated with panic. 'You want to understand him, but what about me? Shall I tell you what it's like being me? Every minute of every day I watch myself, terrified I'll see him in me, the crazy son of a crazy father. That's what frightens you, isn't it? And what about Jo? I know what you think. I don't blame you, but this –', he brandished my notes. 'This doesn't help.' I stared at him. I forced myself to touch his hand. He said, 'Do you honestly wonder that I tried to keep this from you? Would you still have married me – and if not, where does that leave Jo?'

He was right: like him I was watching, waiting for him to betray himself. I'd wondered over and again during the past months just how much of Charles's huge capacity for love twisted into obsession, his spirituality diverted and turned inwards, had been passed on to Jonathan and, through him, to Joanna. Now I told myself that if his father had been unstable and violent, his mother had been a gentle woman, much put upon but patient. Gentle Jonathan, I used to call him in the early days. Surely that instinct was surer. Surely he was his mother's son.

In April I heard from Leonard again. It was a Sunday, the sort of spring day that has you planning picnics and outings to the seaside. We'd had lunch in the garden. I love the way the smell of the food mingles with the scent of the flowers, the way the butterflies hover and swoop.

Joanna dipped her fingers in the last of the gravy and gave them to Barney to lick. Jonathan encouraged her, pretending to be afraid I'd tell them off. She's so like him, with her dark glossy hair and eyes like freshly hulled chestnuts. And her smile. She has a beautiful smile, like Jonathan's – like Charles's.

The telephone rang. Funny the way bad news alters the flow of time. There's happy-time, and there's bad-news time. The one bumbles along like the puppy in the Andrex ad; the other stills the blackbird's trill.

I took the call in the kitchen. The smell of roast lamb and garlic hung on the air. I gave my number, eyeing the pans stacked in the sink. From the garden came the sound of Joanna playing with Barney.

'Alex?' I didn't recognise the voice. 'It's me.' He clipped his words like a miser. 'Leonard. Alex, can you come? I need you. He's asking for you.'

Charles had been admitted to hospital early that morning. 'Of course I'll come,' I whispered. I could feel his pain, I wanted to hold him, draw him into the family circle. I felt helpless. My throat rasped and inside I was screaming. I traced the line of the terracotta-stencilling bordering the door, and listened to the blood thrumming in my veins. He was telling me about the bad nights, hopeless exchanges with the doctors, the ambulance journey. He needed to impose an order on what was happening. As he talked, I thought about my meeting with Charles, how terrified I'd been of having my liberal judgements and smug rationalisations overturned. What if they'd lied to me, Leonard and the others? They claim to love him, despite everything, but what if he turns out to be a monster after all?

The telephone line crackled. Leonard said, 'Are you there, Alex? You'll come?'

I nodded, and felt foolish because he couldn't see me. I said, 'Will Nickie be there?'

'He's with him now. Try to get Jonathan to come.'

Replacing the receiver, I leant against the wall and closed my eyes and took a deep breath, inhaling the homely smells, the exquisite fusion of warm paint and garlic.

I wanted to cry, but felt myself freezing up inside. No time for tears. And even when it's over I'll have to keep a grip, for Leonard's sake.

I crossed to the sink and turned on the tap. When the water ran hot I filled the roasting tin and saucepans. In the garden Joanna squealed. She and Jonathan were playing. She was on her back, he was leaning over her, teasing her, tickling her bared tummy with a broad blade of grass. She clutched at him, trying to fend him off, and Barney skittered round them, crouching low over his paws, barking to the rhythm of her screams. And then Jonathan sat back on his heels and lifted her high above his head, and she laughed and kicked her bare feet. As she wriggled, the dark crow's wing of her hair fell forward across her cheek.

Drying my hands, I smoothed down my tee shirt, and went out into the garden.

2

I hate hospitals. When Joanna was born I told Jonathan, never again. It wasn't so much the pain as the smell of disinfectant, the rattle of the pill-trolley, the incessant good-natured chivvying. What was it doing to Joanna, how much of my abhorrence had been transferred to her? – bringing us back to the same old problem, that we never can tell what we pass on to our children.

I got lost looking for the ward. The place was made up of identical prefabricated units with every block and corridor identical to every other block and corridor.

I found Charles's room. The nurse fetched Leonard. He looked amazing. Not bedraggled or unshaven but upright and crisp in a dark green shirt buttoned to the neck. He'd made the same adjustment I had: his own pain must wait, Charles mustn't be allowed to see his death reflected in Leonard's dishevelment.

I said, 'I got here as soon as I could.' His smile snapped like an elastic band. 'Jonathan wouldn't come. I'm sorry.' I didn't tell him what Jonathan had said as he drove me to the station: 'I don't care if he's dying. I don't want anything to do with him. He should have died years ago. They should have hanged him.'

'What about Leonard? He needs you – you used to be fond of him, he was almost a father to you . . . .'

'Who told you that?'

'Aunt Helen, your father.'

'He could have stopped it, you know.' He gripped the lower rim of the steering wheel and stared out of the windscreen. 'Leonard could have stopped it. He knew what was happening, how dangerous my father could be. But he just sat by and let it happen. Jesus Christ – he bloody made it happen!'

138

Poor Leonard. Jonathan expected too much of him, we all did. He stood beside me, everybody's friend, everybody's confidant. I said, 'Shall we go in?'

The room was dim and warm and musty. There was a blue carpet and yellow curtains and a white cotton blind drawn down against the bright afternoon sun. Nicholas was standing by the bed. Though empty-eyed with grief, like Leonard he was smartly dressed and carefully groomed. He gave me an almost imperceptible smile, then made room at the bedside.

Charles was asleep. At least, it looked like sleep. His eyes were closed and his face all shuttered up like an abandoned house. It was as though he was being eaten away from the inside; at any minute his body might collapse in on itself in a whisper of dust. The least movement, the merest distortion of air, might bring this about. I caught myself watching the rise and fall of his chest, listening to the thin rasp of air between his cracked lips.

I whispered, 'Is he in pain?' Nicholas shook his head.

'Of course he's in pain.' Leonard's anger imploded with a thud. 'Look at him. How can he not be in pain?'

He was right. If this was sleep, it was an odd, unnatural sleep. There was too much tension. His jaw was clenched, the creases round his eyes less relaxed than they should be. I stared at him, and realised how much I cared for him. He'd shared things with me he'd not even shared with Leonard. I knew him better than I was ever likely to know anyone, Jonathan and Joanna included. Charles had treated me not as a confidante, but a confessor, as if my forgiveness was his first step to redemption. If I could forgive him, then maybe so could she.

Charles. I touched the dry hand lying splayed on the coverlet. I forgive you, I've seen it all, been with you into the abyss and back again, and I understand.

Obsession. It was his major flaw. He was obsessive about every-thing he did. At first it had worked to his advantage, got him away from his mother's debilitating influence, propelled him to the top of his profession. But with Sophie it had turned against him and he'd had to look for another means of defence. He'd used both Jonathan and his mother to fight her, but they were frail weapons;

the battle had gone on for too long, his strength had failed him, forcing him to a last act of self-preservation.

3

Neither of Charles's sons bear much physical resemblance to their mothers. True, Nickie is stockier, and Jonathan's hair glossier and less thick than his brother's, but that's about it. When it comes to personality, the genetic cocktail is more interesting. Though Nickie, like Jonathan, shares Charles's reserve, his tendency to withdraw into himself, he is also his mother's son. It's a tantalising combination, fascinating to watch this solitary man playing the extrovert, clothing his isolation with sharp suits and sharper ties.

Jonathan said Nickie was the son Charles should have had, that he could have been proud of him. I'm not so sure. Jonathan's hostility leads him to oversimplify.

The day I called on Nickie to collect his mother's diaries, I walked under the security cameras guarding the wharf-side development, announced myself on the entryphone, and wondered whether Charles had ever been here and, if so, what he'd made of his son's embattled tower.

The lift was smooth and silent, it hardly seemed to be moving. I wanted to jump up and down, make it shudder, reassure myself that the mechanism hadn't died on me.

Nickie lived on the top floor. The pine-planked landing had floor-to-ceiling windows at either end, and lush ferns spread against the whitewashed walls. Answering the door, he allowed me as far as the lobby but blocked the way into the main body of the apartment. Beyond his shoulder I could see the bright expanse of living area and, at the far end, a short flight of steps leading to the elevated kitchen section.

He said, 'Everything you need is in here.'

He handed me a Harrods carrier, one of the white paper ones from the Food Hall. It was heavy. I peered inside. It was crammed with scruffy red exercise books. 'Have you read them all?' He shook his head. 'Are you sure you want me to? They're so personal.'

'If it helps. Leonard insists it will.'

'Well, Leonard would know, wouldn't he?' He gave a little shrug. I waited, then grew impatient. 'Come on, Nickie, aren't you going to offer me a cup of coffee?' Irritation flickered across his face. I waited. I wanted more than just his mother's diaries. I wanted to lift every stone, watch the exposed bugs scurry for shelter. That's what Jonathan says. Reluctantly he stepped back and let me in.

He retreated to the raised kitchen area and clattered about making coffee. I dumped the carrier bag on the cream leather sofa. Between the sofa and the picture-window was a long coffee table made out of a slab of inch-thick glass supported by two blocks of rough onyx. The table was bare apart from a bird's-eye maple photograph frame containing a portrait of his mother. The only other likeness I'd seen had been the punting pictures, taken when she was much younger. Here she's in her forties; the colour of her hair is less strong, and the curls have been teased into a wave. She's laughing and her lips are drawn back from her strong teeth; her eyes dance and the skin round them crinkles like sunbursts.

'Like a fire crackling in a grate,' Jonathan had said.

I looked away. Beyond the window was a balcony with a concrete parapet. I said, 'Is it okay if I go and look at the view?'

'I'll join you.' He left the coffee to brew and we stepped outside. Way below a heavy barge trailed a larger ship out to sea. Over to my left, hazy with summer heat, I could see the fairytale turrets of Tower Bridge.

'It's a great spot, Nickie.'

He shrugged. 'I suppose.' He sounded unconvinced. I turned to look at him. He was wearing a blue silk shirt. It both suited him, and didn't. Strange – as if there were two Nickies. He said, 'He built it, you know. My father. And my mother designed the interiors. This place was her fee.'

'I thought you lived out of town.'

'We moved when I was five, but she kept the place on. We'd come here in the school holidays, do the galleries and theatres. We used to go jogging in the early mornings. She loved that, with the mist on the river and the empty streets.' He leant forward, almost as if he expected to catch sight of her. 'We'd go to Bermondsey, the antiques market. Friday mornings, four o'clock, searching for bargains by torchlight.'

'It sounds a wonderful relationship.'

'So everyone tells me. But she was too much sometimes, you know?'

'I can imagine.' I smiled. He didn't smile back.

He said, 'If my father had been there maybe it would have been different. I used to ask her about him, but she just stonewalled me. So, d'you know what I did? I'd wait till she was asleep, then creep out here and stand just like we're doing now – except that at night it feels different, like the whole world's stretched out in front of you in a glittering orange-peel carpet. And the sounds, they're different at night, remote and yet clear, and you can see the traffic, the headlights moving across the bridges . . . and I'd try to send messages to him, willing him to come back to us. I'd think, if he's alive, then maybe he'll hear me. If he isn't, this is as good a place as any to try and contact the dead.' Uncanny now, how the tone of his voice, the suppressed urgency, remind me of Charles. Even the way he stood with his hands gripping the balcony rail, his eyes fixed on something other than the view, holds echoes of his father.

'Stupid,' he hissed to a passing seagull. 'All that effort and grief when all the time he was just round the corner. I could have walked to his office from here.'

'What would you have done, if she'd told you?'

'Does it matter? She lied, she stole from me. He'd built this place – I knew his name, it was on the billboard by the gate, I went past it every day – but she let me think he was just another customer, the unknown head of a client company. It's not as if I didn't give her every chance to tell me. I'd ask her about him, who my father was, what had happened to him, and she'd take hold of me and put her face close to mine and say, "Why d'you need to know, Nickie?" ' There was a cruel edge to his voice. ' "Aren't I enough, Nickie.

Come on, Nickie, I'm enough for anyone, aren't I? We don't need anyone else, you and I . . ." '

Down below, a police launch whizzed past, the sound of its motor a bumblebee whir. 'It wasn't true, Alex. When I saw them together – the way he touched her, the way she looked at him, I knew I didn't matter to her, not any more, only him. She didn't love me for myself, only because I was all that was left of him. I was a substitute, a stopgap . . .'

'No, Nickie.'

'I couldn't bear it, I'd had her to myself too long.' He no longer saw or heard me. 'I won't share her.' His voice was hard, his hands gripped the balcony rail. 'I won't. I won't.' He stopped, as if his words startled him. He stared at the river, a dark, isolated figure standing guard on his dark tower.

Seeing him like that, rigid with defiance, reinforced my growing conviction that my fears for Jonathan had been misplaced. His childhood may have held echoes of his father's, but he had me now, and Joanna. It wasn't Jonathan who was at risk.

Sarah

1

On a bleak November day, Charles had gone to Sophie's shop, and she'd made love to him, and sent him on his way. He should be bitter, but he wasn't. Being with her had somehow freed him. The world looked different, brighter. She'd shown him that change was possible. Helen commented at Christmas that he laughed more. He turned a deaf ear to his mother's needling and, instead of leaving at the first polite opportunity, stayed on through the evening, playing cards with Brian and the children.

Early in the New Year he sat with Peter Knight reviewing the contract for the last unit on the Essex site. He took his time, lingering over the clauses, taking a sensual delight in the thick beribboned paper and the dark ink. Up until the moment of exchange, any of his schemes might miscarry. He signed his name with a flourish and snapped the cap back on his fountain pen.

'Not bad, eh?' Peter squinted at him. 'From the first twinkle in your eye to final exchange in what? Two years?'

With a sudden, acid clarity he remembered the auction room, the cold seeping through the soles of his shoes and the drone of the auctioneer's voice.

And a pair of grey eyes, flecked with gold.

Peter said, 'An excuse to celebrate.' He banged two tumblers down on the desk and poured a generous measure of Scotch. Charles raised his glass in a salute. Peter sank into his chair. 'So, what new schemes have you got tucked up your sleeve?'

'This and that.' The whisky was good. Peter had a league table of clients and his drinks cupboard was ordered accordingly. Only the finest malts for those at the top of the league.

Peter laughed. 'Playing it close, eh? You're a canny bastard, Charles.'

'Prudent.'

Peter topped up their glasses. They went back a long way. As a junior clerk, Peter had dealt with Charles's first ever sale. He was now a senior partner.

Charles said, 'How's my brother doing? Pulling his weight, is he?'

'You know Anthony, he's a thorough worker . . . .'

'But lacking in flair.'

'Perhaps.'

'And totally unlikable. Peter, I'm eternally grateful to you for employing him.' He drained his drink and, swinging his briefcase up on to his lap, checked the locks. 'I must go,' he said, and stood up.

Peter held the door for him, and he stepped into the outer office. It was blindingly bright. A glossy, semi-tropical plant stood balanced on the corner of the desk, and Leonard Prentice stood behind it, talking to Peter's secretary. In the moment before he straightened, Charles saw how thin his friend's gauze of blond hair had become. Then Leonard raised his head and smiled; it was a personal, critical smile.

He was glad to escape. As Thompson edged the car into the traffic, Charles gazed out through tinted windows that leeched all colour from the winter sunshine. He rested his head back against the seat and closed his eyes – and saw Leonard bent over the desk, Leonard flushed with excitement, examining a concert programme. Life was simple for Leonard, his enthusiasm a brilliant spotlight focused now here, now there, always carrying the image of its last object over to the next. Charles had seen the evidence arranged systematically round Leonard's immaculate flat: programmes for opera, ballet and jazz, posters announcing exhibitions of modern art and photography.

Thompson braked. Charles was jerked forward, then pressed back against the seat. Thompson glanced over his shoulder to apologise and explain. A brown estate car, its rear window clogged with zoo stickers, had cut in front of them.

Charles shifted his position. The car was stuffy. He opened the window. Thompson braked again, this time because a blonde girl in a white jacket and black mini-skirt had stepped off the kerb to dodge between the cars. He watched her swinging along the far pavement, moving ahead of the traffic. She was tall and slim, with long hair rippling across her narrow shoulders.

Sarah. Why did the girl remind him of her? Apart from height and colouring, they had little in common. The one assumed ownership of the world, the other seemed half afraid that at any moment someone might tell her her ticket was invalid.

He'd met Sarah at Cathy's birthday party. 'She's had a hard time,' Cathy had confided. 'Bad marriage, spiteful divorce. Be nice to her, I've put her next to you at dinner.'

Sarah smiled as he held the chair for her. Married and divorced she might be, but she scarcely looked more than a schoolgirl. No, not so. He noted a slight graininess to her complexion. The illusion of extreme youth derived from the fact that she was out of her depth, an impression enhanced by the blue powder smudging her eyelids, giving them a bruised, fragile look.

Mid-twenties, he decided, and really quite lovely. Delightful how the peppermint green of her dress emphasised her pale skin. When she bent over the first spoonful of soup she hooked back a loop of hair, tucking it behind her ear to reveal a tiny, flushed lobe pierced with a pearl stud. His eye slid the length of her delicate neck, to be startled by the clumsy black velvet ribbon and cameo choker. Aware that he was watching her, she glanced at him; he smiled and she blushed and looked away. He felt a faint but persistent pump of desire.

He felt it now, as the car crawled through the afternoon traffic. The memory quickened his heartbeat, raised the temperature in the car. He lowered the window further. They were driving along Bond Street. She worked somewhere round here, didn't she? In a gallery owned by one of James's cronies. Whatever was the name of the place? He'd only been half listening when she told him; it had been disturbing to find that she too was involved in antiques, albeit in a peripheral way.

Sarah was startled to see him. She was sitting behind a desk at the back of the gallery and when she recognised him, a splash of crimson stained her cheeks. She stood up, and he saw that she was taller than he remembered, though she stooped slightly, as if to conceal her height. 'Charles,' she said in a whisper, then corrected herself, 'Mr Wade.'

'Charles will do fine,' he said. She smoothed her skirt and edged round the desk, knocking a stack of papers to the floor. He turned away, leaving her to gather both herself and the papers. He listened to the rustling behind him as he browsed amongst the marble-topped credenzas and flimsy French chairs. He leant forward to examine an ormolu clock that was remarkably similar to one he had at home, and caught his reflection in the speckled plate of a mirror. He was dismayed by how old he looked.

A movement in the mirror made him focus on the figure now standing behind him. She did look dreadfully young.

Why have you come here?

I don't know.

Yes you do. Because of a flicker of human feeling felt not once, but twice. Because you're lonely and tired, and she's lonely too, and frightened.

Still facing the mirror, he met her eyes in the shadows of its plate. 'Would you like to have dinner?' he asked softly.

'I'd love to,' she said with a bright, childlike smile. 'Thank you, yes, I'd like that very much.'

2

Helen swirled the greasy roasting tin round the washing-up bowl. Charles stood behind her, tea-towel at the ready. 'Remember what Dad used to say,' he said with a little laugh, 'about how one washer-upper should be able to keep two dryers going.'

She remembered. She still missed Dad. What would he have

made of Sarah Bannerman? *Nice kid, but a bit young, eh lad?* She could hear him so clearly.

She wedged the tin on the draining board. In the garden, Brian was explaining to Sarah his summer-planting plans. She listened with her pretty head cocked on one side, never once looking towards the house, though she must have wondered what they were saying about her. Little brother brings his latest lady for his sister's persual. Latest! Had there been others? He'd never let on. And why was he avoiding the subject? Ploughing through the washing up they'd discussed all manner of things; Brian and his work, the kids, Mum's rheumatism, a site Charles was after, anything but Sarah Bannerman.

Charles shook the remaining suds off the roasting tin and gave it a rudimentary swipe. Helen tipped the water away and ran a cloth round the bowl. Drying her hands, she confronted him. He gave in. 'Okay,' he said, 'what's the verdict?'

From the garden came the sound of Sarah laughing. Brian took her by the elbow and ushered her into the greenhouse.

Helen said, 'She's very young.'

'That's bad?'

'Not necessarily.' She filled the kettle and reached the brown pottery teapot from the cupboard. 'How long have you known her?'

'Couple of months.'

'And it's serious, otherwise you wouldn't have brought her here. I take it you're going to marry her. Are you in love with her?'

He gazed out of the window to where the shadowy figures of Sarah and Brian moved to and fro in the greenhouse. What did he feel for Sarah? He couldn't in all honesty say he loved her, but there was something touching about her. He felt protective to-wards her – sometimes. At others her vulnerability touched a vicious nerve.

She'd come to London to escape her failed marriage. Her husband had been repeatedly unfaithful. She'd found out, and di-vorced him. She seemed bewildered by what she'd done. He suspected she saw him in much the same light as Sophie saw Michael. He was a haven, a father-figure. The idea was abhorrent.

At first he'd tried to impress her, nosing the big black Rolls up the narrow back street to her flat, whisking her off to dinner at expensive restaurants. Why not? Isn't that the way they do it in films? Not until the third or fourth time did he realise how much she hated it. It was too formal, required her to be something she wasn't, and she was a poor actress. Gradually he became aware of the cracks in her performance. He watched her struggling with her discomfort like a bumblebee trapped in honey, saw how she leant away from the waiter as if avoiding contamination, the way she constantly realigned the banks of cutlery flanking her plate, and the way she ate sparingly, with painful precision, as if expecting to be poisoned.

He said, 'Is something wrong with your fish?' The critical edge to his voice turned a kind inquiry into an accusation.

She shook her head. 'Oh no, it's lovely.'

He thought, you're lovely too. Why can't I tell you, why do the words jam in my throat? I would like to kiss you. Not the chaste peck on the cheek that usually ends our evenings, but something more.

She bent over her plate, carefully flaking the fish. The clumsiness of the cameo choker, the blackness of its ribbon, stressed the wishbone frailty of her neck. He wanted to unfasten it, release her, find something more delicately fitting to snare her fine throat.

That night when she asked him up for coffee, he accepted.

She was proud of her flat. She led the way up the tight stairway, explaining that, having married straight from home, she'd never lived on her own before. Fumbling with the lock, she let them in and helped him off with his coat. Hanging it on a tatty 1930s plywood hallstand, she smiled up at him. He took her face between his hands and her cheeks grew hot as he kissed her. It was still a very restrained kiss, he was alert to any sign of rejection. But she didn't seem alarmed, only flustered. And pleased. He was sure she was pleased as she slid her hands down his shirt until they found the steady pump of his heart.

After a moment he eased her away. He wanted to look at her. She was embarrassed and turned her face aside. 'You'd better come through. I'll put the coffee on.'

Her front room was smallish, and furnished in Art Deco. He knew such objects were considered stylish, but to him they were just old-fashioned. He caught his reflection in the fan-shaped peach mirror hanging on the chimney-breast. On the mantelpiece below was a spelter figure of an attenuated lady attended by two Salukis. He was confused. Being here, in her flat, required him to reassess his attitude towards Sarah. Until this evening she'd been no more than a cipher, relevant only to the extent that she fulfilled or thwarted his needs. But this room betrayed an independent life, independent tastes, a surprising depth of personality.

He sat on a threadbare armchair. In the middle of the glass and chrome coffee table stood a plaster Pierrot, a ghastly, gaudy thing with a crescent mirror on its shoulder. Sarah had gone out God knows where, and paid good money for it – it was an act of will, an expression of taste that was beyond him.

The kitchen door banged open. Sarah tottered through with the coffee. He was thirsty, too much wine at dinner. He took a hasty sip. It was hot and too bitter. He placed the cup carefully on the edge of the table; glancing round the room he said, 'Must have taken some finding, all of this.'

'Yes. D'you like it? Some people can't stand it. I suppose it's a generation thing.'

He said, 'I grew up with stuff like this. When they could afford something better, my mother threw it out.' He stopped. She looked crestfallen. 'I'm sorry.' He gave an embarrassed laugh. 'I seem to have the knack of saying the wrong thing. You shouldn't let me get away with it, you should fight back.'

He took more trouble after that. He asked what sort of restaurants she liked and they found a little Italian place not far from where she lived. The proprietor was called Mario and he and his staff made a great fuss of Sarah. The waiters flirted shamelessly. Charles reached across the table and laid a possessive hand over hers.

But the question of the plaster Pierrot remained. What made her want to fill her home with such objects? What did she do on those evenings they didn't spend together? It was almost as if the moment the door closed behind him, she folded herself up and hooked herself on to a coat hanger until next needed. The idea that she had her own life was irksome. When he quizzed her about it, she solemnly listed her activities, ticking them off on her fingers.

She read a great deal, and liked to cook, she went to the cinema quite often, enjoyed old films on television. 'Bette Davies and Joan Crawford, all padded shoulders and melodrama.' She liked music too. She wasn't very good, but every Thursday she had a guitar class. The tutor was a friend, she often spent an evening with him and his wife, Polly. It would be nice, wouldn't it, if Charles met them. Maybe she'd ask them to supper one evening.

It was shortly after this that Charles suggested Sunday lunch with his sister. By the end of the day he wondered if it had been such a good idea. Trust Helen to turn everything upside down with her questions. Are you in love with her? Are you going to marry her?

How should I know whether I love her? He buttoned his pyjamas and slipped into bed. As for marriage, that really is going too far.

He flicked off the light and lay back against the puffy pillows. The linen stretched across him was cold and shiny. Emmy had a thing about starch. He slid down between the sheets. What would it be like to be married? Not to Sarah necessarily, but to anyone – the loss of privacy, endless intimacies, someone else's clothing tangling with his in the wardrobe.

That's easily solved, buy another wardrobe.

But there were other things. Finding someone else's flannel in his bathroom – alien oils and shampoos clogging his cabinets and shelves.

The sleeping together; not sex, but literally the sharing of a bed. What could be more appallingly intrusive than that?

And yet, there was something to be said for having someone with whom to share the little frustrations and triumphs. He was fond of Sarah, but didn't love her. Did that matter? Surely friendship could grow into love. He already cared about her, desired her. Did he desire her? He stretched against the starched sheets and felt a stiffening and a hollow flickering in the pit of his stomach. They had a future, he was sure of it. If he could come to terms with the toe-curling intimacies, with the dresses in his wardrobe and the flannel in his bathroom and the body in the bed beside him making its sleepy exhalations all through the night, then yes, when the time was right, he would marry her.

3

The decision was made. He felt a thrill of anticipation, a shower of adrenaline like a flurry of snow pattering through his body. He would be a good husband, provide for her, protect her. She wouldn't regret it.

No? The question jumped from nowhere. What if Sophie came back? What then?

She won't.

Can you be sure? If she did, could you withstand her? Imagine another firework party, with Sarah as your wife – and Sophie coming to you out of the flames, leading you by the fingertips into the house and up the stairs to her room . . . . Would you be a good husband then? How would you protect your wife? By not telling her?

It won't happen. Sophie's made her choice. It's over, done with. The door's locked and I can't remember where I left the key.

Still, no point in being rash, in tumbling to his knees, blurting his proposal just yet.

In the middle of a meeting with his accountants, he has a vision of the Pierrot standing on the marble and gesso table in his hall. And Emmy in a tutu, dusting it with a bunch of feathers on a stick.

Yet if he could come to terms with alien clothes in his wardrobe, and the invasion of his bathroom, surely he could handle the Pierrot. With a bit of diplomacy he might get it relegated to somewhere a little less prominent. Like the attic.

Yes. It would work, with a little effort it would all come right. He rang Sarah at the gallery and suggested dinner. She countered with an offer to cook. His next phonecall was to the florist. Red roses; no point in being too subtle.

He made an effort to be on time. She answered the door immediately, as if she'd been standing waiting. He felt a flicker of fear. It was as if she knew.

She looked wonderful. She'd piled her hair on top of her head and her face, robbed of its frame, was more vulnerable than ever. Her dress, of some soft lilac-grey material, had a cowl neckline and was very short. It clung to her, outlining the dip of her thin waist and the almost imperceptible swell of her hips. When she moved, he heard the rustle of something silky beneath. She greeted him with a smile that was a fraction more confident than usual, and led him through to her living room.

A table had been laid for dinner. She'd drawn the curtains and the room was lit by a series of table lamps assembled from other rooms and balanced precariously on chairs and shelves. His flowers had been arranged in a hideous green and orange pottery vase which stood on the low table next to the Pierrot. She said, 'They're lovely, Charles. No one's ever bought me red roses before.'

He shrugged. 'It's a bit corny.'

She laughed. 'I don't care.'

He kissed her. A wonderful warmth filled him. He thought, God, I've been stupid. None of that with Sophie was real; it was just a way of clearing the ground. This is love, this ache to enfold and protect.

She pressed her hands against his chest, easing him away. She said, 'I've made beef olives for dinner. Would you like a drink?'

The beef was overdone, and not an olive in sight. The wine was good – he'd brought it himself. He topped up her glass. She barely noticed, she was talking animatedly, telling him about the gallery. 'I was terrified to start with,' she confessed. 'The people, you know? They turn up in huge cars, and all that fur and jewellery, like the inside of a Crunchy bar!' They both laughed.

After dessert, a baked lemon cheesecake with a crack down the middle, he settled himself in an armchair with a glass of brandy. Sarah went to make coffee. The whisky she'd given him on arrival had been cheap and unpleasant, but the brandy was quite good. She'd bought it at Christmas, had been keeping it for a special occasion. He closed his eyes. This is a special occasion, is it, Sarah?

She came back with the coffee. He downed his brandy and put the glass down with a bang – the tabletop was closer than he realised. She said, 'I'll fetch you some more.'

He watched her cross the room. Her legs were long, but rather too thin, her ankles pinched like squeezed putty above the heels of her mauve shoes. She kicked them off with an apologetic smile and returned wielding the bottle like a trophy.

She stood beside him, unsure again. He encircled her wrist. Her pulse tapped against the pads of his fingers. She perched on the arm of the chair, leaning over him to refill his glass. He tilted his head against the chair to look up at her. Lifting her captured hands to his lips, he kissed the palm, then slid his arm around her waist and drew her down on to his lap. She was so lovely with her bright eyes and satiny hair just beginning to slip from its pins. She looked like a tousled, sleepy child. He pressed his face to the hollow of her neck and she was with him now, ahead of him even as she caressed his brow and temple and stroked his hair. His unpractised fingers fluttered at her breasts and she eased back his head and kissed him with an assurance he'd not expected, her lips parted and her tongue darted against his and he thought yes, this is what I want, to be with her, like this. Sarah!

The chair confined them. He moved to make room for her and the arm dug into his back. He said, 'This is ridiculous.'

Her bedroom was green, pastel green like the dress she'd worn the night they met. The light from the sitting room cast a yellow path across the carpet of the darkened room. They kissed again. He fumbled with her zip; the fabric of the dress caught in the metal teeth, but it didn't matter, they struggled until finally she was free, the dress a shaded pool at her feet, her silk slip glimmering like moonlight on water. She slid her arms round his neck; her bare skin scuffed against the stuff of his suit. He eased her back to sit on the end of the bed. Dropping down onto his heels, he slipped his hand under the clinging silk to release her stockings, rolling them slowly down, first one and then the other, kissing the newly bared flesh, then down to cradle the high arch of her foot, to feel the shy curl of her long toes.

She bent over him, kissing the top of his head, and they laughed as she struggled to help him with his tie and shirt buttons. Then

157

they were swimming beneath the covers, touching and stroking and learning one another, and her fragile fingers spun a web about his flesh and there was no urgency, no mysticism, only a sensual tenderness and the wish to please, which combined with his hope and the wine and the brandy and the sweep of her hands to bring him to a peak of real desire so that, smiling at her through the dark haze, he entered her. And lost her. All gone, all need, all sensation vanished, nothing left.

Nothing but fear. And an empty ache. And the draught from the open window chilling his back.

He rolled away, dreading the sound of her voice, knowing any minute now she'd say something inane, like 'it doesn't matter'.

He gathered his clothes and began covering himself, fastening buttons and zips with fingers that would scarcely function. He could hear her erratic breathing. She was crying. Why should she cry when he was the one who'd been made to look a fool?

Why had this happened?

He should never have embarked on this, should have stayed safely celibate. It had never been a problem, his regrets had been confined to the knowledge that there was a form of companionship, a closeness to another human being he would never experience. It had been a particular type of friendship he regretted, not the act, not this appallingly intimate and messy act – how did people bear it? How could any woman subject herself to such intrusion?

Especially a woman like Sophie.

Which was why she'd left him. At last he understood. And he was like her. She'd said so often.

No. This was no explanation. He'd wanted Sarah, right from the start. From the moment he met her, he'd desired her.

Desired, indeed. He'd wanted to fuck her, that's all.

He made a bad knot in his tie. Dropping his cufflinks into his jacket pocket, he went through to the other room. He poured himself more brandy. He was hot, the back of his neck glowed and his hands were clammy. He had the start of a headache.

Sophie. He'd thought it was over, but it would never be over. She filled his mind with her gold-flecked eyes and her laughter.

'Charles?' – A real voice this time, breathless and frightened. Not reproachful. She ought to be, she ought to be angry.

'It doesn't matter,' she said.

'I had a feeling you'd say that.'

'Charles!'

Good, now she reproaches me. He clenched his fingers round the glass.

'I don't care if you despise me for saying it.' He heard the tremor of defiance. 'It's true. You're tired, you work too hard, you've had a lot to drink. . . .'

'I am not drunk.'

'That's not what I said.'

'Nor am I particularly tired. You don't have to rummage around looking for excuses. It just happened.'

'I'm sorry.'

He turned. She was wrapped in a flamingo-pink kimono with her hair all ruffled and her mascara smudged and trailing down her cheeks. What she was apologising for – for trying to make excuses for him, or for being an inadequate object of desire?

'Oh Sarah,' he whispered. 'God, just look at you. It's me should be sorry. Come here.' He pulled out a handkerchief and tried to rub away the black marks on her cheeks.

'Don't.' She pushed him away. 'Don't treat me like a child.'

'Then don't act like one. Look at you.' Suddenly he was an outsider eavesdropping on this couple, on this obnoxious man and the crying woman. 'Look at you, snivelling like a baby. It happened, Sarah, just one of those things – God, what a cliché – but the world doesn't end because of this; it's not so important, you know. For God's sake, stop crying!'

'Stop shouting!' she shouted. 'Stop taking it out on me; it wasn't my fault.'

'Wasn't it?'

'No,' she wailed. 'Please no.' And her long fingers plucked at the sash of her kimono and he was sorry, so sorry.

He took hold of her hands and tried to quiet them, massaging her fingers, rolling her rings beneath his thumbs. He said, 'I shouldn't have said that. Of course it's not your fault.'

'It's all right, really it is. Oh Charles. . . .' She leant towards him, as if to kiss him – and he drew back. She shook herself free.

He said, 'I'm sorry, Sarah. . . .' But she didn't hear him. She slammed the bedroom door behind her. He finished his drink, and left.

4

Sophie's baby died. Michael rushed her to the hospital and the doctors did what they could, but it made no difference. The baby was dead.

Sophie rested her head back against the deck chair. The wooden cross-piece dug into her thighs; overhead a bee bumbled in and out of the crimson tassels of the sun-canopy. With the minimum of imagination she could have been in a bedouin tent or a courtesan's boudoir.

A thrush watched her from the border. His fat breast was speckled like a slice of fruit-bread. This was his hunting ground; the flourishing weeds contained the moisture and the dark, earthy places beneath yielded him a harvest of snails. Only this morning she'd found a clutch of empty, punctured shells lying by the back door. She admired his audacity and skill, yet pitied the helpless snail who'd thought his home a fortress. Silly creature. No fortress is impregnable. You should have asked me, little snail; I'd have told you, find somewhere better to hide.

Mattie had called this morning. Mattie was in her seventies and scurried round the village like a little dun-coloured beetle. Sophie often used to visit her and they'd drink tea. Sometimes they wandered down the long shaggy garden to where tawny chickens scrabbled in the dry earth. Sophie loved collecting the eggs, dusty and smooth, some of them still warm.

Mattie grew the best strawberries in the village. Blood fruit, spreading their suckers across the garden, their bloated visceral clusters parting the lush foliage. She protected them from the birds with netting and Sophie would muse about circling vultures, and Mattie would pinch her arm and say she had a rum mind, and why didn't she give up this antique lark and have a family. Had she ever said anything of the sort to Michael? He'd have agreed with her. He'd been cock-a-hoop when she told him she was pregnant. Poor Michael, he tried so hard, but his efforts irritated her.

Mattie called round most days. They'd sit in the kitchen drinking tea and eating biscuits, and Sophie would clench her hands in her lap as Mattie went on about her having 'lost' the baby, as if a card in the village shop or a few lines in the Lost and Found section of the local paper might bring about its safe return. This morning she'd brought some eggs, all brown with just the lightest shower of freckles, and one of them with a curled feather still stuck to it. 'Now be sure and have one for your lunch. Nice boiled egg and a bit of bread and butter, do you the world of good.'

The thrush hopped closer. Did it have a mate nearby, and a nestfull of fledglings? She fingered the daisy chain lying in her lap. Where did it come from, this primordial urge to deck herself with flowers? Pretty things, daisies. Common as sparrows and just as lovely. She liked the way the slender stems were overlaid with a film of silvery hair. Lifting the end of the chain, she pressed her thumbnail into the stem. The sap bled as the filaments parted. She selected another flower from the pile and threaded it on to the chain.

She had told Charles Michael loved her so completely he'd forgive her anything. Even adultery. She could have put it to the test, told him the baby wasn't his.

She draped the daisy chain round her neck and fastened the ends.

What would Michael have done? And what would Charles do if he knew? Did she have the right to keep it from him?

Sweet voice of temptation! It had whispered in her ear from the start. Three times during the months of her pregnancy she'd picked up the phone and started to dial his number. And three times she'd banged down the receiver before completing the sequence. She'd written too, but never posted the letters. After she got back from the hospital she'd taken them down to the end of the garden and burnt them.

The thrush cocked its pretty head on one side. 'So?' she demanded. 'It was for the best. No point upsetting him.' Then, 'It's all right for you, you don't know what he's like.'

He's my dark side, my negative image.

A fluttering sensation in the pit of her stomach made her hunch forward. If I'd told him about the baby, what would he have done?

She plucked another daisy from the pile and fretted at its fragile stem. She knew what he'd have done. He'd have come here. He'd have parked his fancy car in the drive and she'd have let him in because, well, she could hardly leave him standing on the doorstep in full view of Mattie and the rest of the village. He'd have come in, followed her to the kitchen, and she'd have made him some of that dreadful scented tea he liked. He'd have taken charge, taken hold of her hands and leant over her – she could see him so clearly, the stubble darkening his jaw and neck, his glittering eyes the colour of chestnuts, and those wonderful creases under them, radiating down to his cheekbones. And she could hear him telling her to leave, go to London, marry him.

From the cottage came the faint trill of the telephone.

The thrush took flight. The phone rang on. When it stopped, she went back into the house.

5

Driving home through the empty streets, Charles fretted over what had happened. He'd lost control, hit out. It was unforgivable.

He pulled up at a red light. The streets were deserted, no cars, no people. His fingers drummed impatiently on the rim of the steering wheel. He wondered what Sarah was feeling. Miserable, embarrassed? Well, she was young, she'd get over it, soon forget him.

But he couldn't forget her. He missed her. The next day, he caught himself stacking up things to tell her, little anecdotes, the inadvertent comedies, triumphs and frustrations. At night he lay in bed, stretched out under the starched sheets, almost smelling her perfume on the air, feeling the press of her high-arched foot on his palm.

Two days later, he rang to ask if she'd meet him for lunch. She was reluctant, but agreed.

When he arrived, she was already there, sitting at a table in the far corner, sipping mineral water. He joined her. They ordered tortellini and green salad. The waiter underlined their order with a flourish, and left.

He said, 'Thank you for coming.' She shrugged. 'I wouldn't have blamed you if you'd said no. I would have done, in your position.'

'Would you?'

'Yes.'

'But you're not in my position, so how would you know?'

'Sarah. . . .'

'Tell me.'

'I miss you. The things I said, the things I implied – they were dreadful and I was wrong. None of it was your fault. It's all down to me.'

The waiter slopped the wine into their glasses; it was rough and unpalatable but seemed appropriate, a penance. Sarah said, 'What do you want? Why did you phone me?'

'To make amends. Because I miss you. I'm very fond of you.'

'Well, I'm not fond of you. I love you – oh it's all right, don't look so worried, I know you don't love me. But you love her, don't you?'

'Who?' His voice cracked.

'I don't know. Someone. There's someone, isn't there?'

He said, 'Yes.' And tried to ignore the sharp laughter rattling inside his head. 'Yes,' he said again, 'there is.'

6

Charles told Sarah about Sophie, spilled it all out, and it was okay, she understood. He'd been hurt, his trust had been betrayed. She knew the feeling. She'd loved Roger, believed his lies, and the shock of the truth had been intolerable. 'I know how you feel,' she whispered. 'But it gets better. It does. I promise.'

Their relationship changed. They ate in more often, she'd cook and he'd bring the wine, and afterwards they'd sit on her shabby sofa and talk. She told him about her childhood on the family farm. Sometimes her stories seemed pretty far-fetched – like the one about the night the pigs escaped and she and her brother had to hunt them through the dark woods, their torch beams cutting great yellow swathes through the undergrowth. He laughed and said he couldn't quite see her as a swineherd. She said, 'It's fine when you're ten or twelve, but after that who wants to paddle around in a mucky old farmyard?'

And then one night she told him she thought it was time he met some of her friends – and that she'd arranged for them to have supper with her guitar teacher and his wife. She gave him strict instructions: he wasn't to wear a suit – Bob and Polly were very informal – and they should take a taxi, it was a rough area, best not to be conspicuous.

Polly served spaghetti and French bread and Chianti on a scrubbed deal table. Though they all made a gallant effort, they didn't have much in common. Polly taught at a primary school, Bob was a music teacher in a nearby comprehensive. The conversation touched on politics, but Charles preferred not to be drawn. They considered the inadequacies of the education system. Charles listened and now and then asked what he hoped were pertinent questions. Over coffee Bob asked him what he thought of Sarah's playing. He was forced to admit that he'd never heard her.

'Come on, Sarah. Show him what you can do,' said Bob. They chose 'Scarborough Fair'. Polly led the singing and Sarah leant forward over her guitar, her pale hair cascading forward, hiding her face, making Charles wonder that she didn't get it caught in the strings. At one point Bob lifted his hand away from his instrument, allowing Sarah to play alone. He watched her with an indulgent smile, and Charles was jealous.

When later he demanded to know what they'd said about him, she bit her lip and said, 'Bob found it difficult. He says it's hard to grumble about your latest rent rise to a man who owns half London.'

'That's an exaggeration.'

'You can see his point though.' She laughed, then became serious. She had something to say. He waited. She said, 'Isn't it your turn now?'

'What?'

'I've never met any of your friends.'

He told her it had already occurred to him. He thought he'd invite a few friends and colleagues to dinner. She said she'd rather meet his friends two-by-two than all at once.

'It'll be fine. Cathy'll be there, and James. You'll enjoy it. Let's go to the house now – you can meet Emmy, get the feel of the place. What d'you say?'

The moment she stepped into the marble-tiled hall, he saw how well she suited his home, like a fine piece of furniture purchased especially.

From the hint of a frown accompanying her greeting, it seemed that Emmy didn't agree. She'd had no objection in principle to the dinner party – that very morning they'd shared a pot of coffee as they put together the guest list and outlined the menu – but now she'd met Sarah she seemed less enthusiastic. Lightly touching her arm, he smiled reassuringly and suggested she make them some tea.

They began their tour in the dining room. Sarah stood at the end of the Regency table and he could see the ghost of her reflection in the gleaming mahogany surface. She looked stricken. He said, 'You don't like it.' It sounded like an accusation.

She said, 'Oh no, it's very nice. But a bit, I don't know – cold, forbidding, like a boardroom. Don't be cross. It just takes some getting used to.'

He hardly trusted himself to respond; so often there seemed a gulf between what he said and the way he said it. Instead, he touched her cheek. She smiled. He said, 'It's much better when it's all laid out. You'll be amazed at what Emmy can do.'

'Flowers, will she do flowers? It'd soften it, don't you think?'

'Just tell her what you want.'

She laid her hand over his, pressing his palm against her cheek. He drew her closer. He thought, what if I asked her to stay the night? Since that last dreadful occasion he'd kept his distance and, for all her new-found courage, she'd not challenged him. He lifted back a loop of hair, elusive as water, it trickled between his fingers. She leant against him a little, nothing too obvious, just letting him know that it was okay. He kissed her. It couldn't happen again, surely? His need for her was less intense than his need for Sophie, but Sophie had been the breaking of a fast and that made a difference; no one could live their entire life on such a level. What he felt for Sarah was gentle enough to last a lifetime. Pressing his face against her hair, he closed his eyes against the autumn sunlight, and the gilding shades of ginger and gold and paprika and bronze.

And deep within the Temple, somebody battered their fists against a barred and bolted door.

Emmy wanted everything perfect, and she was none too happy about Sarah's choice of flowers. Pink roses indeed. Bedroom flowers.

Sarah arrived early, wearing a shimmering white dress. Charles ushered her into the drawing room where he gave her the necklace he'd bought that afternoon from a jeweller's in Covent Garden. He'd chosen an opal. They were supposed to be unlucky, but he defied superstition – he was captivated by its simplicity, by the subtle glimmer of pinks and blues beneath the milky surface. Seeing it now, cupped like a teardrop in Sarah's palm, he was pleased with his choice. She put it on, fastening the fine gold chain at her nape, and it nestled in the hollow of her throat, winking as she moved, like moonlight passing through clouds.

The guests began to arrive and they greeted them together. Fair and dark, light and shade, they made a striking pair. He enjoyed his friends' reactions. James almost leered. The fractional shift in Peter Knight's right eyebrow asked a whole battery of questions.

He'd invited a dozen people and they sat six on either side of the long table, with himself at one end, Sarah at the other. Unlike the evening with Bob and Polly, conversation didn't flag. After the meal they returned to the drawing room and, as they crossed the hall, he caught her by the waist and whispered that she looked gorgeous and was doing wonderfully. 'They love you,' he said. 'Look at James, he's jealous as hell.'

James was less jealous than mischievous. Charles stood by the window sipping his drink, watching how Sarah managed to hold a conversation with Cathy and at the same time maintain her surveillance on the rest of their guests. He saw her simultaneously nod in response to Cathy and smile at someone on the far side of the room. She accidentally caught his eye and he saluted her with his glass. And James said, 'Got to hand it to you, Charles, you've done wonders with Sarah; she used to be such a little mouse. And you, what about you?' He slapped him on the shoulder. 'Didn't think you had it in you, not until that little matter with Sophie MacKenzie, that is. You're a dark horse, Charles – which reminds me, I didn't tell you, I bumped into her the other week.'

'Who?'

'Sophie. I bumped into Sophie. Mind you, I barely recognised her.'

Slowly, very deliberately, he unstoppered the decanter and topped up James's glass. Replacing it carefully on the table beside him, he said, 'Has she changed so much then?'

'Very peaky. She lost a baby. Hadn't you heard?'

Out of the fire she'd come, a cold black shape issuing from its heart, his cream-skinned, flame-clad priestess stepping towards him through the flames.

The whisky scorched his throat. He tightened his grip on the glass, saying, 'No. I hadn't heard.' He stopped. 'When?' So calm. How was he able to sound so calm?

'Back in the spring, I think.'

'I see.' He took a breath and, in a slightly over-loud voice, changed the subject. He asked James about some new premises he'd acquired.

'Warehouse just off Tower Bridge Road,' James enthused. 'Good site, close to the market. . . .'

James talked on. Charles nodded and smiled without really listening. All around him the room buzzed with unheard conversation. But louder than this, and inescapable, was the tidal-wash of memory.

Because now, after so many months of darkness, he remembered everything. The way she looked at him, through him, the shiver of her voice in his ear, the slide of her skin against his.

Behind the bolted door, someone moaned.

Damn her. She had no right coming blundering back into his life like this. Tonight of all nights. I hate you, Sophie MacKenzie.

7

What should he do? Pretend there was nothing remarkable in what James had told him, that it was sad for Sophie and Michael, but just one of those things. Or admit to the possibility that the baby wasn't Michael's at all. . . .

And if it wasn't Michael's, if it was his? What were the consequences for him and Sarah? If he didn't find out the truth it would haunt him forever.

As he drove to Cambridge he tried not to think of what lay ahead, tried to focus on Sarah. She'd known something was wrong. He'd said goodbye to the last of the guests and gone back to the drawing room. She'd come up to him, and he'd half turned away, saying 'I'll get Emmy to fetch your coat. Thompson'll run you home.'

She bit her lip and tugged gently at his lapel, saying, 'It went all right, didn't it?'

'Of course. You were exceptional.'

'Charles. . . .'

He laid his hand over hers and kissed her cheek, hating himself for not being able to love her properly. He said, 'It's late. You'd better go. It'll be okay. Trust me.'

And she had trusted him.

He pressed his foot down on the accelerator. The sooner he got to Cambridge, the sooner he could get this over with. He wanted answers from Sophie MacKenzie, to lay her troublesome ghost once and for all.

It rained heavily as far as Bishop's Stortford. After that it was just wet. Great dark puddles stretched from the sides of the road, encroaching towards the centre, threatening to flood. Cambridge was sodden. He parked in the multi-storey by the Round church and, making his way along Trinity Street, had to run the gauntlet of hurtling bikes and impatient traffic and oily puddles seasoned with cigarette butts. Avoiding a particularly frenetic cyclist he stumbled into one of the puddles and water spilled into his shoe.

He dodged off the main drag and cut up Rose Crescent. There it was, Dragon's Lair. The shop bell jangled. The place looked drab, the tables and chests and chairs lacked their usual clutter; there wasn't a chandelier in sight and there were gaps on the walls and empty hooks where goods had been sold and not replaced. He heard movement in the back room. He clenched his fists in his coat pocket and braced himself. Enid bumbled out, drying her hands on a frayed orange towel. She was startled to see him, but pleased. She said, 'She's not here. Hardly comes in these days. You can tell, can't you?' She gestured towards the empty shelves. 'I try to keep things ticking over. She's been ill, did you know?'

'I've just heard.'

'Tragic. It hit her hard. She's at home, why don't you go and see her? Cheer her up no end that would, she always enjoyed your visits. I'll give her a ring, let her know. . . .'

'No. No, don't do that. I'll suprise her.'

The shop door banged shut behind him. It had started to rain again, a heavy, malevolent downpour.

You don't have to go through with this. You can back out, go home, back to Sarah.

But I have to know.

He crossed to the market. He ought to take her something. He edged his way between the stalls until he found one selling flowers, and hesitated in front of the sodden display. With Sarah he usually left the choice to the florist.

A woman with a tartan shopping trolley bumped into him, and a canvas awning dribbled rainwater on his head.

'Want some help, luv?' called the stallholder across the mountain of blowsy blooms and damp foliage. She had tightly curled grey hair and a man's check scarf wound round her neck. 'How about some roses,' she suggested, 'brighten up the lady's day.'

'No,' he said. 'Not roses. Roses are not appropriate.' She gave him a sideways look and he found himself hassled into a choice. He plucked a dripping bunch of yellow chrysanthemums from an enamel pail and passed them across to be wrapped. Clutching them to his chest, he ducked his head and ran for cover.

By the time he got back to the car he was soaked. He tossed the flowers on to the back seat, switched on the engine and turned the heater up full. His hands were clammy with the wet and the cold and his hair clung to his head like a shiny black skull-cap.

He left Cambridge on roads he knew intimately. Every bend and junction had been mapped and stored, even the potholes seemed familiar. And yet this was Sophie's territory, he was a trespasser.

The closer he got, the slower he drove. What the hell was he going to say to her?

I heard you lost a baby – wasn't mine by any chance, was it?

And as if she were beside him, he heard her say, 'What's it to you?'

'I wanted to be sure, I need to know, I'm getting married. . . .'

Laughter croaked in his throat. He pulled into a farm gateway. The musty smell of the chrysanthemums filled the car. The windscreen wipers swished and whirred. His hand shook as he switched off the engine.

Silence. He leant back in his seat. The rain spattered against the roof and jewelled the glass; the side windows began to steam up. A passing lorry churned a wave of muddy water against the side of the car.

She should have come to him. Surely she didn't think he'd turn her away. She'd treated him badly, it was true, but a baby changed things. He'd have looked after her, got her the best medical care, and then the baby would have lived.

Might have lived.

All she needed to have done was pick up the phone. But no, she didn't need him. As soon as things got tough, she went and hid in that bloody Temple of hers.

Well, if that's the way she wants it. . . .

The cottage was as he remembered it, only wetter. The gravel glistened amber and blue, and the heavy fronds of the evergreens were beaten out of shape by the rain. Wedging the flowers in the crook of his arm, he dived for the porch, rang the bell and waited. He brushed a shower of silvery drops from his sleeve. The damp air heightened the earthy smell of the flowers. They smelt of open graves. They were a bad choice. Best get rid of them. Before he could toss them into the shrubbery, the door opened.

She was frail, fragile as petals on a dying flower. And small. He'd forgotten how small she was. Her energy had always made her seem taller. Now the vitality had drained out of her. He thought suddenly of his mother's house at Christmas, of vases crammed with silver Honesty and Chinese Lanterns – paper pods the colour of flame, fire without heat.

It seemed they stood there for an age. Long enough for him to absorb the changes in her. The thinness of her face gave her cheeks a sucked-in look, sharpened her jawline. Her skin was translucent and taut, her entire facial structure teetered on the brink of disintegration. The slightest movement might make the bones jut through and split the fragile parchment.

He said, 'You've cut your hair.' He stared down at the bubbling halo framing her emaciated face. Halo! Oh no, not a halo. No angel this, but Sophie his demon, snapping at his heels year in, year out.

Behind him, water dripped from the porch guttering, spattering his shoulders. He'd clutched the flowers so tight that the wrapping had turned to mush against the crushed stems.

Embarrassed, he said, 'It suits you.' Then, because she still didn't respond, 'Enid thought it'd be all right to call.'

'Did she.' Her voice was thin, like a membrane passing between them. 'You'd better come in, then.'

He followed her along the hallway, past the table with the telephone and the spiky spider plant, and through to the kitchen. As she moved the soles of her feet sucked against the tiled floor and her skirt swayed, drifting and clinging to her calves. It was one of her Indian skirts, filmy layers of Imari colours, deep blue and iron-red. The way she dressed always confused him. Like this, barefoot and flowing, she was fey and feminine; in jeans and the suede jacket with the embroidery scrolls she was more brittle and unpredictable.

He dumped the flowers on the table and sat down. She stood with her back to him, filling the kettle. He said, 'I don't want coffee.' She turned off the tap. 'I've spoken to James.' Moving with deliberate slowness, she replaced the mugs in the cupboard. 'Sophie? Did you hear what I said. . . .'

'I heard.' She dragged out a chair, scraping it against the quarry tiles.

They'd sat at this table before, drinking coffee, eating toast, whiling away a Monday morning; and they'd stood on either side, stretching strudel dough. Now it was a barrier. At one end his flowers, at the other three jars of home-made strawberry jam, their shiny cellophane caps dipped in the middle, gathered in a ruff round the rim. Like a baby's bonnet.

He said, 'You should have told me.'

She tugged at the soggy red and black paper cone that wrapped his flowers. 'I don't know why you brought these,' she said. 'I hate chrysanths. They smell.'

And he ached for her, to see her like this, out of control. He could imagine how confused she must be. The mind is all, the body nothing; now her body was dictating her life. A life within, a life destroyed and a riot of careering hormones throwing everything out of kilter. 'Oh Sophie, look at you,' he whispered. 'You're not well. What's Michael thinking of, letting you get like this? You should see a doctor.'

'I have. Depression, he says.' She gave a hoarse laugh. 'Only to be expected, in the circumstances.' She looked him full in the face. 'Hilarious, don't you think? He hasn't the faintest idea what the circumstances are. Nobody has. Only me, and now you.'

'You should have told me.' She shook her head. 'For God's sake, Sophie, why d'you have to be so bloody stubborn. . . .'

'I'm not being stubborn, I'm being realistic.' She sounded cold, distant. 'D'you think I haven't been through this – over and over. You tell me I should have told you, but if I had, what would you have done?'

'I don't know. Tried to help.'

'Like now? But you're not helping, Charles. You should have left me alone. I don't need you. I was doing okay. I don't want you here, try to understand that. There's nothing for us, there never was. It was never going to work. Face it. We're not a couple, we never have been. I don't want you, I don't need you, and I certainly don't love you.'

8

She kicked him out. She told him there was no point in his being there, that Michael would be home for lunch any minute. 'He worries,' she said. 'He watches over me.'

She slammed the door behind him and stood with her back pressed against it, listening to the scrunch of the gravel, the sound of his car door opening and closing, then a brief silence followed by the luxurious pussy-cat throb of the engine. Very slowly she slid her back down the door, rucking her skirt, until she sat hunched on the mat, her head on her knees, her arms folded over it as if protecting it from a blow.

It would never work. We're not a couple, we never have been.

Why hadn't he argued with her?

How could he? She'd been so fierce, had rejected him totally. What possible argument could he have offered?

But he might at least have tried. He should have been able to see through the lie, recognised her revolt against dependence – because we are dependent, Charles. Alone we amount to nothing. One is not a number – where had she read that? That One requires Another to stand alongside it, to give it meaning.

She had told James about the baby knowing he'd pass the news on to Charles, and that Charles would mount his charger and come dashing to her rescue. But he hadn't come to rescue her, he'd come to reproach her, to satisfy his curiosity. And what he'd found was her coping as she always coped. She didn't need him. He'd taken everything she'd said at face value, and then left.

The next morning, long after Michael had left for work, she sat over the debris of their breakfast with a sheet of notepaper spread in front of her. The letter was to Michael but, apart from his name, she'd written nothing.

What would it be like never to see Michael again? The least obvious choice for a husband, that's what her friends had said. They'd been together, off and on, since school, and she always came back to Michael; Michael was safe. When she asked him why he put up with her, he said, 'Because I love you, because I can't be like you, but I can watch you, share you.'

This time, no matter what happened, she would not come back.

It was a slow train. The carriages racked and rattled. The force of its passage sent the raindrops scurrying across the window like demented tadpoles. She closed her eyes and conjured Charles's face as he'd sat facing her across the kitchen table. He'd looked older. There was grey in his hair, and a sluggishness about the way he moved, as if he were unbearably tired. Charles. She mouthed his name to the echo of her face in the window. She tried to remember what it felt like to hold him, to stroke his cheek, run her fingers along the line of his jaw; she felt the weight of his body pressed against hers. It would be good to be with him again, to shed the lies and pretence of the last months.

She took a taxi from King's Cross. Settling herself shakily into the seat she wondered why she felt so bad. Was she ill or just frightened? There was a foul smell in the back of the cab, she didn't dare think what it might be; it caught in the back of her throat and made her gag. She wound down the window. The moist air was thick with diesel.

After an age of darting from lane to lane between the heavy traffic, the cab signalled and turned off the main road and into a suddenly peaceful, elegant square with a central garden enclosed by black railings. It wasn't quite what she'd expected. Or rather it was, but more so. The scale was huge, the silence tangible, there was an emptiness, a rain-drenched stillness to the place.

She had no business here. This was the home of the man she'd met in the sale room, not the man she'd taught to punt. Perhaps she should tell the cabby to turn round, take her back to the station. No, that's the coward's way. What's the worst that can happen? That it turns out his visit to Cambridge really was just a duty call, that everything James said about this woman he's seeing, the beautiful Sarah, is true.

No, she didn't believe it. Dumping her bag on the pavement, she hunted for her purse. The cabby gave her the once over, taking in her jeans and clogs and the suede jerkin. As she handed over the fare he said, 'Sure you're in the right place, luv?'

'Beaufort Square?' He nodded. 'This is it, then. Thanks.' He shrugged and, with a brief wave, drew away from the kerb. As he left the square he lit up his "For Hire" sign. Desertion. Ridiculous, but it felt as if the only person who cared about her – a cabby concerned enough to check he'd brought her to the right address – had upped and deserted her.

Very slowly, she turned on her heel, taking in her surroundings. The big houses, their black-painted doors approached by stone steps flanked by doric columns, bore down on her like a ring of mother abbesses frowning beneath their cowled roofs.

Thirteen. He lived at number thirteen. The big black numbers were painted on the right-hand column. She checked her watch.

Four o'clock. He was probably still at his office. What if his housekeeper refused to let her in? What would she do?

Bluff, of course; it's what you're good at.

She lugged her bag to the top of the steps and tugged at the bell. The paint on the door was hard and shiny as enamel. There was a massive, facetted brass handle and beneath that a vicious-looking letter flap. She was about to ring again when the door swung open. She felt like a Victorian waif begging alms. No. Think like that and she won't let you in. You've got to behave as if you've a right to be here. She straightened her back and smiled and said, 'Emmy. You must be Emmy. Charles has told me all about you. I don't imagine he's home yet – may I come in?' She took a step forward. Emmy blocked her path. 'It's all right,' she said, adjusting the strap of her shoulder-bag. 'I know him.'

'If you'd like to leave your name, or come back later.'

'Emmy, no . . . .' She put out a hand to stop the closing of the door. 'I have to see him. If you don't let me in, I'll sit out here till he comes.'

'Then I shall have to call the police.'

'No, you won't.' Emmy frowned. 'I know you're only doing your job, I do understand, but this is different. Listen,' she said, taking a gamble on Emmy's underlying curiosity. 'Do you remember how he used to go away regularly, every weekend? He was staying in Cambridge, with my husband and me. He's my friend, Emmy, I need to talk to him.' Still Emmy hesitated. 'Why not ring him, tell him I'm here, see what he says?'

It was a risk, he might tell Emmy to send her packing, but a risk worth taking. Emmy yielded. She allowed Sophie as far as the hall. 'Wait here,' she said.

Sophie set her bag down on the chequered marble floor. She stood for a moment, eyes closed, breathing deeply. The house smelt of wax and tea and old leather. She felt herself begin to smile. She opened her eyes, and was overwhelmed by what she saw. Naturally she'd known his address was a good one – she'd teased him about it often enough – but she hadn't been prepared for the scale. The hall was wide and high. To her left a curved oak staircase led to a galleried landing. Against the wall to her right was a heavily decorated gesso consul table with a green marble top, at the centre of which stood an ormolu clock encrusted with fat cherubs. Behind this was a massive gilt-framed mirror the smoky plate of which reflected, in a mildly distorted form, the facing hallway, stairs and upper landing.

A ripple of professional excitement skittered through her. She wanted to run up the stairs, fling open the doors, find out what other treasures he'd got hidden away. Luckily Emmy came back. She said, 'He's in a meeting. I've left a message for him to call back.'

9

It was gone five-thirty before Charles could bring his meeting to a close. He returned Emmy's call and listened without comment, barely able to grasp the reality of what she was saying. He said, 'So Sophie – Mrs MacKenzie – she's there now?'

'In the kitchen having tea. I didn't think I should give her the run of the house.'

'It's all right, Em.'

'But I couldn't just send her away. She doesn't look well, and she came expecting to see you, so I don't suppose she's got anywhere else to stay.'

'I'm sure you're right. It's okay, Em. You did the right thing.'

How could he have foreseen this? She'd been adamant, left no room for doubt. *We're not a couple, we never have been. I don't love you.* The memory cut like a hot knife.

He said, 'She can stay, Em. You're right, she's been ill. Make her comfortable, see she eats something and gets an early night. I'll be late. No need to wait up.'

He gently replaced the receiver. What are you doing? She's invaded your home, won Emmy to her side. Did you hear Emmy's voice? There's no way she'd have turned her out. She's already changed sides.

Who says there have to be sides?

Of course there have to be sides – and there she is, all tucked up and cosy in your home, and what are you going to do? Where are you going to go?

I don't know. I need time. If I see her now, I'll say something I'll regret.

He told Betty to let the janitor know he'd be staying late. And before going home, would she bring him the papers for the Cobham site.

After she'd gone, he spread the papers, the architects' proposals and the accountants' costings, across the desk. He stared down at them, listening as the familiar sounds of the building leaked into stillness – no more distant hammering of typewriters or trilling of telephones; no more voices in the corridor, stilling to a murmur as they passed his door.

He shuffled through a file looking for his Project Manager's report. He glanced through the closely typed sheets. He agreed with the recommendations. The site was in a good residential area, it made sense to pitch it at the luxury end of the market.

And still it was only six-thirty.

He stood up. In the darkened window, his reflection looked back at him. He'd put on weight. Too many Italian meals, too much pasta. Sarah. He should have thought of it before. He'd go and see Sarah.

He didn't warn her he was coming and, because she wasn't expecting him, she was dressed casually in a pale pink polo-neck sweater and a pair of royal blue slacks that flared out over the fluffy toes of her slippers.

'Charles!' Her eyes glittered with pleasure. Then she frowned. 'What is it? You look terrible.' She fussed like a mother over an injured child. She took his coat and made him sit down, hovered over him saying, 'I wasn't expecting you. Shall we go to Mario's? Or I could make a chilli . . . .'

'I'm not hungry,' he said. 'Sit down.' He drew her on to the arm of the chair.

She tried to pull away. 'Some tea, I could make some tea.'

He tightened his hold on her arm. 'Stop it, Sarah. There's something I've got to tell you.'

'What?' Her voice came muffled.

There was no gentle way to break it. He said, 'She's back. Sophie's back.' He felt the jolt of her shock. She turned her head away and her hair tumbled down, obscuring her face. 'I'm sorry,' he whispered. 'But you had to know. Sarah, I need your help. What do I do?'

Still without looking at him, she said, 'Why? Why has she come back?'

'I don't know. I haven't spoken to her. Emmy rang to say she was at the house . . . .'

She turned, frowning through the strands of her hair. 'Emmy let her in?'

'You mustn't blame Em. Sophie can be very commanding.'

'I bet she can.'

'Sarah, please. This isn't my doing. I don't know what she wants.'

'Don't be silly, it's you. You she wants.'

'No. She told me – last time I saw her – she made it clear how she felt. She doesn't love me, or want me. Whatever her reason for coming here, it isn't that.'

'If you say so.'

'You must trust me, Sarah.'

'Of course I do. What will you do?'

The decision sprang like a trap in his mind. He said, 'Talk to her. Tell her about us.' Strange how certain he suddenly was. Being with Sophie weakened him, being with Sarah made him strong again. That ought to tell him where his future lay. He looked up at her, at the way her fair hair snaked across her candy-coloured shoulders. 'Listen to me,' he said, his voice shivering with excitement as he drew her closer so that her hair strayed across his brow. 'I have to see her, otherwise she'll just go on haunting us. You do understand?'

'Yes. But you'll send her away?' He nodded. 'Promise me.'

'Yes.' He squeezed her waist and nuzzled his face against her breasts. 'I promise, Sarah. I promise, I promise, I promise.'

10

He delayed as long as he could. It was gone eleven when he got home. Surely Sophie would be in bed and asleep.

He should have known better. An unwelcoming glow spilled from the fanlight above the front door, a chink of light showed at the drawing-room curtains. He drew the bolts on the front door, took off his coat and went through to the study to see if Emmy had left him any messages. He took a steadying breath. He couldn't put it off any longer – and what was all the fuss about anyway? She was just a common or garden fire-breathing dragon who'd temporarily relocated her lair. No big deal. He switched off the light and crossed the hall to the drawing room.

The dragon waited enthroned on his wing-chair. She had one leg tucked under her, his newspaper lay folded on her lap. The only light came from the fire and from the lamp on the table beside her.

He said, 'You needn't have waited up.' She shrugged, and the devil's halo of her hair glittered in the firelight.

Three days ago he and Sarah had hosted their dinner party, exchanging smiles across this very room, and he'd been entranced by how she suited his home. But he'd been wrong; the judgement had been rash and superficial. She blended in, certainly, toned with his furnishings; the golden mahogany of the dining room was the perfect backdrop for her particular pale beauty. Had one of James's designer friends been set the task of producing the perfect consort for a man like him, living in a house such as this, Sarah, or someone very like her, would have been the result; but it was Sophie who really belonged. Sitting there in jeans and sweater, her clogs kicked skewwhiff on the hearthrug, her bare toes wriggling against the tapestry seat, she sat at his fireside as if of right, and he was the intruder.

He poured himself a drink, and sat facing her across the fire. Her presence froze him. The mechanism of the carriage clock tapped away on the mantelpiece. Beneath the floorboards, the central-heating pipes creaked. The house was a living organism and it protested at her presence.

She said, 'I'd almost given up on you.'

'I was busy. There was no rush. Emmy was looking after you.'

'Yes.'

'What are you doing here? I know it's not for my benefit, you've made your feelings on that score plain enough.'

She tossed the newspaper on to the floor. 'All that about us not being a couple?'

'What else?'

'You don't know me at all, do you?' She rubbed her palm against the arm of the chair. 'Or don't want to, perhaps. Maybe you don't care. I'm an embarrassment, aren't I?'

'Don't be ridiculous.'

She said, 'James told me, you know. About your new girlfriend.'

'I'm sure he did.'

She leant forward, rocking over her knees. Her auburn halo glittered like bronze. She said, 'It wasn't true. It hurt seeing you again, that was all. I said the first thing that came into my head.'

He felt dizzy. He said, 'Not now, Sophie. This isn't the time. You're tired, not well . . . .'

'I'm fine.' She dug herself deep into the chair. The wing cast a shadow across her face, obscuring her expression.

He said, 'You're not. You should rest.' And then he demanded, 'What about Michael? Does he know you're here?'

'No.'

'He'll be worried.'

'It's a little late to be worrying about Michael.' And before he could argue she said, 'Tell me about her, Charles. You were with her tonight, weren't you?'

'Yes.'

'James says she's very lovely. And young, and crazy about you.'

'She seems fond, certainly.'

'And you? Are you in love with her?'

'Yes.'

She laughed, and relaxed. Stretching out her legs she curled her toes in the heat of the fire. 'You're a lousy liar, Charles.' She considered him, her head on one side. 'Have you told her about me?' He nodded. 'And the baby?' He didn't respond. 'You've not told her about him?'

He shook his head and took a sip of his drink. 'Him', he thought, she said 'him' – a son. My son.

'Why not?' Her sharpness startled him.

'What?'

'Why haven't you told her? Are you ashamed?'

'I've hurt her enough. Why are you doing this?'

Ignoring him, she said, 'So you're worried about hurting her, but not about hurting me.'

'You don't need me. You never have. If I thought you did . . . .'

'I do.'

'No. You say that now, but it isn't true. She's different.'

'She does need you?'

'Yes.'

She drew her feet up on to the chair and gripped her ankles till her knuckles whitened. Presented with the curly crown of her head as she hunched forward over her knees, he said, 'You're perfectly capable of taking care of yourself.'

'Is that what you think, or what you'd like to think? Look at me, Charles.' She lifted her head to look him full in the face. 'No, you don't see it, do you? You don't want to. A baby died. Your baby.'

'I know. I told you, if I'd known at the time. . . .'

'You would have done something.' Sarcasm loaded her voice. 'Of course you would. Only you didn't know because I didn't choose to tell you. I could so easily have done, I could have forced you to share the responsibility, shoulder some of the pain, but instead I took it all on myself. And that's all right, that's fine, it was my choice. I excuse you your absence.'

'There's nothing to excuse, I didn't know!'

'But you found out. You see, that's where the responsibility starts. You found out and you came thundering up to Cambridge demanding to know whether it was your child that had died, and you never gave a thought to how I might feel. You opened the wound, you woke me up. Do you understand what I'm saying? I coped, yes. But how? I'll tell you. By not being there. I'd pricked my finger and gone to sleep but you, my hero, you came battling through the thorny thicket and woke me up, but I hadn't outslept the pain; it was still there, waiting.'

He stared at her, at the transformation anger had wrought, the play of light and shadow making her face all flat planes and sharp angles, a cubist confusion that distorted understanding. She leant back in the chair and closed her eyes. 'All right,' she said in a voice that was suddenly flat and tired. 'No more riddles. Listen. Last Christmas I found out I was pregnant. I was going to have your baby and I was happy and frightened and excited and angry – but who could I tell? No one. I had to keep it to myself, lock it up inside me. Can you imagine that? It was like I was rotting from the inside. Sometimes I think that's what killed him. Just think of it, he didn't even live long enough to breathe fresh air.

'He died and I couldn't mourn him. Oh, I showed all the conventional signs of grief, but it wasn't for him, it was for Michael's child, a child who'd never existed outside Michael's imagination.

'But it's all right.' She banged her fist against her denimed thigh. 'It's okay. Fine. Grief is grief, no big deal, I can cope. Look at me, Charles, wouldn't you say that one of life's eternal truths is that Sophie can cope?

'So I shut it all away inside me and started living on the outside. Only that's not living. I functioned, responded without feeling, and everyone thought I was going out of my mind – except the doctor, he said it was natural depression. Interesting combination that, natural and depression.

'No matter. It's all in hand. Under control. But then you come blundering along, tearing down the thicket so the light pours in and Michael's child vanishes but ours is still there, our son, and he's real and solid and unmourned and all that anger and fear and excitement came flooding out and with it the guilt – because it really was as if I'd killed him, and even if I hadn't, I should have mourned him and because I didn't, because I haven't, he's still here.

'He's here now, Charles. I can't cope any more, not on my own.'

He threw himself into the chair she'd just vacated and dug himself back against the rough tapestry. The dying fire sighed, collapsing in on itself in a cascade of grey ash. The room had grown cold. As he'd helped her to her feet, her elbow had dug into his palm bringing an inappropriate rush of desire that sucked the breath out of him. The voice inside him screamed – I don't want this, I don't need it, I'm an intelligent, capable man, I can conquer this.

But the flesh still shakes. Body and mind, intellect and flesh, can they be torn apart, separated one from the other, yet the greater part still live? I want to think they're distinct, that I can choose; but can I? Do I have free will, or am I ultimately the victim of this need, this barbaric drive? No, I can't believe that. It can be changed, transmuted and transformed into revelation, animal need as an instrument of the divine, laying down the path to God.

Or is that too grand, just another way of justifying the animal act of procreation, transforming it into a weapon against boredom, the last refuge of a degenerate race?

11

Sophie closed the door and switched on the bedside lamp. The muslin drapes tumbled milkily from the half-tester. God, she was tired, worn out with the travelling and with the waiting and the recriminations. She'd been hard on him, but he deserved it, staying out like that. Still, at least she'd left him in no doubt as to how she felt, even if he had tried to fob her off, telling her she looked pale and ought to rest. He had a point though, they needed time to gather themselves, regroup – terrible how readily the military metaphor sprang to mind.

She kicked off her shoes and, nuzzling her feet against the deep pile of the egg-yellow carpet, thought how different this pretty room was from the rest of the house. She found his home depressing, like a stage set. Everything in it, every rug and vase, had been placed just so. There was nothing personal, no family photographs or inappropriate bits and bobs cluttering the surfaces, presents from nephews and nieces, that sort of thing. It could have been anyone's house. How could he bear it?

She knew how. She'd seen it that day in the sale room, and like a fool she'd set out to rescue him from the sterility of it all.

Do I know you? Of course I know you. You're me, my other self. There but for the grace of God. . . . What are we doing to each other, Charles? We're tormenting each other, that's what. I taunt you with my independence, then confuse you by denying it. And you take shelter with this girl – Sarah!

Oh but it hurt, thinking of him with someone else. That evening, as it dawned on her where he was, a chill had gripped her, pressing like a frozen pebble in the pit of her stomach. She'd never felt like this before, so devastated, so alone. She'd never been jealous, never cared enough about anyone to care.

What was she like, this Sarah? Young, according to James, and beautiful. But how young, and in what way beautiful? Some think the Mona Lisa's beautiful, or Liz Taylor, or Twiggy. The word is infuriatingly imprecise.

The next morning she woke to the sound of running water. It was ten to eight. Presumably he was getting ready to go to work. Slipping out of bed, she bathed quickly, pulled on a skirt and a cheesecloth top, brushed and ruffled her hair, then went out on to the landing.

Emmy was helping him into his coat. She recognised the burgundy silk scarf he'd worn on his last visit to the shop. She remembered the seductive brush of its fringe against her hand, the way the dust from the blanket and the chaise had made them gag, how they'd laughed when he stubbed his toe on the fender. She'd turned down a number of offers for that chaise longue over the past few months.

Emmy saw her, and murmured to Charles. He looked up. She

thought how she loved his eyes, but not as much as his smile. He wasn't smiling this morning. He looked formidable, stern and upright as Emmy ran the clothes brush over his shoulders. With a discreet gesture he dismissed her and crossed to the foot of the stairs. She came down a few steps to meet him. The waxed oak tickled her bare feet. She felt unsteady, and leant slightly against the banister.

He said, 'Did you sleep well?'

'Yes thank you.' It didn't look as though he had; his face was strained and there were dark shadows under his eyes. He came closer, stepping up on to the bottom tread.

He said, 'There are things I need to do that I can't get out of. My board. . . .'

'I see.'

'I'm sorry. It's an important meeting. There's a site at Cobham. . . .'

'Cobham?'

'I'll be back as soon as I can.'

'It's okay. You don't need to worry about me.'

'Sophie, don't.' He climbed another two steps. She was close enough to see the creases in his neck, the shadow of stubble under his newly shaven skin. His hand rested on the banister rail and he slid it along until the tips of their fingers touched. She heard the sigh of air between his parted lips as he moved his hand up her arm to her shoulder. His touch was warm. Her skin glowed. She leant towards him, encouraging him, and he bent his face, pressing his lips to hers so that she felt the rasp of his chin. The nudge of his teeth and the thrust of his tongue startled her as they joined in a way that was somehow more intimate even than penetration, and he held her tightly, and she grasped at his coat and her body flowed open for him until the question came, filling her mind and spilling into the air around them – who taught him this? He didn't use to kiss like this.

Sarah. The name like a knife sliced between them. She pushed him away and saw how flushed he was, his lips parted and moist, his eyes heavy-lidded. She said, 'You'd better go.' He drew breath to argue. 'No.' She shook her head. 'Go on. It'll be all right.'

12

His day began with a meeting with his Project Manager. He barely heard what he had to say, but it didn't matter, it was all on file, this was simply an exercise in personnel management.

What the hell was he going to do about Sophie? He'd forgotten how strong her effect on him could be, the way his need for her could fill him to the brim, obliterating everything. Last night he'd lain hour after hour in his rumpled bed, reliving every word that had passed between them, experiencing again and again the shock of her touch.

He'd been fooling himself over Sarah. Had he never met Sophie, perhaps they'd have had a future but now, present or not, Sophie demanded a level of commitment that left no room for Sarah.

Sometimes he really did hate her. If she didn't want him, why couldn't she let him be happy with someone else? He'd been angry with her last night, for turning up out of the blue, for fitting into his home so neatly. But he couldn't sustain that anger. Gradually it had been replaced by a deep, rumbling pity.

Their son, the secret she'd carried inside her – how could he ever understand what that had been like? How could he ever hope to make it up to her?

It was late afternoon before he brought his board meeting to a close. He arrived home a little after four. The house was silent. An unnatural fear glided through him. The air was chill; shadows gathered against the ceiling and in the corners like smoke-soiled cherubs.

Fool! He put down his briefcase. The metal studs on the base scraped the marble floor. Sudden laughter clattered up from the kitchen. He started towards the back stairs, then stopped. He felt like an intruder. The kitchen was Emmy's domain. But the house was his. With a self-defying shrug, he went down the stairs and threw open the kitchen door.

The room was humid, tropical. Condensation streaked the walls and the air was sweet with the smell of soap. Over in the corner, the washing machine rumbled. Emmy was ironing a shirt and Sophie was perched on the table, engrossed in a story, swinging her legs and illustrating her tale with fluttering gestures of her hands.

His arrival froze them. He said, 'I thought I'd let you know I was back.'

Emmy wedged her iron on the end of the board and, untying her pinny, said, 'We weren't expecting you so soon. I'll make some tea.'

'Don't bother. You carry on. I'll be in my study.'

He leant back in the familiar chair; the buttoned leather creaked. Next to the telephone was the oak-framed photograph of his father. His mother had never noticed its absence. He picked it up. 'What should I do, Dad?' He searched the face in the frame for an answer. 'Fight her? Or give in?' It was so unfair that the one person in whom he might have confided was beyond his reach. He put the photograph back on the desk. For once his study offered no refuge.

The drawing-room fire had been laid but not lit. He set a match to it, then dug his newspaper from under a chair.

Sophie and Emmy. What were they finding to talk about? What had they been laughing about? Him? What else did they have in common?

He closed his eyes. The kindling sticks crackled and spat, the coals dropped and settled in the grate. His sleepless night was catching up with him. He felt light-headed. The fire grew warm; the house was quiet. Emmy's kitchen flickered against his closed lids: Sophie perched on the table, Emmy sweeping the hot iron across the glacial expanse of his shirt, the hiss of fire and ice, a cloud of steam and the smell of starch. And he remembered Sophie in her kitchen. He'd helped her bottle fruit once, wedging thick glass jars into a huge galvanised bin placed on top of the Rayburn. Jam too; she'd had him standing over the wide pan stirring mounds of white sugar into the crimson strawberries, and later tipping it so that she could ladle the contents into sizzling hot jars. Playing house, she called it. None of it was for real; she didn't particularly want the bottled fruit or the jam, but she enjoyed role-playing. She looked the part too, with her long flowing skirts and her hair caught up in an emerald bandanna. . . .

He woke with a start. The dream was so vivid that he could still smell the sweet fumes of the fruit, still feel the weight of the pan's handle digging into his palms.

He heard a movement, there was someone in the room. He opened his eyes. The curtains had been drawn and the lamps lit, and Sophie stood over him, all gold and grey with her hair the colour of the forest floor caught in a band of the setting sun. She bobbed down on to her heels and brushed her fingers against the back of his hand. She said, 'It's getting late. We let you sleep. You looked sweet, like a little boy!' Her voice mocked him, but the nostalgia of the dream blocked his anger. He heaved himself upright, rubbing the sleep from his face. He was stiff and his back ached. She said, 'Are you hungry? Dinner's ready.'

She and Emmy had made the chicken and Calvados dish she'd cooked on his first visit to Cambridge. As Emmy served, Sophie said, 'Remember?'

'Vividly.' He poured the wine.

She smiled, and raised her glass in a silent toast. Last night's anger had gone. She seemed sad now, and he understood her sadness. Back then, at the beginning, they'd been like children, their lives uncomplicated by adult love and physical craving. But it had been spoilt, he had spoilt it.

As he ate, he watched her. She sliced through a piece of chicken and he saw with a shock that she'd removed her wedding ring. His mind emptied of everything but hope and panic. They finished the meal in silence, and went through to the drawing room.

He suggested Cognac with the coffee, but she said, 'No. Look.' And produced a bottle of apricot brandy. She poured them each a glass, then sat cross-legged on the rug in front of the fire.

He said, 'Why not sit in the chair? You'll be more comfortable.' She shook her head and he saw the way the auburn curls swirled round her crown, at her pale nape, revealed as she bent forward.

Rummaging the poker between the crimson coals, she said, 'Charles, about last night. I'm sorry.'

'There's no need to apologise.'

'Of course there is.' She gave a little laugh. 'I was totally over the top. Tired, I suppose. That's no excuse. I shouldn't have come down here like this. You've made yourself a life that doesn't include me, and I'm glad for you. If I can stay here tonight, I'll get out of your hair tomorrow, okay?'

'No. You don't have to leave. Where would you go?'

'I've a friend, Jazz; she's in the antiques business. She'll put me up.'

'That'd just be running away. You've come here because we need to talk, you can't just take off again.' As he spoke, she continued to clutch the poker, using it to fidget with the coals, pushing them back and forth, making them flare into life. Now she wedged it carefully against the fender and looked up at him. He forced a smile. She nodded as if in agreement, and rested her cheek against his knee. A rash of tickling pinpricks like the sting from a nettle chased up and down his spine. He said, 'You can't be comfortable. Go and sit in the chair.'

'I told you, I'm fine.' She looked up at him. The gold in her eyes glittered like firelight on tinsel. The need to touch her was too great to withstand. He tentatively brushed her brow, then easing her head back against his knee, slid his hand lower, bringing it to rest against her nape.

Heat radiated from her.

Can fire inflame fire?

He reached for his glass. The thick, golden liqueur coated his tongue.

The silence between them filled up with memories. A celery-scented fenland field, a shower of fireworks, a cloud of dust and a battered chaise longue. He said, 'You look so tired. Go to bed, we'll start again tomorrow.'

The door closed behind her. He listened to her barefoot tread on the stairs, and the faint bang of her bedroom door. If he'd tried to go with her, what would she have done? Faced with his over-whelming need for her, he had chosen denial.

Pushing himself out of his chair he poured some whisky and the sharp spirit cut through the cloying liqueur.

How long could this continue? How long could he hold himself apart? And if he succeeded tonight, then an identical battle would await him tomorrow night, and the night after. . . .

He drained his glass. His body raged, caught in the pincer grips of anger and desire; every pulse throbbed dangerously against the restraining flesh.

Another drink. . . .

Don't be a bigger fool than you already are.

In the dark he might hide from her, hide from himself. He went upstairs. His room was a refuge. He felt a faint movement of air against his burning cheek.

What now? Sleep? Sleep was not a choice. What would another man do in his position? Go to her, that's what. Not to do so, is that strength, or weakness?

God it's hot. I've got a headache coming. Shouldn't have had whisky on top of the brandy. Excuses, you're always making excuses. The heat increased. The back of his neck became damp, also the small of his back. Tugging at the buttons of his shirt, he stripped to the waist and threw open the window.

The night was frosty. The sharp air prickled his skin, but didn't cool him. The chill draught was like a fingernail caress.

Our Father which art in Heaven. . . .

He'd almost forgotten how to pray. The words dissolved into the night. What was the point? I regret nothing. I repent nothing.

I don't understand. Why her? Why not Sarah, or any other woman?

Because she's not just any other woman. She's unique, all-powerful, and her vision enfolds and includes me, and I love her.

Choice! There isn't any choice, there never has been.

The night air feeds the fire as he augments his need with reasoned argument. Stepping back from the window, he pulls down the sash and closes the curtains. He finishes undressing and, putting on his dressing gown, makes his way along the passage to her room.

13

The billowing bed-hangings engulfed the room in mist. From the garden came the chatter of birdsong. He could almost have been back in Cambridge, except that there he'd slept in a sparse room, in a narrow bed, alone.

He fought back the rising laughter, and rolled his head on the pillow. Sophie stirred and moved against him. He could feel her moist breath warm against his shoulder.

In the end it had been easy. He'd hung around outside her room, trying to think of an excuse for being there, then thought, don't be a fool, it's obvious. He tapped at the door – a very gentle tap; he half hoped she hadn't heard him. She opened the door and stood looking up at him. The man's nightshirt swamped her shoulders but yielded to the press of her breasts. She stepped aside, and let him in.

The room glowed; the lamp on the pedestal fired the brass spindles to gold. She knelt on the bed, waiting for him. The houri-drapes clashed with the fire of her hair. His hands shook as he fumbled with the sash of his dressing gown. She helped him. Then, settling back on her heels, she peeled off her nightshirt.

Flesh of my flesh.

His chest rose and fell sharply beneath the press of her hands. She taunted him with fingers and lips, coaxing and repelling, drawing him on to greater intimacy, then laughing and falling back under him – and the fire and the ice of her hair flared against the snow of the pillows, and the hangings rose like steam from the clash, and her laughter became a moan, became laughter again, and he heard himself cry out as the spasm ripped through him and his lungs roared with the effort to breathe and the bite of her nails brought him back to the bed and to her wide, shining eyes.

The next time it was gentler. At first. They'd slept, then woken to darkness and silence. They sought one another out, cajoling and teasing, their fingers gliding butterfly-light, discovering one another's bodies as a blind man learns a face. As once she'd caressed the belly of an antique jug, so now he slid his hand down the dip of her waist, then out over the swell of her hips and round to her tight-curled nest and her moist parted lips – and surely his broad hand was too large for such a private place – but she moved for him and rested her hand over his, guiding him as she rocked against him and round him until her breathing changed and her back arched and she admitted him and became fierce and so did he, and she cried out as he filled her and she cried out again as he withdrew. The act didn't satisfy her, it increased her hunger.

And we have a lifetime of this – his heartbeat slowed – and I'll never tire of her because I've lived too long without her.

He slept again, waking to a new day and a body heavy with exertion and pleasure. She was lying on his arm. He had pins and needles. He tried to ease himself away, and she stirred and smiled and stretched her arms over her head. Her breasts stood proud. He touched them, felt their quiver of response, and she touched his hair, his cheek, his chin. He kissed her. She ran her hands down his back and her rippling fingers made his nerve ends tingle.

He pulled back. He could hear Emmy downstairs, the front door opening and closing as she brought in the milk, the snap of the letter flap as she withdrew the newspaper. He reached for his dressing gown.

'What are you doing? Where are you going?'

'Emmy's up. I'd better get back to my room.'

'And do what? Rough up your bed so she thinks you've slept in it?' She was laughing at him and she was right; it was ridiculous. But he went just the same.

Half an hour later, shaved and dressed, he went downstairs. The dining room was empty. Two places had been set either side of the broad mahogany table. He sat down and started to flick through the pile of envelopes. He couldn't be bothered. He tossed them aside and glanced at his watch. Why was Sophie taking so long?

According to Sarah, his dining room was like a boardroom. He had to agree. It was rather formal, the regency samovar, the landscape paintings in their gleaming gilt frames – thank God he'd resisted James's suggestion of fake family portraits.

If Sophie stayed, she would expect to make changes. The idea of Sarah putting her mark on his home horrified him. Sophie was different; she had style. Sarah liked Art Deco.

The stairs creaked. He looked up. Standing in the doorway, she gave a half smile and a self-conscious wave.

She insisted she wasn't hungry, that she just wanted coffee. Emmy served Charles his eggs and bacon, and poured coffee for them both.

He felt awkward, being alone with Sophie. The cutlery seemed heavier than usual, the silver handles cold against his palm. He ate slowly, aware of the faintest scrape of knife against plate. As he ate, he watched her.

As with the rest of the house, she'd taken possession of the room the moment she entered. Her eyes flickered over his possessions. He recognised the glint of professional assessment. She caught him watching her and laughed. 'Relax, Charles,' she said. 'I'm impressed. You really were slumming it in Cambridge, weren't you?'

He didn't understand. She'd become hostile again, as if trying to put a distance between them.

She said, 'Take this, for example.' She outlined the wavy rim of her cup. The stroke of her fingers made the hair on his nape prickle. 'Rockingham, yes?' He shrugged. She lifted the cup to one side and tipped over the saucer. 'There. See.' She pointed to the mark on its underside. 'The puce griffin. The lady knows her stuff. Do you break much?'

'I don't think so.'

'But you see what I'm getting at? Most people would keep a service like this locked away in a cabinet, strictly for show. But not you.' She softened and smiled, pulling the sucrier towards her. As she sugared her coffee, she spilt a scattering of grains across the table top. She said, 'You're a strange man, living all on your own in a place like this, using Rockingham the way other people use mugs from Woolies. Why? Who comes here, who are you trying to impress?' And then she tossed her head and laughed and said, 'No one. Am I right? It's to keep them all away, pull up the drawbridge, stir the boiling oil!'

And he said, 'I always knew you'd understand.'

14

Her moods changed so rapidly he couldn't keep up. At first she'd been reproachful and angry, later the memory of her behaviour had embarrassed her. Later still, she'd overcome that embarrassment, had been almost happy, the old Sophie again.

And now she'd changed again. There was something frantic about her as she insisted they go out. She needed some air, some space, a taste of the city.

The autumn day was cold and damp; pinhead pearls of moisture traced the intricate pattern of a cobweb spanning the railings. She insisted they take the tube.

The train was crowded. They had to stand. He held on to an overhead strap, she held on to him. They must have looked an odd couple, he in his dark overcoat and burgundy scarf, she in the suede jerkin with the green embroidery.

She wanted to go to the river. 'Father Thames, the axis of trade.' She laughed and pinched his fingers.

The embankment parapet was high, making it difficult for her to see over comfortably. He helped her up and she sat with her back to the water, craning to look along the curving stretch of river, at the overblown buildings marking its course. She said, 'It's the scale I like. London's such a solid city, massive, monumental.' She gave a mocking laugh. 'Days of Empire, and all that!'

He leant against her, resting his hands on her denim-clad knees. He said, 'Sophie, help me. None of this feels real. What happens now?'

'I don't know. What do you want to happen?' She forestalled him. 'Don't answer that.' She took his face between her hands and kissed him.

He thought, she's hysterical. He pulled away. 'I have to know. Are you staying?' With an irritated grimace she hopped off the wall and started to walk away. 'Sophie!' He caught her by the shoulder and swung her round. 'Don't do this. Stop playing games. Tell me you're not going back to Michael.'

'All right. I'm not going back to Michael. Satisfied?'

'Or anywhere else – to stay with this friend, what's her name?'

'Jazz. No, I shan't go to Jazz. Come on, Charles, don't be such a bore. I want to go sightseeing. Take me to Trafalgar Square.'

Her assurances lacked substance. She'd told him only what she would not do.

'There,' she crowed triumphantly as they arrived at Trafalgar Square. 'See what I mean about scale?' He laughed as she pointed to the steps and pediments of the National Gallery, and Nelson's arrogant column. 'Not exactly subtle.' He commented that the modern world was taking its revenge, the masonry was blackened by diesel fumes and streaked with birdlime.

Sophie marched towards the column. He had to hurry to catch up, dodging round a small child who was running amongst the pigeons, scattering them in a rush of air and a shower of feathers and excrement. At the base of the monument, she clasped his hand and gave it a squeeze. 'Come on,' she said, 'give me a leg-up.' Standing on tiptoe, she rested her foot on the ledge of the plinth. 'I want a closer look.'

'What for? It's only a statue.'

'Don't be such a philistine. Are you going to help me, or do I accost a stranger?'

She was capable of doing just that. He glanced over his shoulder. He half expected an audience to have gathered. Then suddenly he felt exhilarated. So what if they did attract an audience, what did it matter? Catching her by the waist, he half lifted, half propelled her to stand between the massive bronze paws of Landseer's lion.

She grinned down at him. 'There,' she said. 'Not so difficult. No tumbling walls, no lightening bolts . . . .'

She looked vulnerable, standing above him, dwarfed by the

massive maned head. She said, 'You're not going to stay down there, are you? You always play it safe – why? Hey, I know why – someone might recognise you.'

This time when he glanced behind him a middle-aged couple – they had to be American with their plaid scarves and garlands of cameras – gave him a friendly wave and an encouraging smile. He turned back and gripped the edge of the plinth; a smell of stale urine rose up from the stone. He glanced at Sophie. She seemed to have forgotten him. She stood lost in thought, stroking the tamed muzzle and outlining a fang with her forefinger.

With a thrust and a jump, he joined her. A muted cheer rose up from below; the American couple waved, and went on their way.

Sophie perched on one of the lion's paws and drew her knees up under her chin. He said, 'You do realise, don't you, that if anyone does recognise me, that's it – it'll start rumours about my sanity. . . .'

'Share prices will fall . . . .'

'Bankruptcy. Penury. All your doing.'

'Such power. Delilah to your Sampson. What do you think?'

He thought she was closer than she realised. If she stayed, how could he divide his life between her and his work? If she left, would he have the heart to continue?

He stood tall on the lion's plinth and the possibilities spread themselves before him. Whichever course he took, his life was changed forever. So be it. With a shrug he tried to dismiss his disquiet. Over by the fountain the pigeon-chasing child was sitting on the parapet, trailing its fingers in the water. Charles leant against the lion. Lost in thought, he caressed its muzzle, outlining with a forefinger its perfectly sculpted nostril. Realising what he was doing, he withdrew his hand in disgust and wiped it on his handkerchief. She was watching him, he could feel it. Laughing at him. He stuffed his handkerchief into his pocket and bobbed down to face her. He said, 'Sophie, we've got to straighten this out. You're going to marry me.'

She nestled her chin against her knees and rubbed her hand up and down her shin. Tentatively he touched the fragile skin where her wedding ring had been. She said, 'I was thinking just now, about Edwin Landseer.'

'What?' He took hold of her fingers, stroked them and raised them to his lips.

'He was like you; he never married. He had his lions and stags and melt-eyed dogs for company, and you've got your stocks and shares and buildings.'

He shifted his grip to circle her wrist. He said, 'It's not enough.'

That evening he took her to the restaurant that had so intimidated Sarah. With Sophie it was a very different experience. At first the waiters eyed her Indian cottons and chose to condescend. This amused her. When the menu came she quizzed the waiter then, beckoning him closer as if to convey a personal request, demanded to know why the grey-haired man on the next table was wearing a ginger hairpiece.

The waiter made a choking sound. Charles laughed out loud. After that, the waiter took delight in guiding Sophie through the menu, drawing her attention not to the chef's recommendations but to his own personal favourites.

A little later Sophie leant across to draw Charles's attention to the city type sitting near the window who was trying to impress his companion by lighting his cigar from one of the tapered candles, and succeeding only in spilling candle wax down his tie.

Charles felt uneasy. When he'd dined here with Sarah, had there been someone like Sophie observing Sarah's constant rearranging of the cutlery and evident fear of the waiters?

On Sophie's insistence, they returned home by bus, travelling at the front of the top deck with the dark road and glittering head-lights stretching out like a river. The bus dropped them a few yards from Beaufort Square. She tugged his hand saying, 'Race you.'

She ran, and he followed. Their footfalls echoed off the empty pavements. He imagined the flicking of curtains as the other residents responded to the unaccustomed noise.

She took the front steps two at a time, then turned to wait. He arrived all out of breath with his coat flapping and his shoes splashed from the puddles. He thought how small she was as he trapped her against the door. He gripped her hand until the pain registered on her face. He felt a sudden, vicious need to assert his physical ascendancy.

'That's enough, Charles. You're hurting me.' She started to turn away. As she did so, a flustered Emmy opened the door. Before she could say anything, the drawing-room door flew open and Michael MacKenzie said, 'Soph? Is that you? Charles? What the hell's going on here?'

15

Damn, damn, damn – why were they all so intent on rushing her? First Charles trying to force her into a commitment, now Michael. He'd invaded Charles's house and his teddy-bear shoulders filled the doorway as he demanded to know what was going on, looking first at her, then at Charles as he both saw and refused to see the way things stood.

He said, 'You look dreadful, Soph – worn out. You shouldn't be out all hours like this. She shouldn't . . . .' He turned to Charles. 'This is your doing – if she gets pneumonia it's down to you.' Charles's hand slipped from her shoulder to her waist. She felt the warmth radiating from him. Michael said, 'For Christ's sake, I've been out of my mind . . . .'

Charles said, 'Why don't we go through to the drawing room?' He sounded calm and businesslike, but she could sense the tension beneath. He was wary. Afraid. Did he think she'd go back to Michael, hadn't she promised him she wouldn't?

But it didn't follow that she'd stay with him. She looked from one to the other. Michael was the port, Charles the storm. Shelter too long in port and you'll never reach your destination. Sooner or later you have to brave the tempest, even if it destroys you.

The drawing-room fire had been lit; the silk-shaded lamps threw inverted cones of light against the walls. Charles closed the door. Michael said, 'You needn't stay.'

She said, 'He's staying. I want him to. What are you doing here, Michael?'

And Charles came up behind her, murmuring, 'Gently. Take it gently.' To Michael he said, 'Let's sit down.'

'No . . . .'

'Sit, Michael,' she said.

Stay, Charles echoed silently.

Sophie lowered herself into a chair. Michael hesitated, then moved stiffly across the room to sit facing her. Charles stood alongside her, his elbow resting on the chair's wing. Out of the corner of her eye she could see the way the point of his tie rose and fell with each carefully controlled breath. She leant towards him slightly, hoping he'd understand. They would face this together.

To Michael she said, 'How did you find me?'

'Mattie. She saw his car in the drive. And Enid. He went to the shop. Soph, I've been frantic, why didn't you say you were coming here? I've been imagining all sorts of things – I was going to ring the police, but then I spoke to Mattie . . . . Why didn't you tell me, Soph?'

'Don't call me that. I hate it. I've always hated it . . . .' She heard the rising pitch of her voice and felt Charles's hand come to rest on her shoulder.

'Don't do that!' Michael shouted at him. 'Don't touch her, you've no right.'

And Charles said, 'Tell him, Sophie. It's cruel like this.' His fingers curled, biting her shoulder. 'Do you want me to?'

'No.'

'Tell me what?'

'I'll tell him,' she hissed. But how to make him understand? Tell him a story? Once upon a time . . . . Charles in her car that day in the fens; Charles in the storeroom, his jacket covered in dust, cobwebs clinging to his socks. Instead she said, 'The baby.' A spasm caught the corner of Michael's mouth. 'The baby that died.' As if there had been another.

'What about it?'

'It was mine,' said Charles.

Michael's hands jerked in his lap. His pain snapped out. All those years he'd sheltered her and the one thing he'd wanted in return, that he'd believed she'd almost given him, even this was to be stripped from him.

He said, 'Do you hear him, Soph? Do you hear what he's saying? Please, don't let him . . . . He's made a mistake. Tell him. Tell him Sophie, please.'

'No, no mistake. I'm so sorry, Michael.'

'Sorry? What's sorry to do with it? It isn't true. It can't be.' His hands clenched in his lap. He rocked forward, leaning over them as if the pain was in his stomach. 'It's not possible, it's been too long . . . .'

She said, 'James's party. You didn't want to go. I went on my own.'

He continued to rock back and forth over his knotted hands. He said, 'He was there?'

'Yes.'

'Did you know – did you know he'd be there? Is that why you went?' She shook her head. 'So if you had, you wouldn't have gone. Right?'

'I didn't know he'd be there, but I hoped he would, I was glad you didn't want to come.'

'Glad?' She nodded. 'I see.'

She waited. He had nothing more to say. No argument, no protest, nothing.

Charles crossed to the drinks table. He removed the stopper from the decanter and, laying it down, took great care not to break the silence. Glancing over his shoulder, he offered her a raised glass. She shook her head. He came back to the fire, handing a glass to Michael before perching on the arm of her chair. He rested his glass on his knees. She could smell the fumes of the alcohol.

Michael finished his drink in a single gulp, then banged the glass down on the little Chinese table. His palm grated against his beard. Eventually he said, 'I don't believe it, any of it. Not a word.'

'Why should we lie?' asked Charles gently.

'I don't know.' His voice was flat. 'It doesn't matter why. These things don't happen, not in the real world, not to people like us. You were my friend.' His head jerked up; he challenged Charles to meet his eye. 'I trusted you.'

'I know. I'm sorry.'

'Sorry? Don't be sorry, nothing happened, nothing at all, just a mistake. Oh Christ, what's going on?'

'I tried,' Charles whispered. 'When I realised what was happening, I stopped coming.'

'But you started again! Why are you doing this, saying all these horrible things about my baby, that it was yours? It wasn't, it was mine, my son. And you! You of all people! Never would have thought it, not of you, not a lady's man our Charles – more a man's man, little boys, that sort of thing . . . .'

'Michael!'

'No, Sophie, it's all right.' Charles stood up. 'He's upset, he doesn't know what he's saying.' He went to refill his glass.

'I do know. Ask him, Soph, go on, see what he has to say for himself. A man like him, his looks, money – don't you think it's funny he hasn't married? Should have a wife and a whole string of women, but he hasn't. Why not, Charles? Why not?'

Her heart kicked with rage. She stood up. 'Go home, Michael. Make him go, Charles.'

'Oh, I'll go.' Michael stood, swaying, then steadied himself against the chair. 'What, still nothing to say, Charles?' He took a step towards Sophie. She took a step back and Charles placed himself between them. Michael said, 'He hasn't denied it, Soph. You do realise that, don't you? He hasn't said it isn't true.'

16

Sophie wriggled to the edge of the Rolls's deep leather seat and, tapping Thompson on the shoulder, said, 'Could you drop me somewhere please, anywhere you can pull over.'

Charles said, 'Sophie, I'm not so sure . . . .'

'It's got to be done. I've sorted out Michael, now it's your turn

– anyway, there's some shopping I need to do; you'll have to fill the time somehow!' She laid her hand over his. 'It'll be okay, you'll see.'

Thompson held the door for her and she scrambled out into the crush of Oxford Circus. She checked the fastening on her bag, pushed her hair up and back off her brow and watched the car ease back into the flow of traffic. She could see the back of Charles's head framed by the rear window. He did not, as she would have done in his place, turn and wave.

Earlier that afternoon they'd gone to see Peter Knight. Charles had explained that they needed someone to act in her divorce; Knight suggested his junior partner, Leonard Prentice. That had seemed to surprise Charles, but he hadn't commented and Knight had sent for Mr Prentice who whisked her away to his office.

She liked him. There was a sparkle about him, a glimmer of mischief. He was older than her, but younger than Charles. He had the most remarkable almond-shaped eyes. It was easy to tell him about Michael and their marriage, about Charles – though not about the baby.

As she talked, Leonard Prentice leant forward, every so often making a note on the pad in front of him. When she'd finished, he laid down his pencil, glanced at her over the rims of his half-moon specs, and told her to leave everything to him.

Back in the car she started to tell Charles what Prentice had said. When he didn't respond she glanced at him. His face had a closed look. He wasn't listening. No doubt he was finding it disturbing, all this talk of divorce. But he was the one who'd insisted on a commitment, and this was the result. For God's sake, she was the one getting divorced. She felt adrift, as if she'd let go of the side of the pool without being sure she could swim. If only he'd say something. But he just sat there, his face blank and his hands splayed on his thighs. Those hands. She wanted to clutch at them, be rescued by them. I can't swim, Charles. But she didn't do or say anything, just allowed herself to be fascinated by his hands, by the contrast between their well-manicured softness and their breadth and strength. There were labourers in his ancestry for certain – a grandfather perhaps, an Irish navvie digging the roads of Victorian London. She smiled. They belong to her now, those hands. She knew how gentle they could be, and how spiteful.

She touched the base of his wedding finger. He shifted restlessly in his seat and turned to look at her. His face was strained; deep-cut lines bracketed his mouth. He moistened his lips. 'I've been thinking.' She waited. 'I'm going to have to tell Sarah.'

Sarah. Of course. She should have known it was Sarah on his mind. 'She needs me', he'd said. Well, she was going to have to do without him.

On impulse she said, 'Go now.'

'What?'

'Go and see her now. Get it over with. When does she finish work?'

'The gallery closes at four.'

'If you go now, you'll catch her as she leaves.' He drew breath to protest. She said, 'Best to clear the decks. I've some shopping to do. I'll see you later.'

It was a lie about the shopping. She stood on the kerb, jostled by the crowd, watching the car vanish, and all around her the massive buildings teetered, the traffic roared and the wash of the fumes made her giddy.

How will Sarah react? Will she cry, or shout at him? Or reproach him with a suffering silence? He was going to have to be strong.

She couldn't face traipsing round the shops. Nor could she go back to Beaufort Square; it was too alien, she hadn't yet put her mark on it.

Jazz – she would go to Jazz. Hidden in her bag, lurking amongst the crumpled tissues and half-used biros, was her diary and, in the back of this, a list of telephone numbers.

Jazz lived in Battersea, a modern infill in a row of Victorian houses. She only used the first floor herself; the downstairs rooms she rented out to a series of lodgers – poets, musicians, GLC councillors.

She greeted Sophie with a shout from an upper window. Tossing down her keys, she said, 'I'll open a bottle. Red or white?'

'Red. I'm feeling bloody.'

The room where Jazz lived and slept was large and sparsely furnished. A double mattress, covered with rust-coloured chenille, lay directly on the floor. It was scattered with tapestry cushions against which Jazz lounged, cigarette and ashtray in hand, bottle of wine at her elbow. Sophie dropped down beside her. The only other seating was a series of beanbags, each one bearing the impression of the last occupant. The walls had been painted white and draped with silk shawls and oriental rugs. Arrangements of inverted paper parasols hung from the ceiling and a further swathe of chenille covered the window, plunging the room into a state of permanent gloom. The variety of fabrics and the ancient Turkey rug captured the musty odours of occupation, food and wine and burnt-out joss-sticks.

Jazz handed her a glass of wine, and lit another cigarette. 'What's up?' she enquired languidly. 'You're the least bloody person I know.' Sophie didn't answer. Now she was here, she couldn't think why she'd come. She should have gone home to Emmy. It would have been less personal, safer.

Jazz glanced sideways at her and said, 'You're looking better. Fantastic.'

She took a sip of wine. It was rough. Charles would not approve. She said, 'I've left Michael.'

'Hurrah, bravo!' Jazz laughed and beat the bed with the flat of her palm. 'I always said it was wrong – you're not cut out for marriage. Admit it. I was right.'

'No, you were wrong. I was a good wife, I used to make cakes and bake bread and bottle fruit . . . .'

'Playing games. Who the hell did it fool?'

'It fooled Michael.'

'Men! What do they know? Only good for one thing.'

'Chamberpots.'

'What?'

'Great when you feel the need, but best kept out of sight.'

'You got it.'

They laughed and leant against one another, and she thought, I was right to come here. Jazz reacted at gut level and on that level her judgements were either incandescent with insight or barbarically wrong. But she made you think.

'Tell me.' Jazz rested her cigarette on the big plastic pub ashtray and laced her fingers over her knees. 'What made you do it?'

Sophie thought of Charles, and tried to imagine him in this room. She couldn't do it; it was too absurd. And Jazz would never be able to understand how she could love a man like Charles. She'd never be able to see past what he was to who he was.

She'd understand about the baby though. Sophie held out her glass for a refill, and told her. Jazz said, 'How come you never told me this before? Who is this guy?'

'I didn't tell you because I knew you'd go on about it.'

'Too right I would. Leave Michael by all means, but going off with someone else . . . . I suppose he wants you to marry him? Sure he does. They're all the same, bloody men, just want to muscle in and take over – and we let 'em, we bloody let 'em.'

It was dark by the time she got back to Beaufort Square. Charles was already home, shut away in his study. Emmy said he was funny about being disturbed in there, and maybe Sophie'd better wait. Sophie shrugged off the suggestion, knocked and went in without waiting for an answer.

The room was dark apart from the desk lamp which threw a puddle of light on to the pristine blotter and his clenched hands. His face was in shadow. She closed the door and went to stand behind him. Resting her hands on his shoulders, she could feel beneath his jacket the rigidly locked muscles. As she massaged them she said, 'Have you been back long?' He shook his head. 'You saw her?' Releasing him, she perched on the edge of the desk. 'Was it bad?' she said. 'Was she terribly upset?'

'Of course she was upset. What d'you expect? We were going to be married.'

'I didn't know it had gone that far.' She couldn't keep the viciousness out of her voice. So much compassion for Sarah! A terrible scraping jealousy raked through her. She wanted to know if she'd touched him, held his hand – he might have taken her in his arms, just to comfort her of course. He might even have kissed her. She was being ungenerous, but she begrudged Sarah every moment she'd ever spent with him.

The telephone rang. He answered with a dismissive bark, then listened to the shrill, accusatory voice of a woman crackling at the other end of the line. If the woman was Sarah, he was well rid of her.

He snapped at his caller, 'Who told you that?' He ran his thumb along the edge of the desk, deliberately working a splinter into the fleshy pad. He listened for a moment, then said, 'I might have known he'd have something to do with it. . . . No, I don't intend to talk over the phone . . . I said no . . . I'll come over.'

He almost threw the receiver back on its cradle. 'Who was that?' she demanded.

'My mother.' He stood up. 'I have to go out.'

'Is she ill?'

'My brother's stirring up trouble. I've got to sort it out.'

She caught him by the arm. 'I'll come with you.'

'No. Not a good idea. It'll be all right.' He kissed her cheek. 'I can handle her.'

17

Nosing the car through the evening traffic, he congratulated himself on how confident he'd sounded. He doubted Sophie had detected the least hint of the leaden dread his mother's phone call had evoked.

Waiting to turn right across the flow of traffic, he wondered how the hell Anthony had found out so soon. Bernstein's should keep a better standard of confidentiality. From what his mother had said, it wasn't the divorce that had given rise to such fury, but the matter he'd discussed with Peter after Sophie went off with Leonard. He had intended to tell them, but in his own good time – certainly not today, hard on the heels of seeing Sarah.

He wriggled in his seat. He didn't want to think about that, didn't want to remember her tears and repeated assurances that she understood, and loved him, and if ever he needed someone to talk to – just talk – all he had to do was pick up the phone.

Why did she have to be so bloody understanding? Why didn't

you shout at me, you stupid woman, chuck one of your hideous vases at me, kick me downstairs and out into the street? Why do you never fight back, just accept everything that happens to you?

He turned into his mother's street. The cars were bumper to bumper and he had to park several houses away.

Anthony answered the door. He let Charles in, then retreated quickly to the sitting room; he had no intention of being left alone with his brother.

Their mother was in her favourite chair by the hissing gas fire. Her slippered feet rested on a worn leather pouffe, a cup of tea stood on the table beside her. The torn wrapper of the opened packet of rich tea biscuits flapped like a flag. She didn't stand up to greet him, or hold out her hand, or offer her cheek for a kiss. Not that he expected such signs of motherly affection; it was just that nowadays he noticed their absence more keenly.

'Well,' he demanded, 'what's the fuss about?'

'Don't be rude, Charles. I didn't bring you up to be rude. Take off your coat and come and sit down.'

With deliberate slowness he tugged off his gloves and fed them into his pocket. He unbuttoned his coat. Glancing round the room, he drew up a rexine-seated chair and sat down. He folded his hands in his lap, and waited for his mother to speak.

He saw her look at Anthony. Anthony looked back impassively. Neither of them looked at him. He knew this technique; their silence was intended to trap him into a self-defensive indiscretion. It hadn't occurred to her that he'd learnt a trick or two himself over the past thirty years. During the course of his career he'd used this very method to stunning effect. Amazing that his mother still saw him as a frightened schoolboy ripe for intimidation.

He waited. The flickering blue flames of the gas fire sighed; the ceramic waffle glowed orange. It was Anthony who broke. He said, 'You've been to see Knight.' Charles neither confirmed nor denied the statement. 'People are talking. Rumours flying.'

'Is that so.'

His mother leant forward. 'What have you got to say for yourself?'

Ignoring her, he said to his brother, 'Would you care to tell me the precise nature of these rumours? If you're just going to hint, you're wasting my time.'

'Keen to get home, are you? Waiting for you, is she?'

'Yes.'

'It's true, then?' his mother spat. 'About this woman and her divorce. Charles, have nothing to do with it. Think of your position, your reputation. . . .'

'I rather think my reputation might be enhanced.'

'Never mind your bloody reputation. . . .'

'Language, Anthony!'

'He's right,' Charles intervened. 'This has nothing to do with my reputation, commercial or moral. There's something else on Anthony's mind. Let's hear it.'

'We want to know,' said his mother, 'if what Anthony's secretary told him is true.'

'So that's how it got out. Gossip over the tea urn. Peter will be interested to know about this. You do realise you've probably got the poor girl the sack.'

'Just tell us.'

He looked from one to the other. It was true, what they'd heard, that he'd asked Peter to look into setting up a Trust for Sophie. There was a lot of detail to be sorted out, it hadn't even been drafted yet, let alone signed, yet already his family was at his throat. He hated the way money brought out the worst in people, revealed them for what they really were. While he was alive neither mother nor brother gave a damn about him, but they would rip him limb from bank balance after he was dead.

18

Swamped by her emerald and gold kaftan, glowing from her bath, Sophie sat cross-legged in front of the fire gently towelling her hair to a tangle of damp curls. She watched the play of firelight on the steel fender and thought of Jazz and her house, the incense and the parasols. Jazz had given her a hard time over Charles. She'd wanted to know what he did, how he made his money, and when Sophie told her, she'd said, 'Oh Christ, not a fucking capitalist.' And Sophie had laughed, saying, 'Absolutely right. On both counts!'

It didn't seem so funny now. She tossed the towel aside and stretched her arms and spread her fingers against the heat of the fire. She wished he'd come home. What was so urgent that he had to drop everything and go tearing over to his mother's like that?

She knew so little about his family, just the basic facts: that his mother was a harridan, his father was dead, and he didn't get on with his brother. There was a sister, too, Helen. He did seem fond of her.

Charles's key scraped in the front door lock. She straightened her back and ruffled her curls. He came into the drawing room and crossed to her side. As he bobbed down on to his heels she laughed and caught him by the wrist and pulled him off balance. Sprawled beside her, he wrestled with her until he had her pinned beneath him. His eyes grew heavy and his lips parted and he reached for her. She said, 'How did it go? How was your mother?'

He released her. 'Vitriolic,' he said, and rolled away on to his side.

'That bad?'

'Worse.'

She felt sorry for him. He looked so incongruous lying there. Pound to a penny he'd never seen the room from this angle before. She began idly to loosen his tie. 'Why did she want to see you? Why did you have to rush over there?'

'Because . . . ' She bent over him and he wound a coil of her hair round his finger. 'Because my brother got wind of our visit to Peter and decided to give the hornets' nest a stir. But don't worry. I can handle Anthony.'

'If you say so.'

'I do. Listen.' He pulled her closer. 'Will you grow it?'

'What?'

'Your hair. Grow it again. For me. I love your hair.'

'If you like. I only cut it as a penance.' She stopped. She

shouldn't have said that. It brought it back, an icy wind cutting across the dank black fen. She sat up. 'How about a drink?'

She unstoppered the decanter, thinking how large and awkward and out of place he looked. She said, 'Why is your mother so upset? Set her sights a bit higher than a divorced antiques dealer, had she?'

'Something like that.'

'She must have been put out about Sarah. She's just a glorified shop assistant. . . .'

'She liked Sarah. She didn't consider her a threat.'

'But I am?'

'Yes.'

'Why?'

He caught her arm in a grip so tight that it was almost a Chinese burn. He pulled her down beside him. She tried not to show how much it hurt. He was trying to distract her. Two could play at that. As the fire from his fingers roared through her, she put her face close to his, coaxing his lips with her tongue, their breath fused as he sucked her in, then freed her. She tugged at his loosened tie and slid her hands under his jacket to feel the pounding blood and the reassuring thump of his heart. And then she pulled back and said, 'What would your mother say if she could see you now?'

He moved away. He took a gulp of whisky. His broad hand encased the cut crystal. She could see the blue rib of the vein along its back. He said, 'That I should know better at my age.' He hesitated, then said, 'I don't think my mother likes me very much. I don't know why not – God knows I've tried – but I've never been able to please her. When I was a child she'd nag me for not doing well enough at school; why couldn't I be more like Anthony? Then, when I was successful, she didn't like it because it took me away from her. She couldn't tell me what to do any more; or rather, she carried on telling me, but I didn't take any notice. Sometimes I think she'd like me to be one of those cardiganed bachelors who live at home and do the shopping and walk the dog and gossip with the postman.'

'Poor Charles,' she mocked. 'Nobody wants you, nobody loves you, I think you'd better eat worms. . . .' He didn't laugh. She hugged his arm. 'What about your dad?'

'Dad?' His voice became tender. 'Dad was special. Now he

wasn't ashamed of me. Anyone he met in the street had to listen to the roll-call of my achievements. My mother hated that. She used to go on and on at him. Why did he make such a song and dance about me but never a good word for Anthony? Anthony'd stayed on at school, gone to university, got all the right qualifications, married, had children. She liked that. She puffed him up, fed his jealousy – he'd worked hard and I hadn't; the way she saw it, what I had came easily. And Anthony believed her; he hates me for it.' He drained his glass and perched it on the edge of the table. 'For all his diplomas and letters after his name, he's never really made it. Even the job with Bernstein's was a favour to me.'

'Does he know?'

'He chooses to forget.'

'You're a strange family.'

'You should think seriously about what you're getting yourself into.'

'I have,' she said. 'And by the way – you are.'

'What?'

'Loved.' She started to unbutton his shirt. 'So you can pass on the worms.' Pushing him back, she pinned him to the floor, straddling his legs. He laughed and gave in. He slid his hand under her kaftan, along the slope of her thigh. His fingers roved upwards till he touched her and parted her and felt her pulse and moisten. His lids quivered and he inhaled sharply as she released the tab of his trousers. As she eased down his zip he caught her wrist, stopping her – but at the same time pushed her hand hard down against him. 'Don't,' he hissed. 'What if Emmy comes in?'

She laughed softly. 'She won't,' she promised. 'She's having an early night.'

An hour later, weary and ravenous, they went down to the kitchen. Sophie set him to whisking eggs while she melted butter in a pan. When the eggs were beaten to a froth he started on the toast and Sophie made the omelettes, pleating the golden eggs to rumpled silk, then folding them and sliding them on to the plates.

He marvelled at the joy of it, the way his body glowed and his skin tingled, at how his mother's wrangles and his brother's hatred dwindled to insignificance.

They ate at the formica-topped kitchen table. She broke off small pieces of toast, buttering each fragment individually before popping it into her mouth. He loved the way the melted butter made her lips glisten. All that mattered in the world was here in this room. He could block the windows and seal the doors, and feel no loss, no grief at their isolation. He said, 'It's going to happen, isn't it? You're going to marry me.'

'It's tending to look that way.' She ground black pepper on to her omelette.

'When?'

'Oh, you'll need to ask Leonard that.' She raised a forkful of peppered omelette to her mouth. 'Apparently it depends on how hard Michael fights.'

'There's nothing to fight for.'

'Yes there is, the shop, the stock, my share of the cottage . . . .'

'You don't need any of that. Look at this place – I've enough for both of us.'

'Granted it's a beautiful kitchen; but that's hardly the point. It's yours, Charles, not mine. I worked hard to build up that business, and what comes from it is mine. I don't want to be dependent on you.'

'Don't be so bloody proud. Look at me, I'm dependent on you.'

'I don't mean like that. Be reasonable.'

He grunted and straightened his knife and fork and pushed his plate away. He didn't want the past dragged into their new lives; he wanted her to cut loose. With all my worldly goods I thee endow.

'You don't need anything else.'

'I do. Try to understand. Okay, call it pride, but all this, you and your name and this house, it swamps me. I want something of my own, something I've worked for. Surely you can see that.' He looked away. 'God you can be obtuse sometimes, Charles. Why does everything have to be such an issue with you?'

'Me? You're the one standing on principle. You want your pound of flesh not because you need it, but to make a point.'

'I want something of my own, that's all. Is that so hard to grasp? I don't understand you . . . .' She stopped. He saw a flicker of consternation, as if she'd uttered a revelation. In an awed voice she said, 'That's it, isn't it, that's the problem. I've blithely assumed that I know all there is to know about you, that I understand you, but I don't.'

'You know me better than anyone.'

'I know what you are, but not what makes you what you are. I knew before I came here the kind of life you led, but not why you led it, why you live alone, never married.'

In the silence that followed he felt the gulf widening between them. Lulled by her sense of their sameness, she'd lost sight of their differences. There was a husky note to his voice as he tried to make light of her question. 'That's no mystery. I've been too busy . . . .'

'Making money?'

'Yes.'

'And that's it?'

'Yes.' His throat was dry. He said, 'Leave it, Sophie. Don't pry.'

'I only want to know. If we're to have a future . . . .'

'All right.' He closed his eyes, shutting out her glittering gaze. 'I haven't married because I've never got close enough to anyone. I don't find women easy. They frighten me. Satisfied?'

Of course she wasn't satisfied. She said, 'And me, do I frighten you?'

'Yes. You do. You terrify me.' And he saw that she knew it to be true. Up to a point. Did she see the difference – that though afraid of her, it wasn't in the way he feared other women, women like Cathy? It was change he feared, and she was the agent of change. When she came into his life the focus shifted, an era came to an end.

Sophie. Her name scraped like a fingernail dragged down a blackboard. Sooner or later he would marry her. She could become Mrs Charles Wade. The feeling this engendered was very different from that brought on by the prospect of marriage to Sarah. That had filled him with optimism. This filled him with foreboding, a feeling of claustrophobia. His narrow life hadn't widened by association with her; it had narrowed still further so that all his experiences and aspirations were focused on one point. He would never be free of her, would be always with her, always returning to her from every corner, every aspect of the day.

Forever and ever. For as long as he lived.

19

The house was too big, too impersonal. She needed somewhere of her own. She chose a room on the second floor, overlooking the garden.

She threw open the sash and leant out of the window. 'What d'you think?' She turned and propped her bottom on the window ledge. He shrugged. It was pleasant enough. The wallpaper had a pattern of grey ferns, bending and waving, hinting at vistas beyond. He said, 'No doubt you'll make it very cosy. Are you going to sleep up here?'

She laughed and said, of course not, she wanted it for a sitting room. He was to help her. A tour of the house produced a selection of furniture, a two-seater sofa, a bergere chair, a low table and another larger one to stand by the window as a desk. From one of the downstairs bedrooms she appropriated a set of mahogany bookshelves, an alabaster table lamp and a watercolour of a Scottish loch with tumbling hills and a scraggy gibbet of a tree haunting the foreground. They were in the process of hanging this last – his arms aching as she debated its exact position – when they heard the front door bell.

He wasn't expecting anyone. They wedged the painting against a chair and crept out on to the landing, clutching one another like guilty children as they peered over the gallery. 'My sister,' he whispered.

Sophie craned forward, then whispered back, 'Ask her up.'

It was a clever move, Sophie decided, getting Helen to come upstairs. It wrong-footed her. Sophie smiled as she leant against the doorjamb, watching them. Helen said the room was very pretty; she admired the view, but thought the watercolour a bit grim. Charles concentrated on rolling down his shirtsleeves and fastening the cuffs. Sophie said, 'Charles, why don't you get Emmy to make some tea.' He looked doubtful. 'Don't worry, we shan't claw one another's eyes out the moment your back's turned!'

Curling herself in the bergere chair, she kicked off her clogs and tucked her bare feet under her. Helen said, 'You don't mind my calling on spec like this?'

'Of course not.'

'Only Charles went to see mother last night. She's very upset.'

'I think she's overreacting, condemning me sight unseen like this.'

'Maybe. I suppose that's why I'm here, to find out what you're really like.'

'And what am I like?'

'I expected you to be different, somehow. More . . . I don't know. Just different.'

'More like Sarah?'

'Perhaps. My mother and brother . . . .'

'What?'

'Think it's his money you're after.'

Sophie laughed and nudged an abandoned clog with a bare toe. 'Hardly,' she said.

'You can't blame them, not with all this stuff about him putting money in Trust for you.'

'He's done what?'

'A Trust Fund – don't tell me you didn't know.'

'Of course I didn't know. Are you sure?'

'Yes. Peter Knight's dealing with it. The whole family's up in arms.'

'Of course they are. Helen, I'm so sorry. I really didn't know.'

'I don't mind for myself – and it's not as if any of it affects us immediately.'

'No, but it's the long-term prospects they're worried about, and who can blame them? It's all right, Helen. I do understand. I'll talk to him, I promise.'

20

Charles didn't discover the reason for Helen's visit till after she'd gone. 'You should have discussed it with me.' Sophie was livid. 'Your family think I'm a money grubber.' She clattered the cups and plates on to the tray. 'And I don't blame them.'

'It's nothing to do with them. Or you for that matter. It's important to me.'

'They'll never accept me, not now . . . .'

'Helen understands.'

'Helen, yes. But not the rest of them. They're your family, Charles.'

'You're my family, my duty is to provide for you, and for our children . . . .'

She left the room, slamming the door behind her. Damn you, Helen, why the hell did you have to interfere?

But Helen turned out to be their ally. She rang him at work, told him not to worry. She liked Sophie. She was direct, honest. Helen promised she'd work on Mum and, in the meantime, why didn't he and Sophie come over on Sunday?

All during lunch, Brian made comparisons. Brian had liked Sarah. Sophie saw it, and dealt with it. Charles watched as she regaled them with tales of the antiques trade, gave a comic account of her meeting with Charles in the sale room, exaggerated her awe at discovering who he was. She made them laugh, and all the while she kept an eye on Brian, including him with a glance and a smile, inviting his response, coaxing him into the circle of her admirers. Helen was captivated both by Sophie herself and by the idea of himself and Sophie as a couple; the boys could hardly take their eyes off her. By the end of the day they were all of them, including Brian, won over.

His friends were more wary. Peter was typically cautious, asking if the Trust Fund had been Mrs MacKenzie's idea. Normally this would have thrown him into a rage, now he merely laughed and said he ought to know him better than that. But it wasn't just Peter. As Christmas approached there were various functions he was obliged to attend. It was a thrill to have Sophie at his side, but his colleagues disliked her. Some of them had met Sarah; to them the contrast must have seemed bizarre. Sarah deferred to them, but not Sophie. She challenged them eye to eye, her handshake was firm and commanding. Had they encountered her in a business context, they would have been voluble in their admiration, but meeting her socially they disapproved. The same was true of those who had no direct comparison to make. They saw an inappropriate partner to a man in his position, a pixie of a woman who made no concession to dress, who, while he was constrained by dinner jacket and dickie-bow, flounced in flowing cottons and jangled her bracelets and clicked her earrings so that he overheard one of the other wives whisper to her husband that maybe they were about to have their palms read. Rage made him half turn and scowl in the woman's direction. She had the grace to blush but, before he could speak, Sophie touched his back, her hand fluttering between jacket and shirt, and the scales dropped and he saw how false it all was, this dressing up, this ritualised celebration.

To begin with Sophie treated it as a game, playing it for all it was worth. She made fun of the men and mimicked the wives. They'd lie awake for hours reconstructing and rewriting the evening, laughing till the tears rolled. But then it started to irritate her. Instead of storing away their absurdities for later dissection, she became impatient; her responses, hitherto designed to lure them to even greater foolishness, became sharper. He saw that they viewed her as a freak. Had anyone mentioned palm-reading now, he would have retaliated.

Maybe somebody had said something, though not in his hearing. Something had sent Sophie into a rage. In the car she sat in sullen silence staring out of the window at the black night and the reeling

Christmas drunks. The moment the bedroom door closed, she exploded.

'Who the hell do they think they are?'

'Who?' He was bemused by her vehemence. 'What's been said?'

'Oh, nothing specific. But Christ, Charles, they're so bloody patronising, all of them.' She tugged off her dress and kicked it, along with her shoes, into the far corner. 'You should hear the way they talk about you – all hushed and holy, like I should be honoured to have your name mentioned in my presence. Don't laugh, Charles, it isn't funny.'

'You're exaggerating. You're different, that's all; they don't know how to react.'

Kneeling on the bed she unclipped her bra and hurled it after the dress and shoes. It caught on the arm of the chair, dangling like an abandoned catapult. 'I'll tell you something else. Not one of them has ever asked me anything about myself, not who I am or where I come from or what I do or think. I'm nothing to them but an appendage. . . .'

He laughed. 'Speaking of appendages. . . .' He stepped towards her.

'For God's sake, Charles.' She rummaged her nightshirt from under the pillow and tugged it over her head. 'Now will you take me seriously?'

'I'm sorry.' He turned away. Unfastening his cufflinks, he dropped them into the drawer. 'Just don't rush it, Sophie. Give them time, let them get used to you.'

'Did they need time to get used to Sarah?'

'Sarah was different. There's no comparison.'

'But there is. That's the point. They're making comparisons all the time.'

21

She ripped through his routines like a whirlwind. He couldn't bear being away from home, was desperate for the sound of her voice, for her touch like fire licking his body. The files piled up on his desk. When he could stand it no longer, he sent for the car.

More often than not he'd arrive home to find Sophie was out. Where did she go? Why the hell couldn't she be there when he needed her?

'Don't be so bloody possessive.'

'I'm not, but is it too much to ask that you should be here when I get home?'

'God, you're so Victorian. . . .'

'Sophie!'

'You never come home the same time two days running. What am I supposed to do? Sit by the fire knitting and waiting? That's not my style, you should know that – not unless there's a guillotine in the vicinity.' He wouldn't look at her. 'And you wouldn't have me any other way, right?'

'Right.' All the same, it worried him, this need she had to hold part of herself back. He continued to pester until eventually she gave in. Up to a point. Some of the time she spent with Jazz.

Jazz. He remembered the night she'd threatened to leave him, go and stay with Jazz. She said, 'That's precisely why I didn't tell you. I knew you wouldn't like it. She's a good friend, I've known her years, far longer than I've known you. . . .'

'I know. You don't have to tell me.' He took a breath, tried to be reasonable. 'Why don't you ask her here, introduce us.'

Sophie laughed, and told him it would be a disaster, that they each stood for the things the other most despised.

And that frightened him. It suggested a gulf between them. And gulfs have a habit of widening.

He needed commitment. The fact that she shared his house, his bed, wasn't enough. It was too fragile. A word could smash it. When he demanded to know whether she loved him, she said, 'I'm here, aren't I?' And he wanted to shout – meaning what? Here or gone, in and out like the weather-man and his wife. She loves me . . . she loves me not. I don't know where I stand, I don't trust her, I don't understand her.

Then there was her divorce. Why was nothing moving? She'd come to him in October and now it was December and nothing had happened. She said Michael was dragging his feet, letters went unanswered, his own solicitors were having trouble pinning him down. Charles was due to meet Peter. Perhaps he should call on Leonard, see if anything could be done to speed things up.

What did Leonard make of it all? He and Sophie seemed to get on wonderfully. They were on Christian name terms. On at least one occasion they'd had lunch together.

He decided against seeing Leonard. He went shopping instead. From a jeweller's off Bond Street he bought an antique emerald and diamond ring. Afterwards he browsed for a while, and found himself on Regent Street, outside Hamleys. He went in. The shop was crammed, children surged between the displays waving their finds at harassed mothers; a father distracted his two small sons so their mother could smuggle their Christmas presents to the till. His mother would never have engaged in such subterfuge. Dad might have, given the least encouragement. He made to leave. He had no place here.

He found himself facing a rack stacked with soft toys. In the middle was a huge tawny teddy bear. Carefully dislodging it, he wedged it on his hip and gazed into its amber eyes. It was four feet tall and in one ear wore a yellow tag bearing the name 'Steiff'. It was a handsome bear, and expensive. The perfect counterpoint to the ring. He imagined Christmas morning, handing Sophie first one, then the other. It was irresistible.

The next day he arrived home during the afternoon to find a fir tree had been installed in the corner of his drawing room. It was huge. Its top scraped the plaster cornice and its tiered skirt swooped down, flounce upon flounce, almost brushing the floor. In front of it were two cardboard boxes, their lids tilted to one side, their tissue-paper entrails spilling on to the carpet. In the midst of the mess sat Sophie and Emmy. They were making so much noise they didn't hear him. He said, 'What's all this?' and they jumped like guilty children.

Emmy made to get up. Sophie laid a restraining hand on her arm. To Charles she said, 'You're early. Emmy says you don't usually have a tree.'

'No.'

'Why not?'

Emmy said, 'Maybe it wasn't such a good idea.'

'It's a brilliant idea.' Sophie cocked her head on one side, peering up at him. 'He needs time to get used to it, that's all.' He could think of nothing to say. She shifted her position, tucking her leg more tightly under her. The gold glittered in her eyes; her tousled halo needed a brush. She said, 'My, you are in a bad mood.'

'No.'

'Yes, you are. And since you are, I might as well tell you my other news.'

She's pregnant – the thought sawed through him. He bobbed on to his heels and put his face close to hers. She was still speaking. She said, 'Charles? You haven't heard a word. I said I've invited your mother for Christmas. Helen thinks it's a good idea.'

Disappointment unbalanced him; he rocked to and fro on the balls of his feet. He lowered himself beside her. Emmy left. He leant forward and disentangled a porcelain unicorn from the crumpled tissue paper.

'What d'you think?'

'Very pretty.'

'Your mother, Charles.' She snatched the unicorn from him.

'I think it's a terrible idea. She loves Christmas, it's a great opportunity for a row.'

She leant forward, dropping a skein of golden tinsel round his neck and arranging it carefully against his dark suit. 'It won't be like that. Helen will help. It'll be okay.'

22

He woke early on Christmas morning. He moved about the room pretending to be quiet, but allowed the wardrobe door to bang, and left the bathroom door open in the hope that the machine-gun prattle of the shower would waken her. He dressed, then paced the room, stood over her for a moment, then crossed to the window. He parted the curtains. The square was deserted, unnaturally silent. Sophie slept on. He felt more alone than if she'd been in Cambridge with Michael, or across the river with Jazz.

Wake up, Sophie, please.

He sat on the edge of the bed. The mattress sank beneath him. Sophie stirred and stretched. She was clear-eyed and alert. 'You've been awake all along.'

It was typical of her to torment him like this – lying there smiling and tracing her initials on his knee with her fingernail so that he could not sustain his anger. He caught her hand and kissed her fingers, then fetched the bear from the back of the wardrobe. The gold foil barely disguised it. From the bedside pedestal he took the small, neater package, the ring-box. He insisted she open this first. She was suspicious. She took it warily, glancing sideways at the larger parcel. 'No,' he tapped the little box, 'this first.'

She knew what it was before she snapped back the lid. She stared at it but didn't take it out of the box. She said, 'According to Jazz, when a man gives a woman jewellery it's an act of domination. Acceptance a sign of submission.'

'What do you say?' If she refused to accept it, what would that mean? That they had no future, or that she didn't appreciate his taste in jewellery?

She said, 'I think she's over-politicising. Hogwash, basically.' She gave him a sly smile and slipped on the ring.

When she unwrapped the second parcel she laughed and, holding the bear aloft, said, 'I must remember to ask Jazz about the ruling on the giving and receiving of teddy bears.'

This year Emmy didn't go to her sister's for Christmas. She confided to Sophie that she was grateful for the excuse. Sophie and Charles dressed and went down to the kitchen. Emmy had been up for hours. The turkey fizzed in the oven, the steam from the Christmas pudding condensed on to the walls and dribbled down the tiles to collect in pools along the edges of the worktop.

The sweet smell of the roasting bird mingled with brewing coffee. As they ate toast and Gentleman's Relish, Emmy told how the bear, christened Bertie, had spent the last two weeks on top of her wardrobe. Sophie laughed, and confided that, as a child, she'd had an infallible knack for finding the presents and guessing what they were, however heavy the disguise. She learnt early to feign surprise.

Charles listened. Memories of his own started to surface. He leant forward, elbows on the table, nibbling at a slice of toast, remembering himself and Helen tipping the contents of their stockings onto the pocked fields of their eiderdowns, jewelled piles of tangerines and walnuts and toffees, plus for him a tin train and for her a doll. She wedged the doll astride his train and they took her for a ride round the room. By lunch-time the train was broken. Anthony had 'accidentally' trodden on it, crushing the little tender, creasing the paintwork and bending the wheels.

Emmy said, 'Look at the time. We ought to get on.' She set him to peeling the potatoes and parsnips. They worked in silence, Emmy making bread sauce, Sophie brandy butter. Emmy switched on the radio. They joined in the carols and Sophie confessed her favourite to be 'We Three Kings' – only not all of it, just the second verse. She demonstrated, her voice low and sepulchral at the part about 'sorrowing, sighing, bleeding, dying, sealed in a stone cold tomb. . . .'

The door bell rang. Emmy switched off the radio. Charles tossed the potato peeler into the bowl. Sophie said, 'They're here, then.'

She unfastened her apron. 'Emmy, let them in and give them some sherry. I'll be up in a minute.'

She draped her apron over the back of the chair and, turning to him, straightened his tie and smoothed down his shirt. She said, 'Agreed?' He covered her hands, pressing them against the lift of his chest. 'I'll go up, you give me a few minutes alone with them, okay?'

'I'm not sure. . . .'

'We agreed.'

'I think we should do it together.'

'No.' She pulled away. 'It'll look as if you're escorting me. I've got to welcome them in my own right.'

He let her go. As she reached the top of the stairs Emmy came out of the drawing room saying, 'They're all here now. Helen and the others arrived as I was letting them in.'

'Right.' She heard the breathlessness in her voice. She was afraid. A moment ago she'd been so sure of herself, certain she could carry it off, maybe even heal some rifts.

Emmy said, 'She quizzed me about you.'

'What did you say?'

Emmy assumed a mock-serious expression. Gripping the sides of her skirt, she bobbed a curtsey. 'Mistress'll be here directly, ma'am.'

Emmy left. Sophie heard the kitchen door bang, the faint rumble of Charles's voice. She questioned the vanity that had prompted her to take this on. Life was complicated enough without such George and the dragon confrontations.

The marble floor chilled her feet. Charles had suggested she wear shoes to meet his mother, but she'd said no, no concessions.

She stopped in front of the gilt-framed mirror. Behind the ormolu clock the smoky antique plate held captive the image of a small woman in a loose-fitting black cotton top. The fringe of the matching skirt tickled her bare ankles.

From the drawing room came the sound of hushed voices, the chink of decanter against glass. They were making free with Charles's hospitality.

The woman in the mirror shrugged. The black top slithered sideways to expose her pale shoulder. His mother would disapprove. She smiled, and made the necessary adjustment. The emerald on her finger gleamed reassuringly in the depths of the mirror. The captive woman smiled at her; Sophie grinned back and, ruffling her curls, opened the door.

The drawing room seemed crowded, and very bright after the dimness of the hall. She blinked. Her voice rang unnaturally loud in the sudden silence that greeted her. 'Hello,' she said. 'Merry Christmas, everyone. Charles will be here directly. Helen, how are you?'

And Charles's mother said, 'You're not what I expected.'

'That's exactly what I said.' Helen laughed. She took Sophie's arm. 'This is Anthony,' she said. 'And Susan.'

Everything Charles had said about his brother had fed her curiosity. That curiosity was, if anything, intensified by their meeting. She looked up into a face older than Charles's, and both like and unlike him. He was of about the same height and build as Charles, yet somehow faded. His eyes were less dark, his hair more grey. Even his features, though sculpted on the same model, were smudged and ill-defined. The most obvious difference was that he lacked his brother's presence, the innate authority which, according to Helen, had contributed to Charles's success rather than arisen from it.

She said, 'It's good to meet you at last.' She smiled. He scowled. She hadn't expected his hostility to be quite so blatant.

Helen said, 'I love the trimmings, Sophie. I've never seen this room look so pretty. Don't you think so, Mum?'

'Very festive.'

'And the holly berries – and that's bay, isn't it? Emmy let you cut her bay tree?'

'I think it's all rather overdone.' All eyes turned to Mrs Wade. 'Showy. I can't think what possessed Charles to let you bring half of Epping Forest into the house.'

'Easy,' said Charles from the doorway. 'She didn't consult me.'

'Anyway,' murmured Sophie with feigned innocence, 'isn't Epping Forest deciduous?'

Halfway through the first course, Sophie admitted she'd made the most terrible mistake. The meal was degenerating into a chimps' tea party.

They had decided that putting her at one end of the long table, Charles at the other, would make a point about joint authority. Stupid idea. At least she'd had the foresight to keep Helen by her.

Sophie took a mouthful of salmon terrine. It was perfect. She'd made it the day before yesterday so the flavours of the brandy and the fish could blend and mature. Charles's mother did not appreciate this subtlety. She poked at the fish suspiciously, and shifted the garnish round the plate to give the impression that she was eating.

'Don't you like it, Mrs Wade?' She used what Charles laughingly called her business voice. She felt the amused flicker of his eyes, but refused to meet them.

'I don't see the point,' said his mother, 'in messing up perfectly good food. Pay all that money for salmon, then mix it up so's you don't know what you're eating. . . .'

'Fresh salmon, smoked salmon, butter, brandy and wine.' She recited the litany with a smile.

Ben said, 'Why don't you make stuff like this, Mum?'

'Too much like hard work. It's lovely, Sophie.'

Charles replenished Susan's wine glass, saying to Helen as he did so, 'Has Sophie told you we're going to revamp the whole house in the New Year?'

'About time.' She laughed. 'You should start with his bedroom. . . .'

'I know – it's like sleeping in an hotel room.'

'You seem very much at home in my son's house, Mrs MacKenzie.' His mother abandoned the salmon and pushed her plate away.

'I live here.' Sophie gave her sweetest smile. 'It's my home now.'

'Probably is,' sneered Anthony. 'He's probably signed over the deeds along with everything else.'

After lunch came present-opening. Sophie sat cross-legged under the tree handing round the parcels. Helen loved the bisque figures – a shepherd and shepherdess – and Charles's mother hated her shawl. She held it up. It was made of cream silk embroidered with apricot-coloured flowers. Helen exclaimed, 'Oh Mum, it's lovely. Try it on.'

Mrs Wade fingered the shawl. The silk slithered through her

fingers and her face contorted with distaste as she said, 'It's second-hand.'

'Antiques frequently are,' murmured Charles.

To her chagrin, Sophie found herself on the brink of tears. She was furious. She'd gone to a lot of trouble finding gifts for them, and had been particularly pleased with the shawl. She stood up. Placing herself in front of Mrs Wade she took the shawl from her. She said, 'If you don't like it, let's give it to someone who does. Here, Helen,' she held it out, shaking it so the fringe shimmied in the firelight, 'take it.' To Charles's mother she said, 'I promised Charles this wouldn't happen, I didn't believe you were so selfish as to want to spoil our first Christmas together. I would like you to leave now.'

'How dare you.' The old lady's back became rigid. She turned to Charles. 'Are you going to allow her to talk to me like this?'

Sophie heard a movement behind her, felt the pressure of Charles's hand in the small of her back. He said, 'I'll get Emmy to fetch your coat.'

His mother left, and Anthony and Susan went with her. The swiftness of their departure left a lingering unease. It wasn't very charitable to kick your own mother out of the house on Christmas Day. On the other hand, she'd been abominably rude to Sophie. Helen said, 'Don't make such a fuss, it's traditional to have a row at Christmas – except it's usually you that goes off in a huff.'

He laughed, and realised he was happy. With his mother and Anthony out of the way suddenly they all felt free to enjoy themselves. The boys and Sophie played cards, sitting in a circle on the floor with Brian and Helen and Charles leaning over them, offering advice. Emmy brought the tea and Charles went round the room switching on the lights and drawing curtains. As he shovelled more coal on the fire, Sophie looked up from a hopeless hand and said with a grin, 'Chestnuts!'

Emmy and Sophie and Helen piled the chestnuts onto the shovel and wedged it in the fire. Soon they were rummaging under chairs and tables, trying to recover the exploding nuts, and Charles laughed at the sight of the women sprawled under his furniture, pouncing on their victims with cries of 'Got you!' and 'Here's another one.'

'D'you remember when we were little?' said Helen as Charles handed her the chestnut he'd just peeled.

'Don't I just. The rows, and after lunch having to be quiet so as not to waken Gran. Then more rows after tea.'

'Being careful how we opened the presents, folding the paper so it could be used again, and the endless lists of who gave what to whom.'

'Then all day Boxing Day writing thank-you letters. . . .'

'Stop! Stop! My heart bleeds for you,' Sophie exclaimed.

'Easy for you to mock, times were hard when we were young, isn't that so, Helen?'

'Ah, and to escape the hardships you became a property speculator – the ideal antidote,' Sophie teased him, and her eyes sparkled in the firelight and he was struck by how readily, with his mother gone, they'd metamorphosed into a family. Leaning forward he rested his hand on the back of her neck. She smiled at him, and he kissed her. Then Steve tugged at her sleeve to bring her back to the card game, and Charles remembered Helen saying that both her sons were more than a little in love with Sophie. And it didn't matter; they were a family, of course they loved one another. If only he hadn't wasted so much time chasing meaningless goals, he might have had this years ago. If only he'd had the sense to pause in his helter-skelter progress through life.

23

The memory of Christmas lingered like that of a fine meal. He was replete. Content. And he failed to notice when things started to go wrong. At some point it began to drift. It was as if he'd gone to sleep in harbour, and woken alone in an open boat.

There was nothing overtly wrong. Sophie was preoccupied with refurbishing the house. She supervised the work on their bedroom and the dining room, made plans for an assault on the drawing room, and day after day came home laden with wallpaper books and fabric samples. The drawer of the buhl desk in the corner of the drawing room was crammed with business cards of designers and dealers, purveyors of the ornamental for the homes of the elite. She tried to involve him, drew sketches, demanded his opinion on the shade of this fabric, the drape of that – although if he did give an opinion, more often than not she'd shake her head and smile as if to say that only he would think such a thing.

At least she was at home more often. He'd arrive to find the house buzzing with the voices of workmen, the rattling tinny tones of their radio, and Sophie standing, hands on hips, persuading them to approach the task her way, not according to the rules of their trade. Again and again her teasing laughter softened the edge of her determination, and she got her way.

She was absorbed in her work, but it didn't seem to make her happy. It gave her pleasure – colours and textures excited her, she loved to run the fabric between her fingers to test its weight and pliability – but it was a short-lived, sensual pleasure, not real happiness.

The bedroom was finished first. Apart from the addition of a tub-chair and a dressing table, the furniture remained the same, yet the whole ambience was altered by the new decor. His old, lumpy furniture, now set against the flamboyantly patterned yellow and cream wallpaper, glowed as if permanently glazed with sunshine.

It was the end of March when they moved back into the room. A week or so later he woke with a start. Something was wrong. He was alone in the bed. He could hear the faint tap of the clock. The darkness was impenetrable. He was blind. He had to fight the sudden rasp of his breath, force himself to be calm. There was a movement. He rolled over. The room wasn't totally dark after all. Silhouetted in black against the almost-black of the window, a figure was hunched in the chair. From deep inside him came the sound of whimpering. The figure moaned – and he knew what was wrong.

He went over to her. Her arms were clenched round Bertie as she rocked back and forth to ease the pain.

She'd never told him the exact day on which their baby had died, but he knew it was about this time of year. Last year. He held her and they rocked together, sharing the grief. Beneath the sharpness of loss he sensed how, with the passing of time, his relationship with the dead child had altered. From its position at the periphery of his life – its death no more than the route by which Sophie found her way back to him – it had moved steadily towards the centre. As it did so, it lost its anonymity, acquiring both a personality and a gender. This child that had died before he'd known of its existence – his son, concrete proof of their love, the visible token for which he ached and ached and ached.

What would he have been like, their son? The questions raced and jumbled and the answers tumbled and changed, certainty and contradiction wrapping each other round, sharpening the focus. Questions not answers give meaning to life. A child, a son – would he have embodied their differences, or cemented their similarities? And why did he feel like this now, after so long? Why had the vague longings of the past months suddenly crystallised into a craving which had all the intense physicality of sexual desire?

As he rocked her like a baby, the enigma of a directionless, powerless Sophie, he wondered where he went from here. To tell her of his need was more than he dared. He couldn't bear the thought of stirring up all that pain. Yet, could he go back to the waiting, the hoping – almost praying, had he still been capable of prayer – that she might take matters into her own hands and present him with a fait accompli?

He could only wait, and hope that one day she'd whisper the news he hungered to hear. But she didn't. His debate turned inwards. The arguing voices ricochetted off the corridors of his mind and one voice rang louder than the rest, demanding to know if he really wanted a child. Wasn't this just another ruse for tying her more tightly to him?

Daily she moved further from him. Less and less of her truly belonged to him. He had to share her – with Jazz, whom he'd never met; with his own sister, and with Emmy. Would a child bind her closer, or exclude him further?

He had deluded himself. It was his son, the child that had died, that mattered. There was no guarantee that what he felt for him would have any relevance to future children. The world was unreliable, human nature too variable. No child was assured of a welcome.

By mid-May the dining room was all but finished. Charles arrived home one evening just as the decorators were packing away. Unusually, Sophie was out.

When the workmen had gone, he went into the dining room to sneak a look. The furniture had been moved into the hall, the carpet taken up and the floor swathed in buff drugget. Nevertheless, he had a strong sense of how the room was going to look. Maroon silk tented the ceiling and draped the borders of the pale gold walls. He knew the carpet and curtains were to be the same colour as the tenting. The effect would be voluptuous. He turned slowly on his heel, imagining his golden mahogany furniture glowing against the walls. It was a fine line, but he thought the effect would be stunning rather than vulgar. Sophie had a startling eye for colour; a fine sense of the dramatic.

As he left the room, sliding the door carefully over the drugget, the telephone began to ring. He answered it in his study. It was Gregory Barlow of the Pentangle Gallery. He wanted to discuss Mrs MacKenzie's offer for the chandelier. Was that Mr MacKenzie?

'No.'

'Could you tell her I rang?'

He banged down the receiver and dropped into the creaking leather chair. He knew Gregory Barlow by sight – he was Sarah's boss – but had never spoken to him. How could Sophie have done that? She had all London to trawl if she needed chandeliers, but oh no, she had to go there, indulge her curiosity regardless of the pain she might cause.

But maybe Sarah doesn't care about me any more. Probably she's seeing someone else and no longer thinks of me. Even so, it must have been disturbing for her to have Sophie turn up out of the blue. Damn you, Sophie, you had no right. It was all too easy to imagine it. Sarah nervous, wondering what she should say.

Sophie bright and confident, exploring the shop like an inquisitive monkey hunting for fleas. He could see her, hear the tone of her enquiry as she demanded the price of this and the origin of that. Poor Sarah.

He heard a key in the lock. Opening his study door he called to her, 'Sophie, come in here a minute, would you?' In just such a tone he'd have summoned an employee for a dressing-down.

Sophie didn't seem to notice. She slipped off her shoes and came towards him, her curls bouncing, a wide grin splitting her face. 'Hello. I'm late, I know. Have you been home long?'

Following him into the study she closed the door and leant against it. The gold of her eyes glittered against the grey. He said, 'You've been to see Sarah.'

'Ah.' The gold faded. The grin was downgraded to a smile. 'How did you find out? Did she ring to complain?'

'Barlow rang. Something about a chandelier.'

'It's for the dining room, it's perfect – just what I'd been looking for.'

'Did you have to buy it from there?'

'It was too good to resist. If I'd known you wanted me to boycott the place, I'd have got Jazz to go in.'

'Did she know it was you? Sarah – did she know?' Sophie shrugged. She thought it was funny – what was wrong with her? Couldn't she see how angry he was? He took a step towards her. 'Sophie,' he warned, and her lips twitched with laughter. His anger broke and he grabbed her by the arm, shouting, 'It's not bloody funny, Sophie. You can't do things like that. You don't give a shit about other people's feelings, do you?' He gave her a vicious shake. She winced. 'Nothing to say? Go on, tell me I'm being unreasonable.'

'You know you are. What's the problem? You want to know if she's pining away for love of you, is that it?' He tightened his grip. 'Let go, Charles. You're hurting me.'

'Did she know who you were?' She tried to prise his fingers apart but he only gripped her harder, reddening and bruising her arms as he pressed her back against the door. 'Did she know you?'

She stopped struggling. Tilting her head back against the panelling, she met his eye and said, 'Not at once. Though she cottoned

233

on when I gave the address, and she was two digits ahead of me all the way through the telephone number.'

'Bitch,' he hissed, releasing her. All his strength left him. His breath also.

She said, 'It's no big deal, Charles. She wasn't that upset.'

He turned his back on her. He had a headache.

'Charles!'

He didn't answer. He couldn't.

'Oh for God's sake.'

She slammed the door behind her. He felt dizzy. Pressing his fingers into his eyes, he rubbed them until they ached. Coloured stars gyrated and burned against his lids. When he opened them he thought he'd misunderstood, that she was still in the room. But no. Not her, not the real Sophie, the other one. The priestess was back, the woman in white with the halo of fire, the one that mocked and tormented him from the inside.

He'd forgotten how fond of Sarah he was. It was her afternoon off and she opened the door dressed in her silk kimono, her hair twisted up in a towelled turban. He felt a rush of tenderness. It seemed so absolutely right that he should be here.

She hesitated for a moment before stepping back and letting him in. He followed her through to the living room. Nothing had changed: the flat was still crammed full of Art Deco; the lady with the two Salukis still looked down her nose at the plaster Pierrot.

She said, 'I was thinking about you. . . .'

'You don't mind my calling like this?' The day was sultry hot. She slid her fingers under the collar of her wrap, easing it away from her sticky skin. He felt a tingle of excitement. He hadn't expected this. To see her, tell her he was sorry for what Sophie had done, make sure she was all right – these were his flimsy reasons for coming here. He said, 'It's been so long, hasn't it.' Then forced a smile. 'Corny as red roses, right?' She nodded. 'How have you been?' She lifted her shoulder in a half-hearted shrug. He took a step towards her, and whispered her name.

She stepped back. There was an hysterical edge to her voice as she said, 'Fine, I've been fine.' Then, with an effort, 'What about you? You look well. Younger.' She edged backwards towards the bedroom door. 'I was in the shower,' she explained, 'when you rang the bell. I'll get dressed. Get yourself a drink.'

He started towards the drinks cupboard. Then noticed she'd left the bedroom door ajar. He followed her. Her bedroom was also as he remembered it, the walls a cool peppermint green, the silk coverlet matching the deep pile of the carpet. She had her back to him. She'd flicked her long hair forward over her shoulder to dry the ends. He could see the full length of her downy nape. He moved closer, and brushed the delicate sweep with the tips of his fingers. She lifted her head, and the damp tangle of hair slithered down over his hand. Without turning she said, 'I met your Sophie yesterday.'

'I know. She shouldn't have done that. I'm sorry.'

'I thought that was why you were here.' She resumed drying her hair. 'It's all right,' she said, her voice muffled by the towel. 'I know how she felt. I'd have done the same. Well, no.' Her head jerked up as she forced herself to be honest. 'No, I wouldn't. I'm not that brave. I've been curious too, you know. But I didn't dare do anything about it. I'm glad she came, I'm glad I've seen her.'

Her frankness left him breathless. She confronted him, looking into his face. He was surprised by her sudden confidence as she touched him, laughing as she stroked his cheek. In a bemused whisper he said, 'I've missed you.' And at that moment it seemed an overwhelming truth, that the last months had been shot through with a sense of her absence.

'I've missed you too.' She was close now. He could feel the warmth emanating from her, could smell the shampoo on her hair. He was acutely aware of the movement of her body beneath the thin fabric of her wrap. His own body's responding kick stunned him. He gathered a handful of her hair. It was damp against his palm, cool when he pressed it to his face. She was even closer now, but the move had been hers, not his. She didn't stop him when he untied the sash of her kimono. It was only as he began to pull at his tie and unbutton his shirt that she clutched at his hands, saying, 'Are you sure, Charles? You must be sure . . .' and he said, 'I'm sure.' And clutched her against him so that she could feel just how sure he was, and then they were sinking back onto the bed and thought was condensed into pure sensation as he put into practice all that he'd learnt of this art over the past months. He saw and understood her responses as he drove her on ahead of him, leaping from rock to rock towards the peak, so that she arrived ahead of him. He withdrew and hung suspended over her and she, perhaps remembering the last time, whispered, 'What is it? What's happened?'

And he laughed and said, 'Nothing. It's all right. Relax.' And she did, and they began the climb all over again.

24

While Charles was with Sarah, Sophie was shopping. The intention was to look for something to wear at Helen's birthday party, but her mind wandered, and so did she. Without knowing how, she found herself standing outside the Pentangle Gallery.

The chandelier still occupied the prime spot in the window; its facetted drops glinted like water splashing in sunlight. A red 'Sold' label dangled from a sweeping branch. She'd been right to buy it, it would be perfect for her wonderful, over-the-top dining room.

Why did Charles have to be so bloody unreasonable? The way he was carrying on, anyone would think he still cared for the woman.

After their row last night she'd stormed up to her little sitting room and sat hunched and fuming, watching the summer dusk turn from honey to treacle. Leaning out of the window she tried to catch a whisper of air, but there wasn't a murmur of movement. She remembered the owls that had haunted her Cambridge garden, and the night one of them had come to perch on her open casement. She felt a tug of longing – not for the cottage or for Michael, but for lost innocence. How could she have got it so wrong? Her intentions had been good, she'd cast herself as

Charles's saviour but had forgotten how alike they were. If he was flawed, then so was she.

The flesh is nothing. That had been her battle cry, but it was an assertion of defiance, not conviction. Her need for him scraped away inside her, weakening her. Shame and defeat scorched her from the inside. Hot tears stretched the skin of her cheeks and dried unwiped. She leant on the still, her head cradled in her arms, listening to the sluggish sounds of the overheated city.

She woke to a stiff neck and a sky white with incandescent heat. Lifting her head, she inhaled the thick air. There was something explosive about the city this morning, as if it had held its breath too long, as if at any minute its pent-up energies might burst and rip and submerge buildings and people in a bloody morass.

They'd taken to having breakfast on the terrace. Charles was already there, a caricature of a husband, coffee at his elbow, his head buried in his newspaper. He barely looked up as she sat down. When she offered him more coffee he responded with a grunt and a shrug. She wanted to scream at him, pour hot coffee in his lap, anything to flush out this self-righteous anger. How dare he treat her like this. All she'd done was buy a chandelier, a cascade of tingling glass, a bauble – it didn't warrant such fuss.

Standing outside the gallery, she wondered if she should tell them she'd changed her mind. Would that satisfy him? She doubted it. It was as if he wanted to be angry with her, was looking for something to justify an outbreak of temper. Of violence. She rubbed her arm. The bruise had formed quickly, grown darker and uglier overnight.

She turned away. The weather was unbearable. The malevolent sun clamped its steel hand hard down on the city, making it scream. The burnt air conducted every sound, the grinding of gears and the turning of engines, the rumbling, clicking, scraping sounds of city life. The fumes hung like gas in the trenches, poisoning, corrupting, distorting.

She should have stayed at home. Compared to the scorching streets and scalding stone of the buildings, the house in Beaufort Square was cool as a cave. But that didn't fool her. The house was hostile. Its sheer passivity threatened to absorb her, suck her into its fabric, subvert her, lose her, destroy her individuality. She would not allow herself to be reconstructed, gutted, rebuilt and refashioned into a more appropriate vessel for Charles's affections.

No more. It was no good brooding. She could go and see Jazz, except that Jazz was rabidly anti-Charles, refusing to let the fact that she'd not met him modify her opinion. 'I know the type,' she said. 'Only interested in possession. Wants to own you, like a bit of land or a building. Get out, Sophie, while you still can.'

Is that really what I am to him, a site for redevelopment?

She halted outside a dress shop, examining the faint echo of her reflection in the window. Then, slowly, her focus shifted and she was looking down at a display of summer dresses, their skirts flared out across the floor, their bodices stuffed with scrunched-up tissue paper. The smaller window on the other side of the door contained an emerald-green suit primly fitted on to a tailor's dummy. In that dummy she glimpsed her refurbished self.

She went in. The shop door swung to behind her. A holy hush filled the lavender-scented space. Two female attendants and a small, balding man in a suit lined up to greet her. The man paused, giving her a sense of being assessed, then motioned the most junior attendant to step forward. Her voice, as she asked if she could help, betrayed reluctance and doubt. Suddenly Sophie saw herself through their eyes: an unremarkable woman dressed in cheap hippie-cum-gipsy cottons, unlikely to be able to afford their in-flated prices.

She asked to try on the emerald suit.

The changing room was unnecessarily large. It had a deep pile carpet and pink floral curtains and a small gilded chair with a red plush seat. A mirror took up all one wall. She undressed with her back to it, then slowly pulled on the tight linen skirt with its slithery satin lining. Next the jacket. It was short, with military-style epau-lettes and brass buttons. Only when these were fastened did she turn to confront her image.

Terrifying how easy the transformation had been. Both colour and style suited her, though the effect would have been enhanced had her hair still been short. She moved closer to the mirror. The lining rustled, the skirt gripped her thighs, shortening her steps.

Is this it? she demanded of the absent Charles. Is this what you want?

To the ill-disguised surprise of the shop assistant, she bought the suit and a blouse to go with it. At the next shop she added a pair of court shoes and a handbag to her haul. Then she went in search of a cup of coffee.

She chose the café because it was the antithesis of the dress shop and everything Charles stood for. It was old-fashioned and drab. The varnished wood counter was topped by a glass cabinet displaying a selection of sandwiches and sausage rolls and some sad-looking buns with a tired crust of pink icing. She bought a cup of milky coffee and carried it to a table near the back. The coffee was disgusting. She eyed the packages on the chair facing her and tried to imagine Charles's reaction to the glossy monogrammed bags with their smart fold-over tops and crimson cord handles. Was this all it took to fit in to his world, a new outfit and a pair of patent leather shoes?

His friends would approve – Peter Knight and his drabby little wife. What did she have in common with people like that?

I'm not used to it, Charles – she pushed the coffee cup away – being relegated to the second division like this.

She straightened her back. She'd been coasting for far too long. It was time to take control, make a decision. Quickly, too. Things were changing fast. She pressed her hand against her stomach. Stupid to buy a tight skirt she'd hardly have a chance to wear. She was going to have to pay for that monumental weakness of hers, was going to have to tell Charles that she was pregnant. Either that or make the decision not to tell him, and to leave.

25

As soon as was reasonable, Charles made his escape from Sarah's flat. Hands dug deep into his pockets, jacket looped through his arm, he ploughed through the thick summer heat to the end of the street and hailed a cab.

Betty was startled to see him in his shirtsleeves but by the time she brought him his letters to sign, he was back behind the barrier of his desk with his jacket on and his skin chafing at the weight and the heat of it.

He stared down at letters he'd dictated only this morning. Nothing about them was familiar. Even the flourish of his signature seemed to belong to someone else.

He was a man displaced.

But he had displaced himself. No one had forced him to go to Sarah, and having gone, he could have said no. He'd lain back against her lace-edged pillows, breathless from exertion, and she'd pressed her radiating body against him and he'd felt her hot breath on his neck. When she reached for his hand and knotted her fingers with his, he'd had to fight the impulse to pull away.

The air was close and every breath was a conscious effort. The sulphurous heat gathered in the curtained room, fermenting like yeast in a vat. Sarah's cloying body moved against him. Shyly stroking his chest, she leant over him. Strands of her hair clung stickily to his skin.

He couldn't bear it. He had to get away. He sat up. She released him. He could feel her watching him as he pulled on his shirt. The cotton dragged against his damp skin, the tight collar scraped his neck. Why didn't she say something – ask him to stay, or demand an explanation? Didn't she want to know why he'd let it happen? Or was she afraid of the answer – that what had happened stemmed not from any residual feelings for her, but from his anger with Sophie?

And now he was going back to Sophie, to try to find a way of bridging the rift which, day by day, widened between them.

How?

He put his signature to the last of the letters and tossed the file into the tray. All very well to say, I did these things, said these things, I was wrong, I'm sorry; but he knew Sophie, she wouldn't let him off so lightly. He'd done too much, gone too far. For the first time he questioned whether he'd be able to find his way back.

When he got home Emmy told him that Sophie was out on the

terrace. He wasn't ready to face her. He went upstairs. He'd intended to take a shower, but changed his mind and ran a bath. He relished the discomfort as he lowered his hot body into the scalding water. He hadn't bothered to open the window and the steam combined suffocatingly with the lingering heat of the day to make him feel mildly sick and dizzy.

He closed his eyes and lay back in the water. The hard rim of the bath dug into the back of his neck. He had two choices. Pretend to innocence, or confess.

'*Another*,' said the voice inside his head. '*Another choice.*'

He opened his eyes. Blurred by the glare from the window and the wreathing steam, the Priestess watched him.

'What other?' he whispered. She laughed. The late sun drenched her robe with blood. He looked away. The water was stained also, a redness flowed from the gashes in his wrists – such a quantity of blood, flowing and dispersing through the water, swirling, writhing, sinking. . . . Is blood heavier than water, will it sink; when I've none left inside me, will I float?

No!

He sat bolt upright, shaking his head and his arms, and the water – pure, unbloodied water – sprayed and showered against the tiles; his hands shook as he pressed them to his face to blot it out, the sight of the blood in the bath and on the Priestess's robe.

What was happening to him? What he'd done today, it wasn't so very terrible. Everybody did it. Most people. But it was new to him, he needed to adjust.

No. Not that simple, not for him. He had to tell her. If he didn't, she'd find out. She was like that. You couldn't keep secrets from Sophie.

The balm of confession. He'd tell her, she'd forgive him. That would be the end of it.

He rotated the soap viciously against his palms, working up a good thick lather which he transferred to his arms, rubbing it into the curling black hair as he tried to scour away the invisible mark of betrayal. Finally he heaved himself out of the bath and went through to the bedroom. After the steamy closeness of the bathroom the air was almost cool. His raw skin tightened as it dried.

From the chair by the window, Bertie squinted at him. In a

moment of irritation he flicked the corner of the towel at the bear, knocking it to the floor.

Entering the drawing room, he heard voices and laughter coming from the terrace. He paused just inside the French widows. Emmy and Sophie were laying the table for an al fresco dinner. The silver cutlery shone surgically against the swathe of white damask. At either end tapering pink candles had been fixed into bronze sphinx candleholders that he couldn't recall having seen before. He heard Sophie say, 'Call him, Emmy. Tell him to hurry.' Striking a match, she applied it gently to the virgin wicks.

He waited until she'd finished and was shaking out the match, then stepped out onto the terrace. She heard him, and looked up, smiling.

The hair on his nape prickled. Reverse alchemy, gold to base metal. The fire of her greeting vanished. He felt the sting of the adulterer's brand.

She moved. Her black skirt trailed and caught against the tablecloth. Her devil's curls tumbled across her shoulders.

He held her chair for her. She sat with her back to the garden. He took his place facing her. Emmy brought the first course, a chilled soup which he barely tasted.

Their spoons chinked lightly against their bowls.

Dusk fell. Just beyond her shoulder a cloud of gnats gathered.

He told her about his day – his morning – trying to recapture normality as he described a conversation he'd had with Peter, and passed on Abigail's best wishes.

She gave no sign that she heard him. She was so far away that, had he shouted, she might just have noticed a slight displacement of air, might have thought a gnat had flown too close. He imagined her brushing away his words with a dismissive flick of her hand.

It was no surprise to Sophie when Charles refused dessert and took his coffee in the study. She made no comment, barely looked at him as he tossed his napkin on to the table. She let him go, then pinched out the candles, watching as the grey wisps of smoke trailed upwards from the charred wicks, smudging the darkness before merging with it.

Only hours ago she'd thought the matter settled. She'd come

home and taken her purchases into the yellow bedroom. Suddenly secrecy had seemed very important. She'd hung the suit in the wardrobe and stuffed the handbag and shoes behind the spare blanket. Only when the door was firmly fastened did she feel safe. She lay on the bed and gazed up at the clouds of milk-vat muslin sweeping up to the half-tester rails. She came to a decision. She would stay. For the baby's sake.

But what if it goes wrong? What if the baby dies?

It won't. No reason why it should. What happened before was a chance in a million, everyone had said so.

It was decided then, she would tell him over dinner.

Except that the moment she saw him she knew something was badly wrong. Quite what had alerted her she couldn't be sure – something about the excessively casual way that he stood framed by the French windows, a wariness, a reluctance to meet her eye.

And when he did meet her eye, she knew. It was so sudden, so absolutely certain, as if he'd confessed out loud, that he'd been with Sarah.

All through dinner he prattled about nothing and she didn't, couldn't hear him. She set herself to understand what had happened, trying to persuade herself that if it was so, it had been Sarah's doing. Charles would never willingly betray her.

Nonsense. She'd seen Sarah, seen how weak she was, lacking in fire. The truth sat facing her, etched against the summer night. He had sought her out, whether from pity or anger didn't matter, and having found her, he'd stayed.

Because of this, all her choices were plunged back into a melting pot white-hot with indignation, jealousy and hurt. Her eyes ached with unshed tears. Something in the night, a scent released by heat, caught in her throat like incense, reminding her of Jazz – she even heard her voice hissing across the garden, 'Get out, Sophie. Go now. Leave the bastard.'

26

Safe in his study, Charles stared into the buttery puddle of light thrown by the desklamp onto the blotter. Stalking beneath this unlikely spotlight, the events of the day displayed themselves in chilling detail. What had possessed him? All his life he'd prided himself on his self-control, the elevation of reason, the suppression of passion, and now that stood for nothing, demolished by an act of primitive betrayal.

And she knew, of course she did, without his ever having to tell her. She knew it as surely as if she'd been there, a demon sprite perched on the bed-end, watching and chuckling as they damned their souls. And what was she doing now? Hugging that knowledge to her? Honing it like a weapon, the skilled assassin judging the moment to strike.

If only she'd come in, confront him, allow him to explain. 'I didn't mean it to happen . . . it was an accident.'

Accident? He accidentally found himself at Sarah's flat, in Sarah's bed?

'Well, not an accident exactly, but a mistake.'

It had been that, all right.

He switched off the light. His private film-show didn't cease, it carried on and on inside his head, and all the time, with another part of his mind, he listened to the sounds of the house, waiting for her step in the hall, the knock on his door that never came.

When he went down to breakfast she was already there, feeding croissant crumbs to the sparrows. She greeted him with a glance. He sat down. She offered him coffee. As she reached for the coffee pot her sleeve rode up to reveal a cluster of mustard-coloured bruises.

Question and answer flew simultaneously into his mind: who did that? I did that.

She stirred then sipped her coffee. She started to go through her post. One of the envelopes was thick and crisp and white. He thought it might be from Bernstein's. He ached to know what was happening, how much longer this divorce was going to take. But he no longer had a right to that information. He choked the question down with a gulp of hot coffee, and crumbled his croissant. She read without comment, then folded the letter and slipped it back in its envelope. Only then did she look at him. She said, 'Shouldn't you be going? You don't want to be late for work.'

'I've not much on this morning. I thought we could spend some time together.' The calm grey eyes considered him. Only the tiniest flicker of a crease between her brows betrayed her. He said, 'We need to talk.'

She laid the envelope on the table and smoothed down its flap with the flat of her hand. 'About what?'

His mouth was dry, as if full of hot sand. He forced himself to speak. 'About the other day. About yesterday.' Swinging her bare foot, scuffing her toes against the paving, she waited. 'I'm sorry. Sophie, I'm so sorry. It got out of hand, went too far . . . . It was a mistake. I love you.'

'A mistake.'

'Yes.'

'I see.'

'Do you?' He couldn't keep the hope out of his voice, the absurd hope that this might be all there was to it: it was a mistake, I'm sorry, forgive me.

'Why did it happen, this mistake?'

No, he should have known she'd never let it rest. He said, 'Because I was angry, I suppose.'

'Angry?' She picked up the envelope and her fingers clenched against the stiff white paper. 'Well, that explains everything. That's your standard response to anger, is it?'

'Sophie, please . . . .'

'Please what? I don't know what you're trying to tell me. You

245

think you can brush it off just like that. You put on that helpless, bemused look and say it was all a mistake and I'm supposed to . . . what? Smile sweetly, say yes, of course, I understand. In your position any man would do the same. The woman he's supposed to love makes an ill-judged purchase and sure, naturally the first thing he does is go fuck an old flame.'

'Don't. Don't say that.' He hated it when she used language like that, it made him shake inside. It didn't help that she was justified, he deserved her contempt. He'd been a fool, she'd given him so much, more than he'd any right to expect, and he'd thrown the better part of it away in a fit of temper. Now all he wanted was to grab her and bundle her upstairs and lock her in some back room so that he could be sure of her forever.

She stood up. The ridiculous fear jumped into his mind that she'd managed to tap into his thoughts.

Tapping the envelope against her palm, she hesitated, as if she had something else to say, then thought better of it and made to leave. He moved to block her way. She stood perfectly still, waiting for him to move. He stayed where he was, his weight concentrating itself, pushing down to the soles of his feet, welding him to the paving.

And then he heard her sigh, felt the touch of her hand and his own hand flick in a flinch as the gold light of irony arrowed across her eyes. 'What a pair we are,' she said. 'Look at us. And I'm no better than you, I can't live according to what I preach any more than you can. We're flawed, Charles, both of us and in the same way. The Temple is all, the flesh is nothing. Remember? God, I'd almost forgotten.'

He nodded. His throat was so tight that even had he been able to think of anything to say, he'd have been unable to utter it. As it was, her words took him back to Cambridge, to the room behind her shop and the dusty chaise and the cobwebs and the ache of desire and the dizzying fear that he would lose her.

She said, 'If it's true, about the Temple, then it doesn't matter, does it – about her and you? I've been so blind – but it's all right, I understand. What you and she did happened on the outside, it's not even skin-deep.'

27

Wales was Peter's idea. Charles had remarked that he'd like to get away for a few days, and Peter had told him about the cottage he and Abigail used most summers. It turned out the cottage had already been let, but the owners put him on to another.

Sophie was none too pleased. He'd gone about it the wrong way, set his mind to it, booked it without consulting her. 'I wanted to surprise you,' he defended himself.

'You certainly succeeded. What about Helen's birthday party?'

'It's not till Sunday. We'll be back by then.'

'I haven't got her a present.'

'We'll get her something there, a costume doll or a musical spinning wheel or something. We need to get away, you know we do.'

The drive was long. It was dark and he was dead tired by the time he acknowledged they were lost. He said, 'If we don't find it soon, we'll look for an hotel.'

She said, 'Let me see the map.' He pulled into a lay-by. She switched on the overhead light and he handed her the piece of paper on which he'd jotted the instructions, a vague list of land-marks and road numbers. 'What the hell d'you call this? Haven't you got a proper map?' She rummaged in the glove compartment. 'There. Let's try again.' She spread map and paper on her lap. He watched her as she pored over it. He liked the idea of being lost. He massaged his neck, admired the tumbling fall of her hair and the businesslike way in which she traced with her forefinger their route so far.

She'd been odd lately, distant and self-contained. They'd made love only once since Sarah. It had been in the dark, and at his suggestion. He hadn't much liked it. She'd been silent and submissive. It frightened him.

'Here,' she tossed her head and jabbed her finger at the page. 'We're on the wrong side of the main road. If we go down here a bit, there should be a crossroads. If we turn left, that should do it.'

She was right. Once they'd crossed the main road they had no trouble following his handwritten instructions. He eased the ponderous car down the narrow lanes and she read down his list, itemising their progress: past the pond, road bears right at telephone box, pub on the left.

They were supposed to collect the key from the pub. He left her stretching her legs in the car park and went in. The room fell silent, the locals clustered round the bar watched him, eyeing up his suit and silk shirt, condemning him as a wealthy interloper. He explained who he was and the key was handed over. As the door banged shut behind him, he heard the lilting chatter and laughter resume.

They found the house, revealed as a denser patch against the dark night. There was nothing welcoming about it. He said, 'I've a feeling we've made a mistake.'

'It can't be as bad as it looks. Where's the key?'

The large iron key had a rough wooden tag with 'Heron Cottage' singed across it. With much rattling he managed to fit it into the mortice. It turned with a scrape and a clunk. As he pushed open the door a billow of damp air greeted them.

He found the light switch and snapped it on. A bare bulb dangling immediately above his head glowed a reluctant yellow. The lobby was tiny, the stairs steep as a ladder. Sophie said, 'Who was it recommended this place?' He could hear laughter in her voice.

'It wasn't exactly a recommendation.'

'I bet it wasn't. Still, we might as well find out the worst.' She edged past him and led the way to the kitchen. 'Not bad,' she said. In the middle of the room stood a scrubbed deal table and two stick-back chairs; the stone butler's sink, the tap with its rubber spout, reminded him of his mother's house. An ancient Rayburn crouched in the chimney alcove. Sophie nudged a loose quarry tile with her toe. 'At least it's clean,' she said. 'Spartan, cold, but clean.'

'I vote we forget it. There must be an hotel round here somewhere. Even the pub'd be better than this.'

'Don't be a defeatist. I'll light the stove and get the kettle on. You take the cases upstairs.'

Two of the bedrooms were tiny, the third just small. Attractive, though. The old-fashioned mahogany bed had an inlaid pattern of seashells. There was also a little iron fireplace with panels of orange and yellow tiles. Next to the bed was a small bamboo table, but there was no wardrobe, they'd have to keep their clothes in the other rooms. He smiled, and felt suddenly light-hearted. Coming away had been the right thing to do, despite the cottage. In fact he rather liked it, it reminded him of Cambridge.

Downstairs the Rayburn was smoking and Sophie was pouring tea from a brown pottery pot into some rather ugly orange and brown cups. He said, 'You're right. It's not so bad. You should see the bath, it's got feet – vicious-looking thing.' She laughed and handed him his tea. 'Bedrooms are a bit on the intimate side though.'

She smiled and, cradling her mug, began to tell him about holidays she'd had as a child. In Devon and Cornwall mostly, walking the cliff paths and visiting stately homes. He responded with his own muddled memories of dusty boarding houses, of bread and marge and tinned salmon, and pebbly beaches and stag-beetles in the bath.

They were tired. Maybe it was the drive, or the country air. They went upstairs; he went through to one of the smaller rooms to change. As he undressed he could hear the floorboards creaking in the next room as she padded to and fro.

He hung his clothes on a rough wooden hanger in the rickety plywood wardrobe and pulled on his pyjamas. Slowly he buttoned the jacket, then smoothed down his hair. Instead of going straight through to her he stood in the cramped space between the wardrobe and the narrow bed, listening to the pounding of his heart and the rush of his blood. He clenched and unclenched his fingers. This was ridiculous. Anyone would think this was their first night together. Their wedding night.

It had felt good to book the cottage in the name of Mr & Mrs Charles Wade.

He stirred himself and went out on to the landing. At first he thought the other room was in darkness but, as his eyes adjusted, he became aware of a faint irregular glow and a shadowy pattern smoking across the wall. He went in. She'd conjured a candle from somewhere and placed it on a saucer in the middle of the bamboo table.

She smiled. She was sitting up in bed and she was naked. Her skin rippled in the candle-shine.

His chest pounded and his breathing was so erratic that if he'd tried to speak he'd have gaped like a fish gasping for air. It would be too easy to drown.

She said, 'Aren't you a bit over-dressed?' Peeling back the covers, she made room for him.

It was unlike anything they'd experienced before. When she enfolded him, he knew himself forgiven, accepted and absorbed as they fused in a union that went far beyond the pivoting of the flesh, that strained to a climax not of the body but of the mind, to a blinding explosion of white-gold fire that seared the sin right out of him.

She'd said that what had happened between him and Sarah didn't count. How could he, how could either of them, have doubted it? The two experiences existed on unutterably different planes. The mechanical grappling of the one faded to nothing beside the numinous fire of the other. This was his only reality – now, and for all time.

They woke huddled against the cold. A thick blanket of mist pressed against the window. The shock, after the sweltering heat of the city, sent them wriggling back under the covers.

They emerged again two hours later. Braving the cold, Charles went over to the window and declared the mist to be thinning. By midday Sophie insisted she could sense the patch of warmth that indicated the sun. By one o'clock it had finally burnt through.

It was an idle time. Neither of them had any desire to be out and doing day after day. They sat in the garden and drank home-made lemonade, went for strolls, cooked together on the cranky Rayburn – she taught him how to make lasagne.

First thing in the morning he'd creep out of bed and set off for the village to buy milk and bread. On the outward journey he'd go by way of the orchard adjoining the cottage and across the meadow. By the time he'd made his purchases he was eager to be back and so he'd hurry along the road with the first daggers of sunlight striking down from the crags and striping the asphalt.

Only once or twice did they take the car out. On one occasion they stopped off in the nearby town in the half-hearted hope of picking up Helen's musical spinning wheel. In the end they settled for a pair of nineteenth-century Worcester vases, discovered in Caernarvon the day before they were due to return home.

Helen was thrilled with the vases – and also very taken with Sophie's emerald suit. So was Charles. She paraded in front of him and he told her she looked stunning. She could detect no irony, no hint that he recognised how far this woman was from the one who'd been with him in Wales.

Things had started to go wrong the moment they left Heron farm. They argued about the route, disagreed over where to stop for lunch. And then, when they arrived at Helen's, what was supposed to have been a small buffet lunch for a few friends turned out to be a full-scale family do.

Sophie was furious. Helen avoided her but eventually she caught up with her in the hall and, grabbing her by the elbow, propelled her into the kitchen. 'What the hell are you playing at?' She banged shut the door and leant against it.

'Sophie, calm down . . . .'

'You said they wouldn't be here.'

'She's my mother, I couldn't not ask her to my birthday party. Bend a little, Sophie, please. She doesn't mean any harm, she's old. . . .'

'How can you say that? She's done him so much harm over the years, can't you see that? And now he's happy, she can't bear to see it. If you want her here, fine. But leave us out of it.'

She went looking for Charles. All the guests had drifted out into the garden and were scattered in clusters across the lawn. Except for Anthony. He came towards her, brandishing a bottle. 'You haven't got a drink,' he accused.

'I don't want one. We're leaving.' She could see Charles talking to Brian.

'Dear me,' snarled Anthony, 'you're becoming as dull as my brother. What's the harm in half a glass . . . .'

'I said no.' He shrugged – the gesture belonged to Charles – but stayed where he was, blocking her route to the garden. 'Excuse me,' she said.

'You're not a very friendly lady, are you?'

'You're not a very friendly family.' She stepped to one side. He blocked her.

He said, 'You hardly know us. Do you know Charles though, I wonder? Do you know about him and Prentice, for example?' She stared at him. 'Leonard Prentice. He's dealing with your divorce, you'll recall. Interesting choice that, under the circumstances.'

'I don't know what you're talking about.'

'It's not difficult,' he sneered. 'Not much of a riddle, but I'll unravel it if you like. Time was – not so long ago – they were bosom buddies, my brother and Mr Prentice. But I'm sure you know that, don't you?'

28

Two hours later she was huddled in a cab on her way to Islington.

'He'll deny it,' Anthony had said. 'Bound to. If you don't believe me, go and see Prentice, ask him, judge for yourself.'

But Charles had denied nothing. He'd been evasive. Confronted with Anthony's revelation, he'd shrugged and said, 'You know what Anthony's like . . . .'

'He's very sure of himself . . . .'

'He's jealous. Leonard got the partnership he thought should have been his. He's killing two birds with one stone, making trouble for me and for Leonard; you should have more sense than to get sucked in.'

Two things struck her: that this was what Michael had suspected all along, and a certain something in the way Charles said Leonard's name. He used to call him Prentice. Today his Christian name flowed naturally from Charles's lips.

So she took Anthony's advice. She went to see Leonard – though what she'd say to him she couldn't imagine: 'Good afternoon, Leonard. Hope I'm not disturbing you, just wanted to check. I've heard a rumour. Is is true that you and Charles were lovers?'

She laughed out loud. The cabby checked on her in his rear-view mirror. She rested her cheek against the cab window and closed her eyes.

It didn't matter, not in itself. What did matter was that he'd lied to her.

Leonard Prentice lived in a basement flat in a terrace of Georgian houses. She stood on the pavement, summoning her nerve. The hard sunlight bleached the stucco. From an open window the strains of a violin sliced the heavy air like wire through cheese.

She descended the area steps, her hand trailing the iron railing. The windows glittered like cut diamonds. She had to ring the bell twice before the music stopped and the door opened. 'Sophie!' He seemed pleased to see her. She'd almost come to think of him as a friend. Last October he'd invited her and Charles to supper. Charles had said that it wasn't appropriate, Leonard was only a junior partner. She'd called him pompous, but he'd been adamant and she'd let the matter drop. Leonard had taken no offence. She realised now that he was probably all too well aware why Charles had refused.

She said, 'If you're busy I could come back another time.'

'No need. Come in.'

His flat was open-plan with a polished pine floor and the kind of moulded modern furniture she disliked intensely. He said, 'How was Wales? Peter told me,' he explained when she looked startled. 'Wasn't supposed to be a secret, was it? An elopement?'

'Of course not.'

'No.' He smiled. 'That's hardly Charles's style.' It struck her that whereas Charles spoke of Leonard as a stranger, Leonard always used Charles's first name, and unfailingly enquired after his wellbeing.

He was speaking. She started. He said, 'Would you like a drink? There's some wine in the fridge.' He went round the dividing counter to the kitchen to open a bottle. She tried to divine from his stance and movements whether he'd guessed why she was here.

He gave no clue. She turned away.

In the alcove beside the fireplace hung a large photograph of the Thames at low tide, a rusty bicycle lodged in the mud of the foreground. On the table beneath stood a crude but effective life-size bronze head mounted on a granite plinth. Leonard said, 'What d'you think?' He handed her the wine. 'Antique of the future?'

'I wouldn't know.'

'But do you like it?' She shrugged. 'Charles gave it to me.'

The wine was too cold, too sweet.

Leonard said, 'Birthday present. Shall we sit down?'

She sank into the chair, wriggling her elbows against the warm, sticky surfaces of the smooth plastic sides. Speaking carefully she said, 'Charles has always given the impression – has always implied that he doesn't know you that well.'

'Has he?' Did he sound sad, or was she imagining it in her effort to fit everything he said into the picture Anthony had painted?

'Only in a professional capacity,' she qualified.

'I see.'

'It isn't true, is it?'

Very gently Leonard released the glass from her clutching fingers. 'Who have you been talking to, Sophie?'

'Nobody.' It was almost a shout. She took a long, steadying breath. 'I just wondered. Nobody gives presents, valuable bronzes, to mere acquaintances.'

'No.' He stared into his wine. She could see his scalp through his thinning hair.

She said, 'Did he give you many presents?'

'Just the one.'

'Something to remember him by.'

'What are you doing here, Sophie, what's he told you?'

'Anthony. It wasn't Charles, it was Anthony.'

'You should be careful. There's a lot of bad feeling there.'

'I know. And between you and Anthony.' He looked up, met her gaze and held it. 'Charles told me, about the partnership. With that and our marriage, and all the fuss about the Trust fund, this could just be spite, an attempt to split us up, reinstate himself and his family, get his own back on you. What do you think?'

'Sounds very plausible.'

'Yes, it does. But if that's all it is, why didn't Charles deny it?'

'Didn't he?'

'Not really. That pleases you – it means something to you . . . .'

He was silent. At last he said, 'It was a long time ago. I thought he'd forgotten.'

'Forgotten what?'

He shrugged, and rotated the glass on his knee. 'I never really knew what I meant to him.' He drained his drink and put his glass with hers on the table. She waited. He would tell her. This was something he'd waited a long time to tell someone.

He said, 'It was five years ago. These days he barely acknowledges me – I don't blame him, he's in a difficult position.' He spoke softly, without bitterness. Frowning at the rug he went on, 'I made an error of judgement. When I met him he was verging on middle age, attractive, unmarried and unattached, and I jumped to the obvious conclusion. I was desperate to see what I wanted to see. I misread the signs – and poor Charles,' he glanced up and smiled, 'he was horrified. He ran away so fast,' he gestured to the pine floor, 'it took three years to polish out the skid marks.'

'So Anthony was lying.'

'Yes.'

'If you're telling the truth, why didn't Charles defend himself?'

'Maybe he thinks it is true – he's got a finely tuned sense of sin, the thought's the same as the act.'

'If you've gone so far as to think it, nothing to be lost by doing it . . . .'

'Maybe that's how it was with you. I wasn't so lucky.' He stopped. 'I'm sorry. I shouldn't have said that. It's good that he's found you, Sophie. Really. He's been alone too long.' Fetching the wine bottle from the counter, he topped up their glasses. He said, 'I'd been working for Bernstein's a month. I barely knew who anybody was. I did know that Anthony Wade's brother was our biggest client. I had something I needed to take up to Peter's office. Charles was there.' He paused and leant forward, elbows on knees. He was now openly eager to tell his story. 'He can be sharp sometimes.' He smiled, inviting her collusion. 'He was giving Jill, Peter's secretary, a hard time. I felt sorry for her, she needed rescuing.'

'And a knight in tarnished armour, you leapt to the fray?'

'Something like that. Peter was late for their appointment; I offered to take him to lunch. I was entertaining a client. There was nothing personal at that point.'

'At what point did that come?'

'He sent the wine back for being the wrong temperature.' Despite herself, she laughed. She knew how imperious Charles could be. It was easy to imagine the effect it had had on Leonard. He said, 'It was my mistake, Sophie. You must believe that.'

She nodded. She could hear the truth of what he was saying, yet she could see them sitting together at that restaurant table. They looked so at ease, so right together.

Leonard said, 'I was never his lover.'

'Did you want to be?'

'That was my weakness, not his. Don't blame him, Sophie. You've something I'd give the world to have, don't squander it in a fit of misplaced jealousy.'

She turned down his offer to ring for a cab. He kissed her cheek and waved her off. She could hear from several streets away the chimes of an ice-cream van.

Michael had been closer to the truth than she'd realised. He'd implied something of the sort when they'd first met Charles. She'd laughed. He wasn't like that. She could tell.

She hadn't been able to tell with Leonard, though.

How had Charles reacted to Michael's accusation? He'd refilled his glass, and said nothing, had allowed the apparent absurdity of the allegation to speak for itself.

Leonard said it wasn't true. Was he lying? Did it matter? It was a long time ago.

It nagged at her.

It had grown dark. She'd hardly been aware of her progress through a succession of narrow streets hemmed in by tall buildings. She knew she'd crossed a broad highway, strident with garish neon; she started at the way the echoing pavements threw the sound of her footfalls back at her. But it was all background to the arguments inside her head.

At one point a black shadow pinpointed with silver emerged from the darkness and coalesced into a policeman. He seemed about to speak, but thought better of it.

She had principles. The flesh is nothing. She'd abandoned the creed during her stay with him, but it had remained strong enough to save her from her ravening jealousy over Sarah. Why wasn't it working now?

Because now she understood. Now she recognised the undercurrent of feeling when Charles referred to Leonard, regardless of whether he used Christian name or surname. There was a warmth, a tenderness, totally absent when he spoke of Sarah. Whether or not he realised it, Charles loved Leonard. Whether or not that love had ever been or could ever be physical, was irrelevant. It was a feeling that violated the basic premise of their relationship, and it gave the lie to everything they stood for as a couple.

29

She found her way back to Beaufort Square. Her feet were sore and her fingertips tingled. Stepping off the kerb she turned her ankle in the gutter. She waited for the pain to ebb, then crossed to the central garden. Trailing her hand along the railings, she edged round until she was facing number thirteen.

How could she ever have called this place home? She rummaged for her key. As she inserted it in the lock, the door opened. Emmy said, 'Thank goodness. We've been so worried. Where have you been? Are you all right?'

'Fine. Don't fuss.'

'Fuss, she says. We've been out of our minds . . . .'

'Let her alone.'

It was Charles. He looked awful. He stood in the drawing-room doorway with his hair all ruffled and his face flushed – though being Charles the crumpled shirt was still buttoned to the neck, the tie, though askew, firmly fastened at the collar. He turned back into the drawing room. Sophie followed him. He'd been drinking. The whisky decanter and a glass stood on the table by his chair. The decanter was almost empty.

'What did you expect,' he said, 'that I'd sit calmly reading the paper, whiling away the time till you saw fit to come home?'

She shrugged; the movement made her sway. He took a step towards her. She stepped back. 'Sit down,' he ordered, 'before you fall down.' She planted her feet firmly on the carpet and gripped the back of the chair. This was no time to give in to a mistimed bout of morning-sickness. He said, 'What's going on? Where the hell have you been?'

She answered with a question of her own. 'Why didn't you tell me?'

'Tell you what?'

'About Leonard. It mightn't have been so bad if you had.'

'Anthony hates me. He'll say anything to cause trouble between us.'

'And Leonard? Would Leonard lie? I've been to see him.'

'I see.' He sank into his chair. Leaning forward he pressed his hands against his face. His voice came muffled and indistinct. 'Tell me what he said.'

She didn't want this. It was hurting them both and it was unnecessary but it had gained a momentum of its own. She said, 'It looks like you.'

His hands dropped from his face. He looked older. His skin sagged. 'What does?'

'The bronze. The one you bought him for his birthday.'

He clasped his hands in his lap, kneading his fingers, tugging at the pad of skin next to the thumbnail. He said, 'You wouldn't understand, even if I tried to explain.'

'He tried. He told me how you met. He took you to lunch.'

'No.'

'He was lying?'

'I mean no, it wasn't how you make it sound. Just because Leonard's the way he is, that doesn't make me the same.'

'What did you do, what did you say to give him cause . . .?'

'What?'

'To hope. He loves you.'

'Did he say that?'

'He didn't need to.'

'Christ.' He bent forward again, burying his face in his hands, and his shoulders rose and fell, then rose and hunched. She wanted to know what he was feeling. She didn't understand. Leonard had made it sound so one-sided and she'd wanted to believe him; but it was becoming less and less credible.

She said, 'And you? Did you love him? Do you still?'

'We were friends. I was fond of him. That's all.'

'Then why aren't you still friends? Tell me that.'

'Let it rest, Sophie. I've told you all there is.'

'No, you haven't. You let me think you hardly knew him and nothing you've said explains why you lied. Help me to understand. Can't you do that?'

He shook his head. She looked down at the open texture of his thick hair, the flecks of grey marking time like the rings of a tree – and felt a wave of frantic tenderness. All she asked of him, all she wanted, was a single word of denial. It didn't even have to be true.

30

He'd lost her. She was still in his house, yet nothing of her or of them remained. They barely spoke, she slept in the yellow room with the half-tester bed, he lay night after night willing himself not to go to her.

Every morning she appeared at the breakfast table just as he was rising from it. She was rarely around when he got home. Emmy accused them of behaving like children, said they should talk it through. Easier said than done. Even assuming he could swallow his pride she was hardly ever there.

He hated this limbo. He hated the silences, the absence of communication, the complete cessation of physical contact. The void was absolute. His body screamed to be touched. Why is she doing this? He lay alone in his bed and his eyes ached against the dark. I didn't tell her because there was nothing to tell. He was my friend. That's all.

Then why are you no longer friends?

Because he wanted more. For the first time he admitted the reason their friendship had failed. He wanted more, but I didn't realise, not at first; I took it at face value. I was fond of him. Why does that alter what she feels for me? Does the mere possibility repulse her? She came to terms with what happened with Sarah with astonishing ease, why couldn't she extend the irrelevance of the flesh to include Leonard?

And then, quite suddenly, he understood. It would have been easier if it was true but, because his fondness for Leonard wasn't weighted down by the needs of his body, their friendship threatened her. Whether or not his flesh had engaged with another's was of no consequence. It was the untouched territory, the virgin land of his emotions that mattered. That was what had been violated.

He had no space in which to manoeuvre. He'd admitted his affection for Leonard to her and to himself. There was no going back. He clenched his fists and dug his nails into his palms. Stretching against the sheets, he found a cold patch at the bottom of the bed, and recoiled. Rain spattered against the window.

If only he could still believe that the flesh was irrelevant. So much had changed since he'd met her. The years of physical and emotional continence had been easy – there was no virtue, nothing he'd fought to overcome.

He was afraid. He was metamorphosing. Something violent was hatching inside him. There was a bitter taste on his tongue.

A sound. His bedroom door opened and closed. Sophie. Sliding into his bed without explanation or apology. He had no control, only ravening hunger. His body gorged itself on the feast. There was no finesse, no spiritual union. Losing the holy fire meant only carnal dependency remained. Where was the glory in that? Where the wonder? She was right. What he felt for Leonard was pure, not like this corrupt and putrid coupling.

Heartfelt love untainted by desire. That's what he felt for Leonard. It was how it used to be with her. In the beginning. On the day he'd stood on the edge of the wind-whipped fens silently confessing his love for her. Why had it changed, why had he let it? It's come to this, now this is all there is. What gives her the right to do this to me?

Her hands slide along his flanks, flicker over his back, down towards his thighs. She knows all the tricks, the secret places, where and how to touch him, make him gasp and moan. As if he were a machine.

How dare she abuse me like this, how dare she – how dare she. . . .

'You're hurting me.'

Good, yes. I'm stronger than her.

'Charles!'

Don't listen. Teach her. Teach her she can't treat you this way with impunity.

She twisted beneath him. 'I said you're hurting me.'

So I am, and about time. When have I ever hurt her – and it's so easy; that's the amazing thing, so very, very easy.

He opened his eyes. He held her arms pinioned above her head. She strained against his grip. He saw what he had done, and released her.

She sat up, massaging her reddened wrists. He couldn't see her eyes but her mouth was working. Was she about to cry? He couldn't bear it, not Sophie, strong Sophie always in control. He snatched at his dressing gown and fled.

He could breathe more easily with a closed door between them, though he still felt dizzy and had a pain in his chest. He fastened his dressing gown and sat on the top step of the stairs. Below, the streetlight streaked through the fanlight, casting a bright path across the tiled floor of the hall. He could just make out the dull gleam of the ormolu clock in front of the shimmering mirror. Its tick filled the well of the hall like a mechanical heartbeat.

He'd enjoyed it, God help him. His strength was the only advantage he had over her, and he was weak enough to use it.

Shivering, he gathered up the tails of his dressing gown and drew his knees up under his chin. He used to sit like this as a child, drawn from his warm bed by the sounds of quarrelling, listening to the harsh tones of his mother's staccato accusations and the occasional rumble of his father's defence. Sometimes they'd wake Helen and she'd come and sit with him, taking his hand, squeezing it tight as he said, 'That's never going to happen to me. I'm never going to get married. Never, never never . . . .'

He rocked forward, rigid with cold.

Someone was sitting beside him. But not Helen. Sophie.

He loved her. The admission soared through him. That would never change.

'I'm sorry,' he whispered, but could make no excuse. 'I'm sorry.'

'It's over, Charles. You know that. It's gone too far.'

'Because of just now?'

'Not just that. We've tried so hard. But it doesn't work. We're damaging one another. Charles, it can't continue, it just can't . . . .'

'What should I do?'

'Nothing. It's me. I'll leave.' The blood drained out of him. Her hand slid down his arm, but he couldn't feel it. 'You'll be all right.' She peered into his face. 'I know you will. But I have to go. You see that, you do see, don't you?'

Alex

It was a shock when Jonathan's father broke off his narrative and got up to draw the curtains. It took such an effort to heave himself out of the chair. He bore down heavily on his walking stick. I'd forgotten how old he'd become. I'd been caught up with the younger Charles, Sophie MacKenzie's lover. When Leonard spirited Joanna away with the promise of a boiled egg and some marmite fingers, I nodded and smiled my approval, but barely disengaged my mind from the task of dovetailing what Charles was telling me into the information I'd gathered from Aunt Helen and Sophie's diaries, and Leonard himself.

Charles had described Sophie's decision to leave him in a calm, matter-of-fact way. I'd wanted to touch him and say, it's okay, don't mind me – scream if you want to.

But he was screaming. Pity flickered in the pit of my stomach. He'd drawn the curtains and switched on the lamp. His back was turned to me. His right hand clenched round the knob of the walking stick. His other hand gripped the edge of the table.

If it was wrong to encourage this act of exhumation, it was too late to stop it now. The doctors had compelled him to confess and the futility of the experience left him bitter. This was different. He was doing it not for himself, but for me, for Jonathan and Joanna.

He slowly crossed the room. When he sat down I saw the colour had gone from his face. His breath was shallow as a puddle. A child can drown in a puddle. I said, 'You don't look well. Shall I call Leonard?' He shook his head, managed a faint smile. Then, re-membering the wail of "if only" that had ululated from Sophie's diary, I said, 'If you'd only tried to find her, gone after her. Why didn't you?'

'I did.' He tugged at the pad of skin beside his thumbnail. 'Emmy and my sister said they didn't know where she was. I didn't believe them. I remembered Jazz had a stall at Camden Passage. I went there and asked around until I found her.

'It was raining. The canvas stall covers were saturated; I can still remember the smell. She had a yellow sou'wester and sold the sort of things Sarah liked, marble clocks and spelter statues.' He paused and took an unnaturally deep breath before going on. 'She knew who I was. I must have looked out of place, like that day in the sale room.' He'd made his thumb bleed. 'She couldn't stand me, I could see that. Said she didn't know where Sophie was, even if she did she wouldn't tell me. I was angry. I shouted at her, told her she was lying and if she didn't tell me she'd be sorry; the man on the next stall threatened to call the police. Imagine it, getting arrested on top of everything else.' He gave a dry, gasping laugh. 'Might have been a good thing. Jazz would have had to tell her, wouldn't she? She wouldn't have been able to resist making me look a fool, proving to Sophie she'd been right to leave . . . . But I don't think Sophie would have seen it like that. What do you think, Alex? It could have been different. Could it have been that easy?'

I knew the answer. I'd read it in the diaries. I knew how Sophie felt. She was staying with Jazz and she was miserable. The feeblest of excuses would have sent her back to him. He didn't have to make any wild declarations or get himself arrested. Knowing he'd been to the market would have been enough.

Charles was talking, telling me what it had been like, going back to the empty house, to Emmy red-eyed and accusing, to the endless silence and tantalising glimpses of a familiar figure vanishing round corners, lurking in the depths of the mirror. Sometimes it was Sophie. More and more often the other one.

Out of the blue he said, 'I went to church.' He leant against the cushions sucking the blood from his ragged thumb. 'I don't know why. It was cold. The dead were in the air like dust. I was breathing them in. How could I be sure I'd breathed them all out again?

'All around me, deceit, false promises – God's love, Christ's sacrifice . . . . I tried to pray. Where are you? I said. Come back to me. Help me. Why have you abandoned me? I looked at the cross over the altar and thought, why is it hung like that, tilted forward?

I knew the answer. To intimidate, instil fear. I was frightened. I said to Him, to Christ or God or whoever, I want You. Do you hear me, I want You, but I won't be intimidated.

'And then I couldn't breathe. Everyone was praying and the dust caught in my throat and the air was thick, like breathing through wool. I couldn't move. I couldn't put my hands together, or lower my head. I was frozen. I thought, this is it, I'm going to die. Just like that. Surrounded by strangers. What is it, a heart attack, a stroke? It doesn't matter, dead is dead when you're the corpse – who'll mourn for me, Alex? Who'll cry when I die?

'And then the figure on the Cross bent towards me and there was something odd about it, something I couldn't fathom, and I thought, no one will mourn. No one cares, not really. Everyone has their own life, there's no one left to weep for me . . . .

'And then I saw her. She was weeping. Her eyes were full of gold and her white gown shimmered as she stepped down off the Cross and came to stand in front of the altar. Her hair burned like a pyre. Her arms were outstretched towards me. The voice in my head was speaking, but I couldn't understand . . . .'

He stopped. His eyes shone with terror. I could feel the coldness and the awfulness of the vision he'd seen and was seeing again now, hearing again the voice that told him who it was who cared, who would grieve for him when he was dead.

It was the Priestess who sent him to Leonard.

Leonard

1

Leonard lay on the floor listening to Paganini. He couldn't remember the last time he'd played this record. It was an indulgence, it held too many uncomfortable memories. He felt a prickle of panic, like holly beneath his shirt – the usual sensation when he ventured to take a glimpse at the path his life was following. He didn't do it very often. Less and less as the years passed. It was such a bloody featureless path.

The violins snatched and jumped.

Path was a misnomer. Morass was nearer the mark – or void. He was drifting through a void; no direction, no purpose. It was a dangerous state. Out of sheer loneliness and boredom, and not for the first time, he might slide into an unsuitable relationship.

Only this afternoon Stephen had left yet another message on the answering machine.

Stephen, Danny, Ian, John . . . . The names were different but the personalities merged together in the quicksand of memory. Quicklime. Eating their bones, reducing them to ash.

Bitterness made him unjust. Stephen was a nice boy with a sharp mind and lively intelligence. He offered companionship, conversation, love – the happiest combination.

But the last item always eluded him. Without it, what were the others worth? The question returned again and again. If he made the compromise of two out of three, how long would the relationship last? If previous experience was anything to go by, a month, six at the outside. Then he'd be on his own again. It wasn't worth it.

He had to deal with Stephen, he wouldn't let go, thought he was in love. Rubbish, of course. He was young. Hopeful. Leonard envied him.

Perhaps he should take a holiday. Run away. Run to – where? Venice. Venice is beautiful in September.

The first time he'd gone there it had been September. He'd been in love. Not infatuated or obsessed but genuinely, deeply and for the first and only time, in love. The sensation outstripped even his over-romantic imagination. The memory rippled through him like a cascade of silk. He remembered a quiet campo far from the heaving mass of tourists, away from the canals with their tang of seaweed and salt. He'd sat at a café sipping expresso so strong it made his nerve-ends tingle, writing a postcard to Charles. '*Venice smells no worse than the north Norfolk coast – let no one tell you otherwise. Regards, Leonard.*'

He'd known Charles just over a month – knew he had to tread warily. He had very little experience of older men – not recently, at least – and the combination of maturity and innocence puzzled and tantalised him. He'd had no doubt that he'd assessed Charles correctly, but winning his trust would be a slow process. He felt surprisingly secure at going on this holiday which had been booked months ahead.

It hardly bore thinking about, how utterly wrong he'd been about Charles.

Suddenly he'd had more than enough of Paganini. He lifted the record from the turntable and slipped it into its sleeve. As he returned it to the stack, the door bell rang. He glanced at his watch. It was just after eight. He wasn't expecting anyone.

The bell rang again, this time accompanied by a pounding on the door. Damn you, Stephen, there's no need for this.

It wasn't Stephen. It was Charles. He was out of breath, perspiring, as if he'd been chased here. Leonard half expected to see his pursuer leaning over the area railings.

Charles said, 'I shouldn't be here, I know – but I've got to talk to someone.'

'You'd better come in.'

'Are you alone?'

'Yes, I'm alone. For God's sake, Charles, come and sit down. You look dreadful.'

Charles dropped into a chair. He was exhausted. Leonard said, 'Drink?' Charles nodded. Remembering, aching with the precious familiarity of it all, Leonard poured him a scotch. Perched on the edge of a chair, he leant forward, elbows on knees, and waited. He knew – he'd always known – that patience was essential with Charles. Try and push him, and you got nowhere. He'd learnt it the hard way.

At last Charles said, 'I've no right to be here. I didn't know what to do. I've nowhere else to go . . . .'

'I see.' He sounded bitter. More gently he said, 'What's happened?' No reply. He persisted, 'Sophie?'

'She came here.'

'She's quite something. You're a lucky man.'

'She's gone.' Leonard stared at him. 'Left,' Charles insisted. 'I don't know where she is.' He rocked forward and sat head bowed, hands clenched between his knees.

'I don't understand. It doesn't make sense. She loves you.'

'What did you tell her?'

'Ah.' He swirled his drink round the glass. 'It's my fault, is it? What d'you think I told her? I cooked you dinner a few times; we went to some concerts; you lay on my floor listening to Paganini and when you finally understood what was going on, you ran. That's what I told her. Alpha and Omega. Was it enough to make her leave?'

'I don't know . . . .'

'There has to be something else. Much as you'd like to blame me, what happened or didn't happen between us isn't enough to make her do this.' He stopped. He could hear the harshness in his voice, the tears that threatened under the weight of unjust accusation. He finished his drink. Banging down his glass he said, 'I told her. What happened, how I felt about you, how you despise me for it.'

Charles half lifted his head. He sounded bewildered. 'I don't despise you.'

'No?'

'No. Did it seem that way? I never meant it, I swear. I've missed you – our friendship. If you knew how often I almost phoned . . . .'

Leonard reached forward. Plucking Charles's glass from his hand he went to refill it. With his back towards him he said, 'If you say so. But that doesn't throw any light on why she left you. She loves you; she wouldn't have gone without a good reason. She wouldn't have gone because of me.'

2

The story emerged in no particular order. Leonard heard about the baby that had died, how Charles and Sophie had met, and how she'd rejected him over and over again. Then, Charles told him about Sarah. It was too much. He was appalled by the matter-of-fact manner in which the information was relayed; as if it were of no consequence. Perhaps it wasn't, if you subscribed to Sophie's view of the world. The flesh is nothing, the Temple is all. A tempting philosophy. Perhaps he should try it.

Refilling Charles's glass, he rested his hand on his shoulder. He felt the shock of radiating warmth, soft flesh beneath the shirt. He withdrew quickly. Charles did not respond. Probably he'd not even noticed.

Leonard found himself increasingly uneasy with the story he was hearing. Charles gave every impression of openness, but something was not quite right. Then it struck him. The facts were all true, it was the characterisation that was wrong. It was as if there were two Sophies. One he recognised, the other terrified him.

It was gone midnight when he put an exhausted Charles into a cab, having first made him promise to come to supper the following evening. He watched the cab to the end of the street, then turned back into the flat.

Rinsing the glasses, he upturned them on the draining board and made himself a glass of tea. This whole Sophie thing puzzled him. He cut a careless wedge of lemon. Even discounting the doppelgänger aspect, the actions of the Sophie he knew baffled him. She loved Charles, he was sure. He'd been certain that, following their conversation, she'd gone home to patch things up. But he hadn't been privy to all the facts. What the hell had made Charles go and sleep with this Sarah woman?

Then there was the divorce. It had been made absolute weeks ago, but she hadn't told Charles. Which meant her decision to leave predated Anthony's interference. But it couldn't be that clear-cut, otherwise Sarah would have given her the excuse to leave. It was almost as if she didn't know what she was doing. It wasn't like Sophie to be so indecisive.

Rotating his glass in its stand, he leant over it, absorbing the fragrant steam. What did it matter why Sophie MacKenzie had walked out? He'd be far better applying himself to what it meant to him personally.

It meant Charles was back in his life. A thrill rippled through him. Charles had come to him because he'd needed a specific, uncritical sympathy. So now what?

The flesh is nothing. Could he live by such a doctrine?

Too easy to imagine the easy slide into renewed friendship, cosy togetherness, but it would go no further. So back to the old question: is love enough?

He would make it enough. The kick of purpose, the whiplash of self-denial made his body rock. Charles was worth more than all the Ians and Johns and Stephens rolled up together. Why else had he gone on loving him during these years of exclusion and denial?

It was enough. It was too much. The void had become full, it bubbled and overflowed with purpose. He was no longer drifting; he had found his direction.

Charles worked out a plan for survival: identify the routine and stick to it. Routine would provide a framework just as it had in the time before Sophie.

The Rolls slid to a halt. He could see St Paul's up ahead. Around him engines revved, fingers drummed on steering wheels and dashboards. A bob of auburn in the crowd fixed his attention. No. Too tall. He closed his eyes. Routine. Leave the house at eight, cram the day with project and budget meetings and site visits, then home at six-thirty precisely. Leaving only the evenings to be filled.

Twice a week he dined with Leonard, and came close to forgetting. Then went home to his empty house. Empty, yet holding her imprint the way a recently vacated bed retains the shape and scent of its occupant. But more than that, more frightening than the phantoms of his mind, was the actual haunting, the shadowy figure lurking in the corners of the rooms, in the grey places deep within the mirrors.

He must do something. Act. React. A positive assertion of his own self. But what to do? His choices were limited and stark, reduced to yes or no, black or white, live or die.

The car edged forward. Stopped again.

Which would take the most courage, resisting the call of oblivion, or answering it? And if he answered, what then? Did he believe in hell? What did he believe it to be? As his mother claimed, a place of fire and brimstone, or as Sophie had once suggested, a state of conscious exclusion, of being locked out of yet another temple.

Or maybe there was nothing but non-existence after life. He was light spinning in a void, then no light, just void. Nothing beneath his feet, no sense of touch or taste, of here and now, of me or you. If he could be sure, he could choose. He didn't dare to be sure.

A few days later he received a letter from Sarah.

The blazing summer that had consumed Sophie had slumped into a damp autumn. Soggy leaves clogged the gutters and the tangled, crone-crooked branches of the trees meshed the lowering smudge-grey sky. The days of breakfast on the terrace were long gone. Emmy served bacon and mushrooms in the overblown dining room with the crimson silk tenting.

He recognised Sarah's writing immediately. The envelope was smooth and crisp and lavender coloured. The message was brief. She'd heard about what had happened – from Cathy, he assumed – and wanted him to know that if he needed anyone to talk to, or if he just wanted company, all he had to do was telephone. She'd understand. He wasn't to think she was being pushy; she just wanted him to know that she was there.

Three weeks later he telephoned Leonard, said he wanted to call round. He made his way to Islington partly by bus, partly on foot.

It was raining. Where the worn paving slabs had flaked, shallow puddles reflected the streetlights and the lights from uncurtained windows. A family was having tea in a basement kitchen, parents and children clustered round a cluttered pine table; dusty cacti lined the window ledge. Further on, a young boy watched television and the darkened room flickered with the grey light issuing from the screen.

Charles dug his hands into his pockets and quickened his step. The rain chilled his face and curled the hair on his brow. The area steps were slippery; he stumbled. Catching hold of the sopping handrail, he swung himself down the last few steps.

Leonard helped him off with his coat, touching his arm as he did so. He said, 'You're soaked. Go on through, I'll fetch a towel.'

The table was laid for dinner. 'I've already eaten,' Charles lied.

Leonard handed him a towel. He said, 'I assumed . . . .'

'I said I'd call round.' His voice came too loud as, drying his hair, he called above the buffeting of the towel, 'That's all.'

'I see.' Leonard removed the pans from the stove. He called over his shoulder, 'The wine's already open. Pour yourself a glass.'

He smoothed down the damp tangle of his hair and picking up the bottle, glanced at the label. 'Okay,' Leonard took it from him, 'it's nothing special; you can be a real snob sometimes. Why don't you sit down.'

They faced one another across the dining table. Leonard said, 'It was boeuf bourgignon. I remembered you liked it; I had one in the freezer.'

'I told you, I've eaten.'

'I know. I'm sorry, I assumed you'd want to eat.'

'You're always making assumptions.' Charles slid his glass back and forth between his hands. 'You've no right.'

'You'll spill that.' Leonard warned, touching the glass with steadying fingers. 'What is it? You've finally heard from her, is that it?'

'What?'

'Sophie. You've heard from Sophie.'

'No.'

'Then what?'

He said, 'I thought I could handle it. I've been alone before; it never worried me. But now,' he shrugged. 'Now it's different. I get so lonely.'

'We all get lonely.'

'No.' He took a defiant swig of wine and put his glass down with a bang. Out of misjudgement, not anger. 'I used to like being on my own. She changed that. I got used to her being there, having company around me.'

'That's why you come here.'

'Yes. But . . . .'

'But what?'

'Sarah wrote to me. I told you about Sarah.' Leonard fingered the stem of the glass. 'I went to see her. Just to talk. I've seen a fair bit of her since. We went to the theatre last night.' Leonard's fingers pinched snap-tight round the slender stem. Charles said, 'Aren't you going to say something? Aren't you pleased for me?'

'What did you see?'

'What?'

'I also like the theatre.' Pain soured Leonard's voice. Charles was sorry, he hadn't realised it would be as bad as this.

'I'm sorry,' he whispered.

'For what, exactly?'

'She knows about Sophie. I told her – she's even met her. Sarah understands me.'

'I understand you.'

'It's not the same. Surely you can see that. I need more. I'm going to marry her.' Leonard reached for the bottle, refilled their glasses, then replaced it on the table between them. Charles said, 'I have to.'

'Why?' Leonard s. ered. 'Are you pregnant?'

'You're supposed to be my friend.'

'You don't have to marry her, Charles. There's no reason why you should.'

'I need to move forward, I can't stay where I am, I can't stand it. You don't know what it's like.'

'Don't I just! Don't be so bloody arrogant, Charles, you're not the only one this has ever happened to; we've all suffered; we've all been hurt. Christ, have you never stopped to think how you hurt me that time?'

Charles's heart banged against his ribs as he searched for something to say.

Leonard said, 'It's all right, don't upset yourself. It doesn't matter; it was years ago.' He sat back in his chair and crossed his legs. 'By the way,' the tone was too casual. 'I don't think I told you – I'm going away.'

'Away? When?'

'Soon.'

'You can't.'

'I was thinking of taking a month or two . . . .'

'I need you here.'

'You don't need me. You've got Sarah. She understands you.'

'Don't do this.'

'It's just what you need. I'll get out of the way, leave plenty of room for Sarah.'

'No.'

He said, 'Come with me.'

A stiletto of pain jabbed downwards from the crown of Charles's head. He closed his eyes. The words resonated – come with me, come with me, come with me.

'Well?' The voice was a long way off. 'Yes or no?'

He wanted to say yes, but the word stuck in his throat. Say it, go on. You've lost everything, there's nothing left to lose. You're answerable to no one, and you're being given another choice. A different choice. Say yes.

The pain increased. From the point of impact it spread and throbbed. He felt himself sway. He opened his eyes. Leonard's face, the room, even the wine bottle were blurred and smudged like a watercolour left out in the rain. He could feel nothing, neither the floor beneath his feet nor the table top. Leonard's voice was indistinct as he said, 'I'm sorry. Forget it. I should never have suggested it.' A hand came to rest on Charles's shoulder. He couldn't feel it. The fingers clenched. Still nothing. It had happened before, this disorientation, this loss of sensation.

Don't give in.

He dug his nails into the back of his hand, but there was no pain. Only the endless aching and spinning of his brain. Then Leonard's voice ringing from the far side of the abyss, 'What the hell are you doing? Stop it, Charles.' And pale fingers tore at his hands, wrenching them apart. The touch was warm. Leonard was saying, 'Christ, look at you, look what you've done. You're bleeding.'

'It doesn't matter. It's nothing.' Leonard still had hold of his hand. He made no attempt to pull away. He said, 'I want to know – about what you were saying. The holiday. Where would we go?'

'It was a mistake,' Leonard whispered.

'No. Tell me.'

'Italy. I thought Italy.'

'And then?'

'What?'

'Afterwards. When we get back. What happens then?'

'Nothing happens then. You know that. No Italy, and no afterwards. It was a dream, a silly dream, nothing more.'

3

This time, Sophie's baby lived. Nothing to worry about, the doctors said. Just feel him kick! Yes, she could feel him, a tiny, precious parasite restless as a kitten inside her, fidgeting away in the dark, both part of her and separate.

Ironic to think how adamant she'd been that she didn't want any souvenirs. She'd left the house in Beaufort Square taking nothing to remind her of Charles. It had taken Jazz to point out the futility of the gesture since the ultimate souvenir was lodged inside her.

She could have stayed with him. It would have been safer, easier. Better for her son. She felt so alone.

Nickie was a summer baby, and it was such a hot summer. There was no real pleasure in holding him, sticky skin against sticky skin. She was afraid that he was too hot, what would she do if he became ill? She stripped him of his clothes and cooled him with a lacquer fan. Then, terrified that he might catch a chill, she wrapped him in a blanket.

I'm no good at this. Nickie, what are we going to do?

It was too much. As if she didn't have enough to do, a business to run. She wasn't maternal, had no instinct for this kind of thing.

Can't give up though, can we Nickie. You're here now.

She would just have to learn. She'd done it before, had taught herself to upholster chairs and repair furniture. She went to the library and came home with an armful of books. Curled on the sofa with Nickie snuggled in the crook of her arm, she began to read. She didn't get very far. The books seemed to be written for someone else. 'Your mother's a Martian,' she whispered to her son. At the sound of her voice he woke and blinked at her, almost as if he understood. 'This isn't for us. We'll have to do it ourselves, make it up as we go along. What d'you say, little one? You and me against the world.'

Defiance, yes – the surest defence. We'll make the best of this, my sweet. She laughed softly. He really was the most glorious baby, his hair as soft and black as coal dust, his eyes just like his father's.

Nicholas MacKenzie, an exquisite replica in miniature of everything she had lost.

4

It was the week before Christmas. Leonard had been trying to clear his desk for the holiday, but had suspended operations for half an hour to deal with a client. It was a divorce case in which he was acting for the husband, a man he disliked intensely and who was fighting the settlement for the sheer pleasure of giving his wife a hard time.

The client left. Leonard shuffled the papers back into the file, tossed it into the wicker tray and lit a cigarette. He sucked in a deep, dragon's tongue of smoke. The action of smoking, the sensuous raising of the cigarette to his lips, the inhaling and exhaling, the sting of satisfaction, calmed him.

He liked Christmas. It was a shame the way people needed to denigrate it. Okay, so it's all a bit commercial, but there was fun to be had. He flicked open his diary. The days prior to and following the twenty-fifth were full. The day itself he'd spend alone. He'd enjoy it, he always did. He'd cook a meal, open a bottle, read, listen to records.

How would Charles spend the day? He'd seen him only once since the wedding. They'd met for lunch in Soho, in a place better known for its food than its decor, where they were unlikely to encounter any of Charles's acquaintances. Conversation had been spasmodic, with brief forays into the economy and politics, the latest production at the Royal Court, an exhibition at the Tate. In between were long silences. He felt calm. Trusted. Almost loved.

Nothing was said about the marriage. Leonard didn't even enquire after Sarah's health, though her presence was implicit in Charles's mention of the Tate. How had she persuaded him to go? How did Charles respond to Matisse? Try as he might, he couldn't imagine them in front of 'Deux Fillettes' or 'Intérieur Rouge', couldn't think what they might have said to one another. Funny, but with Sophie it was easy – fun even – to imagine them together. If he substituted Sophie at the Tate the occasion sprang to life, the scarlets and yellows and zig-zags of the paintings, Sophie holding Charles's arm, her head bobbing and her hair clashing horrendously with the paint as she pointed and talked, and Charles laughing, a deep pit-of-the-stomach rumble. It would have been easy had Charles married Sophie.

The first time Leonard met Sarah was at the wedding. He had dismissed the suggestion that he should be best man, but offered a hand with the preparations. He and Emmy hit it off from the start. They shared a sense of humour and concern for Charles. He recognised, though she was too discreet to say, that she disapproved of the wedding, disliked the bride. She was also irritated by Charles's insistence on holding the reception at the house.

Leonard suspected this to be a matter of principle. Had he married Sophie MacKenzie, he'd have done it in style.

On the day itself he arrived at the house a little after nine o'clock. The caterers and people from the florist's were already there, their vans cluttered along the kerb as, like worker-ants, they carried their baskets of flowers and trays of food into the house.

He greeted a flustered Emmy with a hug and a grin. 'It's a mess,' he said. 'Don't fret, we'll sort it. Where's Charles?'

Charles was upstairs, keeping out of the way. By ten-thirty order was beginning to return. The caterers had finished laying out the buffet, the flower-people had transformed the whole of the downstairs into a microcosmic Kew. Emmy closed the door on the last of them and leant against it with a sigh of relief. 'Some tea I'd say, wouldn't you?'

'No time for that!' He plucked a rose from the bowl on the hall table and pinned it to her fading hair. 'Lovely,' he said. 'It's you he should be marrying, Em!'

She gave his hand a light slap. 'You're a wicked man, Leonard Prentice.'

In the registry office, two hours later, he stood beside an Emmy resplendent in a pink suit and pillbox hat with a wonderfully frivolous candy-floss froth of net, craning to watch a stunned-looking Charles threading the ring on to Sarah's finger.

His first impression of Sarah had been that she wasn't quite adult enough to be marrying Charles. She was like an overgrown child in her long, pale blue dress, her hair all looped up and studded with tiny blue flowers. More bridesmaid than bride.

It was impossible not to make comparisons. Doggy comparisons – an edge of hysteria crept in. Sarah was sleek and docile, a golden retriever, he saw her draping herself in front of the fire, her chin resting on Charles's knee, pawing at his shin as she courted attention; Sophie was a Jack Russell, first here, now there, barking and skitting, constantly snapping at his heels.

He poured another glass of wine. Anthony Wade glanced in his direction, then whispered something to his mother. How much of a threat was Anthony? Would he cause trouble with Sarah as he had with Sophie? Charles said he doubted it. Certainly Sarah didn't present the same financial threat as Sophie.

Emmy touched his arm. She'd made him up a plate of assorted canapés and vol-au-vents. He kissed her cheek; as he straightened he saw Charles's sister watching him from just inside the dining room.

The guests were an uncomfortable mix of business colleagues, family and friends. Sarah knew the Petersons, they'd been responsible for introducing her to Charles, but apart from that she wasn't very well represented. She seemed velcroed to her mother, a large, grey-haired woman in a nondescript buff dress. Her father, Ted, stood by the fireplace fingering an onyx table lighter. Leonard half expected him to pocket it. He decided to look the other way – just in time to see Sarah finally sever herself from her mother and, like an out-of-depth swimmer, attach herself to Charles's arm. She was tall. Their faces were very close. He saw Charles say something, and Sarah smile before shyly kissing him on the lips.

The wedding had been two months ago. Apart from their Soho lunch date, he'd not seen Charles since.

He stubbed out the Sobranie. The office was quiet now, everyone had gone home early to get ready for Christmas. He liked being in the office after hours. As a child he'd liked to sneak back into the classroom during the break or dinner hour. Still smiling at the memory, he finished tidying his desk, pocketed his pens and slipped on his coat.

He was halfway to the tube station when the big black car docked alongside him. Charles wound down the window and said, 'Merry Christmas.' Leonard approached. Charles looked tired, overwork most likely. It was typical of him that as soon as things got tough at home he took refuge in work.

Leonard pulled himself up short. He had no grounds for supposing the marriage to be unhappy. He leant against the car. On the far side of the road a traffic warden eyed them. Perhaps she was going to book them for parking, or report Charles for kerb-crawling; Leonard felt the twitch of a grin. Charles didn't notice; he stared straight ahead. He said, 'I called on Peter yesterday. I almost dropped in to see you.'

'You should have.'

'I had another appointment.'

Leonard nodded. He'd known Charles was in the building, he

always knew. He thought, if he couldn't be bothered yesterday but is prepared to accost me publicly today, what has changed? He took a breath, and a risk. 'Are you in a mad rush?' he demanded. 'Or have you time for a drink?'

Charles told Thompson to come back in half an hour. The wine bar was quite close, down a side street. It was ludicrous taking Charles there. They sat in cramped smokers' bows placed either side of a table made from a barrel. The bare wooden floor was coated with varnish the colour of golden syrup. Painted advertising mirrors cluttered the walls. A girl in a black midi-skirt and wet-look boots took their order.

Charles unbuttoned his coat and adjusted his scarf. His wedding band gleamed inappropriately. Not for the first time, Leonard wondered what had made him agree to such a blatant symbol of his new status.

They sat in silence. Not a comfortable silence. It occurred to Leonard that Charles rarely did anything without good reason. Charles was here because he wanted something. For once Leonard didn't feel inclined to coax it out of him. Instead he said, 'Well, this is fun, isn't it? We should do this more often.' Charles looked up, but still said nothing. 'I was about to ask how you were,' Leonard continued, 'but I can see for myself. A bit world-weary, a little grey, but you'll survive. You're not a loser. How's Emmy?'

'Emmy's fine.' His voice was deep, pained. Lyrics and melody didn't match. Someone should tell him. Someone should ask him why.

He said, 'And Sarah?'

Charles leant forward. He rotated his glass on the barrel top. Leonard's lighter clicked. The Russian tobacco smelt of burnt earth. What was he doing here, what impulse had made him tell Thompson to pull over? Guilt at the way he'd treated Leonard lately, nostalgia for their lapsed friendship? Or perhaps – more likely – the urge to break with routine. Ironic. Only weeks ago routine had seemed his only lifeline. Marriage had changed that.

Routine: arriving home to find Sarah in the drawing room, waiting for him. She'd be wearing something elegant and expensive. She spent far more on herself than Sophie had ever done;

Sophie had always lived within her means, not his. Then again, Sophie didn't have to fight to win his attention.

Each evening he greeted Sarah with a light kiss on the cheek, as impersonal as he could make it. Then he'd go upstairs, bath, change, come down to share a glass of sherry with her before going in to dinner. Night after night the same. He couldn't imagine it ever being any different because what she didn't seem to grasp was that the more she tried, the more she failed. The more exquisitely she dressed, the more she blended into her surroundings. Day by day she became less visible.

Lifting his head, he confronted Leonard. Leonard was angry. Why? He needed Leonard, there was no one else who knew so much about him, who cared enough to help. He said, 'I don't know what to do. It was a mistake.'

Leonard looked past him, out of the window. He said, 'Your car's here.'

'I said . . . .'

'I heard you. It's not news, Charles. I told you. I told you not to get married, I knew it wasn't for you, but you're so bloody stubborn – and now you're stuck with it and I don't know what the hell you expect me to do about it.'

5

Jonathan was at last beginning to accept the logic behind what I was doing. If he could understand his father there was at least the chance he'd stop being afraid. He agreed to read what I'd written so far, not the rough notes he'd flicked through before, but the whole lot. He spent the weekend on it, sitting at my desk with me hovering anxiously, plying him with coffee and bacon sandwiches.

Halfway through Sunday afternoon, he pushed the papers away from him, saying, 'This is all about him and Sophie MacKenzie, and Leonard. What about my mother?'

'What about her?'

'I read this and I almost feel sorry for her. No one's interested in her, she just quietly made the best of things and let us all fall apart round her. It was like she was invisible, we all looked straight through her. And it's the same here.' He dashed his hand against the pile of papers on the desk. 'What was she doing in that house, Alex? Why the hell did she marry him?'

Good question. I know how he feels. It's frustrating, but whereas my sources for Sarah are few and unreliable, Sophie's diaries reinforce, confirm or contradict what Charles and Leonard tell me. Sophie is a brilliant, dynamic presence: a dragonfly, darting and iridescent; a dragon, flaming and deadly – God, she's getting to me now. Not surprising. I've been steeped in her for months, exposed to her fragmented images, every one of them verging on the lethal. Jonathan once described her as a fire crackling in a grate, bright, dangerous, irresistible – everything his own mother was not. Poor Sarah, it's true what Jonathan says, she seems to have been of only passing interest to everybody. For Charles, now as then, she's a shadowy figure. He speaks of her in a puzzled tone, as if unable to work out how she came to feature so prominently in his life.

Jonathan has promised to tell me anything he remembers, but I can't really rely on it. When it comes to Sarah I've only the bare facts as related by Charles and corroborated by Leonard. For Jonathan's sake I'll try to flesh her out. I'll take my scanty ingredients, lightly pepper them with the confessions to which she occasionally made Leonard privy, mix it all together in a big bowl, spicing it up with a dash of guesswork. Sorry, it's the best metaphor I can manage just at the moment.

Something I do know for certain because she confided it to Helen, is that Sarah judged the failure of her first marriage to be down to her. Although Roger had done the sleeping around, she'd been brought up to believe that if a man wandered, it was because his wife had neglected him in some way, kitchen or bedroom, belly or balls. The wife must pull herself together – give him a steak and kidney pud and a good screw, with a hefty dollop of contrition ladled on the side. Sarah couldn't do this. She divorced him. It was the most assertive act of her life.

Okay, okay, I know I'm playing games. It's all window-dressing, guesswork, amateur psychology, but what can I do? There's not a lot to go on, and at least the theory fits the facts.

Probably Charles was a refuge, an upright citizen sixteen years her senior. In an age of sexual rowdyism he was restrained and considerate. Did she wonder about that restraint? Maybe it seemed a small price to pay. If he wasn't in thrall to his senses, he wouldn't roam.

There was something else. They had hurt in common. After their first meeting, Cathy had hinted at a calamitous affair, which explained the slow pace of their courtship. His vulnerability was very touching. Like her he needed healing. He'd been hurt, and she could understand and forgive his occasional outbursts of spite, their disastrous first attempt at making love, the fact that he abandoned her the moment Sophie MacKenzie reappeared. She understood, and none of it mattered in the end because he came back to her. He had come to her and they'd made love and it had been wonderful – or at least good enough to tide her through the lean weeks until their marriage. And the even leaner months that followed.

Poor Sarah. How did she cope when her wedding night turned out to be as catastrophic as their first attempt? He couldn't, he wouldn't. Which? Every night he came to bed, undressing in the dark, tiptoeing about, sharing the pretence that she was asleep, until one night she couldn't bear it any more. She lay listening to the rustle of his discarded clothing, just able to pick out his shadowy movements in the light from the street. As he eased himself under the covers, she said, 'You don't have to creep about.'

She felt the shock of his alarm. There was a moment's stillness. He lowered himself slowly back against the pillows. She was afraid. To bring it out into the open made it real, to stay silent night after night was to pretend that there would come a night that was different. But now she had to go on. She could feel him waiting. She rolled over and lightly touched his arm. It jerked as he checked the impulse to pull away. She said, 'I wasn't asleep. I never am. You creep in every night and lie as far away as you can, right on the edge of the bed . . . .' She stopped. Her heart pounded, as when at school she'd had to answer a question in class. Or when she caught Roger out in some silly lie.

If only he'd say something. Even if he shouted at her it would be better than this, it would give her something to push against. But he just lay there, using his silence as a weapon to silence her. She whispered, 'Please, Charles, talk to me.'

'What d'you want?'

'Not this. This isn't how it should be.' He gave a bark of laughter. She clutched his arm, digging in her nails, hating the fabric that kept them apart. 'I love you. You've had a horrid time, but it's over now. I want this to work, I want us to be happy. Won't you fight it? Help me.' She was crying. She couldn't bear the thought of losing him, adding another failure to her list. 'Charles?'

He moved closer. Her breath snatched in her throat. She'd done it, reached him. His arms were gentle as he drew her to him. She rested her cheek against his chest and felt the rattle of his heart, the hoarse rumble of his voice. He said, 'I'm sorry, so sorry . . . . I didn't mean to hurt you. I rushed things. I need more time. I'm sorry. Sarah, I'm so sorry.'

6

If time was all he wanted, that was easy. He could have as much as he wanted. She loved him, they'd work it out, and if he also needed physical space, so be it.

She moved into the yellow bedroom. She scattered about her bits and pieces of Art Deco to make it feel more personal, but the plaster Pierrot was out of place on the little Regency table by the window, and the Salukis looked shabby.

Moving rooms turned out to be a mistake. It exiled her not only from his presence, but from his thoughts. She no longer existed for him. Sometimes she'd look at her hands, squinting and peering, wondering if she really had become invisible.

But she wouldn't give in. She couldn't reason with him, or bully him, so she resorted to coaxing. He resisted. She persisted. He gave in, but it was an empty victory. She persuaded him to go to the Tate, but her choice of exhibition was a bad one. He'd gone from room to room, barely glancing at the paintings, not uttering a word.

The situation deteriorated. The little signs of tenderness, the occasional brushing of hand or arm, the discreet smile or exchanged glance, the things that had reassured her that it wouldn't always be like this, vanished. He'd withdrawn completely. She no longer recognised the man she'd married, the man who'd come to her flat that stifling summer's day.

When she spoke to him he'd start and scowl, as if she'd dragged him back from somewhere private and beautiful. His eyes would take on a distant, preoccupied look, or else focus and flicker past her; she had to fight the urge to turn and see who was there. Nothing she could say or do stimulated his interest. He slammed door after door in her face, until she stood, gasping with panic, surrounded by a circle of bolted, barred, unbreachable doors.

In June she had a letter from her mother. Mum wanted her to come to Dorset for a couple of weeks. The invitation didn't seem to include Charles. She brandished the letter across the breakfast table. He laid down his newspaper. She felt herself blush under his raking gaze. It was the first time in months he'd really looked at her.

'You should go,' he said. 'It'd do you good to get away.'

She thought, he's right, I'll go – and he'll miss me and when I come back he'll be so glad to see me. . . . The denouements of all the romantic films she'd ever seen flashed before her in a kaleidoscopic jumble. Violins strained to a crescendo. She sat at the little buhl desk and reached for her pen – and the light went out of the stained-glass fire of the kaleidoscope chips. The violins screeched a discord, and died. She wouldn't go. She didn't dare.

That evening he went straight to his study. He always brought work home. She hated the way he rationed his company. Any assault on his reserve had to be achieved between dinner and bed. Well, tonight she wouldn't stand for it. She'd go in, tell him that she wasn't going to Dorset, that she wanted the honeymoon they'd never got around to.

She opened the door without knocking. He didn't like that. He preferred not to be disturbed in his study. 'Sorry.' She pre-empted his rebuke. 'I forgot.'

On the desk in front of him was a pile of legal documents – stiff and beribboned, like death warrants. Behind him, the safe stood open.

She said, 'I've written to Mum.'

He replaced the cap on his fountain pen. 'Good.'

'I'm not going,' she said in a rush. 'I've told her you need me here.'

'I don't.'

'I know. That's why I'm not going. I'm not leaving you.'

'Perhaps you should.'

'No.' He shrugged, and reached for a document. 'Please, Charles, don't do this.' She heard the whining note in her voice. He'd despise her for it, but she couldn't help herself. Her eyes stung. Any moment now she'd start to cry and then he'd really be angry.

But once she'd cried, and he hadn't been angry. He'd been sorry, he'd held her. That wasn't going to happen again. She was wasting her life, waiting for something that was never going to happen, telling herself fairy tales – and believing them. What a fool. Charles didn't want her, didn't love her. She would go to Dorset.

She turned to leave. She would go home to mother. She started towards the door. Charles moved a file, and revealed a small, leather-covered box. A ring-box. She said quickly, half pointing, 'What's that?' He reached to cover it, but she was too quick for him. She snatched it and, before her courage had the chance to fail, snapped it open. The emerald and diamond ring nestled against the faded antique velvet. The quality was stunning. He had never given her anything half as lovely.

He stood up. His face was white; angry lines bracketed the hard contours of his mouth. In a voice barely above a whisper she said, 'Why have you still got this?'

He held out his hand. 'Give it to me.'

'Why have you kept it?'

He stepped round the desk and advanced towards her. She backed against the door. 'Give it to me,' he repeated.

'It's hers – Sophie's – isn't it? You've kept it all this time. How could you? How can it be right between us if you do things like this? Get rid of it, sell it, give it to Helen. . . .' Her attention was fixed on his rigid face and she missed the swift movement that trapped her wrist in a burning grasp. 'Don't!' she cried out. 'Charles!' She struggled to prise open his fingers but he hung on, his nails digging viciously into her flesh, and she wriggled and fought as she shouted at him, 'Stop it. Please, Charles. You're hurting me.'

He froze. His face changed. Impossibly, it became even more remote. She knew that he was neither seeing nor hearing her as, with a final effort, he tore the box from her grip and, pushing past her, fled the room.

The front door slammed.

Her wrist hurt, her hand too. His nails had left crimson crescents indented in the flesh. She started to cry – not elegantly, but the way she used to as a child, in great raucous sobs that shook her body and made her throat sore and her eyes swell. She was angry too, the fury lodged in her throat like a rock. But her rage wasn't directed against him. How could he help himself? No, it was her fault, that woman, that witch. I shan't let you do this, Sophie MacKenzie, you shan't have the satisfaction. She cuffed away her tears. 'I'll fight you,' she whispered to the absent Sophie. 'See if I don't.'

She needed to know the extent of the threat. How deep had this invasion gone? Were there other relics kicking about the house? She would find them, root them out.

Untie the witchlocks and loose the spell.

She began with the desk, opening drawers, rummaging amongst the contents. All she found were pens and pads of paper and boxes of paperclips. Next she tried the filing cabinets. Still nothing. She abandoned the study and went upstairs to his bedroom.

She found it stuffed at the very back of the wardrobe, behind his suits and the row of crisp shirts. The huge, tawny teddy bear had sad eyes and a partly opened mouth. The brass stud in its ear fixed a yellow label on which was printed the name 'Steiff'. 'Hello,' she whispered as she lifted him up. Pressing her face against the soft fur, she hugged the yielding body to her. 'What are you doing hiding away in there? What's your name, Mr Bear?' She gazed into the amber-rimmed eyes. He was about as communicative as Charles. Squeezing him tight, she carried him over to the window and settled him in the little tub chair. 'What a terrible thing to do,' she said as she arranged the cushions behind him. 'Fancy shutting you up in that dark old wardrobe like that. What a wicked thing to do.'

7

The cab dropped Charles outside Leonard's flat. The Georgian facades stretched flat-faced to the end of the dusty road. The stucco glared. Crimson geraniums spattered bloodily against the white rendered walls. He rang the bell, then rang again and banged on the door, bruising his fist and making the paintwork shiver. The girl in the flat above threw open the sash and called down, 'Hey, what's the fuss? He's out, okay?'

'Where?'

'How should I know?'

Shaded by the area walls, he inhaled the dampness that shadowed the corners. Fallen petals darkened the concrete like bloody raindrops. It hadn't occurred to him that Leonard might not be there when wanted. Should he wait, settle himself on the steps, count the falling petals, while away an hour or two? Or pop a note through the door and call back later?

Then he remembered the key. Leonard had given it to him months ago. He'd tried to return it the night he broke the news of his marriage, but Leonard had said, 'Keep it. You never know when you might need a bolthole.'

Charles let himself in. The flat was immaculate. He stood tasting the silence, savouring the faint tang of foreign tobacco. He felt like a burglar. His pulse pattered with the fear of discovery. Odd how the flat contrived to be both familiar and unfamiliar. He knew it well, yet had only ever occupied a tight area of visitor-space.

With a trill of illicit excitement, he began opening doors and peering into rooms. The bathroom was disappointingly conventional. The next room was dominated by a bed draped with a navy blue counterpane. A silk dressing gown of the same shade swung from a clattering wooden hanger on the door. He gathered a handful of cool fabric and pressed it to his face – then felt foolish and let it drop. On the wall facing him was a large photograph of a turn-of-the-century East End street scene. Children played marbles in the gutter; women, prematurely aged, hunched in their shawls, averting their faces from the camera. This was Leonard's private domain. The urge to learn more, to open cupboards and drawers, rummage and pry, was almost irresistible. The spare room was much smaller, gratifyingly impersonal, and showing no sign of recent occupation.

He went back to the living room. He felt uneasy, as if he'd cheated Leonard, been where he wasn't supposed to go, seen what he wasn't supposed to see – though in fact there'd been nothing to give any real insight into the man.

How much longer was Leonard going to be? Who was he with, where had he gone? A crowd of uneasy speculations jostled for attention. For God's sake, Leonard's private life was none of his business. He shuffled through a stack of records. At first the names – Scarlatti, Corelli – meant little to him, then he came across one he did know. Paganini. He mouthed the name, and felt a flicker of consternation. By way of defiance, he slid the record from its stiff sleeve and lowered it on to the turntable. The music jerked and jumped, reactivating his jangled nerves. He lowered the volume.

As he tried to settle on the uncomfortable sofa he noticed the bump in his jacket pocket. Sophie's ring. Typical that she'd taken from the house only what she'd brought into it. The day she left he'd come home to find all his gifts to her, from Bertie the bear to the emerald ring, ranged out on his bed. She was scrupulous; there was even a cheque for an amount exactly matching the initial balance of the bank account he'd opened for her. She had always been meticulous about money, as if from the start she'd never intended to stay.

Of course she'd meant to stay. She'd loved him. Even Leonard said so. Where the hell was Leonard?

He stuffed the ring back in his pocket and did a circuit of the room. The magazine rack contained a *Financial Times* and a handful of holiday brochures. He should have taken Leonard up on his offer, gone away with him instead of marrying Sarah.

The music began to irritate. He switched it off and went through to the kitchen. In the fridge, crammed into the door next to the milk bottles, was an opened bottle of wine. It was nothing special; Leonard didn't know much about wine. About architecture perhaps, music and the theatre certainly, but not wine. Still, quality wasn't a priority at the moment.

He woke with a start to darkness and the sound of a car door slamming, the sibilant hiss of whispered farewells. He sat up. He'd slept awkwardly. His arm was stiff. The car pulled away. Brisk steps descended into the area. A key clicked in the lock, the door opened, the light blared. Leonard was dressed to the nines: pleated shirt, burgundy bow tie and cummerbund. He was smiling as he came in; the smile faltered when he saw Charles.

Relief and anger roared through Charles. 'What time d'you call this?' he demanded. 'Where the hell have you been? I've been waiting for you.'

Leonard gathered himself, moving away from the door with exaggerated languor. 'Out,' he said unhelpfully.

'Where?'

'None of your business.' He tugged at his bow tie and unbuttoned his collar. 'And what d'you mean, you've been waiting? How did you get in?'

'You gave me a key.'

'So I did.' He gathered up the holiday brochures and replaced them in the rack.

'You're not going to tell me where you've been?'

'No.'

'I've been waiting. . . .'

'You've a bloody nerve. I don't see you for months, then you turn up out of the blue demanding to know where I've been, what I've been doing, and with whom, no doubt.'

'I'm sorry.'

'Are you?' Charles shook his head helplessly. Leonard found a cigarette, lit it and inhaled. 'I've been with friends – I do have friends, you know.'

'I'm sure you do.'

Leonard glanced round the room. 'You made yourself at home, I see.' He took the wine bottle through to the kitchen, poured the dregs down the sink and rinsed it under the tap.

Charles blurted, 'I need your help. I need somewhere to stay.'

Leonard dumped the bottle on the draining board. Without turning he said, 'That's why you're here. You want a bed for the night.'

'Is it a problem?'

Leonard switched off the kitchen light. He turned, and Charles could no longer see his expression, only the garnet glow of his cigarette. 'No,' he said with a sigh. 'No problem. Spare room's down here. I'll show you.'

The spare room was no more welcoming than on Charles's earlier visit. He undressed in a hurry and huddled under the covers. Leonard came out of his room and went into the bathroom; he heard the cistern flush, water ran in the sink, a door closed.

Charles tossed and turned, trying to find a comfortable position for his head on the surprisingly hard pillow. He gave up. Closing his eyes, he lay very still under the blanket of the dark. His borrowed pyjamas were too tight across the shoulders. He didn't dare button them in case they tore. His last thought was that, come tomorrow, he must try and find out what he'd done to upset Leonard.

He woke late. Leonard had gone out. His note explained nothing. Charles idled away the day. He went out for a paper, drank coffee, listened to the radio, dozed. He felt isolated. There was something unreal about the situation in which he found himself.

Leonard arrived home and set about preparing supper in silence. Charles watched him, admiring the deft way he chopped the vegetables and pared the meat into slivers, the flourish with which he tossed them into the wok. Eventually, unable to bear it any longer, he said, 'You're still angry.' Leonard didn't answer. 'You're right. I should have shown more consideration. It might have been embarrassing, me being here last night.'

'Yes, I might have brought someone back with me. . . . For Christ's sake, Charles,' he slammed the knife down on the work surface. 'Why the hell should I do that when. . . .' He stopped. 'I'm sorry. I'm in a rotten, piggish mood. Take no notice.'

'Tell me what I've done?'

'Nothing, you've done nothing. No, that's not true. I don't like being taken for granted, I don't like being your last resort in any emergency.'

'It's not like that. Where else would I go? Who else understands? I can see it might have seemed that way, but it wasn't.'

Leonard said, 'If you say so. Let's leave it, shall we? Are you going to tell me what the row was about? Did you start it, or did Sarah?'

'I'm not sure. It just happened.'

Leonard shrugged. Charles opened the wine. They ate in silence and afterwards sat on at the table, surrounded by dirty dishes. Charles topped up their glasses, took a sip then, pushing the glass aside, produced the ring-box. He fingered it before passing it across the table. He said, 'She found this.' He remembered his wife's fingers crone-curling round the box. A terrible bitterness flooded him, choking him like blood in his throat. He could no longer see Leonard, only Sarah's translucent eyes and the creases like white scars pleating her frightened face. He said in a whisper, 'I can't go back. You don't know what it's like living there. I was fond of her, really I was, but I can't bear the sight of her now, the sound of her voice. . . . I can't even touch her any more, can you believe that? But it's what's on the inside that really terrifies me. Do you remember I told you about Sophie, about the night before she left? I hurt her. It wasn't the first time. I enjoyed it. Why should that be? I'm not a vicious man. But I had her pinioned, crushed under me, and it was so exhilarating. I felt free. I'm frightened. What if it happens again? It could. Because I'm not in control – I'm not used to that – I don't exist any more. There's what my body's doing, but that's on the outside. On the inside I'm falling over and over in the dark, falling inwards, like a cat tumbling down a well.

And there's a circle of light above me; it's all right when I can see that, it means there's a chance I can climb out. But what happens when night falls? What happens then? If I don't have the light to guide me, how will I ever find my way out?'

He opened his eyes. The light from the candle stung them. Leonard was leaning towards him across the table, his thin fingers clasped round his wrist. Their skin crackled with transmitted energy. He said, 'But it doesn't matter, not when you're with me. I stop falling. I'm safe. How do you do that?'

Leonard released him. He stood up and began to gather the dishes.

'Leave that, can't you?'

'No.'

'For God's sake, Leonard.' Charles reached for him, and missed. He followed him to the kitchen. He said, 'Don't walk away like that. I need you.'

'No.' Leonard's shout clashed with the cutlery as it crashed against the china.

'Last night,' Charles interrupted, his voice high with panic, the sibilant shivering on his lips as though at a visceral level his body knew what he was about to say before his mind had formed the words. 'You looked wonderful. Amazing. I couldn't bear it. I wanted to know where you'd been, who with, who you wanted to impress. I was jealous.'

'You've no cause,' said Leonard, turning.

How had they come to be standing so close? He could smell the wine on Leonard's breath. The blue, almond-shaped eyes looked steadily into his. He thought, I love him.

At once another, more niggardly part of him began drawing lines of definition: I love him this way, not that. My way, not his.

Call it what you like, it amounts to the same thing: concern, commitment, an overwhelming gratitude and tenderness. Moving slowly, he touched Leonard's cheek. Odd to feel masculine roughness. He spread his fingers, sliding his thumb across the high cheekbone. Leonard held himself absolutely still, the only movement the tremor in his lower lip. Charles moved his hand downward, felt its soft flickering beneath the pads of his fingers. He heard himself say, 'I have to go back, don't I? I can't bear it. Come with me.'

8

Three days later Thompson was called to Islington. Charles and Leonard settled themselves in the deep seats. Leonard had two major concerns. One was Anthony. Charles said, 'I can handle Anthony.' The second concerned Sarah. He told Charles it was unreasonable to expect her to welcome him into her home. He was the man her husband turned to in a crisis, and he was a stranger to her. In her position he would be as jealous as hell. Charles refused to discuss the matter. He hadn't planned to bring Leonard here; until the moment he suggested it, such a course of action had never occurred to him. Yet, once voiced, he saw how right it was. He said, 'Leave Sarah to me. I'll talk to her.'

They arrived back at Beaufort Square. As they climbed out of the car the drawing-room curtain flicked. Emmy opened the door. Leonard bounded up the steps two at a time to link his arm with hers. 'Beautiful Emmy! I've missed you.' He laughed and squeezed her arm. 'Come on,' he drew her into the house, 'show me my room. It'd better be nice – hot-and-cold running and a view of the sea, otherwise I'll want my money back. . . .'

They climbed the stairs, their heads bobbing busily. Charles felt excluded. Fool. Fancy being jealous of Emmy. Get a grip. Time to face Sarah.

When he'd rung this morning, she'd refused to speak to him. Pity tempered his irritation. He straightened his tie, smoothed down his hair. He'd make an effort to be kind.

She stood by the drawing-room window, her pale grey dress fading like cigarette smoke against the bright afternoon light, twisting her wedding ring round and round on her thin finger.

Seeing her like this squeezed the kindness out of him. 'Are you all right?' he demanded, and sounded surly.

'Why shouldn't I be?' Her finger was raw from the burning twist of the ring.

'I imagine you were worried.'

'I knew you'd be all right. You always are.' She sounded bitter. Perhaps she was starting to hate him.

He said, 'Leonard's here.' She didn't answer. 'He's staying for a bit. You must be nice to him.' She stared at him. 'You don't object, do you?'

'Why should I object?' Her voice scraped like rough-edged metal. 'It's perfect, just what we need, a complete stranger taking up residence.'

'He isn't a stranger.'

'He is to me.' Her knotted fingers were clenched so tight that he half expected to hear the bones snap.

He said, 'You can always go and stay with your mother.'

Her mouth gaped. So ugly, so out of control. Why doesn't she leave me? I've nothing to give her.

His muscles strained for release, to punch and rip and kick. He clenched his fists; held himself upright. Keep control, don't let go. She was right, he wasn't fit to be left alone. Wasn't that why he'd brought Leonard back?

'How long?' The question startled him. 'How long is he staying?'

'I don't know.'

'You must know. Emmy. . . .'

'Leave Emmy to me.'

'Don't do this, Charles!' Her voice rose on a whine. 'Don't cut me out like this.'

And he thought, good girl, that's it, fight back. If only she stood up to him more often. His anger drained away. Very gently he said, 'I'm not cutting you out, I promise. Let's try to calm down, shall we? I'm going upstairs to have a bath and change, then we'll all have tea together. How does that sound?'

Bloody patronising, that's how it sounds.

Opening his bedroom door, the first thing he saw was Bertie on the chair by the window. He picked up the bear and held it aloft. Sarah must have found it, must have come rummaging about in here, looking for evidence of Sophie, and found Bertie. Poor Sarah.

There was a knock at the door. Leonard called, 'Can I come in?' He popped his head round the crack.

'Yes. Come and meet Bertie.' He tilted the bear, inclining its head in greeting.

'How do you do?' said Leonard, solemnly taking the bear's paw and shaking it. Charles laughed. So did Leonard.

Replacing Bertie in the chair and adjusting the cushions, Charles caught a flicker of movement in the doorway. Sarah, realising she'd been seen, fled to her room.

9

Sarah could hardly be civil to Leonard Prentice. The man was a virtual stranger, yet she was expected to share her home with him. It drove her mad the way he followed her around, trying to engage her in conversation. She hated him. He was a bad influence on Charles. He had made her an outsider in her own home. And it wasn't just Charles; he'd taken over Emmy as well. Leonard and Emmy down in the kitchen, laughing. Emmy and Leonard discussing menus and sauces, the timings of meals – and that stupid game they played, pretending they lived in a seaside boarding house, making endless witless jokes about weak tea and packed lunches and the wash of pebbles on the beach keeping them awake at night. Sometimes Charles joined in. She hated that, that they could make him smile.

Then Charles announced that Prentice was resigning from Bernstein's to be his legal advisor. A few days later she overheard Leonard telling Emmy he'd put his flat on the market. Sitting in the garden under the shade of the shaggy bay tree, she tried to grasp the meaning of it all. She seemed to have lost her hold on reality. How should she react? She stared down at the paper on the table in front of her. She'd selected a stone from the border and rested it on the pad to stop it flapping in the breeze. The letter was to her mother, but the page was blank. What could she say, what words could describe her situation?

She gave up. Gathering her writing materials, she started back to the house. As she crossed the terrace, her mind still trying to unravel the stray phrases and lost explanations from her unwritten letter, a murmur of voices drifted towards her through the open French windows. Approaching slowly, she saw Charles and Leonard Prentice standing just in front of the fireplace. The gilt-framed overmantel mirror presented their image in disturbing duplicate. Charles stood at a slight angle. Prentice's hand rested on his shoulder as he leant forward, speaking in a soft, urgent voice. She couldn't hear what he was saying, so she stepped closer. They were both far too absorbed to notice.

As she watched, Leonard fell silent and Charles shook his head and gave a hopeless little shrug. Then she heard, quite distinctly, Leonard Prentice speak her husband's name. As though it belonged to him. And Charles smiled.

Right from the start she'd loved his smile; the rarer it became, the more she treasured it. This time, even after it had faded its ghost lingered at the corners of his lips.

And at last she understood. She stepped into the room. The two men started, blinking as they turned towards her, as if they didn't know her.

'I saw . . .' she began. Her voice was hoarse. She was close to tears. 'I saw you.' Charles moved. The hand on his shoulder slid down to grasp his forearm. 'I don't believe it. I never guessed – I never thought. . . . This is what it's all been about.' She shivered, her throat ached. 'This is why – I thought I understood but I didn't. This is why she left you. Because of him. I've been so stupid. I never thought, I never dreamt. But it's all right. Now I understand what he's doing here. I know what he is. And you. And you, and you. . . .'

He hit her. With a roar of rage he broke free of Prentice's restraining grip and crashed his open hand against her face. She couldn't cry out, could only stare at him. No one spoke. Her cheek throbbed. She wasn't crying. She ought to be, but she wasn't.

Charles moved. She flinched as he pushed past her. She wanted to go after him, but the strength had drained out of her. She swayed. Prentice caught hold of her and eased her into a chair. She tried to wriggle away from him. He said, 'You don't understand.'

'I do. Go away. I don't want you here. I want you to go.'

'It isn't up to you. He came to me – asked me to help him.' He dropped on to his heels and reached for her hand. She pulled away. 'Look. Sarah, look,' he whispered. 'He's this close,' he measured a minute distance between thumb and forefinger, 'this close to the darkness.' She stared at him. What language was this? Who was that close to what darkness? He said, 'He's terrified, can't you see that?'

'Of what?'

'Sophie.' The name, like elastic, snapped back at him. Her fingers clenched round her writing pad. She'd held on to it the whole time. It was crumpled, and marked with sweat. He said, 'I know it's hard. But please, you must try to understand.'

A week later Ron Harris, head of Charles's design department, delivered his recommendation for an interior contract on their most recent residential development. He came into Charles's office brandishing the file. 'No contest,' he announced, presenting it with a flourish. 'New company – not been going a year yet, but good, hell of a reputation already.'

'Cost?'

'Not cheap, but competitive. Woman running it's a real firebrand by all accounts.'

Charles flicked open the file. There was a letter. The company was called Palladian Interiors. The letter was signed. Charles stared at the signature.

Harris said, 'I could arrange a meeting.'

'That won't be necessary.'

'Just a thought.'

'Indeed. Leave this with me. Ask Betty to send for Mr Prentice, would you?'

Leonard's office was just down the corridor. When Betty rang to say the boss wanted him, he went like a dog to the whistle. Charles sat straight-backed at the desk, his face almost blank, his breath coming in quick, shallow gasps. Leonard said, 'What is it?'

Charles pushed the file towards him. Leonard picked it up. He recognised the signature. 'Christ,' he whispered. Charles said nothing. Leonard was afraid. He'd never seen him as bad as this, so far gone so quickly. He said, 'Charles?' And knelt down to peer into the older man's face. Nothing. He thought, I've lost him. I was supposed to stay by him, look after him, and I couldn't do it. I should have left him to Sarah.

But Charles had said he could help, that when Leonard was there it wasn't so bad.

'I'm here,' he said, barely hoping to be heard. 'Listen, Charles....' He took him by the shoulders, calling his name, shaking him. Nothing. Silence roared back from the abyss. He teetered giddily, clutching at Charles's shoulders, shaking him till his body rocked back and forth, out of control. Then he began to pinch and scratch at his hands, still calling to him – but Charles was deaf and blind. There was nothing he could do to bring him back.

The Temple doors are carved from bone, the chamber glows red and gold, the Priestess's hair lifts on her scalp at the draught from the open door.

She turns.

He had loved her, but now he knows how dangerous she is. Had she not left, she'd have driven him on and on, further and further towards some dreadful act of annihilation – his or hers, it hardly matters which. It had come so close.

But she had left, and now he is almost safe. All he need do is eject her from the Temple, then seal the doors so that neither she, nor he, nor anyone can ever enter there again.

Can he do it? Is he strong enough?

Oh, but it's hard. He loved her so much.

Or did he? What if all those years ago he'd stayed in the agent's office, drinking bitter mud-coffee and exchanging stilted pleasantries with the secretary. Or if he'd passed by the auction room and gone for a walk instead.

Do I know you?

If he'd kept to his first answer, then his world might not have changed. If only on a night in a red-mahogany bedroom he'd found the will to turn his back and walk away.

Do I know you?

No. I never knew and never loved. My whole life has been a lie, and you come to me and go again, like a flitting, fire-touched butterfly.

But if I could die – the simplicity of it makes him gasp – then there would be no Temple, nowhere for her to hide. If I could bury myself, find some dark place. . . .

'No,' the Priestess sighs. 'There's nowhere you can go that I'd not find you.'

But if I can find a place far enough, unlikely enough that decay might take its toll before I'm found, how then will she know me?

'I will always know you.' The Priestess smiles. 'I am part of you, woven in every sinew, etched on every bone.' The smile fades, the sweetness sours. 'There's nowhere you can go.'

And then she comes towards him, gliding across the floor of the Temple, blocking his path to the door. He must either stand his ground, or go deeper. Her robes brush against him. His body rises to her. The word is no. Say it.

No.

She laughs, and the sound echoes round the domes of the Temple. He has no choice, he dare not go deeper.

She touches him. Flesh against flesh. Forbidden memories surface like scum to poison his future as they poison his past.

The word is no.

'I do not love you,' he whispers to the curving ear that nestles against his cheek.

'Yes you do.'

'No. And you don't love me. You devoured me, a sucking-pig at your feast – I understand now. And the bait. Illusion. The illusion of love. And I had to take it, I had to believe you because I couldn't justify my captivity, capitulation, in any other way. And you call it love! Oh just look at what it's done to us, this lying-love of ours, to you and me and Sarah. . . .'

305

'It was more than that.'

'No, that's all it ever was – and I couldn't see, how could I not have seen?'

She shakes her head, angry but defeated. She moves away from him, backing towards the doors through the billowing clouds of her robe. Her hair has lost its fury and laps about her face like the tired flames of a fire about to die. Tears fill her eyes, magnifying the sunburst of her irises and fragmenting the gold, so that suddenly he cannot remember if he has ever seen her cry.

And she says, 'You are right. I never loved you.'

And now he can no longer see her. He blinks away his tears. When his vision clears, she is gone from the Temple. The light has also faded and he stands alone in a drab, grey chamber which it is now no hardship for him to leave.

10

He felt different – empty on the inside, but sharp as sand outside. He had a sense that things were about to change. He tried to reassure Leonard. It's all right, everything will be different now. The Temple is sealed.

Which meant there was no reason to boycott her company. She was the best, according to Ron Harris, and it would be bad business to let what had been between them influence him. He felt liberated by this decision.

Arriving home that evening he was struck by the vivid shade of the privet bordering the residents' garden, how every leaf stood out clear and sharp against its neighbour, like a child's pop-up book. A sparrow was taking a dust-bath in the gutter. With a laugh and a pinch Sophie had once pointed out the variety of colour in a sparrow's wing. 'Every shade of brown – how can anyone call them drab?' He smiled at the memory. He was still smiling as he went in search of Sarah.

She was on the terrace writing to her mother; it worried him sometimes, what she might be saying in those letters. She looked up as he approached. 'You're early,' she said. She sounded a little disappointed.

Sarah couldn't remember the last time she'd heard him laugh or seen him as animated as he was this evening at dinner. Leonard told them about a production of *The Magic Flute* at Covent Garden, apparently Papageno was excellent. Charles suggested he get some tickets, then began to babble about a sparrow taking a bath. He laughed; so did Leonard. She didn't understand. Leonard laid a hand on Charles's arm. She looked from one to the other. Something had happened, something shared, but for once she didn't feel excluded.

Suddenly she felt terribly tired. She said, 'I think I'll go to bed.' Cupping her elbow in his palm, Charles kissed her cheek. She could still feel the glow of his touch as she snuggled down against the pillows. She replayed the evening's events over and over in her mind. For the first time she found herself moved by the closeness between the two men. Leonard had sacrificed much to be with Charles. If Charles would be her friend again, she might learn to like Leonard a little more. He was very fond of Charles.

But suppose he was more than fond. She shivered, and tugged the sheets tighter under her chin. Why had Sophie MacKenzie left?

Downstairs a door opened and closed. She heard the rumble of Charles's voice as it mingled with Leonard's lighter tones. Charles laughed. Leonard hushed him. They climbed the stairs. Silence. Leonard passed along the passage to his room. She waited for the click of Charles's door, but instead her own door opened.

In the moment before he closed it, she saw Charles's broad silhouette against the landing light. She lay still, afraid that if she moved she'd frighten him away. He crossed the room, she heard the hiss of his breath as he stood over her. He said, 'Are you awake?'

'Yes.'

'I didn't want to disturb you.'

'I couldn't sleep.' He moved. Now she could see him better

against the silvery backdrop of the window. 'Why don't you sit down?' She edged across the bed. The cool sheets slithered against her skin; the mattress sank beneath his weight. She said, 'Should I put the light on?'

'No.' He was sharp. More softly he said, 'I wanted to ask you,' he hesitated. 'The dress you had on tonight, you wore something like it the evening we met, didn't you?'

'Not really.' What an odd excuse for coming to her room. 'I suppose the colour's similar,' she conceded.

'Yes, it's probably the colour I remember.' As he spoke, he reached for her. She flinched as his fingers brushed her cheek. He pulled back. 'I wouldn't hurt you, Sarah,' he whispered. 'I know I did that time, but it wasn't me. You understand that, don't you?' She didn't answer. 'Sarah?'

'I think so.'

'What you said about Leonard – he's the only real friend I have.'

'What about me?'

'You too?' he asked as he bent over her, pressing her back against the pillows. Should she resist? She didn't want him to despise her. But he was so warm and solid, and all the months of privation gagged in her throat. She clung to him, digging her face against his shoulder, clutching him till her fingers ached.

He said, 'I don't deserve this.'

'I know.'

'I've been a complete bastard.'

'Yes.'

Laughing, he said, 'You're not making it easy, are you?'

'No.' She felt his breath on her face, warm and spiced with whisky.

He pulled back. His hand trailed her cheek. She turned and bravely tickled his palm with her tongue. He said, 'If you were to go away, Sarah, if you were to leave me,' her flickering tongue froze, 'no one would blame you.'

'Is that what you want?'

'No. I want you to stay. You and Leonard.'

Living on the outside, that was how Sophie had described what he was doing now. The prospect had appalled her, but it wasn't so bad. Playing the perfect husband was a simple matter of being attentive, remembering to comment on her clothes, her hair, buying occasional presents, and now and again making love to her.

The process was seamless and it came as no surprise when, towards the end of the summer, she told him she was pregnant. Another role, another challenge. Was it still a role? He wasn't sure, but he didn't think so. Sarah was so happy. He wanted that to last. He took control, booked her into a top nursing home, filled the house with flowers, did everything he could to make up for his past neglect.

Everybody was excited, Leonard and Emmy and Helen – anyone would think they had as big a stake in the baby as he did. He laughed at the idea and kissed Sarah and thought how very lovely she was. He had made the right choice. True, there was a limit to the amount of time a rational man could spend arbitrating the relative merits of giraffe or teddy-bear wallpaper, but he enjoyed the endless unresolved debates about names and watched with fascination as one of the spare rooms was converted into a nursery.

Sarah's labour began in the middle of the night. There was a mad rush to the hospital but three hours later he and Leonard were still waiting. The room was hazy with Leonard's cigarette smoke. He ran out and had to go out for more. He couldn't get his usual Sobranies. He grimaced as he waved the lighter flame under the white tip. He glanced towards the door, saying, 'Can't go on much longer, surely.'

'Emmy says it can take hours.'

'Don't,' he said with a shudder. 'Poor Sarah. God,' he stamped out the cigarette. 'I can't smoke these things.' They sat in silence, shoulder to shoulder. Occasional footsteps passed the door; the second hand of the wall-clock made a scraping sound every time it passed the hour. Charles tugged at the pad of his thumb and made it raw.

And then with a flurry the nurse came in, bursting to tell them that Mrs Wade had given birth to a fine baby boy.

A son.

He rose to his feet. Leonard's hand rested on his arm. A dread chill spread through him, from skin to marrow-bone.

A son. Sarah held the creature out to him. Leonard's hand in the small of his back blocked his retreat and nudged him gently forward. 'Go on,' he said, 'take him.'

The soft, heaving bundle gave him a queasy itch in the pit of his stomach. He'd never held a baby before. Laughing, Leonard adjusted his fingers, showed him how to support the frail head. Beneath the mushroom-cap of dark hair, the baby's face was crumpled and red, its lips moist and pursed. He said, 'He looks like a frog.' He stared at his son, wondering how long it would take for the cold that was stiffening his body to reach him and make him cry.

Leonard said, 'Charles, you're hopeless. He's not going to explode, you know. Come on, give him to me.' He glanced at Sarah who gave a shy smile and a nod. 'Come along, tich.' He lifted the baby on to his shoulder and nuzzled his face against the dark fuzz of hair. 'He's gorgeous, Sarah,' he laughed. 'Hey, but your mum's clever, isn't she, little fella?'

Charles watched. It had nothing to do with him.

Leonard said, 'So what are we going to call him?'

'I've decided,' said Sarah triumphantly. 'Jonathan. I want to call him Jonathan.'

Jonathan Wade. Charles closed his eyes. The name ricochetted round his skull and a voice screamed, 'What about the other one, your son who died? Did he have a name?'

His mind toppled. He'd never thought to ask. He knew almost nothing about the baby Sophie had lost. He'd never asked what it had been like for her, standing at the tiny graveside, nor whether she'd buried or burnt him.

Baby Jonathan started to cry. Leonard handed him back to his mother.

And Charles stood alone in the half-light of his half-world, scattering the ashes of the child who had never cried against the closed door of the darkened Temple.

11

The frog grew and the entire household treated him like a prince. Sarah thought of nothing, talked of nothing but Jonathan. The same was true of Emmy and Leonard. When Charles complained to Helen she laughed and accused him of being jealous. Was he? Probably. He was certainly confused. His responses and reactions to Jonathan switched on the spin of a coin. Fatherhood. He'd never really expected it or thought what it might be like. The death of Sophie's baby had slammed a door he hadn't realised was open.

The trouble was the baby, his son, was so appealing. He couldn't deny the seductive allure of the clutching fingers, of tiny limbs padded against harm. Part of him longed to yield, to touch and hold, but another part held back. If he touched the child it was bound to cry, if he held it, pound to a penny it would vomit on him. If he loved it, it would hurt him.

Yet how could he help himself? The house wasn't big enough to keep a distance between them and in the beginning everyone was desperate to thrust him into the baby's company: why don't you feed him, bath him, play with him? He soaped the plump arms and legs without seeing or feeling, ducked away from probing fingers, used the towel as a straightjacket. When his coldness made Jonathan cry, the other were swift to the rescue. Then came the shame. There was such a dislocation between what he felt and what he did.

He had a dream. There was a desk and a receptionist. A row of chairs. He was sitting in one of these. There were no sounds, no smells, no colours. He waited. He sat with his hands splayed on his knees. He stared at them, and couldn't be sure they really were his hands. And then the receptionist beckoned him, steered him towards the door. It was only as she opened it and ushered him through that she said, 'Mrs MacKenzie will see you now.'

The room was all white. White walls, white floor, white ceiling. And it was empty. He waited. The sound of his breathing filled the room, became magnified, like the rush of the sea in a shell, and the white walls became tinged with peach, then darkened to orange and darkened again and began to pulsate and generate heat as they pressed towards him and down on him closer and closer and hotter and hotter.

He woke breathless, streaming with sweat. Sarah lay sweetly asleep. He got out of bed without waking her and went downstairs. With still shaking hands, he poured himself a drink. Hunched in the wing chair, he rocked forward over his glass. Tomorrow he would tell Ron Harris that they would honour their present contract but, after that, they were to have no more dealings with Palladian Interiors.

She's won, then, said the devil on his shoulder.

No. She loses.

But she knows: you care enough to act against her.

He downed his drink. Devil or not, it had a point. Their professional relationship was a statement of indifference.

He made his way back upstairs. The door to Jonathan's room was ajar. He went in. Jonathan was awake. The night-light made his skin glow. 'Can't you sleep either?' he whispered. He bobbed down on to his heels and peered through the painted bars. He loved his son, he had no doubt, but he was also afraid of him. 'I'm sorry,' he whispered as the clutching hands reached for him. 'It's not your fault. I am so very sorry.'

Jonathan grew, and he was an eager, inquisitive child, there was no hope of confining him to the nursery. He explored the house first crawling, then lurching drunkenly from table to chair, stool to sofa, poking around in all the dark corners, curling up with his toys in the most inconvenient places. Emmy would appear with him clinging monkey-like to her hip having retrieved him from the back of the pantry where she'd caught him sucking sugar cubes. Sarah would laugh as she described finding him trying to thread liquorice laces down the telephone mouthpiece.

It seemed to Charles his house no longer belonged to him. Nobody considered him any more. If he left, would anyone notice? Even Leonard had changed, was more critical; his sympathy no longer to be relied upon.

One day he went into his study and found it invaded. Jonathan was sitting at the desk, his mouth smeared red from the Smarties he'd been wolfing, his sticky fingers spread across the tooled leather top. 'What the hell's going on here?' He dashed the remaining sweets to the floor. 'Sarah! Sarah! Do something.' The thump of his hand, the gush of rage, made Jonathan cower. He stared at his son, and saw that he was afraid.

The shock rocked him. But he felt no pity. He wanted to take hold of the child and shake him and shout at him for being a nuisance, for being afraid, for having been born. He took a step towards him. The Smartie-bloodied mouth quivered.

'Charles, no!' Leonard pushed past him, scooping Jonathan into his arms and easing the silky black hair off the sticky, teary face. He said, 'Hey now, what's all this, Jo-jo? No more tears, nothing to cry about, Daddy didn't mean it.'

'Look at this.' His voice shook with rage and self-loathing. 'Look at the mess he's made.' He picked up the unravelled Smartie tube and, brandishing it like a baton, gestured to the sticky finger-marks.

'You've got to fight this,' said Leonard softly. 'He's your son.'

'He's Sarah's son.'

12

Nickie, Nickie, you really are something. Sophie was triumphant. She'd been defiant and stubborn, and sometimes bloody-minded, but they'd come through, the pair of them.

He was an amazing child. Early on he displayed his gift, an eye for colour and a flamboyant nature definitely not inherited from his father. He spent his pre-school years making puppets out of fabric samples and playing cards out of colour charts. The older he grew, the more she involved him in her business. She learnt to trust his instinct; it amused her that some of her most prestigious clients occupied drawing rooms in some part designed by a ten-year-old.

But for all that he was her son, he still looked like his father. That was hard. Disturbing too, the way a gesture or an expression could make her weak with longing. How was it that, never having seen Charles, he could mimic him like this? She rebelled against the biology of it, but there was nothing she could do, only insist on his father's irrelevance. Sometimes it felt like a losing battle. She hated it when he asked about his father. She'd become vague and dismissive. 'What did he do?' Nickie would demand. 'What was his job?'

'Oh, you know, buying and selling, that sort of thing. Come here, Nick.' She unrolled a bolt of blue and crimson fabric, whipping it dramatically across the workbench. 'Tell me what you think of this.'

He could always be seduced by the fall of fabric, a flash of colour.

By the time she'd signed her first contract with Charles's company she already had a reputation. She'd made contacts through her Portobello traders and become known for her vision and strong views. Nickie accused her of being a bully, but her clients adored her. 'Your life is a theatre,' she told them. 'I provide the scenery: this is how you live, you do as I say. Does a leading lady bring on her dog halfway through a performance? Or produce auntie's favourite Crown Derby pot? Just so. Now take that vase/clock/magazine, and scrap it. I decide what stands on your mantelpiece, what books you scatter on your coffee table. It's what you pay me for.'

Performance. Her whole life was an act; she vamped it up and jacked up her fees to match. She loved it, and so it seemed did Nickie.

13

When Jonathan was eight, Charles's mother fell ill. Within six weeks of the diagnosis, she was dead. She might have used those last weeks to make peace with her family, but instead she'd milked the guilt right up to the end. She was going to die a disappointed woman, and it was Charles's fault. She talked about his father – how proud he'd been of his youngest son. Her tone, the theatrical sigh, made it clear that Charles had fallen far short of his father's ideal.

Sophie MacKenzie. She spat the name like a curse. How she still hated her. All his successes, the good things in his life, his career, his marriage, his son, dwindled to nothing in the face of that. Because of Sophie he'd abandoned God and God's laws. That was what she claimed to believe, but he knew that she hated Sophie because she'd given him the strength to break her crippling grip. But she'd never admit to that. For her it was all hellfire and damnation. He was a lost soul. The bloodied jaws of the beast gaped at his feet – Sophie his demon, her hair like dark flame, her bare feet and Imari skirts, her vision merging with his, more tangible than his, more terrible.

You don't argue with the dying. You listen and make a show of contrition. But with her tireless carping she leant against the Temple doors, and the locks and hinges, rusty with disuse, creaked and shuddered beneath the pressure. It would be too easy to add his strength to her weight and throw them wide.

Then the hospital rang to say it was over, and now he stood beneath the vaulted arches of the church she'd brought him to as a child, surrounded by the same old women, starlings in hats, he'd last seen at his father's funeral more than ten years ago.

She'd been a hard woman, a demanding mother and a fearsome wife, but in death she was proof against criticism. The vicar, whose collection box had regularly swelled from her fat purse, whose coffee mornings she'd regularly poisoned, sang her praises either ignorant of, or ignoring, the carnage of broken lives around her.

Charles refused to sing the hymns. He stood, back straight, chin jutting, cursing her for the blight she'd put on his life. If she'd been less severe he might have been less vulnerable to Sophie; he might have met and married Sarah out of love rather than desperation, been able to give Leonard what he so badly wanted. At the very least he might have found it in himself to love his son. To admit to his love for his son.

With much shuffling and coughing the congregation dropped to its knees. Charles perched on the edge of his pew and leant forward, his hands clasped between his knees. It was a long time since he'd been in a church. The shadows that had afflicted him then still flickered beneath the arches, behind the pillars, always just out of sight, threatening to search him out.

The service over, he escaped into the fresh air but was almost at once surrounded by his mother's friends eager to compliment him on how well he looked, and to tell Sarah how pleased his mother had been about his marriage, relieved to see him settled at last. Nodding and smiling, he herded Sarah and Jonathan into the car. Mrs Lloyd leant in at the window. 'Shame you can't come to the house. Lovely spread your sister's put on. Still, if you can't, you can't.' Turning to Sarah, she said, 'He always was his mum's favourite. Always my Charles this, my Charles that. Now don't you forget,' she patted Sarah's arm. 'If there's anything I can do, you just let me know.'

As the car drew away, Sarah said, 'We should have gone.' Charles didn't answer.

'She gives me sweets,' said Jonathan.

'Does she, dear.' Sarah pushed the cascade of almost-black hair away from his eyes.

'When we go and see Gran, they taste like soap.' He pulled away from his mother's fussing hand.

Charles rested his head against the window and closed his eyes. Thank God it was over. He was so tired.

Like a stone skimming water, Jonathan prattled on about Mrs Lloyd. As well as sweets tasting of soap she had a dog smelling of sick.

The water was dark and cold. Sunlight spattered the surface with flecks of gold.

'Shush,' whispered Sarah, 'Daddy's asleep.'

'No he's not, he's pretending.' Charles opened his eyes. 'There,' Jonathan crowed. 'Told you so.'

He stared out of the window. A movement caught his eye. A small woman in a crimson and blue skirt, a man's arm about her waist. Too young.

As the traffic lights turned red, they came to a halt alongside a group of workmen refurbishing a shopfront. The shop's facade was painted in crimson, the fluted pillars supporting the portico were lined with gold. A workman in paint-splashed overalls was sign-writing in a great arc on the window. The name of the shop was Palladian Interiors.

The association between his company and Sophie's had flourished, as had her business generally. He'd heard about her plans for a high street design consultancy – the financial journals had been full of it some months back, but he hadn't realised the project was so far advanced. Had they stayed together, what a team they would have made.

'It's coming, it's coming. . . . Look, there it is.' Jonathan tugged at Leonard's arm and pointed along the platform to the advancing train. 'Why don't you come too, Uncle Leonard?'

'Not this time.' Leonard squeezed Jonathan's shoulder. He and Sarah were going to Dorset for a couple of weeks. Charles had not been invited.

Leonard glanced along to where Charles and Sarah were saying goodbye. They stood apart, very upright, very formal. He half expected them to shake hands. He wondered if they were like that in bed, side by side, straight as billiard cues.

Jonathan said, 'Why are you laughing?'

'No reason.' He ruffled the dark head. 'So tell me, will you miss me?'

'Yes,' Jonathan peered at him from beneath his floppy fringe. 'I wish you were coming.'

'You'll enjoy yourself, all that sea and sand. It's nearly time; on you get.' He ushered Jonathan along the platform. 'Be sure and send me a postcard,' he said as they reached Charles and Sarah. 'And bring me back a stick of rock.'

'I will,' he said, brave and angry, frightened and excited. It wasn't fair; he was too young to cope with such a cocktail of emotions.

Then Charles was saying goodbye to his son. He made a hesitant gesture, as if to lay a hand on Jonathan's shoulder, but thought better of it. Nor did Jonathan encourage him. Over the years Leonard had watched as Charles's feigned indifference gradually convinced his son. Charles had once confided that resentment sometimes became anger and he was so afraid that anger might turn to violence. Leonard wondered now whether the habit of indifference had made it real.

It was time for their train to leave. Leonard kissed Sarah's cheek, aching for his helplessness. He loved her, he loved Jonathan and wanted to help them, but he loved Charles more.

They waved the train out of sight. Or rather Leonard waved; Charles raised an awkward hand, dropping it again almost immediately.

Arriving home, Leonard was struck by the unnatural quietness of the house. Emmy had been tidying; not a single toy peeped from under the furniture, the half-finished jigsaw had been cleared from the table. He said, 'It's horrid without them, isn't it? Empty.' Charles slumped into his wing chair. 'Won't you miss them at all?'

'Not so much as you,' he said. 'Don't look so shocked. I know you'll hate every minute they're away, but it's different for me, you know that.'

'Do I?' Charles flicked some dust from his trousers. 'You've changed,' Leonard accused. 'I used to think I understood, but I don't, not any more. I don't know what you think about Sarah or Jonathan, or even what you feel about me.'

'You're my friend,' he whispered. 'The only one who really knows . . . .'

'Oh yes, I know – all the details, the duff decisions, everything. And I live with the consequences, just like you. How would you react, Charles, if I said enough? If I told you I'd decided to go away.'

'Go where?'

'I said, if.'

Charles tilted his head against the chair and looked up at him. His eyes were bright, but Leonard saw how old he'd grown, saw as if for the first time how grey his hair had become, how deeply etched were the arrowed creases bracketing his mouth, the way the shallower ones sagged beneath his eyes. For the first time he questioned where, if anywhere, this was leading. Why was he wasting his life on these people? They took him for granted, sucked the energy out of him. Maybe he should get out now, while he still had a choice.

He said, 'I'm going upstairs; I've some letters to write.'

He passed close to Charles's chair. Charles caught him by the wrist. His hand was broad, the fingers strong. Looking down, Leonard saw that his own wrist appeared alarmingly frail within that grasp; frail enough to snap.

Charles said, 'Don't go.'

And all the questions gathered in his throat: what do you mean? Don't go now, or don't go ever? Explain yourself. Tell me what you think, what you feel. About me.

But he said nothing. He stared at his friend, locking on to the dark, gaping eyes, and thought how utterly selfish he'd become in his belief that no one had ever loved the way he'd loved, that no one had ever been hurt as he'd been hurt. And they all put up with it because ultimately there was no malice in him. He was as innocent as a child, and as selfish as a child. And he had a child's instinct for getting his own way.

14

Time, Charles thought, was a slippery fish. He peered into the mirror, dragged the razor through the foam mask. Fifty-six. An age since his last birthday, an age till his next. It was too great, the burden of life's passing. And yet. If he looked not at the tedious details of daily existence but at the pivotal points, time was nothing. It was but a moment since his mother's death, since Jonathan's birth, a blink of an eye since Sophie MacKenzie was here.

And she was here still, like him locked out of the Temple, a lost and questing soul – though he tried hard not to hear her, not to see her shadow flickering at the end of the corridors, pretended not to feel her light touch on his shoulder.

What had brought his haunting to the forefront like this, making him wonder afresh if she ever thought of him? Had she remarried, or did she live alone? She used to say they were alike – perhaps she lived as he'd once lived. The thoughts jostled. He longed to say her name out loud. But hearing, who would listen?

They had built a motorway to Cambridge, but he took the old road. He'd had enough of anger and resentment. His marriage was a habit, he didn't trust himself to get close to his son, and there was a real danger he might lose Leonard. He had coasted too long. He had to act. He would go to Cambridge. He didn't expect to see her, but to go there again, to see those places as they were now, rather than as they existed in his memory, might just lay his ghost.

Over breakfast he'd told them he was going off to see a new site. There was no response. Cambridge meant little to Leonard and nothing to Sarah; they associated Sophie with Beaufort Square.

Never had he felt so alone, not even in the dark days before

Sophie. He was truly alone now, on the old Cambridge road. The serious drivers were tearing along the motorway. One would need a special reason to drive a lumbering car like this along such a winding route, through village after deserted village.

Not quite deserted. A couple of boys on bikes hung around a bus shelter. He braked to allow an old man in a gaberdine mac with orange bailer twine trailing from the pocket, to push a wheelbarrow across the road. A woman in a flowing blue skirt and emerald bandanna turned at the sound of the car and raised her arm, beckoning him. No, she was just making a half-hearted attempt to hitch a lift.

He pulled over. She got in. Without looking at her he said, 'I'm going to Cambridge,' and she said, 'Great.'

He accelerated out of the village. She settled herself in the deep seat. Her hands rested in her lap. There was a silver ring on every finger, a cluster of bangles round her wrist. Gipsy or hippie, either or both. He pressed down on the accelerator. She shifted in her seat. He pressed harder. She said, 'Shit! Slow down.' He looked at her. She looked back. Challenging. Mocking. She was young – brown eyes, thin lips. She said, 'Watch the fucking road, can't you?' Dark eyebrows. Black lashes. He snatched at the emerald bandanna. She screeched. A wing of black hair flew across her face. She screeched again and grabbed the wheel turning and turning and he fought her and hit out at her as an oncoming van veered out of their way and they tumbled to the big-dipper spin of the careering car. The impact jarred him; an acid spread of pain scraped through him, merging with the grinding shriek of twisting metal. Then all was still. A geranium spatter of blood stained the pale leather. Through an amazingly intact window the vapour trail of an invisible plane sliced the fading sky.

It was dark and warm inside this place. He wanted to stop, snuggle down and sleep – but he couldn't, he had to keep running, on and on, with all the time behind him the moist, snuffling sound of an animal on the scent and, behind that, the mechanical tick of claws on bone.

There was no light to show him how close it might be, this animal, this beast. His death. He had no choice, had to keep on

321

running round and round, hemmed in by blood and bone, swamped by the dull echo of his pain.

Perhaps he'd died and ended up in hell like his mother had promised. Had she known it would be like this – endlessly fleeing a foe who could never quite catch up, whose form he couldn't see or purpose understand? Onward and round and back again, retracing the lightless route he'd already taken and always behind him, the sound of running feet, the hoarse breath and ever-present gasp of his enemy.

Then silence. Sudden, absolute. And absence: of sound, of movement, of pursuit. He was no longer running, no longer locked within the confines of his skull.

He blinked, but the darkness stayed. Also the silence. He tried to move, but his limbs were pinioned. Then something touched his hand with a terrible, spidery delicacy. He screamed – but no sound came. Or else it came and he couldn't hear it. Which? How could he tell . . . and why couldn't he move? He strained against the paralysis, fighting it, and all his strength and stubbornness was ranged against it until, at the final push, a great dark, thrashing serpent of pain unleashed itself and raised its flattened head and swayed back and forth, sensuous, sinuous, hypnotising – then struck.

Sarah had gone home. Leonard was alone with Charles. Every day for weeks they'd sat by his bed watching, waiting. It was too much for Sarah. It would be easier if they knew how long it was likely to go on, but the doctors were evasive. It was an open-ended sentence.

Massaging his cheek he felt how the skin had grown slack and rough. It was as if he'd taken root beside the bed. Nothing could move him so long as Charles still breathed.

Why?

The inert body had nothing to do with Charles. At regular intervals the nurses came in to rearrange his limbs, check the readings on the flashing screens, adjust the tubes that pumped fluids in and out of his body – the process was functional, impersonal. Reduced to this. If Charles knew, God how he'd hate it. But this wasn't Charles. Charles was somewhere else.

During the first months the doctors had done little more than shake their heads and express sympathy. They were doing all they could, so they said. Sometimes it seemed to Leonard they were doing a great deal, but at others he was sure there was something else, some drug, some technique they were withholding. Perhaps Charles had been judged and found wanting, and this was his punishment.

But now there were fewer tubes. They had disconnected most of the machinery. He was breathing on his own. The doctors had begun to express a cautious optimism.

Sarah took this optimism at face value, never pausing to consider the sort of life that might await Charles should he wake. Leonard had asked, but no one was prepared to commit themselves on the extent of the damage. Sarah had heard the question and its answer, but it hadn't registered. All she grasped was that the line between life and death had been redrawn. 'He's on the mend,' was the phrase she used on the telephone to her mother, and the next day she brought Jonathan to visit his father.

Jonathan was eleven, a withdrawn, studious boy who resented being prised away from his books. He lingered in the doorway, one hand thrust deep in his blazer pocket, the other fretting at the knot in his school tie.

'Come on, Jonathan,' his mother coaxed. 'Come and say hello.'

'I feel sick.'

'Don't be so silly.'

'Don't force him,' said Leonard. 'Charles doesn't know he's here.'

'You can't be sure. You've no right to say that. Jonathan. . . .'

Jonathan came as far as the end of the bed. He stood sullenly fiddling with the chart hooked over the rail. Regardless of whether or not his father knew he was there, Jonathan was still afraid. Leonard saw how he absented himself from the room in the same way that Charles had absented himself from his marriage. They were alike, father and son, cause and effect circling one another like mounted combatants. Trying to read the closed young face was like trying to read a message in tea leaves. He was too young to veil his feelings entirely. There was fear on the surface, but under that something else. What? Sorrow, relief, indifference? Leonard found himself locked out of the boy's mind.

Although Charles had been unplugged from the last of his apparatus and moved to another room, the doctors still wouldn't commit themselves as to the outcome. Only when the bruising to the brain had finally subsided would they know. Leonard caressed Charles's bony hand. At first he'd been morbidly obsessed with the details of the accident – the passenger, the woman who had died, what had she been doing in the car? The police said she was a hitch-hiker. It wasn't like Charles to give lifts to strangers. The van driver and his passenger had both seen the woman trying to wrest the steering wheel from Charles. As the weeks passed these details became less important to Leonard. Now all he wanted to know was what Charles had felt and thought as the car spun out of control, and whether those feelings and thoughts would be altered, what grasp his battered brain would retain on those moments. Stroking the limp fingers, he thought how obscenely healthy his own hand looked. He was so afraid. Anything might happen. Charles might wake blind, or crippled, or with his mind impaired – or all of these things. Or worse. To be aware of the incurable limitations of his mind and body. That would be terrible.

No. I won't let that happen – his fingers clenched round the frail hand – I won't let you live like that.

The hand held clenched in his, stirred. The fingers curled feebly against his palm. He was awake. Charles was awake; his eyes glittered with the effort to focus. Leonard whispered his name. The dark gaze sharpened, a frown pulsed between his brows. Laughter, relief, hysteria cackled in Leonard's throat; he stifled it. 'Hello,' he said inadequately. Charles moved his fingers in response. Lifting his hand, Leonard kissed the dry palm.

Charles closed his eyes. When, after a few minutes, he opened them again, he tried to speak. His breath was hoarse, but his cracked lips parted and his voice, when it came, was like a blunt razor scraping bristle. 'She wouldn't go,' he said. It was as if every word drew blood deep inside him. Leonard stroked the hollow cheek, and shook his head in puzzlement. Charles said, 'I sent her away.'

And suddenly he understood. 'I know,' he whispered.

'I had to.'

'Yes.'

'But she kept coming back.'

After all this time, she was still with him. The fact itself wasn't so surprising, only the immediacy of it. When Charles had described how he'd evicted her from the Temple, Leonard hadn't altogether believed him. At best, he'd decided, he'd buried her deep enough that she wouldn't easily trouble him again. At best. But best was nowhere near good enough – she was still there and always would be, the auburn-haired ghost pacing the corridors of his mind, ready and eager to rattle her chains at the first sign of weakness.

15

When he tried to sit up, he felt dizzy. Once he actually vomited. Sarah recoiled, but not Leonard. Leonard took hold of him and turned him so he couldn't see the mess.

After that he stopped trying. He passed his time making an in-depth survey of the ceiling, mapping the dents in the polystyrene tiles, the splashes of paint and crude holes dug for the service ducts. When he closed his eyes, he could still see it, a crazy network, a root-system, a spider's spoor.

As he contemplated his ceiling the voices, the dash of feet, the clatter of dishes, faded into a uniform hum. But he could never shut out the noise entirely. Nor could he shut out the pain. He had a dull ache in his back as if he'd been beaten with a club and, skittering over the surface, a whole percussion section of twinges, jabs and stabs darted irregularly between the base of his skull and the backs of his knees.

'Stravinsky,' Leonard grinned. 'Sounds like something by Stravinsky.' Charles laughed. It hurt to laugh, and it hurt to cry, to eat, to piss and shit.

He hated this place, the smell, the food, the way the nurses coaxed him, as if he were an educationally sub-normal child. How much longer must he put up with being patronised, with the constant prodding and poking of the doctors? Hardly an hour passed without a new clutch of white-coated technicians arriving to give him another overhaul, gathering round the bed, shining lights in his eyes, testing his reflexes and asking endless questions, the answers to which they bounced back and forth over his aching head as if they were discussing a malfunctioning carburettor.

Afterwards he'd drift into a doze, then wake, still aching, to find Sarah fidgeting with the bedcovers, smoothing his pyjama collar and asking another batch of stupid questions. How did he feel? Was he thirsty? Had he read Mrs Lloyd's card?

Feigning sleep was dangerous. Without the spider-spoor to distract him he hovered dizzily on the brink of the abyss, facing the closed doors of the Temple, knowing it to be occupied, that he'd failed again, hadn't driven her out at all, but forced her to burrow deeper.

By the end of the third month he could walk again, though not without the aid of a stick. His right foot had a will of its own, sometimes dragging behind him, at others jutting to one side and almost overbalancing him. 'Rome wasn't built in a day,' said the nurse. But walking was the least of his problems. Far more disturbing, because it concerned the Temple not the flesh, was that he'd forgotten how to read and write. They said not to worry; these skills he could also relearn.

After four months they allowed him to go home. Leonard collected him. The cab pulled into Beaufort Square. He knew the name but the buildings were unfamiliar; they were too big, too white, they glared disapprovingly at him in the hard light of the November sun.

The door of number thirteen opened. He recognised Sarah. There was someone else, older, plumper. Emmy. She bumbled down the steps, her arms open to embrace him, and he inhaled a delicious perfume of tea and bacon.

The house was bigger than he remembered. The staircase curved endlessly away from him. It was a long, difficult climb to his room. He was aware of Sarah down in the hall, fluttering like a wing-clipped chicken, and of Leonard's voice, comforting and restraining.

He made it at last. Closing the bedroom door he leant against it, struggling to control his jagged breath, crying with frustration and anger. As he crossed the room the knob of the walking stick dug into his palm, crushing and bruising it. In time the stick would become a grafted appendage to his calloused hand.

Don't be bitter, it's not so bad. You might have died. Like her.

Who?

A half memory. A ringed hand. They'd asked him about her. He couldn't remember. She had black hair. He remembered that.

He lowered himself into the tub chair. Thank God he was out of that hospital. He started to relax, the tension eased as his spine began to unwind. His gaze drifted round the room. The perspective kept shifting. Some parts of the room were familiar, others completely alien. Some objects he recognised, some not. The chair in which he sat, the table next to him, these he knew. But not the lamp. It had a brass column topped by a fragile shade with a bead fringe. He lifted the glass tassels, allowed them to trail across his palm. The amber and ruby coloured beads were cool and soothing.

Somebody knocked on the door. Sarah. He was glad to see her. He smiled and said, 'Don't look so worried. Come here.' He held out his hand; she came to him and leant against him – and he remembered about the lamp. It was Sarah's, one of the few things she'd brought into the house.

He hated forgetting the obvious. All very well for the doctors to say take it easy, one step at a time; they didn't have to live with this body that refused to function, this mind that was so slow at interpreting the world around it. It took all his strength to go on living in this shell. There were things inside him the doctors would never cure. Like this sound he was hearing now, as he'd heard it every night since his return to consciousness: the faint, rhythmic hum of the Temple chant.

If there was a drug that could stop it, he'd take it by the barrel-load.

Like the drone of the mystic it throbbed on and on, deep inside the Temple, relentless, wordless, without meaning.

I can't hear you.

Then come closer.

Christmas came and went, and still he rocked between bitterness and resignation. Bitterness when he stared at balance sheets and calculations that were gibberish to him; when he read his notes and saw how he'd pressed so hard with his pen that he'd jabbed a hole in the paper, saw how rounded and childlike was his lettering and knew his elegant flourishes had gone forever. Resignation came as he lay in bed night after night, rigid with fear, contemplating his death. He had come so close, it would have taken just one more step, had he but known.

If I destroy the Temple, where then could she hide?

'*I am woven in every sinew, etched on every bone.*

The Temple cannot fall.'

She left him no choice. He metamorphosed into the perfect patient, meticulously carrying out the instructions of the doctors and physiotherapists, even devising mental exercises of his own. Typically he expected immediate results. Instead there was a gradual dawning, a slow realisation that the world was easing back into focus. One day as Leonard outlined the details of a new project, his interest was aroused. He pulled the papers towards him. The words leapt up off the page, took shape, gathered meaning.

He started going into the office two days a week; by the end of April he was going in daily. The Temple doors were locked and barricaded. And only on the quietest of days, when the wind was in the wrong direction, could he hear the Priestess chanting.

16

It was summer again, a year since the crash. He sat in the cab fingering the carved ivory bear that topped his walking stick, trying not to examine too closely his motives for going to this exhibition. *Landseer at the Tate*, he'd seen the announcement in *The Times* weeks ago and, for the first time in years, remembered the lions in Trafalgar Square. Not that that was reason enough to go. Quite the contrary. But the exhibition was well publicised, there were posters everywhere. Or so it seemed. Today was his last chance, the exhibition was coming to an end.

The cab dropped him outside the gallery. He began the slow climb up the broad steps. Several times he stopped to catch his breath and stood looking down at the glittering expanse of the river. Young people were sprawled up and down the steps, hunched over guide books, eating sandwiches out of crumpled foil packages, chewing thoughtfully, gazing across the viscous flow of traffic to the sluggish Thames beyond. The fumes pushed out by the lorries and buses and cabs, melted the whole scene into soft focus.

Inside it was cooler. He passed through the rotunda and skirted a rust-coloured iron sculpture. The rooms were tall, airy, with light wooden floors. Students in jeans scribbled in notebooks, women in hats looked bored.

What was he doing here?

With a shrug that drew a puzzled glance from a large woman in a frowzy floral dress, he placed himself before one of the paintings and wondered how big a gap there was between what he was seeing and what he was supposed to be seeing.

What he thought he saw was a wounded stag. Its muzzle was moist, its eyes soft and dark and pleading. The jaws of the hounds were smeared with blood.

Sir Edwin Landseer was like you, he never married. He had his lions and stags and melt-eyed dogs for company, and you've got your stocks and shares and buildings. . . .

It was too vivid, this sharp-edged memory that hadn't surfaced for years. He could see her so clearly, a small woman with fiery hair, perched on Landseer's lion, making fun of him. The pain was acid bright, as if the intervening years had never been.

Fool. You haven't changed, have you? Fancy coming here like this, you must have known it'd all come rushing back – not general fears and wordless chants, not the Priestess but the reality. The auburn-haired, grey-eyed reality. But you came all the same, knowing how dangerous it was. You've wasted your life because of her, allowed others to suffer – die even – and she wasn't worth it. All she offered was illusion, fantasy, haven't you learnt that yet? Go home.

He stepped back and blundered into the man behind him. He apologised, and moved on to the next painting, this time a group of spaniels. The contrast made him uneasy. It was as he turned away from the spaniels that he noticed her. She was on the far side of the room, standing with her back to him: a small, neat-bodied woman in a yellow summer dress. Her hair, long and curled, the colour of faded bronze, was tied loosely at her nape with a ribbon a shade darker than her dress. She shifted her weight from one foot to the other. His skin prickled. A draught fanned the fire he'd thought extinguished.

He bore down on his stick. The carved knob dug into his hand. He took a step towards her, and then another. A man brandishing a catalogue at his companion passed between them. Another two steps, and he'd be there.

He was standing very close now. His eyes were drawn to the way her hair curled upwards and away from the restraining ribbon, to the ribbon's tail which heightened the paleness, emphasised the vulnerable crook between neck and shoulder. She moved, and the faintly freckled skin slid over the fine bones.

She turned. She didn't know him. He was a stranger and he was being too forward; irritation flickered across her face.

But there was never a chance that he would fail to recognise her. Sophie would always be Sophie, with her wonderful hair and her gold-flecked eyes ready to dart with anger or fizz with mischief. Oh, she'd changed a little, of course she had. The tender skin beneath her eyes was lightly scored, her hair faded and finely ticked with grey, but it barely showed, it was as if he saw her indistinctly, through a mist.

But she didn't know him. She gave an exasperated shake of her head and started to turn away.

'Sophie.' She swung back to face him. She knew his voice. At least there was something about him that hadn't changed. He said, 'I'm sorry, did I startle you?'

'I didn't recognise you.'

'I know.' He wanted to ask what she was doing here. Was she alone? Was she meeting someone? Could they go somewhere and talk? He wanted to touch her.

She said, 'You've changed.'

'I've been ill.'

'I heard.' As she spoke, her eyes darted round the room. She was looking for someone, or expecting someone to come looking for her. She said, 'I'm sorry. It's a bad time. I have to go.'

'No. Please. Surely you've time for a coffee. . . .'

'I'm meeting someone.'

'I see.'

She said, 'I'm sorry. Maybe. . . .' She stopped. She'd seen someone. Her eyes widened in recognition. He turned.

Jonathan. She was meeting Jonathan? It couldn't be. Not Jonathan. This boy was older, taller, better looking. His hair was thicker and coarser than Jonathan's, but his eyes were the same.

He didn't understand. His mind slowed. The sounds of the gallery became distant. The boy stared at them. Sophie took his arm and he could feel her warmth and smell the citrus tang of her perfume. She said, 'Well, he's here now. I suppose I'd better introduce you.' She drew him reluctantly across the room to where Jonathan's double waited for them. She said, 'Charles, this is my son.' She squeezed his arm. 'This is Nicholas.'

17

It seemed to Sophie also that at every turn she was confronted with posters and reviews for the exhibition. She'd had no intention of going. Which was ridiculous because she rather liked Landseer. On the very last day of the exhibition, she succumbed. She had to bully Nickie into accompanying her, eventually bribing him with the promise of lunch.

Once there, he wandered off on his own. She didn't mind, she was absorbed in the paintings. She loved their theatricality and tactile nature. The exquisite pelts were irresistible; she wanted to touch and stroke the canvas, was fascinated by the contrast of luminous eyes and blood-drenched savagery.

She noticed the elderly man with the walking stick as soon as she entered this room, but there was nothing about the lop-sided stance and the shock of grey hair that was remotely familiar. It was his walking stick that caught her eye. A fine piece, ivory-topped with a silver ferule. His hand closed over the carving before she could see the detail.

She turned back to a painting of puppies which had been paired with its engraving. As she studied them and read the legend alongside, she became aware of someone standing very close behind her. Expecting Nickie she swung round, smiling. But it wasn't Nicholas, it was the old man.

He was leaning to one side, pressing down on his stick. His face was tilted towards her and had the drawn, cadaverous look of someone recently recovered from a severe illness. She was annoyed. She didn't like being accosted by strangers. She started to turn away.

And then he said her name.

Charles. So many years living in the same city, their companies communicating, but not them. Such a long time living with his replica so that now the shock of time passing stunned her to silence. She stared at him. She wanted to touch his ravaged face, wanted him to say her name again. More than that, she wanted him to go before Nicholas came back.

He was saying something about them going for a coffee. When she said she was meeting someone, she knew what he thought.

It shouldn't hurt like this. Not after all this time.

Then Nickie came through from the other room and she had no choice, she had to introduce them. She said, 'This is Mr Wade. We do a lot of work for his company.'

'Oh, right,' said Nickie. They shook hands. Charles's face was a complete blank. That couldn't be right, could it? There ought to be something there, some response, anger or joy, bewilderment even, but not this nothingness. Didn't he see the likeness?

And then she remembered the rumours about the accident, the bits and pieces she'd gleaned from Ron Harris, her contact in Charles's company, and the snippets in the financial sections of the papers. They were very interested in his fate, those papers. Charles was synonymous with his company, if he died the ramifications would be tremendous. But death wasn't the only possibility.

Why didn't he see the likeness? Had he forgotten how he used to look, had his injured brain obliterated the memory?

Then he smiled. It was all right. He saw.

He began asking Nickie what he thought of the exhibition. Nickie shrugged. 'It's okay. A bit prissy, sentimental.'

She still had hold of Charles's arm. She said, 'So what are you doing here? I didn't think art was really your thing.'

'I had some time to waste.' His voice was hard. She dug her fingers more deeply into his arm. He continued, 'Also, someone once likened me to Edwin Landseer.' She released him.

'Who?' demanded Nickie.

'Your mother.'

Nickie looked from one to the other. 'Why?' he demanded. 'Why would you say that, Mum?'

'I really can't remember.'

Charles said, 'It was something to do with the fact that I was unmarried, and likely to remain that way.'

'Whereas now,' she said gently, 'you have a wife and a son.'

'A whole other life.'

'Mum?' Nickie interrupted. 'Shouldn't we be going? You booked a table. . . .'

'In a minute, Nickie.'

Charles said, 'Don't let me keep you.'

'Why don't you join us?'

'Mum!'

'It's all right, Nicholas.' Charles spoke without looking at him. 'I don't intend to gatecrash.'

'Nickie, don't be so rude. Charles, do come. I thought you wanted to talk.'

'Not any more.' He turned to go.

'Charles no, not like this, please. If not today, then let's meet. We really ought to talk. Why don't you come to the house, come for lunch, or dinner. Charles!'

Pivoting on his stick, he swept round to face her. He was furious. As usual she'd gone too far. As always, she'd pushed him to his limit, then pushed again.

'Where?' he said, startling her. She stared at him. 'Tell me where you live.'

He should never have turned back. How could he allow it to begin all over again? The moment he'd recognised her he should have left the gallery. To do so might have involved going through the room Nicholas was in. Would he have recognised him? Probably not, he'd have been so hellbent on getting away from Sophie. It was academic anyway; he hadn't left. He'd gone across to her. Even then it hadn't been too late. He could have pretended not to recognise her – but the idea had not presented itself in time.

He finished shaving and splashed cold water on to his face. Buttoning his pyjama jacket he went through to the bedroom. Sarah sat at the dressing table taking out her contact lenses. He squeezed her shoulder. 'Shower's all yours,' he said, kissing the top of her head. 'Don't be long.' As she closed the bathroom door, he slid under the sheets and rested back against the pillow.

He'd had no choice, he'd had to make himself known to her. And to his son. His son! Had she known she was pregnant when she left him?

Nicholas.

Fists beat against the closed doors of the Temple.

No.

It was Nicholas who had stood between him and Jonathan, not the dead child at all. In some dark corner of his mind he had known or suspected Nicholas.

From the bathroom came the splash and tattoo of the shower. He lay listening to the familiar, domestic sound.

She hadn't recognised him. But then he'd changed so much. He was old. An old man, and a foolish one. All the bad things in his life were down to her. His mother had been right. Sophie MacKenzie danced like a demon, tempting him, luring him to the false sanctuary of the Temple. Why hadn't she warned him of the dangers, the madness that lurked in the corners, flickering just out of sight behind the vaulted arches?

Perhaps because insanity was itself the sanctuary?

No. She hadn't warned him because she'd wanted him destroyed. What had he done to her that she wanted him dead? Dead in body, dead in mind, it didn't matter which, so long as she was free. Was that it? Was she as much enthralled by him as he by her? But she loved me. She loves my son.

He ached with the effort to untangle her motives. Had the accident dislodged some vital connection in his brain so that he never would be able to make sense of it all? He seemed to believe equally in her innocence and her malice.

For some time now no sound had come from the bathroom. He wished Sarah would hurry up, there was no point in his trying to sleep until she came to bed; she'd only wake him and then he'd toss and turn for the rest of the night.

When she did come, it was in a cloud of steam and she drifted towards him, and he saw that she was different. How, different? Something about the way she moved? No. Not her, it wasn't her, it was the other one, walking with a spring in her step, tossing her long auburn hair back off her shoulders as she slid into bed beside him.

Pulling up the covers, Sarah said, 'You look tired.'

'Yes.'

She pressed her hand against his chest and kissed his cheek. His body kicked awake. He saw her recognition and her pleasure and wanted to shout, no, not for you, not because of you. Instead he said, 'I feel so old, Sarah.' And he looked up at her, at her face all stripped of make-up, and saw how painfully deep were the creases lining her thin face. His fault, all of it. Worry for him, concern for their son, unnamed fears about Sophie and Leonard, about his past and their future, these were the things that had withered her. Like the rings that define the age of a tree, her sorrows were carved indelibly on her face.

He lifted her hand. Kissing the thin fingers he said, 'You're tired too. Go to sleep.'

But they didn't sleep. He switched off the light, then returned to her. Physical supremacy. Much good may it do him. Sarah's thin arms clutched him to her, her hungry lips chewed at his as he thrust at her, hurting her maybe – she never would say.

And Sophie, where are you tonight? And who's with you? Do you ever think of me, my foxy lady?

Sarah fell asleep with her arms wrapped round him. He felt swamped. He smelt her peppermint toothpaste, felt the eerie tap of her heart.

Come to the house. The voice leapt out of the dark, making him start. Sarah's grip on him tightened, then relaxed.

Why should she want to see him again after all these years? Perhaps simply so that he could get to know his son. If he hadn't found out, would she ever have told him about Nicholas? Of course not. She hadn't changed. Sophie MacKenzie, hard as ever, clutching their lives in her hands, moulding and shaping, crushing.

But that didn't stop him wondering about her life. Had she shared it with anyone after him? Had she embraced the principle of the Temple – the flesh is nothing – or was there a man who called her his wife, Nicholas his son?

He needed to get an objective view. But there was no one he could talk to, not even Leonard. Nobody mentioned Sophie, and to say her name out loud after so long would cleave his household like an axe through a log.

18

Though the doctors said it was dangerous for him to drive, he'd insisted on retaining a set of car keys. He needed the illusion of autonomy. Sliding open the desk drawer, he took out the keys. Emmy was busy downstairs; Leonard had taken Jonathan swimming, and Sarah had gone shopping. He could slip away now and no one the wiser.

He drove carefully, feeling vulnerable; the new car seemed unduly cumbersome. The journey to Ware took a ridiculously long time but finding the house wasn't difficult. He spotted it fractionally too late and had to drive on until he found an opening wide enough to turn the car. That first glimpse brought a prickle of foreboding. Surely it was too large for just the two of them.

Once she'd told him his way of life was too grand for her, that she would never adapt. She'd adapted now. It was an imposing house – double-fronted Georgian, set well back from the road behind tall iron railings. The deep gravel roared like the sea as he swung the car into the drive and curved round the oval of close-cut grass.

He switched off the engine. He was stiff. He stretched his leg and reached down to massage the calf. There was movement at one of the upper windows. He heaved himself out of the car, rocked against his stick, recovered himself and made for the front door. The downstairs windows had green-painted shutters thrown back against the ivory rendering. The door was flanked by two teardrop-shaped bay trees. He crushed a leaf between his fingers and dabbed them to his nose. There'd been a bay tree at the cottage she'd shared with Michael, though less ornamental, more shaggy, a refuge and nesting place for birds.

He tugged at the bell-pull. The door was opened almost immediately by a rather severe woman in her mid-thirties. He gave his name. She said Mrs MacKenzie was expecting him, but was out at the moment. Would he care to wait?

She showed him into the drawing room. He stood in the middle of the room remembering the transformation Sophie had wrought on his dining room. Sarah had hated it. Leonard had been amused; through him Charles had finally recognised the extent to which Sophie had been playing a prank on him. But this house, this room, was no joke. It was large and light, exquisitely decorated in pale apricot highlighted with royal blue: the mouldings that sectioned the walls were pencilled in blue, the swagged curtains were lined in it and the piping to their tiebacks was likewise picked out in blue. A monumental garniture of Chinese vases filled the space in front of the window; two knole sofas faced one another like gossipy friends, across the hearth. Above the fireplace was a gilt overmantel. At the centre of the carved marble mantelpiece stood a massive bronze of a tiger felling an elephant. The cat's claws and jaws had sunk into the wrinkled hide, the beady eye of the elephant tried to look backwards at its assailant. The only other ornament was the Celtic head.

As the Crucifix represents your faith to you . . . .

He picked it up. He felt a kind of vertigo as he looked down at the almost-familiar stylised features: the curved eyebrow sweeping down to delineate the nose, the blank oval eyes looking sightlessly back at him.

'It's Celtic,' said a voice from the doorway.

'Yes,' he answered softly, 'I know.' Smiling, he turned to face his son. Nicholas leant against the door. Charles was again struck by the self-assurance of this boy who seemed so much older than his years. Nicholas. His feelings were a tangled ball of tenderness, awe and fear. He looked back down at the head, focusing on it, turning it over and over in his hand. He said, 'It's to do with the head being the seat of the soul, am I right?'

'How d'you know that?' The boy's voice was sharp.

'Your mother told me.'

'When?' Why is he so angry? 'When did she tell you?' Nicholas demanded. 'The same time she told you you were like Landseer?'

'No,' he said quietly. 'I think it was before that.'

Nickie said, 'You'd better put it back. She doesn't like people touching it. She always knows.'

'Here.' Charles offered him the head. 'You do it.'

Nicholas edged round the coffee table. His fingers brushed Charles's. He replaced the head on the mantelpiece, carefully adjusting it to its former position. Did he realise the head's full significance, the extent to which his mother had allowed its philosophy to govern her, even though it hurt those she most loved? That's you and me, he wanted to say.

Dangerous ground. It was tempting to be indiscreet. He had a fleeting vision of Sophie coming home to find them reconciled. A crazy dream. He closed his mind to it. Gesturing to the elephant, he said, 'That's stunning, too.'

Nicholas frowned. Charles thought, why does he dislike me so much when he barely knows me?

Running a finger along the rib of the elephant's back, Nicholas shrugged and said, 'I found it in an auction in Norfolk last summer. Only decent thing there; cheap too.'

The severe woman came into the room, carrying a tea tray. Nicholas thanked her, and Charles learnt that she was called Alison. He faced his son across the low coffee table. The sofas were no longer so chatty. After a while Nicholas said, 'Mum didn't think you'd come. When I asked her, she said you probably wouldn't.'

'I almost didn't.'

'Why not?'

Charles shrugged. Nicholas frowned again. Does he see the resemblance, Charles wondered, all the little things, the way he has of moving his shoulders, his smile, the way he narrows his eyes. I see them day after day in my own mirror, and in Jonathan. It won't take him long to work it out, he won't have to be told.

He glanced at his watch. 'Is she likely to be long?'

'I shouldn't think so.'

'Good.'

The silence stretched between them, thin and fragile. Then, out of the blue, Nicholas said, 'May I look at your stick?'

The non-sequitur made him sharp. 'What?'

'The stick. I know someone who collects them, but I haven't seen one like that.'

Charles passed the stick across the table. Nicholas ran his hands along the shaft, caressing it as a blind man might. As his mother might.

Nicholas said, 'Where was it made?'

'I don't know. A friend gave it to me. He said, if I was going to join the ranks of the halt and the lame, I'd better do it in style.'

'Leonard,' said a voice. He looked up. Sophie stood in the doorway, smiling. 'Sounds like Leonard to me. No, Charles, don't get up.'

'Who's Leonard?' The spiky, almost querulous note had returned to Nickie's voice. He looked from his mother to Charles and back again.

Sophie said, 'It's a beautiful piece.' She took the stick from her son and examined it. An enamelled snake coiled the lower part of her arm, its emerald scales glinted as she moved. She said, 'You always did like to have the best of everything, and to use it.'

'Rockingham,' he grinned.

As she returned the stick, Nicholas demanded again, 'Who's Leonard?'

Sophie put her arm round his shoulder. 'A mutual friend.' Nickie sulkily shrugged her arm away. 'Don't be childish, Nickie. What will Mr Wade think?'

'I don't care. You don't usually care what people think either.'

'That depends on the people. Come on, Nickie, I need to talk to Mr Wade.' The scaled enamel tightened its grip on her wrist. Twining her fingers with her son's, she urged him towards the door. Leaning against him, she whispered something as she ushered him out.

She turned back into the room. 'He's a good boy,' she said, 'but possessive.' She sat facing him. She was dressed in white, a tight bodice and a flowing skirt, her waist nipped by another emerald snake. Her faded hair hung loose, mantling her bare shoulders. His eyes were drawn to the rash of golden freckles dancing across her bare arms. A fine gold chain spanned her throat like a cobweb caught in the sun. 'It's good to see you,' she said. 'I didn't think you'd come.'

'So Nicholas said.'

'But you did. I'm glad.' He nodded. His throat was tight and he couldn't speak. She said, 'So how is everyone? How's Leonard?'

'Fine. He's fine.'

'Has he managed to hang on to any hair? Poor Leonard. . . .' The smile dashed across her face, then faded. She was nervous. Of him? Surely not. She said, 'It must have been a shock, finding out about Nickie like that. I didn't want it to happen that way.'

'I don't suppose you wanted it to happen at all.'

'Charles . . . .'

'You never intended me to know, did you?'

'You've no right . . . .' She stopped. Bit her lip. She said, 'I was wrong to ask you here if all we're going to do is bicker.'

'I'm sorry,' he said. 'Could we try again?'

She hesitated, then nodded. He watched as she poured more tea, then tucked her feet under her and settled back into the corner of the sofa. Her feet were bare. Some things never change. Her hands were bare as well, she wore no rings, only the snake bracelet which glittered as it writhed about her wrist and spread its cobra head across the back of her hand. 'So,' she was more composed. 'What do you make of your son?'

'I don't know, I haven't really had a chance. . . . He's a bit prickly, defensive. Like me, I suppose. And Jonathan. At first I thought he was Jonathan.' At the mention of his younger son's name her hands moved in her lap and his overheated brain was convinced the snake-tongue flickered.

There was an edge to her voice when she next spoke, even though it was only to ask after Emmy. 'Is she well?'

'Em doesn't change.'

'Does she remember me?'

'We don't discuss you.'

'I suppose not. Does she get on well with your wife?'

'Emmy gets on with everyone.'

'A gold star for Emmy.' She traced the coil of the snake, bringing her forefinger to rest on the flattened head. Then she looked up, forcing him to confront her. She said, 'What about you? Have you been happy, Charles?'

'What do you think?'

'It's been such a long time.' Her eyes moved past him to fix on something beyond his shoulder. She said, 'I don't know how much of the past is dead, how much still alive. I don't even know why I asked you here, let alone why you came.'

'I know. Because you couldn't resist the opportunity to rake it all over, give the wound a jab, pinch and scratch, make sure you can still make me bleed.'

'No.'

'I know you. And you can, Sophie! Look at me, bleeding here and now, all over your sofa. Does that satisfy you? Does that make you happy?'

'It isn't what I wanted.'

'I told you, I know you. And that's funny, because you don't know me. You've wasted your time. You didn't have to go to this much effort, you don't even have to be there; you're an amputated limb that goes on and on aching . . . .'

'Don't!' She banged her hand hard down on her knee so that the snake convulsed. Anger thickened her voice. 'Don't imagine you're the only one who's suffered. You didn't have to face it alone. All these years you've been surrounded by people who loved you – Helen, Emmy, Sarah, even Leonard – and who have I had, tell me that? No one. All the way through it's been just me and Nickie. There was no one I could trust. Even Jazz – remember Jazz? – I had to get away from her because I couldn't stand the things she kept saying about you. So don't try and tell me how hard it's been, how much you've suffered, because I'm not interested.'

Into the silence he whispered, 'I didn't know. How could I know?' His voice became stronger. 'If you'd told me about Nicholas. . . . You should have told me.'

She laughed. He stared at her flushed face and glittering eyes. She said, 'Now doesn't this sound familiar? We've been here before.'

Ignoring her, he said, 'The night you left – did you know then? You did, didn't you; you knew you were pregnant.' She nodded. 'And did you never consider letting me know? If I hadn't gone to the Landseer, if I hadn't found out for myself. . . .'

'I thought it would just cause too much trouble. It worried me, though. Nickie was always asking about his father. When I thought you were going to die, I almost told him about you. I even wondered about taking him to the hospital.'

'You'd never have got past Leonard.'

'Standing guard, was he? Good old Leonard, loyal to the last. Faithful too, no doubt.'

'You make it sound like a failing.'

'What about Sarah, is she faithful? Dear Sarah, such a paragon – God, Charles, I'm so sorry.' She pressed her fingers against her lips, as if to push the words back in. 'Why do we do this?' As she rocked back and forth her collarbones made little hollows of shadow and the gold chain shifted and slithered. Cursing his slowness, he moved round the low table to sit beside her. He touched her. He lifted a strand of hair back over her shoulder and his fingers brushed her skin. After a while she said, 'I'd like you to tell me about Jonathan.'

His shoulders stiffened. He drew back. He said, 'Why?'

'He's Nickie's brother. . . .'

He edged away from her. He said, 'He looks like Nicholas. He's clever, does well at school, but not much imagination. Bit like Anthony really.'

'You don't seem to like him much.'

'He gets on better with Leonard. Leonard's teaching him to swim and play chess.'

'Nickie's good at chess.'

'Is he?' He felt a stab of pride, then misgiving. 'Who taught him?'

'A friend.'

'He's clever too, then.'

'Not academic, but bright, yes. Quite the businessman. He's been trading through my shops since he was eleven.'

'Does he make much?'

She laughed, bubbling like a geyser. Struggling to catch her breath, she said, 'Oh, Charles! That's so typical.' She slipped her hand into his, and drew him back to her.

He said, 'Jonathan doesn't do anything remotely enterprising.'

'Why should he?' Her fingers curled against his palm. 'Give the boy a chance. Don't keep comparing him with Nickie, it isn't fair.'

She took it for granted he'd stay for dinner. When he protested that he shouldn't drive home in the dark, she said, 'Then stay the night, there's plenty of room.'

After dinner they sat in the drawing room drinking strong coffee from tiny, straight-sided cups rimmed in royal blue and gold. Later, after Nicholas had gone to bed, Sophie poured more brandy. As he cradled his glass, he said, 'He doesn't like me very much.'

'He hardly knows you. He's a bit jealous. Don't rush him.'

'But you'll tell him?'

'When he's ready.' She stood up. 'Come on,' she said, 'I need some fresh air.'

She led him out on to the terrace, down the stone steps to the garden. He could smell the damp grass; bats, like puppets on jerky

343

strings, flitted above them. At the end of the garden was a pad-
dock. He could just make out the outline of a horse or pony on the
far side. Sophie leant against the rail, her profile silhouetted against
a sky not yet entirely dark. A pale wash of lingering blue smeared
the blackness and offered her features for his study. He said, 'Do
you still see Michael?'

'Good God no. Why ever should you think that?'

'I just wondered.'

'You wondered. . . .' He heard the smile in her voice.

'I thought – I'm surprised you haven't married again.'

She laughed. The pony tossed its head and snickered. She said,
'It has been touch and go. My accountant – he taught Nickie to
play chess – proposes about once a month.'

'Persistent man.'

'Yes, but then he is an accountant.'

Without his being aware of having moved, they'd come to be
standing so close that he could detect her perfume mingling with
the scents of the night. He reached out and touched her softly
curving cheek. She lifted her face to his.

From his bedroom window, Nicholas saw the caress, saw his
mother return it. Leaning forward, he pressed his hands against the
glass, watching as his mother took the stranger's arm and turned
back to the house. An hour later he stood with his ear to the door,
making sure his mother's guest spent the night alone.

Charles couldn't sleep. The night was very dark – a country dark –
and very quiet. But inside, the day's events replayed themselves in
technicolor and stereo. Not a word spoken nor a gesture sketched
escaped him. He watched and listened until his eyes stung as if
dowsed in soap, until the ringing in his ears competed with the
silence.

Then he slept, and woke to an unfamiliar room and the distant
murmur of a radio, to a sour taste in his mouth and the realisation
that he'd wasted his life. Nothing could make it right. The sooner
he stopped fooling himself the better.

He refused breakfast, wouldn't even have a cup of coffee.

Sophie followed him to the car. Catching him by the arm, almost
unbalancing him, she said, 'What's happened, why the rush?' He

shook her off and unlocked the car. 'That's it, is it?' She stood, hands on hips. 'Walk out, why don't you. Run away.'

'I'm not running away.'

'No? So you'll be coming back?'

'No.' This time, he thought, I must be firm. 'What would be the point?'

'Nickie.'

'No. Nicholas doesn't need me. Nor do you. It's over. We can't go back, we can't change the past.'

'We can change the future.'

'I'm married.' His voice shook, he felt the ground shudder. 'I have a son. That's my future.'

'You have two sons.'

'One needs me, the other doesn't. You said it yourself – give the boy a chance.'

'I should have fought for you, Charles.' Her face was white as a clown's and she didn't seem to see him any more. 'I should have kept you by me, but I was stubborn. I let it all go, fall away like flesh from a corpse, and I've spent fifteen years remembering, regretting, wishing – if wishes were fishes. . . . You can't do this, Charles.'

'I can.' He was doing it, managing to sound firm, but it left him weak. He needed to sit down. He opened the door and eased himself into the car. He said, 'You'll cope, you know you will. You're a capable, intelligent woman; don't tell me you can't. . . .'

'I was wrong. Is that what you want to hear? I was wrong when I said that; it didn't apply then and it doesn't apply now.'

With fumbling fingers he buckled his seat belt. The distant chanting blurred her voice. When she reached into the car to touch his shoulder, his body tingled from top to toe. He said, 'Please, let it rest, Sophie. Let it die.' But her fingers stroked his cheek and fluttered against his chin and the Temple doors opened a crack on groaning hinges, and a thin, blinding strip of light made him blink, made his eyes water.

She said, 'Come again – next Sunday. For lunch. But don't drive. I'll pick you up at the station.'

He should have said no. He started the engine and slipped the car into gear.

No. He should have said it before, when first she challenged him: *Do I know you?*

19

Sophie watched him pull out of the drive. After years of coping, she no longer knew what to do for the best. She'd bullied him into coming again, knowing that it was a mistake, that he wanted her to tell Nickie who he was, and that Nickie wasn't ready.

She loved Nickie, and she knew him. He could be volatile. She had made him her own, bonding him exclusively to her, and their closeness had salved the ache inside her. He had yielded at first, but as he grew older he began to kick against it. She had used him – how could she have done otherwise? Having lost everything, she channelled her life through his until all her pain, stifled hunger and loss, erupted inside him, scorching his skull, leaving him screaming.

It was dreadful the way her feelings for Charles had come thrusting to the surface. Their power bewildered and enraged her.

So why insist that he come back?

For Nickie – no, for Nickie he should stay away. Not for her son, but for herself. If she pretended to altruism, or claimed the renewal of her search for the numinous, then she was lying. Every time she touched him all her most basic instincts screamed awake. He was old and changed, but she still wanted him.

She went back into the house. In the breakfast room Nickie was hunched over the newly arrived *Trades Gazette*, ringing auction adverts with a fat red marker. She poured herself some coffee. Nickie didn't look up. She reached across the table and snatched the paper from him. He glared at her, but let it go.

She said, 'He's coming again, next Sunday.' Nickie shrugged. 'You don't mind, do you?'

'Why should I mind? Nothing to do with me. Can I have the paper back? There's a sale out near Norwich. . . .'

'Nickie, don't be like this.'

'Like what? How should I be?' He twisted the cap back on the marker pen, then carried on twisting and twisting and twisting. 'How should I be?' he said again. 'Who is he, Mum?'

With a shaking hand, Charles fumbled with his keys, found the right one and inserted it into the lock. He sensed the drop and chunk of the mechanism. The door slid open.

One two, buckle my shoe. Three, four, shut the door.

Nothing was the same any more. Leonard appeared. Charles blinked; he hardly recognised him he was so ragged and pale. 'Thank God,' Leonard hissed.

From the drawing room Sarah called, 'Charles?' She came into the hall. Her eyes were red from crying and her face all puffy. 'Charles. . . .' She took a step towards him, but Leonard stopped her with a hand on her arm. 'We've been so worried.'

He felt dizzy. His brain floated; when he turned his head it took a moment for the swimming mass to reorient itself.

Leonard said, 'I think you should go upstairs and lie down.'

'Yes, I shall.' He felt fragile. He moved carefully, as if holding a bowl filled to the brim with water.

'I'll be up in a minute,' called Leonard.

The wooden banister was slick as glass. The shallow steps snagged at his feet, jarring him so that he splashed crystal droplets of water onto his fingers. Reaching his bedroom he paused, then continued along the passage to Leonard's room.

The room was familiar. Many of its furnishings had come from the Islington flat, pieces such as the photograph of the Thames at low tide, the Edwardian street scene and the bronze head. He sank onto the bed and lay back. The silk counterpane slid beneath his gliding fingers. The murmur of Emmy's radio drifted up from the open kitchen window.

We can change the future – her voice skittered like a moth amongst the shadows on the ceiling. Change the future. How? Aren't they the same thing: past, present and future? How can we isolate them one from the other?

But if we could – just imagine – I would have a choice.

No, no choice. There's never been a choice. I'm trapped in the present. I have to go forward. I'm tired. I don't want to.

Through the rumbling denial he heard the double click of the door opening and closing. No choice in anything. He couldn't even choose to be alone.

The bed sagged as the intruder sat down. He opened his eyes. Leonard said, 'Sarah's terribly upset.'

He turned away, rolling his hot cheek against the cool silk. Why wouldn't they leave him be? They gave him no peace, clustering round him like flies on a corpse – a sentient corpse. He shuddered and blinked; his vision blurred and cleared. He blinked again, but it was no good. She was still there, standing framed by the window with her white gown rippling and her lips curved in a cruel smile. The power of the Priestess would never wane, his thraldom would continue for as long as she lived.

'You don't care, do you?' Leonard spat, and the Priestess vanished. 'You don't give a shit about us. We've been up all night worrying. . . .'

'There was no need.'

'Evidently, but we didn't know that. You're not supposed to drive, Charles – anything might have happened. I've been on to the police, the hospitals. . . .'

'Oh, for God's sake.' He turned and looked up at Leonard, and saw that the almond-shaped eyes were very blue and very bright. 'For God's sake,' he said more softly, 'I came back, didn't I – for all of you, for Jonathan. I didn't want to. I wanted to stay.'

'Stay where?'

'I should have phoned. I didn't think . . . I know – I never do. I'm sorry.'

'And sorry solves everything, does it?' Anger transformed Leonard's face, making the angles sharper, rendering him more catlike than ever. 'Sorry's supposed to set us back on track, stop us asking uncomfortable questions. You've a bloody nerve. We deserve better than this.'

Charles closed his eyes, shutting out the hurt and anger, but

Leonard wouldn't be ignored. He took Charles's hand and his grip was hard. Charles shuddered at the coldness of the lips pressed briefly to the corner of his mouth. 'That's right,' said Leonard, and Charles felt the bitter vibration of his lips, tasted the earthy tang of Russian tobacco on his breath. 'Go to sleep. Do what you always do – run to where the rest of us can't follow.'

It was dark when Charles woke. The house was silent. He moved, and his daytime clothes rasped against the silk bedcover. Somebody had covered him with a blanket. He was too hot. He tossed it aside and it slithered to the floor.

He should never have gone to that exhibition. He'd been doing pretty well up until then. Okay, he and Sarah weren't in line for the Dunmow flitch, but even so, under the circumstances, they'd made a reasonable go of it. Until now. What to do? Sophie had made him promise to go back and he knew that, like the hawk to the lure, he would fly to her.

Her house, sitting in its grounds, spreading its elegant skirts like a Gainsborough lady, held the echo of everything he had lost. He could still feel it, the pale, peachy atmosphere wreathing round him. He was frantically homesick for Sophie and her son.

He'd promised to return, and he always kept his promises. On Sunday he would go to Ware and they'd sit and talk, she'd tell him how she'd spent the years, tell him about her business and about Nickie.

Nicholas. He'd watched his son, listed the ways he resembled himself and the ways he resembled Sophie, saw how everything about him was defined by his genes, innocuous elements that would make him life's victim or its victor.

But what part could he – the real he, not his genetic input – play in his son's life? The boy's reaction to him had veered between hostility and curiosity. Sophie said he was jealous. Why should he be jealous? Because he sees a stranger intruding on their life together. So, it'll be all right when he knows who I am. I won't be a stranger any more. I'll be able to say to him, you're my son, Nicholas.

But what about Jonathan?

They're so different, Sophie's child and Sarah's – like their mothers, one bright and confident and alive, the other self-effacing and nervous.

Then, in a sudden, dizzying flash, he saw them together: kicking a ball around on Sophie's lawn; in her drawing room, their heads bent over a game of chess. Surely they'd both profit from such contact. Nickie would acquire a family, and maybe some of his self-assurance would rub off on Jonathan. Like a spotlit painting, the image glowed. Everyone would benefit when Sophie, who had been his lover, became his friend.

Fool. The harsh voice inside his head dowsed the light and plunged him into darkness so that he clutched at the silk coverlet. You think it'll stop at that? Dream on. You know you want more from her than friendship. Have you forgotten – the way her hair used to coil and snake, the salty-sweet taste of her skin, the way she'd cry out and puncture your shoulders with her nails? Oh yes, you remember it all, you feel it now. Face it, old fool, she'll never be your friend.

The others were already at breakfast. Sarah sat very upright. Her hair was tugged sharply back from her face, revealing the stark line of her bones; her make-up was harsh, presumably to mask the effects of tears and sleeplessness.

Leonard also looked grim. Jonathan sat, head bent, concentrating on his cereal. He felt a rush of tenderness for his son.

Sarah said, 'D'you feel better? You slept the clock round.'

Charles pulled out a chair and sat down without answering. Jonathan pushed his bowl away, saying, 'May I go?'

'I think you should eat a bit more than that, dear,' Sarah gushed. 'You can't go all morning on just a bowl of cereal.'

'Leave him, can't you,' Charles said. 'You treat him like a baby.' He reached for the coffee pot. It yielded only half a cup.

'I'll fetch some more.' Sarah started to rise but Emmy arrived to take away the empty pot. The four of them sat in edgy silence as the plates of bacon and egg cooled and the butter soaked into the toast. Sarah twisted her wedding ring round and round. Jonathan stared fixedly at the tablecloth.

Leonard said, 'We've been thinking,' he glanced at Sarah who became suddenly alert, 'talking things over. . . .'

'We?'

'Yes. Sarah and I. You're tired, Charles. You've done well, but you've been very ill, you should rest. We thought we might take a holiday.'

'No. I can't. Not now.'

'Please, Charles.' Sarah leant towards him. Her hand fluttered towards his, then withdrew. 'It'd be nice. It'd do us all good.'

'No,' he repeated in bewilderment. How could they possibly expect him to leave London, now of all times?

'Think of Jonathan,' said Leonard.

'I am thinking of Jonathan,' he said, and his throat ached and he didn't understand. Why were they doing this? Why couldn't they leave him alone?

He heard the Priestess's laughter before he saw her. She stood behind Jonathan's chair. Her long auburn hair writhed across her shoulders and her fingers hovered above Jonathan's head. '*They'll never do that*,' she said with a half-smile as she lifted a lock of his silky hair. She let it trail over her fingers, then drop. She said, '*Next Sunday. . . .*'

'Next Sunday,' Charles echoed.

'What about it?' Leonard demanded.

'Jonathan and I shall go out for the day.'

Sarah glanced at Leonard, then back at Charles. 'Where? Can we all come?' She was excited and alarmed.

'No.' She was still there, still standing behind Jonathan, her hands resting on the back of his chair. 'No,' he said again. 'This is just for the two of us, for me and Jonathan.'

20

'Where are we going?' Jonathan demanded. They sat side by side. The rhythmic sway of the train rocked them against one another. 'Where . . .' Jonathan began again.

'Ware,' Charles replied with a half smile.

'Where are we going, we're going to Ware,' Jonathan chanted. A rare flash of childish glee flitted across his face. Charles felt a rebuke forming on his lips: don't be a baby, act your age. Why could he never be gentle? He forced a smile. Jonathan wriggled uneasily. Poor kid, he didn't stand much chance; he was Sarah's son through and through, nervous as a rabbit. All the education in the world would never overcome that. Which made this trip all the more important. Jonathan needed a role model. He needed Nicholas.

'What happens when we get to Ware.' The chant was defiant now.

'Wait and see,' he said. Jonathan turned away and started to tug at the pad of skin beside his thumbnail. 'Don't do that. You'll make it bleed.' He reached to still the plucking fingers, and saw the raw patch on his own thumb. He hated this, the constant echo of his own behaviour in that of his sons. He withdrew his hand and said, 'We're going to visit some people I know.'

'Don't Mum and Uncle Leonard know them?'

'Not really. Oh for heaven's sake, sit still, Jonathan, can't you? It won't be long.'

Jonathan became still. Charles rested his head against the seat and closed his eyes. Sarah would never forgive him for this. Not that it mattered. Nothing mattered now. All he wanted was to see them together, Jonathan and Nicholas and Sophie.

'Are we there? Is this it?' Jonathan jumped up, bracing his thin legs against the sway of the slowing train. Charles nodded.

Through the grimy window he saw her waiting on the platform. The draught from the train lifted the mantle of her hair; she tilted her head sideways the better to hear something Nicholas was saying. Nicholas looked sullen.

Charles edged along the compartment to where Jonathan was fumbling with the door catch. 'Leave it,' he said. 'I'll do it.'

The platform was shaded by the station buildings and the air was cool. Sophie, who was standing two carriages along, saw him and her head jerked in recognition. Jonathan was hanging back. Sophie hadn't noticed him. She smiled and raised a hand in greeting. He waved back, and started towards her.

The air shimmered. He was limping more than usual. He kept his eyes fixed on her, his lodestone, willing her not to look past him and see Jonathan. He reached for her and held her, burying his face in her hair, inhaling the evocative tang of her perfume, clutching her so that the knob of his walking stick dug into her back and must surely be hurting her – but she gave no sign as he clung to her, to the lifeline he'd lost hold of fifteen years ago and would never let go of again.

'Mum. Mum, don't. People are staring.' At the sound of Nicholas's voice she stiffened. Pressing her hands against his chest, she began to disengage herself. He held on to her for a moment longer.

'Mum!'

She pushed him away. Nicholas was furious. Jonathan stood with his mouth gaping. As Charles turned towards him, the tears brimmed and spilled. 'Jonathan, act your age, can't you?'

'Charles, don't.' Sophie's hand was on his arm, heavy, shackling. She smiled at the boys, saying, 'You're right, Nickie, this is a bit public. Let's go home.'

Ushering them into the peach and blue drawing room, Sophie closed the door. The boys eyed one another. Nicholas was still angry, Jonathan still afraid. Sophie was – what? Irritated, yes. Also amused. She looked from one to the other, then laughed and said, 'Once upon a time, long ago and in a distant land. . . .'

Nickie scowled.

Charles said, 'We should explain.'

'I thought that's what I was doing. There's no point in stating the obvious. All they have to do is look at one another, compare ages, and they have it.'

'That's right,' said Nickie. 'Obvious.' To Charles he said, 'I thought you were dead.'

'Why should you think that?' Turning to Sophie he demanded, 'Is that what you told him?'

'Certainly not. I told him nothing. I made an art of prevarication.'

'I asked you – you didn't say he wasn't. Anyway, it was better to think he was dead than that he didn't want me.'

'That isn't so, Nicholas. I didn't know anything about you.'

'Mum?' Sophie stared at her son. 'You never told him?'

'There was no point.'

'If I had known . . .' Charles began, then glanced at Jonathan. Jonathan knew what he'd been about to say; it was written in the sharp lines of his face.

If I had known, I would have come to you.

Lunch was roast leg of lamb spiked with rosemary. Charles carved, Sophie distributed the pink-tinged slices. She urged the boys to help themselves to potatoes, braised celery, carrots. They spent the next twenty minutes spreading the food round their plates without eating.

Alison served dessert – apricot sorbet with a white wine sauce. Sophie said to Jonathan, 'Your father tells me you're learning to play chess.' Jonathan shrugged, and scraped the tip of his spoon across the surface of the sorbet; Nicholas pushed his dish away untouched. She said, 'Nickie, why not take Jonathan to your room and give him a game?'

'He's not very good,' Charles intervened.

She turned on him. 'How the hell would you know? You don't play chess. What about it, Nick?'

Nickie glanced at Jonathan. Jonathan shrugged and gave a faint nod. Nickie tapped his shoulder as he passed the back of his chair and Jonathan followed him upstairs.

Sophie said, 'For God's sake, Charles. I don't understand you. Why are you so hard on him? He's sweet.'

'He's no business being sweet. . . .'

'Big boys don't cry, is that it?'

'Nicholas didn't.'

'It might have been better if he had. Why did you bring him here?'

'I thought he might learn something from Nicholas. . . .'

'I said not to rush things. Nickie's not ready for this. He resents you, he can't believe you didn't know about him. He's always been desperate to know about his father. That's another reason I never told him, there's no knowing what he might have done . . . if I'm not careful I'll lose him, Charles. He'll blame me for keeping you apart. It's all right for you, you've got Sarah, and Jonathan and Leonard. Nickie's all I have.'

'I'm sorry. I didn't think of it like that.' She glared at him across the table. 'I know,' he whispered, 'sorry solves nothing.'

Her face softened. 'Well,' she said gently. 'What's done is done. We'll have to make the best of it.'

'What should I do?' She bit her lip and reached across the table to touch his wedding ring. When he turned his hand to capture her fingers, she withdrew. He moved round the table to sit closer to her. He said, 'Help me.'

'You ask too much.' She reached for his hand and stroked his forefinger from root to tip. Tracing the curve of his nail, she said, 'I don't want to lose him. I'm not exaggerating. It's a real possibility. But I can't tell you what to do, not this time. You must make your own choice.'

'Do I have a choice?'

She released him. She said, 'You should go home. You know that. Take Jonathan home, try to persuade him not to tell any of this to his mother. Will he do that?'

'I don't know. If he does, what then?'

'Then you make amends, to him and his mother. This is what you ought to do.'

'You said there was a choice.'

'Perhaps. I don't know.'

'Sophie. . . .'

'Yes,' she said at last. 'Yes, there is. But you know it already. You could come here.' Her grey eyes were sad, the gold flecks motionless. 'You could come here, to us.'

21

Just as they were leaving the house Sophie had given Jonathan a bottle of Coca Cola and a bar of chocolate. Now he and Charles sat facing one another in the train, the chocolate wrapper spread across the window ledge, Jonathan sullenly rotating the half-empty bottle on his knee.

Sophie was right, of course, it had been a stupid thing to do. He glanced at Jonathan. What had possessed him to confront the boys with one another like that? God knows what damage he'd done. He said gently, 'Are you all right?'

'He beat me,' said Jonathan without looking up. 'You said he would.'

'He's older than you. He's been playing longer. Besides,' he forced a smile, 'he was taught by an accountant.'

'What's that got to do with it?'

'Nothing. It was supposed to be a joke.'

'It wasn't funny.'

'I know. I'm sorry. Why don't you tell me what happened when you went upstairs, apart from his beating you. Did you talk?'

'Yes.'

'About what?'

'About you. And her.' He drained his drink and banged the bottle down on top of the chocolate wrapper.

Charles said, 'It was a mistake, taking you there.'

'Why did you?'

'I don't know.'

'What'll happen now?'

He shook his head. 'I don't know.'

'You don't know much, do you?'

356

'Jonathan!'

'Well, you don't. You just push us all around all the time and nobody stands up to you. Mum doesn't, and Uncle Leonard doesn't, not really, he pretends to but he always gives in in the end, and it isn't fair. They just let you do what you like. . . .'

'That's enough, Jonathan.'

'What about her, that woman? I bet she stands up to you; you couldn't bully her the way you bully us.'

'No.'

'I hate her,' he hissed. 'I hate her and I hate him and I'll tell Mum, I will. . . .'

'For God's sake, don't start crying again.'

'I'm not.' He cuffed roughly at his wet cheeks. 'I hate you too.'

'I know.'

'I do.' He leant his head against the window and beat his brow rhythmically as he chanted, 'I do, I do, I do.'

'Did you have a nice day, dear?' Sarah stood at the bottom of the stairs dry-washing her hands as she resisted the instinct to clasp Jonathan to her. She glanced warily at Charles, who refused to respond. Turning back to Jonathan, she insisted, 'Aren't you going to tell me where you went and what you did?'

'We went to Ware,' said Jonathan in a hard, quiet voice.

Leonard forced a laugh. 'Ware? What on earth did you find to do in Ware?'

Sarah said, 'Tell us later, yes?' She took a step towards him and held out a tentative hand. 'Let's have tea; Emmy's made a cake.'

'Don't want any cake.' Jonathan backed away from her, and fetched up against Charles. 'I'm not hungry.'

'What is it, dear? What's wrong, what's happened?' And she reached for him again but he dodged round her and made for the stairs.

She moved to follow him, but Leonard said, 'I'll go.'

'Yes, that's right,' Charles called over his shoulder as he headed for his study. 'Let Leonard go. He's good with little boys.'

He banged shut the study door. Dropping into the chair he leant his elbows on the desk and buried his face in his hands. What on earth had made him say that? He could still hear Leonard's sharp intake of breath, see the explosion of disbelief on his face.

God, Leonard, I'm so sorry.

Sorry? Sorry solves everything, does it?

It's all Sophie's fault. In the end everything always comes back to her.

You could come here, to us. Her voice echoed. The windows shimmered, the walls shuddered and cracked. Someone screamed – inside or outside, himself – her – Leonard; he couldn't tell which or who. What was happening to him? He had to get away. He moaned, and leant against the Temple doors. They moved. Not enough for him to enter, but enough to see the flame-haired Priestess standing before the altar, beckoning.

Come to us.

The rosy light kindled her faded hair. The fire was too bright to look into.

'That was cruel and uncalled for.' Sarah stood in the doorway and, just behind her, Leonard.

He said, 'I know.' Looking past her, he fixed Leonard's stricken face in his gaze. 'Leonard knows I didn't mean it.'

'Then you shouldn't have said it,' hissed Sarah.

'It doesn't matter, never mind me.' Leonard edged round Sarah and approached the desk. 'There's nothing I can't handle, but what about Jonathan? What have you done, Charles? He's locked himself in his room; he's sobbing his heart out.'

'I took him out for the day.'

'Where did you take him?'

'Ware . . .' Charles mused.

'He's not going to tell us,' said Sarah. 'Look at him. We don't mean a thing to him, we might as well not be here, he doesn't even care enough to hate us. Look at him.'

'D'you hear that, Charles? You wife thinks you hate her, and your son, and me. Does that make you proud? Is that what you wanted to achieve? God, we've been fools. Look how we've loved you. And for what? Bugger all. In the end it counts for nothing because none of this was ever anything more than a convenience to you. We loved you; but you've used us, you use everybody. You don't give a shit about anyone but yourself.'

'Why?' His voice turned on a ratchet, stiff and mechanical. From the oak photograph frame on the desk his father watched as the destruct sequence began. 'Why should I tell you anything?'

'Because we've stood by you all these years, tried to help you make some sense of it all – at the very least you owe us an explanation.'

'But it doesn't make sense, and I owe you nothing. There's nothing you've done for me that you've not done for yourselves. Stood by me, is that what you call it? Do you know what you are, shall I tell you? Gaolers, that's all you've ever been, watching over me year after year, building walls round unmentionable subjects, surrounding me with routine, with domestic detail. You talk about responsibility and duty, and you use them to build a prison. Gaolers!'

'Tell us.' Leonard brought his fist down on the desk and the photo frame jumped and the vibration shuddered through him. 'Tell us what you've done.'

'*Tell him*,' said the Priestess.

'I took him to see his brother.'

'His what?'

'Brother . . .' Sarah said on an outrush of air as she sank down into a chair.

'Sophie,' said Leonard flatly.

'Yes.'

'You never said.' Sarah was too shocked for tears. 'You never said anything about a child.'

Charles stared at his hands. The chanting was quite clear now, meandering between his words and theirs, obstructing, distorting, confusing, swaying with the Priestess as her robes swirled in the draught from the gaping door. One more step, just one more step and he'd be with her forever.

He said, 'I didn't tell you because I didn't know.' He fought against the Temple glow, struggling to concentrate on his hands where they rested on the desk. They didn't look like his hands. He turned them over and over and pressed them against the desktop and, though they responded to the command, there was no sensation; he couldn't feel the cool wood or the blotting pad where it scuffed against his little finger.

'You were with her last weekend?'

'Yes.'

'I thought,' Leonard's anger was so fierce that he could hardly articulate, 'I thought you were stronger than this – fight it, Charles, don't give in to her. Not now, not after so long.'

'I don't intend to.'

Sarah said, 'I still don't understand how you didn't know about him.'

'Come on, Sarah, you know how good he is at blinding himself to unpleasant truths. He runs away from responsibility. He always has.'

'Not from this,' Charles said. 'I'm not running from this.'

Leonard leant across the desk. Bitterness flooded his eyes and edged his words with glass. His face was very close, saliva specked his lips. 'No? You're going to face it, are you?' he hissed. 'You're going to make a commitment once and for all. Promise us you'll stay away from her, from both of them.'

'He can't. Leonard, don't you see, he can't.' Sarah's voice came as if pumped by bellows. 'Look at him. How can he promise that, now there's a child? Her son, Leonard. Think about it. Jonathan was my son, never his – but this boy. . . . What's his name, Charles?'

'Nicholas.'

'Nicholas.' She tested the name. 'Oh yes, Nicholas is your son, isn't he? Not my Jonathan. But that's all right; nothing's changed.'

'Oh no, please no.' The hysteria shivered through him like shattered glass. 'Just listen to her; she understands!'

'So she should, after all this time.'

'I do understand, Charles. I know you despise that; you'd much rather be misunderstood, wouldn't you? It gives you an excuse to be angry with us. That's the thing about Sophie. She misunderstands you, that's obvious. So you'll go to her and she'll hurt you all over again, only this time your son will see it all –'

'I'll tell you,' he interrupted, 'I'll tell you what you'll never understand. They're like one another, my two sons. And they're like me, how I was when I was young, except Nickie is more like me. He's got fire, he knows what he wants. He'll go far, will Nicholas.'

'You bastard,' Leonard spat. Charles had never seen him so murderously angry. 'You selfish, arrogant bastard. Do you know what you're saying, what you're doing to us? For twenty years I've loved you and no one could accuse me of being blind to your failings, but I thought I knew what lay behind it. I thought you were a strong man overwhelmed by circumstance and misplaced love. But no, you're weak, Charles, through and through. You run away whenever things get complicated; you don't have the stamina to stay and fight. Just look at you. How could I have loved you? You're ungrateful and selfish and weak. . . .'

'Weak? Was it weakness to survive without her? I didn't want to. And it would have been so easy – so many times, so many opportunities . . . . But oh no, you were always there, my self-appointed guardian, never letting me out of your sight. No, Leonard, I only had one weakness, and that was you.'

22

It was dark by the time the train pulled into Ware station. For the second time that day he stepped down onto the platform. This time he was not met.

The taxi dropped him at Sophie's gate. As it drew away he turned to face the house. All the downstairs lights were on, streaming out of the windows, patterning the driveway and the lawn. The point of his stick and his irregular footsteps munched the gravel as he started up the drive.

Alison looked surprised and a little alarmed to see him, but she let him in. The clash of raised voices came from the drawing room. Alison knocked on the door. The shouting continued unabated. She hesitated for a moment, then went in. The shouting stopped.

Charles stayed where he was, his feet planted firmly on the

Persian rug. The hall, large as a small room, was lit by a central chandelier. Beneath this was a gleaming antique mahogany table upon which stood a modern glass sculpture, cloudy as an ice-cube and massively heavy. He peered into the misty depths, unsure as to what he expected to see.

The opening of the door roused him. Sophie and Alison came out of the drawing room. Alison disappeared in the direction of the kitchen; Sophie came to stand close to him, her fingertips pressed so hard against the burnished table top that her nails whitened. Her face was flushed, her hair dishevelled.

She glanced over her shoulder at the closed drawing-room door. He said, 'I still think you should have told him years ago.'

'I know my son,' she said gently as she turned back to face him. 'He would have made a scene, a grand gesture – turned up on your doorstep most like. How would Sarah have coped with that?'

'I don't know. Hysterically, I imagine.'

'Quite. Still, Leonard would have known what to do.'

He said, 'Leonard's disowned me.'

'Has he now?' She seemed amused. 'Not forever, I shouldn't think. We all forgive you in the end, don't we?' And she framed his face with her hands and pressed her lips against his. 'Even Nickie,' she said. 'Even he'll forgive you one day.'

Alone in the drawing room, Nickie waited for his mother to send the stranger away. Stranger. Man. He couldn't give him a name. All the alternatives were so silly. Mr Wade. Uncle Charles. Daddy. Owen Wilson, his mother's accountant, had once half jokingly suggested that Nickie call him 'Uncle Owen'. She'd laughed and said, 'Why should he do that? You're not my brother!'

Any more than the man called Wade was his father.

Strange how all these years he'd longed to know about his father, and now he did, he wished him back where he came from. Everything that had been precious to him was falling away. Nothing was what it seemed. His mother wasn't what she'd seemed. She had lied to him.

He stood close to the overmantel mirror. Maybe it wasn't true. Maybe he could make it untrue. His breath clouded the plate as he peered at his reflection. One by one he divorced his features from

362

those of the man his mother called his father. Soon there was no resemblance left at all.

Which left Jonathan. Jonathan couldn't possibly be his brother, he was too skinny and his hair was silky like a girl's, and he was useless at chess.

His vision blurred. He blinked. From its place on the mantelpiece, the stone head leered at him. His hand shook as he picked it up. It had to be true. Charles Wade had known all about the head – and the Temple. He remembered coming into the room to find him holding it as if it belonged to him.

That's how he behaves with her, as if she belongs to him.

The mirror image watched him – another boy's face, another man's eyes. It was the truth. The man was his father. His mother had let him think he was dead. She had no right to do that. It was too cruel.

And all that stuff about the Temple – 'it's what's inside that counts,' she always said. Well, what about what's inside me, what I feel, what I want?

It was all spoilt. Everything he had ever believed in amounted to nothing. It was worthless. The stranger who was his father knew their secrets, their mystery. It was all ruined. Nothing could ever be the same again.

Sophie stroked Charles's cheek and at her touch his skin crackled. She said, 'You're tired. Get some rest. We'll talk in the morning.'

The bedroom was the one he'd had last time. He sat on the white counterpane, stark as an altar cloth; the brass bedstead jingled like temple bells. He shook with tiredness. The skin on his cheeks felt stretched and dry. He lay back and closed his eyes.

For as long as he could remember, every choice he had made had been the wrong one. Or else it had been right but he'd been unable to carry it through. Maybe Leonard was right, he was weak. Certainly Leonard wasn't the first to accuse him of running away when things got tough.

So, no more running. Face the future.

Come here, to us.

His head ached, he was hot.

According to Sarah, nothing had changed. She was right. Nothing would ever change. The torture goes on and on. The rack turns, pulling and twisting, and the hands on the wheel are small and strong, the straining arms lightly dusted with gold – and the pain is a hot knife working its way between sinew and bone, parting the joints, butchering him slowly, piece by bloody piece. . . .

The pain wakes him. He lies still, trying to remember where he is. He aches all over – wrists, elbows, knees, ankles. He turns his head. The night is over. He frowns, and tries to focus on his surroundings. A gauzy pink dawn streaks the walls and blushes his hand where it rests on the counterpane. He sits up, and at once knows where he is. And why.

The patterns repeat themselves. Freedom of choice is an illusion. He slides out of bed and sways as he waits for the agony to subside to a faint, sustainable pulse.

Facing the future is not enough. Change the future, she said. . . . He will go to her. His heartbeat quickens and his body hardens. He will go to her – not a young man about to take his bride for the first time, but a raped virgin returning to the arms of his violator.

Out of the fire she had come to him, a cold black shape issuing from its heart. Virgin sacrifice. He smiles and, crossing the room, opens the door to the bathroom. He showers, washes his hair, and shaves.

The landing doesn't face the dawn but there is enough pearl-grey light for him to see the pencil portrait of the Edwardian lady with a garland of ivy leaves in her hair.

One of these rooms belongs to Sophie. Which? This? No, this is empty. This, then? Yes.

The parted curtains stir in the breeze from the open window. As it billows across the pillow, the faded bronze of her hair borrows a rosy glow from the dawn.

Our Father which art in Heaven.

He throws wide the Temple doors.

Destroy the Temple, he'd once thought, and where then would the Priestess go? But the Priestess is a shadow, she follows, she clings, she never lets go.

So. Destroy the Priestess.

Hallowed be Thy name.

Physical supremacy. He drops to his knees and leans over her. Her perfume rises up, releasing his longing like a finger springing a catch. The hand is not his that moves to lift back the coil of burning hair. The sweep of her throat is white as a branch stripped of its bark.

Thy Kingdom come, forever and ever.

Never again – never again to be torn in two by her. . . .

His racked limbs shudder, but he is strong. The choice is his, and he has the strength to make it.

For his father, and for himself – for Michael and Sarah, for Leonard. For Jonathan. . . .

Forever and ever.

Rebuilding the Temple

1

'Forever and ever. . . .' His voice trailed away, blending into the silence of the Chelsea drawing room. The only sounds were the skeleton-click of the carriage clock, its brass viscera eerily visible, and the little popping noises Joanna made in her sleep. Leonard had made a nest for her in an armchair and she lay snug and safe and warm, her little hands clutching at the fragments of her dreams.

Charles sat, his white head bowed, staring at his hands as he plucked at the pad of skin next to his thumb. 'I don't remember any more,' he said mechanically. 'Too long ago. I can't remember.'

Leonard said, 'It's all right. Alex doesn't need any more.' Perching on the arm of the chair, he began to massage Charles's rigid shoulders.

When Jonathan's Aunt Helen had told me what her brother had done, she'd made all sorts of excuses – he was a good man really; it wasn't his fault, he didn't know what he was doing. And I'd thought, so he's crazy, is he? He killed her because he was out of his mind, and that makes it okay. Tell that to Jonathan, tell that to Joanna.

But that was before I'd met him. Now I understand what she'd meant. He'd been a fool, made a whole bundle of stupid mistakes, been mindlessly stubborn, but he'd fought in the only way he knew. He'd been like a man struggling in quicksand. Why had nobody told him to stop? Why had no one pointed out that if he carried on he was bound to go under?

I slid off my chair and bobbed down onto my heels. I took hold of his limp hands. His eyes – Jonathan's eyes, Nicholas's – were dull and blank.

Leonard, who'd continued his massaging, leant forward, saying, 'Charles? You're tired. Time you were in bed.'

Charles nodded and heaved himself to his feet. Leonard handed him his stick. He hesitated, seemed to be testing it, uncertain of its strength, then leant down hard and took a swaying step. Before it was completed, he swivelled unsteadily to face me. Reaching out, he clutched my arm. Though his frail fingers bit surprisingly hard, he was shaking, not just his hand but his whole body. It was the grip of a man about to fall. He said, 'I never meant to hurt her, Alex. I loved her. I wish it could end. I want it to stop. I miss her.'

Leonard took him upstairs and I sank back on to the sofa. I felt battered, confused by my compassion in the face of his brutality. It had been a long day. I ought to go home, Jonathan would be wondering what had happened to me, though I had warned him I'd be late. It was now just after nine, though in this house time wasn't measured by the clock but by the sag of Charles's shoulders, by the brightness or dullness of his eyes.

Above me the floorboards creaked and I heard the low murmur of their voices, Leonard's light and quick, Charles's deeper, heavier. Did he appreciate the fact that he'd had Leonard to come home to? Come to that, did he have any real grasp of the effect his act of defiance had had on those around him? He'd faced up to his problem all right, destroyed the Priestess, but he'd used a scatter-bomb to do it and the wounded screamed on all sides.

To begin with Sarah had depended on Leonard. He'd supported her all through the visits to the police station, the prison hospital, stood by her like a brother. But then the newspapers started to take an interest; the financial pages had reported Charles's car crash, but the story of the fallen entrepreneur had a wider appeal. At first employees and associates were eager to praise Charles as an upright man of principle. There had to be some mistake. But the evidence was incontrovertible. Gradually a different picture emerged. Come to think of it, these same people said, he'd always been a bit of an odd fish, prickly, not very sociable. From there it was a short hop to speculation about the role of Leonard Prentice in the Wade household. At this point, Sarah kicked Leonard out.

'I don't blame her,' Leonard said. 'She needed someone to blame. Who better than me?' What had really hurt though was that Jonathan also turned against him. Like Sarah, Jonathan needed a scapegoat. Unfortunately Leonard wasn't enough. For Jonathan what had happened was as much his mother's fault as it was Leonard's: either of them could have stopped it before it went so far. Jonathan became withdrawn. Sarah couldn't cope. She sent him away to school. By the time I met him the rift was absolute.

I visited Sarah once. She wouldn't talk to me on the phone so I drove down to Dorset. I took my wedding photos. She was very polite. She gave me tea and a slice of cherry cake, but she declined to look at my photographs and when I tentatively told her of my quest she said firmly, 'I think not, Alex. It's over. Let it be.' She struck me as touchingly ordinary and out of her depth; she didn't belong in Charles and Sophie's drama.

So many lives and relationships crumbled as a result of what Charles did, yet the most troubled relationship of all, that between Charles and Nicholas, blossomed. The deepest hatred ought to lie between those two: Nicholas had lost everything because of Charles. His whole way of life was turned upside down. In life his mother had seemed inescapable. Now she had vanished, and the void left him dizzy.

Her will named Owen Wilson, the maligned accountant, Nickie's guardian. Wilson sent Nickie away to school. The school was sworn to confidentiality, but Nickie made the mistake of confiding in one of the boys. Soon everybody knew. He was treated with a mixture of awe and distaste.

Poor Nickie. All he wanted was to belong again – belong somewhere, anywhere. Once again, it was Leonard to the rescue. Leonard, who had also lost everything, began to write to Nickie.

I heard Leonard's tread on the stairs. He said, 'Is Jo still asleep? Good. I'll make some coffee.' I followed him through to the kitchen. He made the coffee in an aluminium expresso pot. Perched on a counter stool, I watched as he filled the bottom half with water, spooned coffee into the basket, then screwed down the top.

'Will he be okay?' I asked, thinking of Charles alone upstairs.

'I gave him something to make him sleep. He'll be fine.' Leonard placed the pot on the hob and adjusted the heat. Easing himself onto the stool facing me, he plucked one of his black cigarettes from its sleek packet.

What a lonely life – what did he and Charles talk about all day?

What did they do? I imagined slow walks in the park, sitting on a bench feeding the ducks. The days were long gone when Leonard might take him to the theatre or a concert; now their common ground is too painful to contemplate. Is this where Nickie comes in? Someone with whom to share the burden? I said, 'I've been thinking about Nickie.' Leonard balanced the cigarette between his long fingers. 'You'd think he'd be more bitter, wouldn't you?'

He didn't answer at once. Placing the cigarette delicately between his lips, he flicked his heavy gold lighter and passed the flame under the wavering tip. He drew the smoke deep into his lungs before removing the cigarette and exhaling slowly. At last he said, 'It was Nickie who found them. Did I ever tell you that?'

'No.' The smoke was powerful in that confined space, it caught in the back of my throat and made me cough.

He went on, 'He strangled her, and put a pillow over her face for good measure. But you know that. Then Nickie came in.' His voice cracked; he took another shaky tug on his cigarette. 'He feels responsible, that's Nickie's particular hang-up. If he'd got there sooner he might have stopped it. He knows it wasn't Sophie Charles killed, it was the part of her he'd fabricated. All the same, if he'd got there sooner, he might have saved them.'

I haven't seen Charles again since that night, though Leonard phones me at regular intervals. Again and again I promise another visit to Chelsea: of course I'll come, and yes, naturally I'll bring Jo. I meant it, but I never made it and now it's too late, because Charles is dying.

The cancer was diagnosed in February, but nobody told me until a few weeks ago. Leonard had occasionally commented that Charles was under the weather, but never elaborated. He tells me now that he didn't want me to feel blackmailed into coming. Good old Leonard, honourable and scrupulous to a fault. When finally he did tell me, it was because the disease had advanced to the point where he had no choice.

And now I stand beside Charles's hospital bed raging with frustration, desperate that he should know why I stayed away; not because I didn't want to see him, because I don't love him, but because there was always tomorrow, and the chance that Jonathan might finally relent. But I say none of this because at this stage in life or death, all reasons have a tendency to sound like excuses.

'It's all right,' I tell him silently. 'Don't be afraid; I'm here.' We're all here now, me and Nickie, Leonard and Helen, the ones who really care. For an hysterical moment I see how bizarre it is, how medieval the way we've gathered round his deathbed, guarding his soul from the devils that perch on his shoulders and snap at his heels. I want to laugh, but don't because I know that the devils are real. I can hear their clicking jaws, feel the wave of heat from their fetid breath as they pant and drool in their lust for his soul.

Every now and again he wakes up and calls out for Jonathan. When that happens, Nicholas stands at my side, his arm draped round my shoulders, pretending to be his brother.

But Charles hasn't woken for some time now. I sit close, holding his hand. Helen faces me on the far side of the bed; Leonard and Nicholas stand by the window talking softly.

I look down at him. I don't even know whether he's sleeping or unconscious. I desperately want to know what's going on inside his head. Is the Temple still empty, or are the cymbals clashing with the promise of resurrection?

It frightens me the way they inject him to dull the pain. I can't help wondering what else they're dulling, whether his last impression of the world is going to be blurred by drugs, his mind struggling like a swimmer in treacle, his final thoughts muddled and incomplete. The awful thing is, no one can take the burden of decision from him, he's the only one who has the right to choose lucidity over pain, and he's beyond choice now.

His hand is very cold, but his breath still rasps and the hospital coverlet rises and falls and there is a white deposit at the corner of his lips. Then he opens his eyes, startling us all, and Leonard and Nicholas crowd against the bed, towering over him, but it's me he's looking at, though not me he sees.

As his eyes fix on mine, the most wonderful smile transforms his face. His smile transforms him, Sophie said, it makes him young. And it's still true, even now. Perhaps especially now.

Disentangling his fragile hand from my clutching fingers, he reaches shakily towards my face and strokes my cheek. But it isn't me he sees, it's her – and suddenly I am her and I know how much he loves me, and how the sight of me beside him like this scatters all his fear. And I do so want to be her, to reel back those terrible years and play her part and do all the things she failed to do and say.

I can save you, Sophie's voice screams inside my head, *I can save you.*

'I can save you,' I whisper to the man on the bed, and the light goes out. His eyes cloud. His hand drops away and his head sinks into the quicksand of the pillow.

The room is silent. The devils have fled. No one moves.

Even now there is a sense in which nothing has changed. There are things that go beyond sense. The light has been internalised, it is inside me now – his smile, her voice, the people they were before the Fall, so that I hold in my shaking hands a beautiful thing, an irrational legacy that goes beyond science, so that at last I understand everything: that Sophie wasn't a charlatan, only that her vision was flawed and narrow; that Charles, whose spiritual insight was so much greater than hers, who should have been released by her revelations, was instead cramped by them. Trusting her, he struggled to contain his cauldron within the framework she provided and it would not, could not fit. The godhead festered within him, lacking the context of the whole – the god within and all within god, the fragmented mirror made whole, the pomegranate soul.

And for us who are left, this means that what he was, I am. And what I am, he was. Past, present and future – there is no difference. He knew that, and now I know it too, and there is more to life than the accidents of the flesh.

2

It's weird being back in Nickie's flat like this. It's somehow not as I remember; it's starker, the walls are antiseptic white and the brash light glares, clashing against the broad expanse of the plate-glass window with its view of the Thames.

From the massive glass and marble coffee table Sophie watches the proceedings from the shelter of her maple photograph frame. We are all here now, though Helen looks uneasy. Two scarlet spots of colour scorch her cheeks as she meets Sophie's eye.

I hear soft laughter, and Charles whispers, *'It's all right now, Alex. Tell her it's all right.'* But I don't get the chance because Jonathan arrives. He's brought Joanna. She's desperately tired. The sharp light makes her blink. She digs her little fists into her eyes, rubs vigorously then lowers her hands to look round the room. She sees Leonard, and begins to laugh.

Jonathan, who refused to the last to be reconciled with his father, stands surrounded by those of us who loved him despite every-thing. I touch his arm. I'm afraid. He seems fragile, but the bewilderment and the hurt are no longer hidden or choked in, they are on the surface, flayed and raw – and that's good, I can bring him through this. I can save you.

Jo starts to fidget. I give Jonathan's arm a little squeeze, and say, 'Let Leonard hold her.' He hesitates for just a moment, then hands her over. She chuckles and clutches at Leonard's nose and ears and what's left of his hair. Leonard laughs and then he cries and Jo trails her fingers through his tears and tastes them and pulls a face. He hugs her close.

Helen goes to make some tea. I need some air. I go out onto the balcony. The city spreads itself before me like a swathe of lurex glittering in the dance-hall lights – a tawdry magic carpet weaving over the rooftops, along the quicksilver line of the Thames, playing ducks and drakes under the arches of the bridges, loop the loop round Big Ben. The vortex of lights makes me dizzy. I think, is this it, is this where it ends? Our lives evaporating like water on a griddle, skittering wildly then gone in a moment?

I want to find a reason, impose an order on Charles's chaos. But it isn't up to me. He's left so many reeling in his wake.

Nickie joins me on the balcony. He says, 'I've something for you.' He hands me a parcel. It is dense, and very heavy. Instinc-tively, I know what it is. He says, 'I don't need it any more. It was hers. You understand?'

I say, 'You'll miss him, won't you? You were close at the end.'

'Hardly. He thought I was Jonathan, remember? That's me, the all-round substitute. D'you think Leonard would have thought twice about me if he'd still had Jonathan? And my mother.' He stops. 'And you – they've all confessed to you and you think you know it all, but you don't.' His voice shakes. He leans against the balcony rail. 'Will you hear my confession, Alex?' I wait. Something about his tone and his stance makes me wary. At last he says, 'It seemed just, you know, that he should be punished. That's what I told myself. But then they released him and Leonard made me go and see him, and he was just an old man. I couldn't tell them, could I?' He gives a dry, breathless laugh. 'You don't know what I'm talking about, do you? He didn't kill her, Alex.'

In the room behind me, Helen sets a tray of antique cups and saucers on the marble and glass table. Leonard and Jonathan lean towards one another, deep in conversation. Jo is cradled against Leonard's shoulder. As he talks, Jonathan strokes her bare arm from elbow to wrist.

'She used to say life was a performance,' he continues. 'And it was true, it was all an act to her. She wasn't what she seemed. She lied to me over and over again. He didn't kill her. I did.'

Speaking firmly, as if to a child, I say, 'You can't argue with the facts, Nickie. He went to her room, she was asleep. . . .'

'Yes. She was asleep, and he put his hands round her throat, and everybody thought it was him. He thought so. But she didn't die.' His hands clench the balcony rail. He says, 'Who could I tell? Then you come along, demanding to know everything. It was me, Alex. Listen. Please. Listen.'

And so he tells me what really happened. It took him a long time to get to sleep that night. Inside his head a perpetual picture-show replays the events of the day – his father, his brother, the truth about his mother.

He wakes early to the sound of water running, and movement in the next room. He lies very still and tense. A door opens and closes. Footsteps creep along the passage to his mother's room.

Another lie.

He follows. She lies on her back with her long, glorious hair smothering the pillow, her exposed neck marred by bruises and red grip-marks. His father is slumped against the far wall, his eyes blank, his mouth open.

His mother moves – not dead then – no time to think, only the fist in his chest, panic and disappointment, and a tidal wash of loss and betrayal as he grabs a pillow and clamps it over her face. He leans over her, using his whole body to still her struggling, and though she kicks and clutches at him, she is weak and battling from instinct and it's so easy, so very, very easy. . . .

And easy too, when it's all over, to remove the pillow and carry it across the room, and place it in his father's cradling arms.

I'm shaking, full to the brim with the confessions of this family. My family. I feel sick. I lean over the balcony rail with the wild idea that I can vomit knowledge away. For God's sake, Nickie, why did you have to tell me?

Down below, the night-time river glitters like gilded jet. I realise I am still clutching Nickie's parcel. I turn my back on the river. The bright window makes a stage set of the apartment. Jo is asleep, Jonathan, Helen and Leonard lean towards one another, speaking in low, earnest voices. A tableau of innocents.

The parcel is heavy, the shiny brown paper firmly bound with Sellotape. I run my nail along the seam and unfold the thick sheet. A gold-coloured chiffon scarf is wrapped round something spherical and hard. I unroll the scarf. Sophie's Celtic head comes tumbling out.

I finger the stone. *As the Crucifix represents your faith to you. . .*

Suddenly I am no longer afraid. I am still full, yes, but knowledge makes me strong. Charles is free, as is Jonathan. Charles smiles, Sophie laughs. The stone resonates. We will heal now, all of us. We have come back to the beginning, we are of a piece, like the stone. One in all, all in one – we are the stones, the stones are the Temple, and the Temple is ours.

Forever and ever.